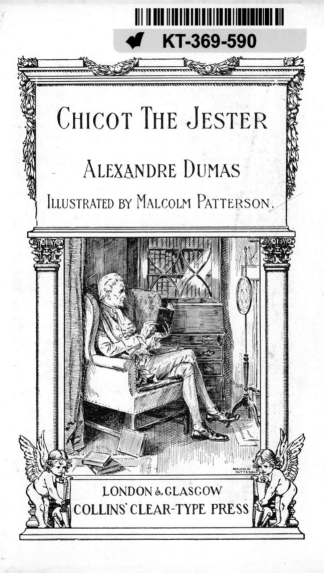

CHICOT THE JESTER

ALEXANDRE DUMAS

ILLUSTRATED BY MALCOLM PATTERSON.

LONDON & GLASGOW
COLLINS' CLEAR-TYPE PRESS

sweetest tones and with the most engaging expression, he replied,—

'Yes, my lord, we purpose coming, though you certainly do not deserve this mark of our friendship.'

Then Mademoiselle Brissac, now Madame de Saint-Luc, humbly thanked His Majesty, who, however, turned away without replying.

'What grievance has the King against you?' asked the young wife of her husband.

'My dear friend,' answered Saint-Luc, 'I will tell you all about that later, when this anger has passed.'

'Will it pass?' asked Jeanne.

'It must,' answered the young man.

Mademoiselle de Brissac had not been Madame de Saint-Luc long enough to insist on this point; she concealed her curiosity, promising herself to find another opportunity of learning the truth.

Henri was anxiously expected at Montmorency House just when our story begins. It was now eleven o'clock, and he had not yet arrived.

Saint-Luc had invited all his own and the King's friends; amongst them being an old acquaintance, the Duc de Alençon—Duc d'Anjou upon Henri's accession. His Grace, who had not attended the feast in the Louvre, seemed to find it unnecessary to grace with his presence the entertainment at Montmorency House.

As for the King and Queen of Navarre, as we have stated in a former work, they had fled to Béarn, where they acted as leaders of the Huguenots, and thus offered open opposition to the King.

His Grace the Duc d'Anjou, as usual, was engaged in an intrigue, but his constant care was to keep himself in the background, whilst employing those of his friends who had not been cured by the example of La Mole and Coconnas, whose terrible death our readers will not have forgotten.

It goes without saying that his followers and the King's lived on bad terms with one another, so that two or three times a month at least duels took place, in which combatants were severely wounded, if not actually killed outright.

As for the Queen-Mother, she had attained all her desires; her beloved son had succeeded to the throne, which she had been so anxious to gain for him, or rather

CHAPTER I

SAINT-LUC'S WEDDING

On Shrove Sunday, in the year 1578, after the popular carnival, and while the echoes of the merry day were dying down in the streets, a splendid entertainment was about to begin in the magnificent mansion which the noble family of Montmorency, a family allied to royalty, and on an equality with princely houses, had just built on the other side of the Seine, almost opposite the Louvre. This private feast formed part of the celebrations in connection with the marriage of François d'Épinay de Saint-Luc, a great friend of King Henri III., and one of his chief favourites, and of Jeanne de Cossé-Brissac, a daughter of a French maréchal of that name.

The wedding feast itself had been served in the Louvre earlier in the day, and the King, who had but grudgingly given his consent to the marriage, had indeed appeared at the banquet, but with severe looks, and demeanour sadly out of keeping with the occasion. His dress, moreover, harmonised with his countenance. He wore that dark brown suit in which Clouet depicts him as a guest at the wedding of Joyeuse. This royal spectre, with aspect so grave, had petrified every one with fear, more especially the young bride, on whom the King frowned whenever she glanced in his direction. Still, this sternness, in the midst of the joyful feast, surprised nobody, for its cause was one of those court secrets which are cautiously handled by every one, like rocks on the surface of the water, which one touches at the risk of being broken to pieces. The meal was hardly over, when Henri rose, and every one naturally followed his example, even some who declared in an undertone their wish to remain at the table. Saint-Luc, glancing at his wife as though he would seek courage from her, approached the King and said, 'Sire, will your Majesty honour me by your presence at the entertainment which I wish to give in Montmorency House to-night.'

Henri turned, half in anger, half in sadness, and as Saint-Luc, bending before him, besought him in the for herself. She reigned in his name, though apparently withdrawn from worldly affairs and concerned only with her salvation. Saint-Luc, thoroughly uneasy at the non-arrival of these royal personages, sought to reassure his father-in-law, who was greatly disturbed by this ominous absence.

Convinced, as every one else, of the friendship which King Henri bore to Saint-Luc, he had thought to unite himself to a royal favourite, and now it would appear that his daughter was marrying one almost in disgrace. Saint-Luc exerted himself to the utmost to inspire him with a security which he himself did not feel ; and his friends, Maugiron, Schomberg, and Quélus, attired in their finest suits, straight and stiff in their magnificent doublets, with enormous ruffs like dishes supporting their heads, increased his fears still more by their ironical lamentations.

'Ah ! good gracious, my poor fellow,' said Jacques de Lévis, Comte de Quélus, 'you are really done for this time, I believe. The King bears you a grudge because you laughed at his friends, and his Grace the Duc is angry because you made fun of his nose.'

'No, no !' answered Saint-Luc. 'You are quite mistaken, Quélus, the King is not here because he has gone on a pilgrimage to the Monastery of Vincennes, and the Duc d'Anjou is away because he is in love with some lady who has not been invited.'

'Come, then,' said Maugiron, 'did you notice the King's expression at dinner ? Was that the fatherly countenance of a man preparing to take his staff and set out on a pilgrimage ? As for the Duc d'Anjou, would his absence, though occasioned as you suggest, prevent his Angevines coming ? Do you see one of them here ? Look round; a total eclipse, not even that swaggerer Bussy.'

'Alas ! gentlemen,' exclaimed the Duc de Brissac, shaking his head despairingly, 'this seems to me a total disgrace. In what particular has my family, always so devoted to the reigning monarch, managed to displease His Majesty ?'

And the old courtier sadly raised his arms to heaven. The young men looked at Saint-Luc, and burst into laughter which, instead of reassuring the Maréchal, caused him to despair. The young wife, thoughtful and absorbed, was asking herself the same question as her

father: in what way had Saint-Luc displeased the King?
Saint Luc himself knew the cause, and, possessing this
knowledge, was the least at ease of them all. Suddenly,
at one of the two entrance doors leading into the reception-
room, the King was announced.

'Ah!' exclaimed the Maréchal, radiant with joy,
'I fear nothing now, and if I could but hear the Duc
d'Anjou announced, my satisfaction would be complete.'

'I, on the contrary,' murmured Saint-Luc, 'am more
afraid of the King now he is here than when he was absent,
for he comes simply to play me an ugly trick. The Duc
of Anjou stays away for that same purpose.'

But, in spite of this reflection, he hurried forward to
meet the King, who had now laid aside his gloomy brown
suit, and advanced, gorgeous with satin, feathers, and
jewels. But just when Henri appeared at one door,
another King Henri, robed, shod, beruffed, and bewigged
in exactly the same way, appeared at the opposite door.
The courtiers, rushing towards the first, stopped as the
waves are stopped by the pile of an arch, and surged back
again, turning about in astonishment from the first to
the second king. Henri noticed the movement, and
seeing before him only mouths wide open, startled eyes,
and bodies revolving round on one leg, exclaimed,—

'Well, my lords, what is wrong?'

A prolonged burst of laughter was the only answer.
The King, naturally impatient, was beginning to scowl
when Saint-Luc approached him to say,—

'Sire, it is your jester, Chicot, who has dressed himself
exactly like your Majesty, and is giving the ladies his
hand to kiss.'

Henri began to laugh. Chicot, at the court of the last
Valois, enjoyed the same freedom as Triboulet thirty
years before at the court of François I., a freedom such as
Langely was to enjoy forty years later at the court of
King Louis XIII. Chicot was not an ordinary jester.
Before calling himself plain Chicot, he had been known as
de Chicot. He was a Gascon nobleman, who had been
badly treated by M. de Mayenne as a result of some love
affair, in which Chicot, in spite of his lower rank, had
triumphed over the Prince. Having fled to King Henri's
court, he there told unpleasant truths in return for the
protection afforded him by the successor of Charles IX.

'Ah! Master Chicot,' cried Henri, 'two kings here. That's a lot.'

'Then, let me go on playing the King in my way, and you can act the Duc d'Anjou in your way. Perhaps people will think it is he, and you will learn things that will enlighten you, not as to what he thinks, but what he does.'

'As a matter of fact,' said the King, glancing round him crossly, 'my brother Anjou has not come.'

'All the more reason that you take his place. It's done! I am Henri and you are François. I assume my duties as King, you go and dance; I shall perform all the necessary antics. Meanwhile you may amuse yourself a little, poor King.'

The King's eye fell on Saint-Luc.

'You are quite right, Chicot; I wish to dance,' said he.

'Truly, I was wrong in supposing the King was annoyed at us,' thought Brissac. 'On the contrary, he is in a charming mood.'

He hurried here and there, congratulating everybody, and himself above all, for having given his daughter to a gentleman in such high favour. Saint-Luc had approached his wife. Though not beautiful, her charming black eyes, white teeth, and a dazzling skin made her face what we may term expressive.

'Sir,' said she to her husband, 'why did they say the King was angry with me? Why, he has not stopped smiling since he arrived.'

'That is not what you told me after dinner, my dear Jeanne; you were afraid of his looks then.'

'No doubt His Majesty was not in a good mood,' answered the young wife, 'but now——'

'Now, matters are far worse,' interrupted Saint-Luc, 'the King smiles, but his lips are close set. I would rather he would look threatening. Jeanne, my poor friend, the King has some treacherous surprise in store for us. Oh! don't look at me so tenderly, I beg you. Turn your back on me even. Ah! here comes Maugiron; take him in hand, monopolise him, and be very gracious to him.'

'Do you know,' said Jeanne, smiling, 'that is a strange piece of advice, and if I were to obey it literally people might think——'

'Ah!' said Saint-Luc, sighing, 'and a very good thing, too, if they thought that.'

Turning from his wife, whose astonishment was now complete, he proceeded to pay his respects to Chicot, who was playing his kingly rôle with most amusing animation and majesty. Meanwhile Henri, following Chicot's advice, joined heartily in the dance; but though thus seeming to take full advantage of his respite from kingly grandeur, he never for an instant lost sight of Saint-Luc. Now he would call him up to repeat some witty remark, which, funny or not, had the power of making Saint-Luc laugh immoderately. Or, again, he would offer him the contents of his comfit dish, burnt almonds and preserved fruit, which Saint-Luc found delicious. Or if the young man absented himself for a moment from the reception-room where the King was, in order to play the host elsewhere, the King immediately sent a friend or officer in search of him, and Saint-Luc would come back, smiling, to his master, who seemed only happy when he saw him again. Suddenly a noise, loud enough to be noticed amid the general tumult, reached Henri's ears.

'Eh,' said he. 'I think I hear Chicot's voice. Do you hear, Saint-Luc, the King is angry.'

'Yes, sire,' said Saint-Luc, without appearing to notice the allusion, 'he is quarrelling with some one, it seems to me.'

'See what is the matter, and come back at once to tell me.'

Saint-Luc went away. Sure enough, Chicot was heard calling out in a snivelling voice, such as the King used on certain occasions,—

'I have issued sumptuary orders, but if those do not suffice, I shall issue others; I shall go on issuing till there are enough; if they are not good, at least they are numerous. By the horn of Beelzebub, my cousin, six pages, M. de Bussy, that is too much !'

Chicot puffed out his cheeks, put his hand on his side, and bent his body slightly, almost deceiving everybody into thinking he was really the King.

'Whatever makes him speak of Bussy ?' asked the King, knitting his brows.

Saint-Luc, who had now returned, was about to answer, when the crowd, falling back, showed six pages, clad in cloth of gold, covered with necklaces, and bearing on their breasts their master's coat of arms, studded over with gems. Behind them came a young man, handsome and proud, his head high in the air, his eye glancing haughtily, and his lip curled scornfully, while his simple suit of black velvet contrasted with the pages' rich attire. There was a shout of 'Bussy, Bussy d'Amboise!' and every one rushed forward to see the young man who had occasioned the shout. Maugiron, Schomberg, and Quélus had posted themselves at the King's side, as though to defend him.

'Hallo!' said the first, alluding to Bussy's unexpected presence, and the prolonged absence of the Duc d'Alençon, to whose retinue Bussy belonged. 'Hallo, here's the valet, and the master nowhere to be seen.'

'Have patience,' answered Quélus, 'the valet's valets were in front of the valet himself, so perhaps the valet's master is coming behind the first valet's master.'

'Look here, Saint-Luc,' said Schomberg, the youngest, but one of the bravest of King Henri's favourites, 'do you know that M. de Bussy scarcely does you honour? Look at that black doublet, I pray; is that like a wedding suit?'

'No,' said Quélus, 'but it's a funeral garment.'

'Ah!' murmured Henri, 'why isn't it his own; why isn't he wearing mourning for himself?'

'More than that, Saint-Luc,' said Maugiron, 'M. d'Anjou does not follow Bussy. Is it possible that you are in disgrace in that quarter, as well?'

These words, 'as well,' struck Saint-Luc deeply.

'Why should he follow Bussy?' rejoined Quélus.

'Don't you recall that when His Majesty honoured M. de Bussy by asking him to join his household, M. de Bussy replied that, belonging, as he did, to the house of Clermont, he had no need to join anybody, and would be content with belonging wholly and simply to himself, feeling certain that he would find himself superior to any prince in the world.'

The King knit his brows and bit his moustache.

'All the same, whatever you may say,' began Maugiron again, 'it seems to me that he is one of the Duc's party.'

'Then,' said Quélus calmly, 'that is because M. d'Anjou is a greater lord than the King.'

This was the most poignant remark that any one could make in Henri's presence, as he had always detested the Duc d'Anjou, in a brotherly fashion. Though he made not the least reply, they saw him grow pale.

'Come, come, my lords,' Saint-Luc ventured timidly

to say, 'show some charity to my guests. Do not spoil my wedding-day.'

These words seemed to turn Henri to a new train of thought.

'Yes,' said he, 'do not let us spoil M. de Saint-Luc's wedding-day.'

As he said these words, he curled his moustache with a cunning look, which was not lost upon the poor bridegroom.

'See,' exclaimed Schomberg, 'Bussy is an ally of the Brissacs nowadays!'

'How so?' asked Maugiron.

'Why, there's Saint-Luc defending him. Good gracious, in this wretched world, where one has enough to do to defend himself, surely one defends only those who are relations, allies, and friends.'

'My lords,' said Saint-Luc, 'M. de Bussy is neither an ally, a friend, nor a relation of mine : he is my guest.'

The King darted an angry look at Saint-Luc.

'And, besides,' the latter hastened to say, thunderstruck, at the glance, 'I do not defend him in the least.'

Bussy had approached gravely behind the pages, and was going to bow before the King, when Chicot, hurt that others were being honoured before him, called out,—

'Eh! Here! Bussy, Bussy d'Amboise, Louis de Clermont, Comte Bussy, since we must give you all these titles before you realise that it is to you we are speaking, don't you see the real Henri, don't you distinguish the King from the fool? That person you are approaching is Chicot, my fool, my jester, who plays so many pranks that sometimes I nearly die with laughing at them.'

Bussy went on his way, and was soon in front of Henri. He was making his obeisance, when the King said,—

'Do you not hear, M. de Bussy? Somebody is calling you;' and, amid the loud laughter of his favourites, the King turned his back upon the young captain.

Bussy coloured with anger; but, restraining himself, he pretended to take the King's remark seriously, and, seemingly deaf to the outbursts of Quélus, Schomberg, and Maugiron, and blind to their insolent smiles, he turned towards Chicot,—

'Ah, excuse me, sire,' said he, 'but some jesters resemble kings so strongly that you will pardon me, I hope, for mistaking your jester for a king.'

'Eh!' murmured Henri, turning round, 'what is he saying?'

'Nothing, your Majesty,' exclaimed Saint-Luc, who seemed to have been entrusted with the office of a peace-maker for the whole evening; 'nothing, nothing at all.'

'That doesn't matter, M. de Bussy,' said Chicot, getting up on tiptoe, as the King did when he wished to appear majestic, 'it's unpardonable.'

'Your Majesty,' replied Bussy, 'excuse me, I was absorbed in thought.'

'About your pages, sir,' said Chicot angrily. 'You are ruining yourself with pages, and, marry, it is encroaching on our prerogatives.'

'Why is that?' asked Bussy, who understood that in coping with the jester, the King would have a sorry part to play. 'I beg your Majesty to explain, and if I really have done wrong, I shall confess it in all humility.'

'Cloth of gold for these clodhoppers,' cried Chicot, pointing to the pages, 'whilst you, a nobleman, a colonel, a Clermont, almost a prince, indeed, are clad in plain black velvet!'

'Your Majesty,' said Bussy, turning in the direction of the King's favourites, 'it is like this; when one is living at a time when clodhoppers dress like princes, it is a mark of good taste on the part of princes to dress like clod-hoppers.'

So saying, he returned the young favourites, in their gorgeous, glittering attire, the insolent smile with which they had greeted him a moment before. Henri looked at his courtiers, who, pale with rage, only awaited his word to throw themselves on Bussy. Quélus had even angrier feelings than the others towards this nobleman, whom, but for the King's express orders, he would already have challenged to a duel. As it was, he had now his hand on his sword-guard.

'Is it for my benefit and my followers' that you say that?' exclaimed Chicot.

While asking this question, the jester assumed a bullying air to such an exaggerated degree, that half the room burst out laughing. The other half did not laugh, and the reason was simple enough: it was at them the others were laughing. Three of Bussy's friends, however, fearing mischief, took up their stand beside him. They were Charles Balzac d'Entragues, commonly known as

Antraguet; François d'Audie, Vicomte de Ribeirac, and Livarot.

As he saw these preliminaries, Saint-Luc guessed that Bussy had come, on the part of the King's brother, to cause a scandal or to issue a challenge. He trembled more violently than ever, for he felt caught, as it were, between the sharp fire of two powerful enemies, who chose his house for their battlefield. He ran to Quélus, who seemed the keenest of all, and placing his hand on the young man's sword-guard, said, 'For Heaven's sake, restrain yourself, my dear fellow, and let us wait.'

'Eh, by my sooth, restrain yourself,' exclaimed Quélus, 'that fellow's impudence strikes you as well as me; whoever says anything against one of us, says it against us all, and who says it against us, says it against the King.'

'Quélus, Quélus,' remonstrated Saint-Luc, 'think of the Duc d'Anjou, who is behind Bussy, watching all the more keenly because absent, and to be feared more as he is invisible. You do not insult me, I presume, by imagining that I am afraid of the servant; it is the master I fear.'

'Marry,' cried Quélus, 'what has one to be afraid of when one is of the King of France's party? If we risk our lives for him, he will defend us.'

'You, perhaps, but what about me?' asked Saint-Luc, in a pitiful voice.

'Ah, by my troth, why did you get married, then, when you knew how jealous the King is in his friendships?'

'Good,' said Saint-Luc, 'each is thinking of himself. Do not let us forget ourselves, then; and since I wish to live in peace for the first fortnight of my married life, let us endeavour to make a friend of M. d'Anjou.'

With this remark he left Quélus and advanced to Bussy. After delivering his insolent address, Bussy had raised his head and glanced all round the room, on the alert to catch any insults which might be launched in return. Every head was turned away, every mouth remained shut: some feared to show their approval before the King, others to show their disapproval before Bussy. Seeing Saint-Luc draw near, Bussy believed he had at last found what he was seeking for.

'My lord,' he exclaimed, 'is it to what I have just said that I am to attribute the honour of this interview?'

'To what you have just said?' Saint-Luc asked, with

his most gracious air, 'what is that ? Indeed I heard nothing. I had seen you and wished to have the pleasure of greeting you, and of thanking you, at the same time, for honouring my house by your presence.'

Bussy was, in all respects, a superior man : brave to a degree, but cultured, witty, and well-bred. He recognised Saint-Luc's courage and understood that his duties as host restrained him from showing his annoyance. To any other he would have repeated his sentence, that is to say, his challenge; but he merely greeted Saint-Luc politely, and replied to his compliment, in a few gracious words.

'Oh,' said Henri, seeing Saint-Luc near Bussy, 'I believe my young gallant has gone to abuse the captain. All very well, but I do not want him killed. Go and see, Quélus—— No, not you, Quélus, you are too hot-headed. Go you, Maugiron.'

'What were you saying to that coxcomb, Bussy ?' asked the King.

'I merely said "Good-evening" to him,' answered Saint-Luc.

'Ah, that was all, was it ?' said the King, fuming with rage.

Saint-Luc realised that he had made a stupid mistake. 'I wished him "Good-evening,"' he went on, 'and added that I would have the honour to wish him "Good-day" to-morrow morning.'

'That's excellent; I suspected as much, hot-headed fellow !'

'I trust your gracious Majesty will keep my secret,' added Saint-Luc, pretending to speak low.

'Oh ! marry, what I say does not need to worry you. Certainly if you could rid me of him, without being hurt yourself——'

The favourites exchanged a rapid glance, which Henri seemed not to have noticed.

'For, really,' continued the King, 'the rogue's impudence is——'

'Yes, yes,' said Saint-Luc, 'still, be sure, your Majesty, he will find his match, sooner or later.'

'When ?' asked the King, shaking his head. 'He handles the sword skilfully enough. Why doesn't he get bitten by a mad dog ? that would rid us of him conveniently.'

And he glanced sidelong at Bussy, who moved about with his three friends, offending and scoffing at those most hostile to the Duc d'Anjou, and consequently the King's greatest friends.

'Eh, gracious,' exclaimed Chicot, 'don't be so rough with my fine gentlemen, good Master Bussy. I can handle the sword, king though I am, as well as if I were a jester.'

'Ah, the rogue,' murmured Henri; 'he sees plainly, upon my word.'

'If he persists in such jokes, I shall have to rebuke him, your Majesty,' said Maugiron.

'No, don't meddle with him, Maugiron. Chicot is a gentleman, and very nice with regard to one's honour. Besides he is not the one who deserves punishment, for he has not been the most impertinent.'

This time there was no mistaking the King's meaning. Quélus beckoned to d'O and d'Épinay, who, occupied elsewhere, had taken no part in what had just occurred.

'Gentlemen,' began Quélus, drawing them aside, 'let us discuss matters. You, Saint-Luc, go to the King, and conclude the overtures of peace which seem to have begun so happily.' Saint-Luc drew near the King and Chicot, who were arguing with one another. Meanwhile, Quélus had carried off his four friends into a window-corner.

'Well,' asked Épernon, 'what do you wish to tell us? I was just in the midst of paying my respects to Joyeuse's wife, and I warn you that if your story is not interesting, I shall not forgive you.'

'I wish to tell you, gentlemen,' answered Quélus, 'that I am going hunting immediately after the ball is over.'

'Very good; what kind of hunt?'

'A wild boar hunt.'

'What fancy has taken you to go in cold weather like this, and get yourself spitted in some copse?'

'Never mind that; I am going.'

'Alone?'

'Not at all, with Maugiron and Schomberg. We hunt for the King.'

'Ah, yes, I understand,' said Schomberg and Maugiron together.

'The King wishes to have a wild boar's head served to him for breakfast to-morrow.'

'With a collar, inverted in the Italian fashion,' said Maugiron, alluding to the plain, lying-down collar, worn by Bussy, in contrast to the high collars of the favourites.

'Ah, good.' said d'Épernon; 'now I understand.'

'What is it all about, then ?' asked d'O. 'I don't see in the least.'

'Eh !' look round you, my fine fellow.'

'Well, I am looking.'

'Is there anybody here who has laughed in your face ?'

'Bussy, it seems to me.'

'Well, does it not occur to you that there's a wild boar whose head would be acceptable to the King ?'

'You think that the King——' said d'O.

'He has asked for it,' replied Quélus.

'Well, so be it; but how are we to hunt ?'

'We will lie in wait; it is surer.'

Bussy noticed the discussion, and suspecting that it involved himself, drew near, with his friends, sneering as he came.

'Do look, Antraguet, and you, Ribeirac,' said he; 'look how they are grouped together; it is affecting; one would say Euryale and Nisus, Damon and Pythias, Castor and—— But where is Pollux ?'

'Pollux has got married, so Castor is left the odd one,' said Antraguet.

'What can they be doing there ?' asked Bussy, glancing at them in an impudent way.

'They must be plotting the manufacture of some new starch.'

'No, gentlemen,' said Quélus, smiling, 'we are speaking of the hunt.'

'Really, my lord Cupid,' exclaimed Bussy, 'it is very cold weather for hunting. Your skin will get cracked.'

'My lord,' answered Maugiron, in the same polite fashion, 'we have very warm gloves and doublets lined with fur.'

'Ah, that reassures me,' said Bussy, 'are you to be hunting soon ?'

'Probably this very night,' said Schomberg.

'There is no "probably" about it; to-night certainly,' added Maugiron.

'Well, since that is the case, I shall warn the King. What would His Majesty say to-morrow, if he found his friends with colds in their heads ?'

'Do not trouble, my lord,' said Quélus; 'His Majesty is aware that we are going hunting.'

'For larks ?' asked Bussy, with a most impudent, questioning air.

'No, my lord,' said Quélus, 'we hunt for wild boars. We simply must have a head.'

'And the animal ? what of it ?' asked Antraguet.

'It has turned aside,' said Schomberg.

'But still, you require to know what direction it will take ?' asked Livarot.

'We shall try to get that information,' said d'O. 'Do you hunt with our party, Monsieur de Bussy ?'

'No,' answered the latter, continuing the conversation in the same way; 'no, indeed, I am prevented from doing so. To-morrow I am obliged to be at the Duc d'Anjou's for the reception of M. Monsoreau, whom the King, as you know, has appointed his First Huntsman.'

'But, to-night ?' asked Quélus.

'Ah ! to-night, too, I am prevented. I have an appointment in a mysterious house in the suburb of Saint-Antoine.'

'Ah !' said Épernon, 'has Queen Margaret come incognito to Paris, for we heard that you had succeeded La Mole ?'

'True; but for some time past, I have given up the inheritance, and this has to do with another person altogether.'

'And this person is to be waiting for you in the Rue du Faubourg-Saint-Antoine ?' asked d'O.

'Exactly; I was even going to ask some advice from you, M. de Quélus.'

'Do so, then; although no counsellor, I flatter myself that I give rather good advice, especially to my friends.'

'The streets of Paris are said to be unsafe : the suburb of Saint-Antoine is a lonely district. Which route do you advise me to take ?'

'By my faith,' said Quélus, 'seeing the Louvre boatman will be waiting for us all night, in your place, sir, I would take the little ferry-boat of Pré-aux-Clercs, and get out at the Tower at the corner; then I would go along the quay as far as Grand-Châtelet, and reach Saint-Antoine by Rue de la Tixeranderie. If you succeed in passing the Hôtel des Tournelles without accident, you will probably arrive safe and sound at the mysterious house of which you have just been telling us.'

'Thank you for the route, Monsieur de Quélus. You say the ferry-boat of Pré-aux-Clercs, the tower at the corner, the quay as far as Grand-Châtelet, the Rue de la

Tixeranderie, and the Rue Saint-Antoine. I shall not diverge from that, be assured.'

Bowing to the five friends, he departed, saying aloud to Balzac d'Entragues, 'In truth, Antraguet, nothing can be done with those people; let us go away.'

Livarot and Ribeirac laughed as they followed Bussy and d'Entragues, who walked off, turning round several times as they did so. The favourites remained calm; they had evidently resolved to understand nothing. When Bussy was crossing the room where Madame de Saint-Luc was, her husband, whose movements she was watching, signalled to her that the Duc d'Anjou's favourite was going. Jeanne understood with that perspicacity which is woman's privilege. Running up to the nobleman, she stood in his way.

'Oh, Monsieur de Bussy,' said she, 'every one is talking of a sonnet which you have composed, which is——'

'Against the King, madame?' asked Bussy.

'No, in honour of the Queen; do repeat it to me!'

'With pleasure, madame.'

He gave her his arm, and walked away, repeating the sonnet she had asked for. Meanwhile Saint-Luc, going quietly back to the King's favourites, had overheard Quélus saying, 'The animal will not be difficult to follow with these steps to guide us; at the corner of the Hôtel des Tournelles, then, near Porte Saint-Antoine and opposite the Hôtel Saint-Pol.'

'Are we to take a lackey each?' asked d'Épernon.

'No, no, Nogaret, let us be alone; let us keep the secret to ourselves. I hate him, but I should be ashamed if any lackey's cudgel touched him; he is too much of a gentleman.'

'Are we to go all six together?' asked Maugiron.

'All five, but not all six,' said Saint-Luc.

'Ah! true enough, we had forgotten that you had a wife now. We were treating you still as a bachelor,' observed Schomberg.

'Indeed,' laughed d'O, 'poor Saint-Luc ought to remain with his wife the first night of his married life.'

'You do not quite understand, gentlemen,' said Saint-Luc; 'it is not my wife who keeps me from coming, although she might be a reasonable excuse, you will agree; it is the King.'

'How is that?'

'His Majesty wishes me to escort him to the Louvre.'

The young men looked at Saint-Luc, and smiled in a way which he was at a loss to understand.

'What would you have, then?' said Quélus; 'the King's friendship for you is so strong, that he cannot do without you.'

'Besides, we have no need of Saint-Luc,' remarked Schomberg. 'Leave him to his king and his wife.'

'Our prey is a difficult one,' observed d'Épernon, with a grimace.

'Bah!' cried Quélus, 'let me confront it. Just give me a boar-spear, and I'll settle it.'

Henri's voice was heard calling for Saint-Luc.

'Gentlemen,' said he, 'you hear, the King calls me. Success to your hunt; good-night.'

He left them, but, instead of going straight towards the King, stole along by the walls of the crowded room, and reached the doorway, where Bussy stood. He was kept by the fair bride, who exerted all her efforts not to let him depart.

'Ah! good evening, Monsieur de Saint-Luc,' said the young man. 'You look scared! Do you happen to be one of this hunting party that is being arranged? It would be a proof of your courage, but not one of your gallantry.'

'Monsieur,' answered Saint-Luc, 'I looked scared, because I was searching for you.'

'Ah! really?'

'And because I feared that you had gone. My dear Jeanne,' he added, 'you might ask your father to try to stop the King; I must say a few words privately to Monsieur de Bussy.'

Jeanne went quickly; she did not understand, but she obeyed the command, feeling it to be an important one.

'What do you wish to say, Monsieur de Saint-Luc,' asked Bussy.

'I wished to say, Monsieur le Comte, that if you have any appointment to-night, you would do well to put it off until to-morrow, seeing that the streets are in a bad state, and if this appointment should lead you near the Bastille, you would be as well to avoid the Hôtel des Tournelles. There is a hollow there where several men could hide. That is what I had to tell you.'

Just then Chicot was heard crying,—

'Saint-Luc, my dear Saint-Luc, come, do not hide yourself; you know very well I am waiting for you to go to the Louvre.'

'Your Majesty, here I am,' answered Saint-Luc, darting in the direction of Chicot's voice.

Near the jester stood Henri, to whom one page was handing a heavy cloak, trimmed with ermine; a second, long gloves reaching to the elbows; and a third, a velvet mask, lined with satin.

'Your Majesty,' said Saint-Luc, addressing himself to the two Henris at once, 'am I to have the honour of bearing the torch as far as your litters.'

'Not at all,' said Henri; 'Chicot takes one direction, I another. My friends are all scamps to allow me to return alone to the Louvre, whilst they enjoy themselves at the Carnival. I was relying upon them, and they have failed me; now, you cannot let me go away unattended. You are a sedate, married man, you must take me back to the Queen. Come along, my good friend. Hallo! a horse for Monsieur Saint-Luc—no, there is no need for one,' he added, 'my litter is big enough to hold two.'

Jeanne de Brissac had been listening to every word of this conversation; she wished to speak, to say a few words to her husband, to warn her father that the King was carrying off Saint-Luc; but Saint-Luc, putting his finger on his lip, warned her to be silent.

'Confound it,' said he, in a low tone, 'now that I have succeeded in disposing of François Duc d'Anjou, do not let us get into the bad graces of Henri de Valois. Your Majesty,' he went on, aloud, 'here I am. I am so devoted to your Majesty that I would follow your Majesty to the ends of the earth.'

There was a great noise and bustle, then much bowing and scraping, finally silence to hear the King's farewell words to Mademoiselle de Brissac and her father. They were very gracious. The horses paved the ground in the courtyard, while the torches cast red reflections on the windows. At length, some laughing, some shivering with cold, the royal courtiers and the wedding guests emerged into the darkness and the fog. Jeanne, left alone with her attendants, went into her own room, where she kneeled down before the image of a saint in whom she believed devoutly. Then she requested to be left alone, and ordered a meal to be prepared for her husband on his return. M. de Brissac did more. He sent six attendants to wait for the young husband at the gate of the Louvre, so as to escort him when he should come out. But, after waiting two hours, one of the attendants returned to inform the Maréchal that all the gates were closed, and that, before closing the last one, the keeper had said, 'Do not wait any longer; it is useless; no one will leave to-night. His Majesty has gone to bed, and everybody is sleeping.'

The Maréchal carried this news to his daughter, as she had declared that she was too uneasy to go to bed, and that she would sit up for her husband.

CHAPTER II

HE WHO OPENS THE DOOR, DOES NOT ALWAYS ENTER THE HOUSE

THE gate of Saint-Antoine was a stone arch, very similar to the gates of Saint-Denis and Saint-Martin at the present day. On its left side it touched the buildings which adjoined the Bastille, and was thus connected with the old fortress. The space to the right between the gate and the Hôtel de Bourgoyne was wide, dark, and muddy. It was very little used during the day, and quite deserted at night, for the streets were dangerous, and a night watch almost unknown. Those who were compelled to use the passage had made a road next to the fortress, so as to put themselves under the protection of its sentry. He could not help them, it is true, but he could, at least, raise an alarm, and so frighten the assailants. Needless to say the pedestrians were even more cautious in winter than in the summer time.

The evening on which the events we have already described and those we are about to relate happened was so cold, so black, and the sky so filled with low-lying, dark clouds, that nobody could have seen the sentry, placed as he was behind the battlements of the royal fortress, and he would have been equally at a loss to distinguish passers-by. In front of the gate of Saint-Antony, towards the town, there were no houses, only high walls. To the right were the walls of Saint-Paul's Church, and to the left those of the Hôtel des Tournelles. At the end of this hotel near Rue

Sainte-Catherine, the wall formed the angle or recess which Saint-Luc had mentioned to Bussy. Then came the cluster of houses between the Rue de Jouy and the Rue Saint-Antoine, the latter having opposite it at that period Rue des Billettes and Sainte-Catherine's Church. Moreover, in certain parts of old Paris not a single lamp was lit. On moonlit nights there rose up, gloomy, majestic and still, the huge pile of the Bastille, standing strongly out against the blue and starry sky. But on dark nights, its place was indicated only by an intenser blackness, broken here and there by the pale light which streamed from its windows. On this particular night, which had begun with keen frost, and was to end in a heavy snowfall, no steps resounded on the causeway leading from the street to the suburb. But, to make up for this stillness, a practised eye could have distinguished several black shadows in the angle of the hotel wall. The movements of these proved that they belonged to unfortunate human beings, hard pressed to maintain an ordinary heat, of which they were being deprived every minute, by the vigil to which, in the expectation of something happening, they had condemned themselves. The sentry on the tower, who could not see the street in the darkness, would not have heard their conversation either, in such a low tone was it carried on. Nevertheless, this conversation was not without a certain interest.

'That mad Bussy was quite right,' said one; 'it is just such a night as we used to have in Warsaw, when King Henri was King of Poland, and if this cold continues, our skin will be cracked, as he prophesied.'

'Come, Schomberg,' answered a second, 'you are grumbling like a woman. It is not warm, that's true; but draw your cloak down on your eyes and put your hands in your pockets, you won't feel the cold any more.'

'Indeed,' said a third, 'it is easy to talk; and one sees very well that you are German. As for me, my lips are bleeding, and my moustache is bristling with pieces of ice.'

'It's my hands that are frozen,' exclaimed a fourth voice. 'Upon my word, I would wager that I have no longer any.'

'Why didn't you bring your mother's muff, poor Quélus,' answered Schomberg. 'That dear lady would have lent you it, especially if you had told her it was to rid her of her dear Bussy. She likes him nearly as well as the plague.'

'Oh, good gracious! do have patience!' cried a fifth voice. 'Presently you will be complaining that you are too hot.'

'May God hear you, d'Épernon,' said Maugiron, stamping his feet.

'I didn't speak, it was d'O,' said d'Épernon. 'I am keeping quiet in case my words get frozen.'

'What were you saying?' Quélus asked Maugiron. 'D'O was saying that presently we should be too hot,' answered Maugiron,' and I answered, 'May God hear you!'

'Well, I believe he has heard; for something is coming along the Rue St Paul.'

'A mistake. It can't be he.'

'And why not?'

'Because he told us of another route.'

'Would it be surprising if he had suspected something and changed his plan?'

'You don't know Bussy; when he says he will go by a route, he goes, even if aware that the devil is waiting in ambush to stop him.'

'Meanwhile, here come two men,' answered Quélus.

'Yes, yes, really,' cried two or three voices, as the truth of the statement appealed to them.

'Well, then, let us fall upon them,' suggested Schomberg.

'Stop a moment,' urged d'Épernon; 'don't let us kill substantial citizens or respectable midwives. Hallo! they're stopping.'

Indeed, the two individuals who were attracting our five friends' attention had stopped, in a seeming indecision, at the end of the Rue Saint-Paul, which looks into the Rue Saint-Antoine.

'Oh!' said Quelus, 'is it possible that they've seen us?'

'Come, come, we can hardly see one another even.'

'You are right,' answered Quélus. 'Hallo! they're turning to the left; they are stopping in front of a house. They are looking for something.'

'Yes, indeed, they are.'

'They want to enter,' observed Schomberg. 'Eh, wait a moment. Can they be going to escape us?'

'It is not he; he was to go to Saint-Antoine suburb, and those two came down the street,' answered Maugiron.

'Eh,' said Schomberg, 'who is to say the cunning rascal

did not give you a wrong clue, either by chance and carelessly, or from deliberate malice.'

'Indeed, that may well be,' said Quélus.

This conjecture made the whole band of noblemen leap like a pack of hungry hounds. They left their hiding-place and, with swords brandished, rushed towards the two men. One had just put a key into the lock, and the door was opening, when the noise made by the assailants caused the strangers to raise their heads.

'What's that ?' asked the smaller of the two, turning to his friend; 'can it possibly be that they have designs upon us, d'Aurilly ?'

'Ah ! my lord, it looks to me very like it,' replied the one who had just opened the door; 'will you give your name, or keep your incognito ?'

'Armed men—an ambush !'

'Some jealous people who watch for us. I was right, my lord, when I said the lady was too beautiful not to have lovers.'

'Let us enter quickly, d'Aurilly. A siege is better with-stood from the inside than from the outside.'

'When there are no enemies within the fortress. But who tells you——'

He had no time to finish his sentence. Quick as a flash of lightning, the young men had crossed the space of one hundred feet or so, which separated them. Quélus and Maugiron, who had skirted the wall, threw themselves between the door and the strangers, thus cutting off their retreat, while Schomberg, d'O, and d'Épernon prepared to attack them in front.

'Die ! die !' cried Quélus, ever the most impulsive of the five.

Suddenly the person who had been addressed as 'My lord,' and been asked if he would keep his incognito, turned to Quélus, stepped towards him, and, crossing his arms proudly, said, with a sinister look and in a melancholy voice, 'I think you said "Die !" to a son of France, Monsieur de Quélus.'

Quélus drew back, his face white, his knees shaking, his hands hanging motionless.

'My lord the Duc d'Anjou !' he exclaimed.

'My lord the Duc d'Anjou !' repeated the others.

'Well,' François inquired, with a terrible look, 'and are we still crying, "Die, die," my good friends ?'

'My lord,' stammered d'Épernon, 'it was a joke; forgive us.'

'My lord,' said d'O, in his turn, 'we did not dream that we should meet your Highness in this deserted quarter.'

'A joke,' answered François, not even honouring d'O with a reply; 'you have singular ways of joking, Monsieur d'Épernon. Come now, since I am not the victim of your ill-will, who is the object of your jest?'

'My lord,' replied Schomberg respectfully, 'we saw Saint-Luc leave Montmorency House and come in this direction. That seemed strange, and we desired to learn why a husband was leaving his wife on the first night of his married life.'

The excuse was a plausible one, for, in all likelihood, the Duc d'Anjou would learn the next day that Saint-Luc had not slept at home, and this would coincide with what Schomberg had just said.

'Monsieur de Saint-Luc? You took me for Monsieur de Saint-Luc, gentlemen?'

'Yes, my lord,' exclaimed the five friends in chorus.

'And when did people begin to make such mistakes about us two? M. de Saint-Luc is a head taller than I.'

'That is true, my lord,' said Quélus; 'but he is the same height as M. d'Aurilly, who has the honour of accompanying you.'

''Tis a very dark night, too, my lord,' put in Maugiron.

'Then, seeing a man put a key into the lock, we supposed that he was the important one of the two,' murmured d'O.

'In short,' said Quélus, 'your Highness cannot imagine that we have had even a shadow of an evil intention toward you; we have not even wished to disturb your pleasures.'

While he listened to the more or less logical answers, inspired by fear and surprise, which were given him, the Duc d'Anjou, cleverly and strategically managed to leave the doorway, followed by d'Aurilly, his lute player, who usually accompanied him in his night expeditions. He thus stood already at such a distance from the door that it could not be recognised, but would be confused with the others.

'My pleasure,' said he sharply; 'what can lead you to suppose that I come here for pleasure?'

'Ah, my lord, in any case, for whatever purpose you

have come, excuse us,' begged Quélus; 'we are going away.'

'It is as well. Farewell, gentlemen.'

'My lord,' added d'Épernon, 'may our discretion, which is well known to your Highness——'

The Duc d'Anjou, who had already moved away a step, stopped and said, knitting his brows: 'Discretion, Monsieur de Nogaret, who asks you to use it, pray ?'

'My lord, we thought your Highness, alone at this time, and followed by your confidential friend——'

'You were mistaken; this is what you are to believe.'

The five noblemen listened in the deepest and most respectful silence.

'I was going,' resumed the Duc d'Anjou slowly, and as if seeking to engrave each word on their memory— 'I was going to consult the Jew, Manasseh, who can read the future in a crystal and in coffee grounds. He stays, as you are aware, in the Rue de la Tournelle. While we were passing, d'Aurilly seeing you, mistook you for archers. So,' he added, with a gaiety that was alarming to those who knew his character, 'like true consulters of wizards, as we are, we were keeping close to the walls and doors, to hide ourselves, if possible, from your terrible looks.'

Meanwhile the Prince had reached the Rue Saint-Paul again, and was at a distance to be overheard by the sentries at the Bastille, should an attack be made. He was but imperfectly reassured on this point by the excuses and respectful attitudes of Henri's favourites, for he thoroughly realised the secret and deep-rooted hatred borne him by his brother.

'Now that you know the truth, and, above all, what you are to tell others, farewell, gentlemen. It is needless to add that I do not wish to be followed.'

All bowed and took leave of the Prince, who walked off in the opposite direction, turning round several times to watch them.

'My lord,' said d'Aurilly, 'I declare these people we have just interviewed had evil intentions. It will soon be midnight; we are in a deserted quarter; let us go back to our dwelling.'

'Not at all,' replied the Prince, stopping him; 'let us rather profit by their absence.'

'Your Highness is mistaken,' said d'Aurilly; 'they have not gone; they have returned to their hiding-place, as

your Highness can see. Do you not see them, my lord,
in that recess, at the corner of the Hôtel des Tournelles ?'

François looked; d'Aurilly had spoken nothing but
the truth. The five noblemen had really taken up their
former position, and were clearly contemplating some
project which the Prince's appearance had interrupted.
They might still intend to spy on the Prince and his
friend, and to make sure that they were indeed going to
the Jew, Manasseh.

'Well, my lord,' asked d'Aurilly, 'what do you decide
upon ? I shall do what your Highness commands, but
I do not think it wise to stay.'

'In sooth !' said the Prince, 'it is annoying to abandon
our project.'

'I am quite aware of it, my lord, but it can be postponed.
I have already had the honour of informing your Highness
that the house is rented for a year; we know the lady lives
on the first flat; we are in communication with her
chamber-maid; we have a key which opens her door.
With all these advantages we can wait.'

'You are sure the door yielded ?'

'At the third turn of the key.'

'By the way, did you shut it again ?'

'The door ?'

'Yes !'

'Without a doubt, my lord.'

D'Aurilly uttered this statement with seeming confidence, yet he was less sure of having shut the door than
of having opened it. However, his self-assurance left his
companion with no more doubt about the first point than
the second.

'But,' said the Prince, 'I really should not mind knowing
myself——'

'What they are doing there, my lord ? I can tell you
that, without fear of mistake; they are met together to
lie in wait for some one. Let us go. Your Highness has
enemies; who knows what they may dare to attempt
against your Highness ?'

'Well ! let us go; but we can return.'

'Not to-night, at least, my lord. I would your Highness
appreciated my fears : I see ambushes everywhere, and
surely I may well be allowed to entertain such fears when
I am the companion of the first Prince of the blood—the

heir to the throne, whom so many people would wish not to succeed to it.'

These last words produced such an impression on François that he decided to go at one; all the same, he grumbled angrily, and inwardly determined to pay back these five noblemen, at a suitable time and place, for the unpleasantness which they had just caused him.

'Very well,' said he, 'let us go home; we will find Bussy there; he must have returned from that wedding party; he will probably have been picking quarrels and will have killed, or will be going to kill to-morrow morning, some of these minions, and that will console me.'

'So be it, my lord,' said d'Aurilly; 'let us put our hopes in Bussy. Like your Highness, I have the greatest confidence in him.'

Before they had turned the corner of the Rue de Jouy, our five friends perceived a horseman in a long cloak approaching from the direction of the Rue de la Tison. The sharp, heavy sound of the horses' feet re-echoed on the hard ground, and a feeble moonbeam struggling with the gloom, and making a last attempt to break through the cloudy sky and snow-laden air, touched with silver the white feather of his hat. He held carefully in check the horse he was riding, and forced it to walk, so that it foamed at the mouth, in spite of the cold.

'This time it is he,' exclaimed Quélus.

'Impossible!' said Maugiron.

'Why impossible?'

'Because he is alone, and we left him with Livarot, d'Entragues, and Ribeirac, who would never allow him to travel unattended.'

'It is he, nevertheless,' declared d'Épernon. 'Don't you recognise his deep hum, and the haughty way of holding up his head? He is quite alone.'

'Then it is a trap,' observed d'O.

'Trap or no trap, it's he,' asserted Schomberg, 'and, since it is he—draw your swords!'

It was indeed Bussy, coming carelessly along the Rue Saint-Antoine, following most strictly the way which Quélus had planned for him. He had been warned by Saint-Luc, but in spite of the very natural fear with which the words had inspired him, he had dismissed his three friends at the door of Montmorency House. This was one of these adventures such as the brave colonel loved. He said:

'I am but a plain nobleman; but I have the courage of an emperor in my breast, and when I read in Plutarch's lives of the exploits of the ancient Romans, there is not a single act of theirs which I cannot imitate if I choose.'

Then Bussy had thought that perhaps Saint-Luc, who was not usually a friend of his, and whose unexpected interest was, in fact, explained by the perplexing situation in which he found himself, had only warned him in order to force him to take precautions which would make him appear ridiculous in the eyes of his adversaries. Now, Bussy feared ridicule more than danger. He had, even in his enemies' sight, a reputation for courage, which must be maintained at the level to which it had raised itself, even should he court the wildest adventures. Like one of Plutarch's heroes, then, he had sent off his three friends, a strong escort which would have caused even a troop of horsemen to respect him, and, with arms folded in his cloak, with no weapons save his sword and dagger, he rode toward his destination. There awaited him, not a mistress, as might have been supposed, but a letter which in token of their firm friendship, the Queen of Navarre sent him on the same day of every month. The brave gentleman, according to his promise to the fair Margaret, a promise which he had kept without fail, went at night and alone, so as not to endanger any one, to obtain this letter. He had come all the distance from Rue des Grands-Augustins to the Rue Saint-Antoine safely, when, on reaching Rue Sainte-Catherine, his sharp eye distinguished in the darkness, along the wall, those human forms which the Duc d'Anjou, not so well warned, had not perceived. Moreover, to the truly brave soul, at the approach of danger, there comes a certain elated feeling which heightens the acuteness of the senses and perceptions.

Bussy counted the black shadows upon the gray wall. 'Three, four, five,' said he, 'not counting the lackeys, no doubt hidden in another corner, to run up at their masters' first call. They evidently expect to make short work of me. Good Heavens! here's a hard enough task, though, for one man. Come, come, that worthy Saint-Luc was not deceiving me, and though the first were to run me through, I should still say to him: 'Thanks for the warning, friend.'

He advanced nearer; only his right arm was now

moving freely, beneath his cloak, which he had unfastened with an imperceptible movement of his left hand. It was then that Schomberg cried, 'Draw your swords!' and the others repeating the cry, rushed upon Bussy.

'Yes, forsooth, gentlemen,' exclaimed Bussy, in a sharp but calm voice, 'so you wish to kill that poor Bussy, it appears! He is that wild beast, then; he is the famous wild boar you were reckoning on hunting? Well, sirs, the wild boar is going to cut up some of you, I swear, and you know I never fail to keep my word.'

'So be it,' replied Schomberg, 'but, all the same, you are a most ill-mannered fellow, my lord Bussy d'Amboise, to speak so to us when you are on horseback, while we listen to you on foot.'

Saying these words, the young man's arm, clad in white satin, stole out from his cloak and shone like a silvery flash of lightning in the moonbeams, before Bussy could guess with what intention. He was about to answer in his usual way, when, as he dug his spurs into his horse's sides, he felt the animal tremble under him. Schomberg, with a skill peculiar to him, a skill he had already manifested in the numerous encounters he had taken part in, young as he was, had thrown a kind of cutlass, having a broad blade heavier than the handle; and the weapon, cutting open the horse's leg, remained in the wound as the woodman's chopper sticks in the branch of an oak. The animal gave a dull groan and fell, shivering, on its knees. Bussy, ready for every emergency, stood firmly on the ground, grasping his sword.

'Ah! wretch,' cried he, 'that is my favourite horse. You shall pay me for this.'

As Schomberg approached, carried away by his courage and miscalculating the range of the sword which Bussy held pressed to his side, just as we may count wrongly upon the reach of the serpent's fangs when it lies coiled, the sword and the arm were unbent, and the weapon entered his thigh. Schomberg gave a cry.

'Well!' said Bussy, 'do I keep my word? One of you wounded already. It was Bussy's wrist you should have slashed at, not his horse's leg.'

In the twinkling of an eye, while Schomberg was binding up his wound, with his handkerchief, Bussy flashed the point of his long sword in the faces, at the breasts of his other antagonists. He would not call out; for to call for help would be to acknowledge his need of assistance, and that was unworthy of Bussy; only, twisting his cloak round his left arm and making a buckler of it, he stopped the attack, not to retreat, but to reach a wall against which he could stand and not be surprised from behind. Parrying ten thrusts every minute, he felt at times that yielding resistance which shows the strokes have found their mark. Once he slipped and glanced mechanically on the ground. This moment was long enough for Quélus to thrust at his side.

'You are struck,' cried Quélus.

'Yes, in the doublet,' answered Bussy, who would not even confess that he had been wounded. And, rushing on Quélus, he struck his sword on that of his adversary with such force as to send it flying ten feet away. But he could not follow up his advantage, for in the same instant d'O, d'Épernon, and Maugiron attacked him with renewed strength. Schomberg had bound up his wound, Quélus had recovered his sword; he understood he was going to be hemmed in, that he had only a minute more to reach the wall, and that, if he failed to make use of that minute, all would be lost. Bussy leaped back, putting three feet or so between him and his adversaries; but four swords quickly thrust at him again, and yet not soon enough, for Bussy had placed his back to the wall. There he stood, strong as Achilles or Roland, smiling at the tempest of blows that rained and clashed all around him. Suddenly he felt the perspiration on his brow and a cloud passed before his eyes. He had forgotten his wound, and these signs of fainting he had just experienced reminded him of it.

'Ah! you are getting weak,' cried Quélus, redoubling his attack.

'Look here!' said Bussy, 'see if I am;' and with the pommel of his sword he struck him on the temple. Quélus reeled under the blow from this iron fist. Then, heated and furious like the wild boar which, after coping with the dogs, falls upon them, he gave a fearful cry and rushed forward. D'O and d'Épernon drew back; Maugiron had lifted Quélus, and stood holding him; Bussy broke the latter's weapon with his foot, and with the point of his sword slashed d'Épernon's forearm. For a moment Bussy had the victory, but Quélus recovered consciousness;

Schomberg, wounded as he was, renewed the struggle; four swords flashed anew. Bussy felt himself losing ground a second time. He gathered all his strength to make good his retreat, and drew back, gradually, to gain the wall again. Already the icy perspiration on his brow, a dull ringing in his ears, a film of blood spreading over his eyes, warned him that his strength was becoming exhausted. His sword refused to follow any more the path marked for it by a dulled brain. Bussy felt for the wall with his left hand, touched it, and was refreshed by its coldness ; but, to his great astonishment, the wall gave way. It was a half-open door.

Then, taking heart again, he made a final effort for this supreme moment. For a second he rained such a succession of rapid, violent blows, that all swords were thrust aside or lowered before him. Then slipping round to the other side of the door, and turning his back, he gave it a strong push with his shoulder. The bolt creaked in the staple. All was over, Bussy was out of danger; Bussy was the victor, since he was saved. With an eye that roved about in joy, he looked through the close iron railing on the pale faces of his enemies. He heard furious sword-cuts falling upon the woodwork, followed by cries of anger. Suddenly the ground gave way beneath him; he saw the wall totter. He advanced a step or two, found himself in a courtyard, fell over and rolled upon the steps of a staircase. Then he felt nothing more, and he seemed to be going down into the silence and darkness of the tomb.

CHAPTER III

DREAM OR REALITY ?

Bussy had slipped his handkerchief under his shirt, and fastened his sword-belt over it, thus making a sort of bandage for the open, throbbing wound, from which the blood flowed like a fiery stream; but he had already lost such a quantity of blood that directly afterwards he fell into a swoon. Whether his brain, over-excited by anger and suffering, was still working, or whether to the faintness had succeeded a state of fever which, in its turn, had given place to a second fainting fit, this is what Bussy saw, or thought he saw, during that period of dim consciousness, which came between the shadow of the two nights. He was in a room which had carved wood furniture, figured tapestry, and a painted ceiling. The figures on the walls, in every possible attitude, holding out wreaths of flowers and carrying swords, seemed to be leaving their place, and endeavouring to reach the ceiling by mysterious pathways. Between the two windows was the portrait of a lady in a blaze of light, only it seemed to Bussy that the frame for this portrait was formed by nothing other than a doorway. Bussy, motionless, held in bed as by some superior power, deprived of all movement, every faculty but sight lost, gazed at all these figures dully, admiring the insipid smiles of the flower-bearers, and the absurd rage of those carrying swords. Had he seen these figures before, or was he looking at them for the first time ? That was just what he could not be sure of, so heavy had his head become.

Suddenly the lady in the portrait seemed to leave the frame, and came towards him, a charming creature, dressed in a long, white robe, such as the angels wear, with fair hair falling on her shoulders, eyes black as jet, long, velvety eyelashes, and a skin so transparent that one could almost see the motion of the blood beneath it, tinting it red. This woman was so extraordinarily beautiful, her stretched out arms were so enticing, that Bussy made a violent effort to get up and throw himself at her feet. But he seemed to be held down by fetters like those which keep the corpse in its grave, while the immaterial soul, scorning the earth, rises to the sky. He was, thus, compelled to look at the bed in which he was lying, and it seemed to be one of those magnificent carved pieces of furniture of François the First's day, with white damask curtains, embossed in gold.

At the sight of this woman, the figures on the walls and the ceiling lost their interest for Bussy. The woman alone held his attention, and he tried to see the blank space left in the frame; but a mist, which his sight could not pierce, hung in front of this frame, hiding all trace of it. Then his eyes travelled back to the mysterious person again, and, bending his gaze upon the wonderful apparition, he began to address some flattering remarks to her in the easy verse which he had a faculty of making. Suddenly, however, the woman disappeared : a solid body came between her and Bussy; this body walked heavily and spread out its hands, like a man playing at Blind Man's Buff. Bussy felt so angry with this ill-timed visitor that he would have thrown himself at him, had his actions been free; it is fair to say he made the attempt, but found it impossible. As he tried, in vain, to raise himself from the bed to which he seemed chained, the new-comer spoke.

'Well,' he asked, 'am I at the place at last?'

'Yes, sir,' said a voice so sweet that Bussy's heart thrilled; 'and you may now remove your bandage.'

Bussy tried to discover if the owner of the sweet voice was the lady of the portrait, but the effort was useless. All he saw was the young and graceful figure of a man, who had just removed his bandage, in answer to the invitation, and was glancing with startled eyes all round the wall.

'Deuce take the man!' thought Bussy, who strove to express this thought by word or gesture, though both were equally impossible.

'Ah! now, I understand,' said the young man, coming near the bed; 'you are wounded, aren't you, my dear sir? Come, we are going to try to put you right.'

Bussy vainly endeavoured to answer. An icy vapour was falling on his eyes, and the tips of his fingers tingled as though a hundred thousand pins were running into them.

'Is the wound mortal?' asked the sweet voice, betraying such a sorrowful interest, that the tears came into Bussy's eyes. It was the same voice that had already spoken, and the wounded man knew it belonged to the lady of the portrait.

'I hardly know yet, but I will tell you presently,' answered the young man; meanwhile, he has fainted.

After this point, Bussy understood no more. He seemed to hear a robe rustling away, then he felt something like a red-hot iron pass over his side, and the part of his brain still active slept again. Later on, he was unable to say how long the unconsciousness had lasted. Only, on awaking, a cold current blew across his face; hoarse, harsh voices grated on his ears; he opened his eyes to ascertain if the figures on the tapestry were disputing with those on the ceiling. Hoping to find the portrait still there, he looked all around. But no tapestry! no ceiling either! As to the picture, it had completely

C.J.   B vanished. On his right stood a man—a butcher apparently—clad in gray, with a white apron, stained with blood, tucked into his belt; on his left was a monk of Sainte-Geneviève, who raised up his head, and an old woman mumbling prayers. Bussy's wandering eyes presently fell upon a mass of stonework, and looking up, as though to measure the height, he recognised the fortress of the Temple; above the Temple was the sky, white and cold, slightly gilded by the rising sun. Bussy was evidently in the street, or rather on the edge of the Temple moat.

'Ah! thanks, good friends,' said he, 'for the trouble you have taken to carry me here. I needed fresh air, but they could have given me some by opening the windows, and I should have been much more comfortable on my bed with the white and gold damask than on the bare ground. Never mind, I have some twenty gold crowns in my pocket, unless you have already paid yourselves, which would have been wise; here, friends, take them.'

'But, noble sir,' said the butcher, 'we had no trouble in bringing you here; this is where you actually were. We found you when we passed at daybreak.'

'Ah, really!' said Bussy; 'was the young doctor here too?' The bystanders looked at one another.

'It's just part of his delirium,' observed the monk, shaking his head. Then, looking down on Bussy, he added, 'My son, I think you would do well to confess.' Bussy regarded the monk with a startled air.

'There was no doctor, poor, dear, young man,' mumbled the old woman. 'You were alone, abandoned, cold as a corpse. Look, there's a little snow on the ground, and you can see the black outline where you were lying.'

Bussy glanced at his aching side, remembered having received a sword cut, and, slipping his hand under his doublet, he felt his handkerchief in its old place, fastened over the wound with his sword-belt. 'It's queer,' said he.

The bystanders had already availed themselves of his invitation, and were dividing the money with many pitying exclamations.

'There,' exclaimed Bussy, when they had finished; 'that's all right, friends. Take me to my home, now.'

'Ah! surely, surely, poor, dear young man,' said the old woman; 'the butcher is strong, and you can have his horse.'

'Is that true?' asked Bussy.

'Perfectly true,' replied the butcher; 'my horse and myself are at your service, noble sir.'

'All the same, my son,' said the monk, 'while the butcher goes for his horse, it would be as well to make your confession.'

'What's your name?' asked Bussy.

'Brother Gorenflot,' answered the monk.

'Well, Brother Gorenflot,' said Bussy, sitting up, 'I hope that moment has not come yet. So, my father, let us do what's most urgent. I am cold, and would like to be taken back to my house to get warm again.'

'And what is the name of your house?'

'Bussy House.'

'What!' cried the bystanders; 'Bussy House!'

'Yes; what is there to astonish you in that?'

'You are one of Monsieur Bussy's servants, then?'

'I am Monsieur de Bussy himself.'

'Bussy!' cried the crowd; 'my lord Bussy, the brave Bussy. Long live Bussy!'

The young man was lifted on their shoulders, and borne in triumph to his dwelling; whilst the monk went away, counting his share of the twenty gold crowns, and shaking his head as he murmured, 'If he is that swaggerer Bussy, I am not surprised he was unwilling to confess.'

Meanwhile Bussy had sent for his usual doctor, who pronounced the wound but slight.

'Tell me,' said Bussy, 'has this wound been dressed?'

'Good gracious!' exclaimed the doctor, 'I can hardly say for certain; though, after all, it seems very much like it.'

'Is it serious enough to have made me delirious?' again asked Bussy.

'Certainly.'

'Gracious! then the tapestry with the figures carrying flowers and swords, the frescoed ceiling, the carved bed hung with white and gold damask, the portrait between the two windows; the charming, fair woman with the black eyes, the doctor playing at Blind Man's Buff, whom I was very nearly falling upon—that was all delirium, was it? and the only real thing was my encounter with the courtiers! Where was I fighting. Ah! yes, I remember. It was near the Bastille, toward the Rue St Paul. I leaned against a wall, the wall was really a door, which, luckily for me, gave way. I shut it again with great difficulty; I found myself in a passage. There, I fainted. Or, was I dreaming ? That's the question. And my horse, by the way ? They must have found my horse dead in the square. Doctor, ring for some one, please.'

The doctor called a valet. Bussy, making inquiries, learned that the animal, torn and bleeding, had dragged itself to the house, and had been found outside the door at daybreak. Immediately the alarm had spread; all Bussy's servants, who worshipped their master, had set out in search of him, and the majority had not returned.

'There is only the portrait, then,' said Bussy, 'that remains like a dream. Is it likely that a portrait would leave its frame to come and talk to a doctor with his eyes bandaged ? It is I who am a fool. Still, when I recall it, the portrait was very charming. It had——' Bussy began to think over the details, and as they came back to his memory, a delicious thrill, warming and stirring his heart, passed with a velvety touch, through his burning breast.

'I dreamed all that !' exclaimed Bussy, while the doctor placed the bandage over his wound.

'By my sooth, it is not possible; one can't have such dreams ! Let us sum it up once more.'

Bussy began repeating for the hundreth time : 'I was at the ball; Saint-Luc warned me that I should be way-laid near the Bastille. I was with Antragues, Ribeirac, and Livarot. I sent them home. I proceeded by the quay, Grand-Châtelet, and so on. At the Hôtel des Tournelles, I caught sight of the men watching for me. They rushed up, and lamed my horse. We had a fierce struggle. I went into a passage; I fainted away; and then:— ah ! there it is ! it's that "and then" that finishes me; there is fever, delirium, dreams after that "and then." Later,' he added, with a sigh, 'I came to myself on the slope of the Temple moat, where a monk of Sainte-Catherine's Church wished to hear my confessions. All the same, I will have a clear account of it,' continued Bussy, after a moment's silence. 'Doctor, shall I have to keep my room a fortnight for this scratch, as I did the last time ?'

'That depends. Come, you can't walk, can you ?'

'On the contrary, I feel as if I had quicksilver in my legs.'

'Walk a few steps.'

Bussy leaped out of bed, and gave proof of his recovery by walking, easily enough, round the room.

'That's all right,' said the doctor, 'as long as you don't ride on horseback, and don't walk twenty-five miles the first day.'

'Good! there's a doctor for you!' cried Bussy. 'I saw another one, though, last night. Ah! yes, really saw him. I have his face before me now; and if ever we meet, I shall recognise him, I promise you.'

'My dear sir,' said the doctor, 'I do not advise you to look for him; one has always a touch of fever after a sword-cut; you ought to know that, however, as you have already received a dozen of them.'

'Oh! my goodness,' exclaimed Bussy suddenly, as a new idea seized him, for his thoughts were entirely taken up with the mystery of the previous night, 'can my dream have begun outside that door, instead of inside? Was the passage not there either, or the stair, any more than the bed with the white and gold damask, and the portrait? Did these brigands, imagining I was killed, carry me to the moat of the Temple, so as to put any witnesses off the scent? If so, I may well have dreamed the rest. If I owe them the dream that is troubling me, mastering me, killing me, I swear I will kill every one of them.'

'My dear gentleman,' said the doctor, 'if you wish to get well quickly, you must not excite yourself.'

'All except that kind Saint-Luc,' continues Bussy, paying no attention to the doctor; 'that's another matter: he behaved to me like a friend. So I wish to pay my first visit to him.'

'Not before this evening, at five o'clock,' the doctor protested.

'Very good; but I assure you, going out and seeing people won't hurt me; keeping quiet and staying alone will.'

'That may be; you are a remarkable patient in every way. Act as you think fit, my lord; I only give you one piece of advice: that is, don't get another wound until this one is healed.'

Bussy promised to do his best in this respect, and having dressed, he called for his litter, and was conveyed to Montmorency House.

CHAPTER IV

HOW MADAME DE SAINT-LUC PASSED THE NIGHT

A SPLENDID horseman and a perfect gentleman was
Louis de Clermont, better known as Bussy d'Amboise.
No man had made more glorious conquests for a long time
past.   Kings and princes had sought his friendship:
queens and princesses had smiled upon him.   Bussy had
taken La Mole's place in the affection of Margaret of
Navarre, and this noble, tender-hearted Queen, who
needed some consolation, no doubt, after the death of
her favourite, whose story we have told, had committed,
for the brave, handsome Bussy's sake, so many indiscretions, that her husband, Henri, a man usually unmoved
by these things, was affected, and Duc François would
never have forgiven his sister's love, had it not won over
Bussy to his side.   This was another occasion on which
the Duc sacrificed his feelings to that ambition, secret
and undecided, which all through his life was to cost
him so much sorrow and bring so little reward.

But, in the midst of all his successes, in war, in ambitions, in intrigue, Bussy had remained exempt from all
human weaknesses; he had never known fear, neither
had he known love.

Henri III. had offered him his friendship, which Bussy
had refused, saying that kings' friends are their servants,
and sometimes even worse, and consequently such
a position did not suit him.   Henri had swallowed this
insult in silence, aggravated as it was by Bussy's choice
of Duc François as a patron.   It is true that François
was Bussy's master, as one who fights with a lion is its
master.   He feeds and attends to it, lest it should devour
him.   Such was this Bussy, whom François used to manage
his own private quarrels.   Bussy realised this, but the
part suited him.

He had constructed a theory after the style of the
Rohan motto, which ran, 'I cannot be King, I scorn to
be a Prince, I am Rohan.'   Bussy said: 'I cannot be
King of France, but the Duc d'Anjou can; I shall be the
King over the Duc d'Anjou.'   As, in fact, he was.

When Saint-Luc's servants saw the formidable Bussy, they ran to inform Monsieur de Brissac.

'Is Monsieur de Saint-Luc at home?' asked Bussy, looking through the curtains of the porter's house.

'No, my lord,' replied the lodge-keeper.

'Where can I find him?'

'I don't know, monsieur. They are becoming anxious in the house. Monsieur de Saint-Luc has not come in since yesterday.'

'Bah!' said Bussy, in astonishment.

'It is as I tell you.'

'But, Madame de Saint-Luc? Is she at home?'

'Yes.'

'Pray inform Madame de Saint-Luc that I shall be charmed to be permitted to pay my respects.'

Five minutes later, the messenger returned, saying that Madame de Saint-Luc would be pleased to see Monsieur de Bussy. Descending from his velvet cushions, Bussy walked up the wide stair; Jeanne de Cossé had come to the centre of the reception-room to meet him. She was very pale, and her hair, black as the raven's wing, gave to her skin a tint of yellowish ivory; her eyes were red from want of sleep, and her cheeks were marked by silver traces of recent tears. Bussy, at first inclined to smile, and ready to address some improvised compliment, was stopped by these signs of real sorrow.

'Welcome, Monsieur de Bussy,' said the young woman, 'in spite of the fear which your presence occasions me.'

'What do you mean, madame? Why should my presence disturb you?'

'There was a duel last night between you and Monsieur de Saint-Luc, was there not? Confess.'

'Between me and Monsieur de Saint-Luc?' repeated Bussy, stupefied.

'Yes, he sent me away that he might speak to you. You are on the Duc d'Anjou's side, he is on the King's; you disputed. Hide nothing from me, Monsieur de Bussy, I beg you. You must know how anxious I am. He went away with the King, it is true; but you could have met again. Tell me the truth. What has happened to Monsieur de Saint-Luc?'

'Madame,' said Bussy, 'truly, this is strange. I was expecting you to ask about my wound, and you are questioning me——'

'Monsieur de Saint-Luc wounded you; he fought!' exclaimed Jeanne. 'Ah, now you see——'

'No, madame, he did not fight at least with me, the dear Saint-Luc; thank goodness, I was not wounded by him. More than that, he did all he could to prevent my being hurt. Besides, he surely would tell you that we are now like Damon and Pythias!'

'How could he tell me, when I have not seen him again?'

'You have not seen him again? What the porter said was true, then?'

'What did he tell you?'

'That Monsieur de Saint-Luc had not been home since eleven o'clock last night. You have not seen your husband since then?'

'No, alas!'

'But where can he be?'

'I ask you.'

'Pray tell me about this, madame,' said Bussy, suspecting what had happened, 'it is very funny.'

The poor woman regarded Bussy with the greatest astonishment.

'No, it is very sad, I meant to say,' Bussy continued. 'I have lost a lot of blood, so I am not in possession of all my faculties. Tell me this sad story, madame.'

Jeanne related all she knew, namely, that Henri had ordered Saint-Luc to accompany him, and that the gates of the Louvre had been closed.

'Ah! very good, I understand,' said Bussy.

'What! you understand?' asked Jeanne.

'Yes; His Majesty carried Saint-Luc to the Louvre, and, once in, Saint-Luc could not get out.'

'Why was Saint-Luc unable to come away?'

'Ah, gracious!' said Bussy, embarrassed, 'You are asking me to divulge state secrets.'

'Still, I went to the Louvre, and my father went too,' said the young woman.

'Well?'

'Well! the guards declared that Saint-Luc must be at his own house.'

'All the more reason that Saint-Luc is at the Louvre,' said Bussy.

'You think so?'

'I am sure of it, and if you wish to be certain——'

'It would be useless my going to the palace, I should

be sent away with the same answer as before. For, if he is there, why should I not see him ?'

'Do you wish to enter the Louvre ?'

'For what purpose ?'

'To see Saint-Luc.'

'But then, if he is not there ?'

'Eh, by my troth ! I say he is there.'

'It is strange !'

'No, it is king-like.'

'But *you* can enter the Louvre, then ?'

'Certainly. *I* am not Saint-Luc's wife.'

'You are confusing me. What can you mean ? You assert that Saint-Luc's wife may not enter the Louvre, and yet you wish to take me with you !'

'Not at all, madame. I do not wish to take *Saint-Luc's wife* there—a woman ! fie ! for shame !'

'Then, you are laughing, at me—and it is very unkind of you !'

'No, no, dear lady, listen : you are twenty years old, you are tall, you have black eyes and a supple figure, you are like my youngest page—do you understand— that pretty youth who looked so well in cloth of gold last night.'

'Ah ! what madness, Monsieur de Bussy !' cried Jeanne, blushing.

'Listen ; there is no other way. You wish to see Saint-Luc, tell me ?'

'Oh ! I would give anything in the world for that.'

'Well, I promise to show you him without your giving anything.'

'Yes, but——'

'Oh ! I have told you how.'

'Well, Monsieur de Bussy; I accept; only tell this young man I require one of his suits, and I will send one of my maids for it.'

'No, no. You shall have a new suit, which I mean these rogues to wear at the Queen-Mother's first ball. I'll send the one which fits you best; then you will join me to-night, in Rue Saint-Honoré, near the Rue des Prouvaires, and from there——'

'From there ?'

'Well, we will go together to the Louvre.'

Jeanne began to laugh, and held out her hand to Bussy.

'Forgive me for my suspicions,' said she.

'Willingly. You are going to provide me with an adventure at which all Europe will laugh. It is I who am indebted to you.'

Taking his leave, he returned home to make preparations for the masquerade. In the evening, at the stated time, Bussy and Madame de Saint-Luc met on the rising ground of the Barrier des Sergents. If she had not worn his page's costume, Bussy would not have recognised her. She was charming in her disguise. After exchanging a few words, they proceeded towards the Louvre. At the end of the Rue des Fossés-Saint-Germain-l'Auxerrois, they overtook a large company which barred their passage. Jeanne was afraid. Bussy recognised the Duc d'Anjou by his piebald horse and the white velvet mantle which he usually wore.

'Ah!' said Bussy, 'you were puzzling your brains, my fine page, as to how you were to enter the Louvre? Well! be easy, you are to make a triumphal entry. My lord,' he called out at the pitch of his voice.

The cry travelled through space, and, in spite of the stamping of horses' hoofs and the sound of voices, reached the Prince's ear. He turned round.

'You, Bussy!' he exclaimed, quite delighted; 'I thought you were mortally wounded, and was going to your house, the Stag's Horn, in the Rue de Grenelle.'

'In troth, my lord,' said Bussy, without even thanking him for this mark of attention, 'if I am not dead, it is nobody's fault but my own. Indeed, my lord, you land me in some pretty traps, and leave me in some happy situations. Last night, at Saint-Luc's ball, it was a regular cut-throat business all round. I was the only Angevin there, and they nearly took every drop of blood in my body, upon my honour.'

''Sdeath, Bussy, they shall pay dear for that, and I will make them count every drop of it.'

'So you say,' said Bussy, with his accustomed freedom, 'and then you smile at the first one you meet. If you would even show your teeth, in smiling, but your lips are too tight set for that.'

'Well!' answered the Prince, 'come to the Louvre and you will see.'

'What shall I see?' my lord.

'How I am going to speak to my brother.'

'Listen, my lord, I am not going to the Louvre to meet with a rebuff. That is all very well for princes of the blood and minions.'

'Be easy, I have taken this affair to heart.'

'Do you promise there shall be fitting reparation?'

'I promise you shall be satisfied. You still hesitate?'

'My lord, I know you so well.'

'Come, I tell you; we will discuss it.'

'This is your opportunity,' whispered Bussy in the Comtesse's ear. 'There will be a fearful scene between these good brothers, who hate each other, and, meanwhile, you will find Saint-Luc.'

'Well,' asked d'Anjou, 'have you decided, or must I pass my word as a prince?'

'Oh, no!' said Bussy, 'that would bring me bad luck. At all events I am with you, and if any one insults me, I can well avenge it.' Bussy stepped up beside the Prince, whilst the new page, following closely, walked directly behind him.

'Avenge it! no, no!' exclaimed the Prince, answering Bussy's threat, 'that is no concern of yours, my brave gentleman. I take that upon myself. Listen, I know your assassins,' he added, in low tones.

'Bah!' said Bussy, 'your Highness has taken so much trouble as to find out.'

'I saw them.'

'How was that?' asked Bussy, astonished.

'I had business at the Porte Saint-Antoine; they met me and nearly killed me, instead of you. Ah! I had no suspicion it was you the brigands were waiting for, otherwise——'

'Well! otherwise?'

'Was this new page with you?' asked the Prince, leaving his threat unfinished.

'No, my lord, I was alone; and you?'

'I was with Aurilly; why were you alone?'

'Because I wish to maintain my reputation as the brave Bussy.'

'And they wounded you?' asked Anjou, with his quickness in parrying the thrusts aimed at him.

'I don't wish them to boast about it, but I have a fine sword-cut right across my side.'

'Ah! the villains! Aurilly declared they had evil intentions.'

'What!' cried Bussy, 'you saw the ambush! you were with Aurilly, who wields a sword as well as he plays the lute; he suspected these people; you were two, they only five, and yet you did not stay to lend a helping hand?'

'What could I do? I had no idea who was to be the victim of the ambush.'

'The deuce! When you saw Henri's courtiers, you must surely have known they were plotting against some friend of yours. Now, as I am almost the only person courageous enough to be your friend, it was not difficult to guess I was the victim.'

'Perhaps you are right, my dear Bussy, but it did not occur to me.'

'All the same ——' sighed Bussy, as though unable to express his thoughts in any other way.

On reaching the Louvre the Duc was received at the gates by the captain and the porters. Their orders were strict, but these, as one may suppose, were not made for him who was first in the kindgom after the King. The Prince entered then under the arch of the drawbridge, along with his suite.

'My lord,' said Bussy, when they arrived at the Court of Honour, 'go to your brother, and remember you have given me a solemn promise; I wish to say a few words to some one.'

'You are leaving me, Bussy,' stammered the Prince, who had been depending on his presence.

'I must; but don't let that hinder you; be assured I will return when the noise is loudest. Call out, my lord, because unless I hear you calling, you understand, I will not come.'

Then, taking advantage of the Duc's entrance into the grand hall, he slipped away, followed by Jeanne. Bussy knew the Louvre like his own house. He went up a hidden stairway, traversed a few lonely corridors, and arrived at a sort of ante-room.

'Wait for me here,' said he.

'Oh, goodness! you are leaving me alone!' cried Jeanne, terrified.

'I am obliged to,' answered Bussy; 'I must clear the way for you, and arrange how you are to enter.'

CHAPTER V

HOW MADAME DE SAINT-LUC SPENT THE SECOND NIGHT AFTER HER WEDDING

BUSSY went straight to the arms-room, which had been the favourite apartment of Charles IX. It now served as King Henri's bedchamber, and had been altered for his use. Charles IX., a hunter, smith, and poet, kept stags' horns, arquebuses, manuscripts, books, and vices in this room. Henri III. had two beds there, of velvet and satin, besides drawings, relics, small scapularies blessed by the Pope, perfumed sachets from the East, and a collection of the finest fencing swords.

Bussy was aware that Henri would not be in this room, since his brother was asking audience in the gallery; but he knew, too, that close at hand was the apartment formerly used by Charles IX.'s nurse, but now appropriated by Henri's favourite. Henri being a prince who often changed his friends, this room had been occupied by Saint-Mégrin, Maugiron, d'O, d'Épernon, Quélus, and Schomberg in turn, and (according to Bussy's idea) would now be Saint-Luc's, since the King had shown him such a marked increase of affection as to carry him away from his wife.

This strange being, Henri III., a prince, at once frivolous and deep, timid and brave, always wearied, restless, and a dreamer, required continual distraction—in the daytime, noise, games, exercise, mummery, masquerades, intrigues; at night, light, gossip, prayers, or debauchery. Henri is almost the only person of this character to be found in modern days. He should have been born in some Eastern town, in the middle of a world of mutes, slaves, eunuchs, pages, philosophers, and sophists; and his rule must have marked a special era of weak debauchery and follies, unknown between the reigns of Nero and Heliogabalus. Suspecting that Saint-Luc would be in the nurse's apartment, Bussy knocked at the door of the ante-room, which communicated with both apartments. The Captain of the Guards opened to him.

'Monsieur de Bussy!' exclaimed the astonished officer.

'Myself, my dear Monsieur de Nancey,' said Bussy.
'The King wishes to speak to Monsieur de Saint-Luc.'

'Very good,' answered the captain; 'inform M. de Saint-Luc that the King wishes to speak to him.'

Through the half-open door, Bussy darted a glance at the page. Then, turning to M. de Nancey, he asked, 'And what is poor Saint-Luc doing?'

'Playing with Chicot till the King returns from the audience he has granted to the Duc d'Anjou.'

'Will you allow my page to wait for me here?' Bussy asked.

'Very willingly,' answered the captain.

'Come in, Jeanne,' said Bussy, and he pointed out a window recess, where she took refuge. Scarcely was she hidden from sight, when Saint-Luc entered. M. de Nancey discreetly withdrew out of reach of the voices.

'What does the King want now?' asked Saint-Luc, in an ill-natured voice, scowling as he spoke. 'Ah, its you, Monsieur de Bussy.'

'Myself, dear Saint-Luc, and first of all——' He lowered his voice. 'First of all, thank you for the service you did me.'

'Ah!' Saint-Luc said, 'that was perfectly natural. It would have hurt me to see a brave man like you murdered. I thought you had been killed, though.'

'I just escaped by a little; but little, in this case, means a great deal.'

'How is that?'

'Well, I escaped with a nasty sword-cut, which I paid back, with interest, to Schomberg and d'Épernon. As to Quélus, he has his thick skull to thank. It's really one of the hardest I have known.'

'Tell me about your adventure, it will amuse me,' said Saint-Luc, yawning sufficiently to break his jawbone.

'I have no time now, my dear Saint-Luc. Moreover, I came for another purpose. You seem very bored!'

'Royally; that expresses it enough.'

'Well, I have come to amuse you. One good turn deserves another, surely.'

'You are right, and the one you do me is not less valuable than the one I did you. People die of ennui as well as of a sword-cut; it is more lingering, but surer.'

'Poor Comte,' said Bussy, 'you are a prisoner, then, as I suspected?'

'In every sense of the term. The King pretends that my humour alone amuses him. The King is very good-natured, for, since yesterday, I have made more faces at him than his monkey, and said more outrageous things than his jester.'

'Well, let us see; can I not do you a service?'

'Certainly,' said Saint-Luc, 'you can go to my house, or rather to Maréchal de Brissac's, and reassure my poor little wife, who must be very anxious and thinking my conduct most extraordinary.'

'What shall I tell her?'

'Eh, goodness! tell her that I am a prisoner under orders not to go out; that since yesterday the King has spoken to me about friendship, like Cicero, who wrote on the subject, and about virtue, like Socrates, who practised it.'

'What answer did you make?' asked Bussy, laughing.

'*Morbleu!* I replied that, as regards friendship, I am ungrateful, and, as regards virtue, I am perverse; that does not hinder him from persisting and repeating, with a sigh, "Ah! Saint-Luc, friendship is only an illusion, then! Ah, Saint-Luc, virtue, then, is only a name!" Only, after saying so in French, he says it again in Latin, and a third time in Greek.'

At this witticism, the page, to whom Saint-Luc had not yet paid the least attention, burst out laughing.

'What would you have, dear friend? he thinks it will affect you. What is twice repeated pleases, and all the more does it please a third time. But is that all I can do for you?'

'Ah! *mon Dieu*, yes; at least, I am afraid so.'

'Then it has been done.'

'How is that?'

'I suspected the truth, and told it beforehand to your wife.'

'What did she reply?'

'She was unwilling to believe it at first. But,' added Bussy, glancing towards the window recess, 'I hope she will be won over by evidence. Ask me to do something else, something difficult, impossible, even; there will be some pleasure in undertaking that.'

'Then, my dear Bussy, borrow for a few moments the winged horse of Astolpho, that fine horseman, and lead it up to one of my windows; I will get on the croup behind you, and you shall lead me to my wife. Then, if you choose, you may continue your journey to the moon.'

'My dear friend,' said Bussy, 'it will be simpler to take the winged horse to your wife, and bring her to you.'

'To the Louvre ?'

'To the Louvre itself. That would be still more laugh-able, would it not ?'

'Oh ! *mordieu* ! I should think so.'

'You would not be bored any more ?'

'No, in truth I should not.'

'For you are bored, you tell me?'

'Ask Chicot. I took an aversion to him this morning, and challenged him three times to fight with swords. The rascal got so angry that I nearly died of laughing. Well ! I didn't move a muscle; but I believe that if this state of things continues, I really will kill him as a distraction—or else get killed myself.'

'The deuce ! don't play any of these games; Chicot is a formidable swordsman. You would be still more loved in your grave than in your prison, let me tell you.'

'I don't know about that.'

'Come !' said Bussy laughing, 'would you like me to give you my page?'

'As my own ?'

'Yes, a wonderful lad.'

'Thank you,' said Saint-Luc. 'I detest pages. The King offered to send for some of my favourites, and I refused. Offer him to the King, he is adding to his household. As for me, when I leave this place, I will do as they did at Chenonceau, have only women to wait upon me, and what's more, I myself will design their costumes.'

'Bah !' said Bussy, insisting, 'try him.'

'Bussy,' said Saint-Luc, in annoyed tones, 'it is not kind to laugh at me like this.'

'But I know what you need.'

'No, no, a hundred times no !'

'Hallo ! page, come here.'

'*Mordieu* !' exclaimed Saint-Luc.

The page leaving the window came forward, blushing furiously.

'Oh ! oh !' murmured Saint-Luc, astonished to recognise Jeanne in Bussy's livery.

'Well !' asked Bussy, 'must I send him away?'

'No, certainly not,' Saint-Luc cried. 'Ah! Bussy, Bussy, I am eternally obliged to you.'

'Remember that, though not overheard, you are seen, Saint-Luc.'

'Yes, that's true.'

He stepped back hastily, for M. de Nancey, surprised at the rather too expressive pantomime, was beginning to listen, when a loud noise, which came through the glass doors, made him start.

'Ah! *mon dieu!*' he exclaimed, 'that is the King quarrelling with some one.'

'I believe it is, really,' said Bussy, pretending to be uneasy; 'I wonder if it can be the Duc d'Anjou?'

The Captain of the Guards, securing his sword at his side, walked towards the corridor, where he could hear sounds of a very lively dispute.

'Have I not managed things well?' said Bussy, turning to Saint-Luc.

'Whatever is wrong?' asked the latter.

'Only that the King and the Duc d'Anjou are abusing each other, and, since that must be a splendid sight, I am going to see it. Take advantage of this squabble, not by trying to escape, for the King would certainly find you again, but by putting this handsome page in a safe place; is that possible?'

'If it were not, it would have to become possible; but, luckily, I am supposed to be ill. I keep to my room.'

'In that case, good-bye, Saint-Luc; madame, do not forget me in your prayers.'

Bussy left the room, overjoyed at having played this trick upon Henri, and reached the corridor, to find the King, red with anger, protesting to the Duc d'Anjou, who was pale with rage, that Bussy had provoked the attack of the previous night.

'I assure your Majesty, d'Épernon, Schomberg, d'O, Maugiron, and Quélus were waiting for him at the Hôtel de Tournelles.'

'Who told you?'

'I saw them myself, your Majesty, with my own eyes.'

'In the darkness, was it? The night was as black as the inside of an oven.'

'I did not recognise them by their faces.'

'By what, then? By their shoulders?'

'No, your Majesty, by their voices.'

'They spoke to you?'

'They did more than that, they took me for Bussy, and attacked me.'

'You? What were you doing at the Porte Saint-Antoine?'

'I was going to Manasseh's.'

'To Manasseh, a Jew!'

'You go to Ruggieri's, the poisoner.'

'I go wherever I wish; I am the King.'

'That is not answering, it is knocking one down.'

'Moreover, as I said, Bussy provoked the affair.'

'Where?'

'At Saint-Luc's ball.'

'Bussy provoked five men! Surely not! Bussy is brave, but no fool.'

'*Par la mondieu!* I heard the provocation myself. Besides, he was quite capable of it, since, in spite of what you say, he wounded Schomberg in the thigh and d'Épernon in the arm, as well as nearly beating Quélus to death.'

'Ah! really, he did not inform me; I must compliment him.'

'*I* shall compliment nobody, but make an example of this bravo.'

'And I, whom your friends attack, not only in the person of Bussy, but in my own, shall know if I am your brother, and if there is one man in France, except your Majesty, who dare look me in the face and is not compelled by fear, if not by respect, to lower his eyes.'

At this moment, attracted by the noise made by the two brothers, Bussy appeared, gracefully attired in green satin of a delicate shade, adorned with pink bows.

'Your Majesty,' said he, bowing before Henri, 'permit me to present my very humble respects to you.'

'*Pardieu!* here he is,' said the King.

'Your Majesty has, apparently, been deigning to think of me?' Bussy suggested.

'Yes,' replied the King, 'and I am relieved to see that, in spite of what I was told, you seem the picture of health.'

'Your Majesty,' said Bussy, 'when one is bled, it clears the complexion, and I ought to have a very fresh colour to-night.'

'Ah! then, if you have been ill-used, lodge a complaint, my lord Bussy, and justice shall be done.'

'Excuse me, your Majesty, I have not been ill-used, and I do not complain.'

Henri was astonished, and glanced at the Duc d'Anjou.

'Ah, well! what were you saying, then?' he demanded.

'That Bussy had received a sword-cut in his side.'

'Is this true, Bussy?' asked the King.

'When your Majesty's brother affirms it,' Bussy replied, 'it should be true; a first prince of the blood cannot lie.'

'And though you have a sword-cut in your side, you do not lodge a complaint?'

'I should only complain, your Majesty, if I were prevented from avenging my wrongs by losing my right hand. Still,' continued this unmanageable duellist, 'I should avenge them quite well with my left hand.'

'Insolent man!' murmured Henri.

'Your Majesty,' observed the Duc d'Anjou, 'you were speaking of justice, well! let justice be done; we ask nothing more. Direct an inquiry to be made, appoint judges, and discover who laid the ambush.'

Henri grew red.

'No,' said he, 'I prefer for this time to let the matter drop, and to extend a pardon to all. I would rather these fierce enemies made peace, and am annoyed that Schomberg and d'Épernon are confined to their apartments by their wounds. Come, Monsieur d'Anjou, which of my friends was, in your opinion, the most outrageous? Tell me; that should be an easy matter since you saw them.'

'Your Majesty,' said the Duc, 'it was Quélus.'

'Indeed it was,' said Quélus, 'I won't deny it; His Highness saw very well.'

'Then,' said Henri, 'let M. de Bussy and M. de Quélus make peace in the name of all the others.'

'Oh! oh!' cried Quélus, 'what does that mean, your Majesty?'

'That I wish you two to kiss here, before me, this very instant.'

Quélus knit his brows.

'Well, signor,' said Bussy, turning towards Quélus, and imitating the Italian gesture of Pantaloon, 'will you do me this favour?'

The speech was so unexpected, and Bussy uttered it
with so much animation, that the King himself began to
laugh. Then, approaching Quélus, Bussy continued,
'Come, sir, the King wishes it,' and he threw his arms
round his neck.

'I hope this does not pledge you to anything,' said
Quélus, in a low tone, to Bussy.

'Be easy,' answered Bussy, in the same tone, 'sooner or
later we shall meet.'

Quélus, red and dishevelled, drew back in a fury.
Henri knit his brows, and Bussy, always acting Pantaloon,
turned on his heel and left the council-chamber.

CHAPTER VI

THE KING RETIRES FOR THE NIGHT

AFTER this scene, begun as tragedy, ended in comedy,
reports of which spread through the town like an echo
escaped from the Louvre, the King, with a feeling of
annoyance, retired to his bedroom. He was followed by
Chicot, who asked for supper.

'I am not hungry,' said Henri, crossing the threshold
of his room.

'That may be,' said Chicot, 'but I am ravenous, and
could eat anything, were it only a leg of mutton.'

The King apparently had not heard. Unfastening
his cloak, he laid it on the bed, removed his cap, which
was fastened by long black pins, and threw it on a chair;
then going towards the lobby leading to Saint-Luc's room,
which only a wall separated from his own : 'Wait for me
here,' said he, 'I am coming back.'

'Oh, don't hurry, my son,' said Chicot, 'I want time to
prepare a little surprise.'

When the sound of Henri's footsteps had died away, he
opened the door of the ante-room and summoned a valet.
'The King has changed his mind,' Chicot remarked,
'and wishes a nice supper for himself and Saint-Luc.
Some good wine especially.'

The valet immediately departed to carry out the orders,
never doubting but that they were the King's.

Henri, meanwhile, had found Saint-Luc in bed, as

he had been prepared for the King's visit. An old servant, who had followed him to the Louvre, and shared his imprisonment, was reading prayers to him, while, in a gilded arm-chair in the corner, with head in his hands, the page Bussy had brought slept soundly. The King took in all these details at a glance.

'Who is this young man ?' he asked Saint-Luc, uneasily.

'Your Majesty told me I might send for a page ?'

'Certainly.'

'I availed myself of the permission, your Majesty.'

'Ah !'

'Does His Majesty repent of having granted me this distraction ?'

'Not at all, my son, amuse yourself, by all means. How are you feeling ?'

'Your Majesty, I am highly feverish.'

'Indeed, your face is flushed; let me feel your pulse, you know I am a bit of a doctor.'

Saint-Luc held out his hand, evidently with a bad grace.

'Ah !' observed the King, 'quite intermittent and disturbed.'

'Oh ! your Majesty, indeed I am very ill.'

'I shall have you attended to by my own doctor.'

'Thank you, your Majesty, but I detest Miron.'

'I shall watch by you myself.'

'Your Majesty, I could not permit——'

'I shall have your bed placed in my room; we can talk all night. I have a thousand things to tell you.'

'Ah !' cried Saint-Luc, in despair, 'you call yourself a doctor, and my friend, yet wish to keep me from sleeping! *Morbleu !* doctor, what a fine way to treat your patients ! What a strange manner of showing your affection !'

'What ! you prefer to stay alone ?'

'Your Majesty, I have Jean, my page.'

'He is sleeping.'

'That is what I wish him to do; at least he does not prevent me from sleeping myself.'

'Let me watch with you; I will not speak unless you waken.'

'Your Majesty, I am extremely ill-tempered on wakening, and only the most intimate friend can excuse all the stupid remarks I make before being fully awake.'

'At least, come with me until I go to bed.'

'And I shall be free afterwards ?'

'Perfectly free.'

'I am a sorry courtier, I assure you. I am nearly falling asleep now.'

'You can yawn as you please.'

' What tyranny!' exclaimed Saint-Luc, 'when you have all your other friends.'

'Ah! a fine state they are in, too. Bussy has seen to that. Schomberg has had his thigh hurt, and d'Épernon's wrist is slashed like an Italian sleeve; Quélus is stupefied with the blow he received yesterday and his embrace to-day; then there is d'O, who bores one to death, and Maugiron, with his sour looks. Come! waken your rascal of a page, and tell him to give you a dressing-gown.'

'Your Majesty, in five minutes I will be with you.'

'Very well, but not more than five minutes, understand; and try to remember some stories, Saint-Luc, that we may laugh a little.'

Thereupon the King, having obtained half his desires, retired half satisfied. No sooner was the door closed than the page woke up with a start, and leaped towards it.

'Ah! Saint-Luc,' said he, 'you are going to leave me. What torture! I shall die of fear here. If I should be discovered?'

'My dear Jeanne, Gaspard,' and he indicated the old servant, 'will guard you.'

'I may as well go away,' said the young woman, blushing.

'If you really wish it, Jeanne,' said Saint-Luc sadly, 'I will have you taken to Montmorency House. But if you were as good as you are beautiful, if you had any feeling for poor Saint-Luc, you would wait a little time. I am going to be so ill that the King, bored with such a gloomy companion, will order me to bed.'

Jeanne cast down her eyes. 'Go, then,' said she, 'but don't stay long.'

' Jeanne, my dear Jeanne, you are charming,' exclaimed her husband, 'trust me to return as soon as possible. Moreover, I have an idea which I mean to develop. I will tell you about it presently.'

'An idea which will restore you to liberty?'

'I hope so.'

'Go, then.'

'Gaspard,' said Saint-Luc, 'see that no one enters. In a quarter of an hour, lock the door, and bring me the

key to the King's apartments. Let it be known that
Madame the Comtesse is safe, and returns to-morrow.'

Gaspard smilingly promised to carry out these orders,
which the young woman blushed to hear. Saint-Luc,
taking his wife's hand, kissed it tenderly, and went to the
already impatient King. Jeanne, left alone, trembled,
and hid herself in the wide curtains which fell round the
bed. There, pensive, uneasy, vexed, she thought of some
means of emerging triumphantly from her strange
position.

On entering the King's presence, Saint-Lux's nostrils
were assailed by a strong, heady perfume. Henri's feet,
in fact, trod upon bunches of cut flowers; roses, jasmine,
violets, gilly flowers, despite the coldness of the season,
formed a soft, scented carpet. The room, the ceiling
of which had been lowered and decorated with fine
paintings on canvas, was provided with two beds,
one so large as to take up almost a third of the space,
though placed against the wall. This bed had a
tapestry of gold and silk, with figures illustrating the
story of Cenée or Cénis, sometimes a man, and sometimes
a woman—a change, one may suppose, requiring strange
efforts of the painter's imagination. The bed canopy was
of cloth of silver, covered with gold and figures in silk.
On the part forming the head of the bed were the royal
arms, richly embroidered. From the middle of the ceiling
hung a gold chain, supporting a silver-gilt lamp, from which
the oil diffused a delicious perfume as it burned. At
the right-hand side of the bed, a gold satyr held a
candelabra, in which four pink and perfumed candles
burned. These candles, large as wax-tapers, cast a light
which, combined with that of the lamp, lit up the apartment.

The King, his bare feet on the carpet of flowers, was
seated on a chair of ebony, encrusted with gold; on his
knees were seven or eight very young spaniels, whose
damp noses rubbed softly against his hands. Two
servants dressed and curled his hair (which was turned up
like a woman's), his moustache, and his fine flowing beard.
A third spread on his face a thick layer of pink-coloured
cream of a unique kind, and with a delightful odour.
Henri, closing his eyes, bore these operations with the
serious majesty of an Indian god.

'Saint-Luc!' he was saying, 'where is Saint-Luc?'

Saint-Luc entered. Chicot, taking his hand, led him to the King.

'Here is your friend Saint-Luc,' he said; 'order him to be cleaned or rather besmeared with cream. Unless you take this necessary precaution, an annoying thing will happen : either he will offend you, who are so well perfumed, or you will appear too scented for him. Now, creams and combs,' added Chicot, stretching himself in an arm-chair opposite the King, '*I* wish to try some, too.'

'Chicot, Chicot,' cried Henri, 'your skin is too dry, it will absorb too much cream; there is hardly enough for me; and your hair is so tangled it would break my combs.'

'My skin has become hardened through exposure on your behalf, ungrateful prince ! and my mane is shaggy because it is always bristling at your contradictions; but, if you refuse me cream for external use, I'll say nothing more.'

Henri shrugged his shoulders, as if little inclined to be amused at his jester's bantering. 'Leave me,' he said, 'you are raving.' Then, turning to Saint-Luc, 'Well, my son,' said he, 'and how is your headache ?'

Saint-Luc lifted his hand to his brow and groaned.

'Just think,' Henri continued, 'I have seen Bussy d'Amboise. Monsieur,' to the hairdresser, 'you are burning me.'

'You have seen Bussy d'Amboise, your Majesty ?' Saint-Luc asked, shivering.

'Yes; just imagine these fools attacked him, five at once, and were beaten. I shall have them well whipped. Had you been there, what then, Saint-Luc ?'

'Your Majesty, probably I should have been no luckier than my comrades.'

'Now, now, what do you say ? I wager you would strike at Bussy ten times for his six. *Pardieu!* to-morrow we will see about it. Do you still practise ?'

'Yes, your Majesty.'

'Often ?'

'Almost every day when I am well; but, when I am ill, your Majesty, I am good for nothing.'

'How often did you——— ?'

'We were nearly equally matched, your Majesty.'

'I am a better swordsman than Bussy. Zounds ! sir,' to his barber, 'you are pulling out my moustache.' The barber knelt down.

'Your Majesty,' said Saint-Luc, 'tell me a cure for sickness.'

'Eat,' the King replied.

'Oh! your Majesty, I think you are wrong.'

'No; I assure you.'

'You are right, Valois,' exclaimed Chicot, 'and, as I am very ill, or have a pain in my stomach, I really don't know which, I am following the prescription.' And a strange noise, like the complicated movement of a monkey's jaws was heard.

Chicot, having finished the supper for two which he had ordered in the King's name, was cracking his jaws noisily while he devoured the contents of a Japanese porcelain cup.

'What on earth are you doing ?' Henri demanded.

'Taking my cream internally,' answered Chicot, 'since I am forbidden to take it externally.'

'Ah, traitor!' cried the King, and turning half round most inopportunely, he received the clammy finger of his valet, and the cream it was covered with, in his mouth.

'Eat, my son,' urged Chicot. 'I am not so despotic as you : for the interior or the exterior, I allow you both.'

'You are choking me, sir,' cried Henri to the valet, who knelt down as the barber had done. 'Bring my Captain of the Guards,' he continued, 'bring him at once.'

'Why ?' asked Chicot, passing his finger round the inside of the cup and then licking it.

'To run his sword through Chicot's body, and make a roast of him for my dogs.'

Chicot drew himself up, and putting his cap to the side : 'Par la mordieu!' he exclaimed, 'Chicot for your dogs, a nobleman for your quadrupeds! Well! let him come, your Captain of the Guards, my son, and we shall see.' Drawing his long sword, he defended himself in such an amusing manner from the hairdresser, the barber, and the valet, that the King could not help laughing.

'But I am hungry,' the King exclaimed, in a piteous voice, 'and the rascal has eaten all the supper.'

'You are a changeable being, Henri,' Chicot protested. 'I invited you to join me, and you refused. You have still your broth, however, I am no longer hungry, and am going to bed.'

Meanwhile old Gaspard had brought his master the key.

'I also,' said Saint-Luc, 'for I should fall down exhausted if I remained standing longer. I am shivering.'

'Here, Saint-Luc,' said the King, holding out a handful of little dogs, 'take them.'

'What could I do with them?'

'Take them to bed with you; the sickness will pass to them, and you will be rid of it.'

'Thank you, your Majesty,' said Saint-Luc, putting the dogs into their basket, 'I have no confidence in the remedy.'

'I am coming to visit you to-night, Saint-Luc.'

'Oh! no, your Majesty, I beg you; you will waken me suddenly, which brings on a fit.'

Saint-Luc thereupon bowed to the King and left the room. Chicot had already gone. The attendants departed in turn. There remained only the valets, who covered Henri's face with a mask made of fine linen, smeared with a perfumed paste. In this mask holes had been placed, for the nose, eyes, and mouth. A night cap of silk and silver stuff fixed the mask on his brow and round his ears. Then his arms were passed into a pink satin sleeping vest, with a soft lining of fine silk and cotton wool, and afterwards the attendants gave him his gloves. These reached to the elbows, and were touched inside with perfumed oil. When these mysteries of the royal toilet were finished, they handed Henri his broth to drink in a gold cup; but, before tasting it, he poured half into a similar cup and ordered it to be carried to Saint-Luc, wishing him a good night's rest. It was now Religion's turn. Owing to his absorption in other affairs, its claims were rather lightly regarded. Henri repeated only one prayer, without even telling his consecrated beads; then his bed being opened up, and warmed with coriander, benzoin, and cinnamon bark, he lay down. Once settled on his numerous pillows, he ordered the flowers to be carried away, as the air was becoming heavy. The windows were opened for a few minutes to freshen the atmosphere. A large fire of vine-shoots was now lit in the marble fireplace, and, quick as a meteor, was extinguished after having shed a warm glow through the room.

The valet then shut doors and drew curtains, and called in the King's favourite dog, Narcissus. With one bound the great dog leaped on the bed, where it kept pawing and turning a minute or two, and finally lay down across its master's feet. Then the pink candles which burned in the hands of the gold satyr were blown out, the light of the night lamp was lowered, and a less powerful wick substituted, and the valet charged with these last duties retired in his turn on tip-toe. Already more peaceful, more careless, more forgetful than the lazy monks shut snugly in their comfortable abbeys, the King of France no longer troubled to remember that France existed. He slept. Half an hour later, the servants who watched in the galleries, and who could see the windows of Henri's room from their respective positions, perceived the royal lamp go out altogether, and the silver moonbeams replace the rosy light which had coloured the panes. They thought consequently that His Majesty slept more and more soundly. At this time all sounds within and without had subsided, and the most noiseless bat could have been heard flying through the dark corridors of the Louvre.

CHAPTER VII

A SUDDEN CONVERSION

Two hours passed thus. Suddenly a terrible cry rang out from His Majesty's room. Yet the lamp remained unlit, the silence was deep as ever, and no sound was heard save this one strange cry. It was the King who had called out. Presently came the noise of falling furniture, the crash of china, of wild disordered steps in the room; then fresh cries, mingled with the barking of dogs. Immediately lights burned, swords gleamed in the corridors, and the heavy steps of sleepy guards shook the massive pillars.

'To arms! to arms! the King calls! to the King!' rose from all parts.

With quick steps the Captain of the Guard, the Colonel of the Swiss troops, the King's friends, the musketeers on duty rushed into the royal room, which was immediately flooded with light. Twenty torches lit up the scene. In front of the bed, the sheets and covering of which were scattered in disorder, Henri stood, a grotesque and terrifying figure in night attire, his hair on end, his eyes fixed. His extended right hand shook like a leaf in the

wind. His clenched left hand grasped the handle of his
sword, which he had instinctively seized. The dog,
quite as disturbed as his master, with paws thrust out
wide, looked at him and howled. The King seemed dumb
with fear; nobody dared break the silence; all looked at
one another questioningly, and waited in fearful anxiety.
Awakened by her husband's cries, half dressed, but
wrapped in a long cloak, appeared the young Queen,
Louise de Lorraine, that fair and gentle creature who
led the life of a saint on earth.

'Your Majesty,' said she, trembling more than any one,
'what is the matter ? Your cries reached my room,
and I have come.'

'It—it—is nothing,' answered the King, never moving
his eyes, which seemed to be regarding some vague form,
unseen by all but himself.

'But your Majesty called,' protested the Queen; 'your
Majesty is in pain ?'

Terror was so clearly imprinted on Henri's features
that it gradually seized upon the bystanders. They drew
back, they advanced, they gazed upon the King to assure
themselves that he was not wounded, had not been struck
with lightning, or bitten by some reptile.

'Oh ! your Majesty,' cried the Queen, 'in Heaven's
name, do not leave us in such misery ! Do you need a
doctor ?'

'A doctor !' said Henri, in the same gloomy tones;
' no, it is not the body, but the mind that ails—
no, no, not a doctor, a confessor.'

The bystanders gazed at the doors, the curtains, the
floor, the ceiling, but saw no traces of the object which had
so greatly terrified the King. The mystery grew darker,
the King asked for a confessor. No sooner was the request
made than a messenger leaped to horse, and a thousand
sparks were struck from the stones of the courtyard.
Five minutes later, Joseph Foulon, superior of the monastery of Sainte-Geneviève, was aroused, dragged from his
bed, and carried to the palace. At his coming the tumult
ceased, questions were asked, conjectures made; some
thought they could guess at reasons, all were afraid, for the
King was confessing his sins.

The next day, the King, who had risen early, issued
orders that the gate of the Louvre should be shut, and
only opened to let the confessor pass. Summoning the

treasurer, the wax-maker, the master of ceremonies, he opened his black bound prayer-book and read prayers. Then he stopped to cut out pictures of saints, and suddenly ordered all his friends to appear before him. Saint-Luc was sent for, but he was feeling worse. He was weak, and thoroughly exhausted. His lethargy had been so profound that alone of all the palace guests he heard no noise during the night, though his room and the King's were separated by a single wall. So he begged permission to remain in bed, where he would offer up as many prayers as the King desired. At this moving account, Henri crossed himself, and ordered an apothecary to visit Saint-Luc.

The King next sent for all the scourges from the monastery of Sainte-Geneviève. He went round, a black-robed figure, distributing these to the limping Schomberg, to d'Épernon, whose arm was in a sling, to Quélus, still dizzy with the effects of his blow, to d'O and Maugiron, who were trembling, and ordered the unfortunate courtiers to scourge one another with all their might. D'Épernon suggested that he should be exempted, as, having his arm in a sling, he could not return the blows given to him. This, he pointed out, would cause a discord, so to speak, in the scale of the scourging. The King answered that his penitence would, on that account, be the more acceptable to God.

Setting the example, Henri, removing doublet, vest, and shirt, struck himself like any martyr. Chicot wished to laugh and joke as usual, but a terrible glance convinced him that the time was unfavourable; seizing a scourge, he chastised his neighbours, and when none came within reach, he began knocking off the paint in scales from the pillars and woodwork. The noise succeeded in clearing the King's countenance, although his mind evidently remained deeply moved. Suddenly he left the room, bidding the company wait for him. No sooner was his back turned than the scourging stopped magically. Chicot alone continued beating d'O, whom he detested, and d'O returned the blows as well as he could. It was a duel with scourges. Entering the Queen's apartments, Henri gave her a pearl necklace, worth twenty-five thousand crowns, kissed her on both cheeks, a thing he had not done for over a year, and begged her to discard her royal apparel and clothe herself with a sack. Louise de

Lorraine, sweet and gentle as ever, consented. She asked why he had given her a pearl necklet, and yet desired her to dress in a sack.

'It is for my sins,' answered Henri.

This answer satisfied the Queen, who knew for what a large number of sins her husband should do penance. She put on her unusual garb, and the King returned, having instructed the Queen to join him. On his appearance the beating began again. D'O and Chicot had not ceased, and blood was flowing from their shoulders. The King paid them compliments, calling them his true, his only friends.

In ten minutes, the Queen appeared with her sack. Tapers were handed to the whole court, and, with bare feet in that terrible frost and snow, fine courtiers, fair ladies, good Parisians, devoted to the King and to Notre Dame, set out to Montmartre, at first shivering, but very soon warmed up by the hard blows dealt by Chicot to all those who found themselves within reach of his scourge. D'O, acknowledging himself beaten, had joined the procession some yards distant. At four o'clock, the gloomy procession was finished, the monasteries had received handsome gifts, all the court had swollen feet, all the courtiers' backs were raw; the Queen appeared in public in a covering of coarse cloth, the King with a necklace of death's heads. They had all wept, cried, prayed, burned incense, and sung hymns. The day had been most successful.

As a matter of fact, every one had suffered from the cold and the flogging to please the King; but nobody could guess why this Prince, who had danced so heartily two days before, should now be mortifying himself. Huguenots, Leaguers, and libertines laughed as the scourgers passed, declaring falsely, like true depreciators, as these people always are, that the former procession was finer and more in earnest.

Henri returned, still fasting, with long blue and red scars upon his shoulders, and did not leave the Queen all day. He had taken advantage of every opportunity, while waiting before the chapels, to promise her new allowances, and to plan pilgrimages with her. Chicot, tired of flogging and hungry with the unwonted exercise to which the King had condemned him, stole away just before the company reached Porte Montmartre, and, accompanied by his friend, Brother Gorenflot, the same monk who wished to confess Bussy, entered the garden of a very famed inn. There he drank spiced wine, and ate a teal caught in the low-lying ground near Grande-Batelière. On the company's return, Chicot resumed his place in the ranks, and walked to the Louvre, scourging the penitents, ladies and gentlemen, in his best style, and giving out, as he said, plenary indulgences.

When night came, the King was exhausted by his fasting, his barefoot pilgrimage, and the hard blows he had dealt himself. He had a slight supper served, his shoulders bathed, and a big fire lit, and went to visit Saint-Luc, whom he found bright and lively. Since the previous night, the King had indeed altered; all his thoughts turned upon the vanity of human things, towards penitence and death.

'Ah!' said he, in the tone of a man disgusted with life: 'God has done right to make existence here so bitter.'

'Why so, your Majesty?' asked Saint-Luc.

'Because man, being tired of life, covets death instead of fearing it.'

'Excuse me, your Majesty, speak for yourself; I don't covet death in the least.'

'Listen, Saint-Luc,' and the King shook his head, 'if you were anxious to do well, you would follow my advice, I say, even my example.'

'Very willingly, your Majesty, provided the example is a good one.'

'What do you say to my giving up my crown and you your wife and entering a monastery? I have dispensations from our Holy Father the Pope; to-morrow we shall take the vows. I shall be known as Brother Henri——'

'Excuse me, your Majesty, you care little for your crown, knowing its value too well; but I care a great deal for my wife, whom I do not know sufficiently yet. So I refuse your request.'

'Ah! you are better, evidently.'

'Very much better, your Majesty; my mind is at ease, my heart filled with joy. My heart is strangely disposed to happiness and pleasure.'

'Poor Saint-Luc!' murmured the King, clasping his hands.

'You should have unfolded your plan yesterday, your

Majesty. Then I was in pain, full of whims, sulky. For the least thing I would have thrown myself down a well. But, to-night, I am a different being, I have passed a good night and a delightful day. *Mordieu !* long live joy !'

'You are swearing, Saint-Luc.'

'Did I swear, your Majesty ? Perhaps so, still you swear sometimes yourself.'

'I used to swear, Saint-Luc, but I shall do so no more.'

'I do not dare to say that. I shall swear as little as possible. That is all I can promise. Besides, God is good and merciful, when human weakness occasions the sins.'

'You think God will forgive me, then ?'

'Oh ! I do not refer to your Majesty; I speak for his subject. The deuce ! you have sinned—yes, as a king— whilst I have sinned only as a common person ; I rather fancy that, on the day of judgment, the Lord will have two sets of scales and balances.'

The King, sighing, murmured a *Confiteor*, beating his breast at *Mea culpa*.

'Saint-Luc,' he asked presently, 'do you wish to spend the night in my room ?'

'That depends,' was the answer, 'what should we do ?'

'We will keep all the lights burning, and you shall read to me the litanies of the saints.'

'No, thank you, your Majesty.'

'You abandon me, Saint-Luc !'

'No. I will not leave you.'

'Ah ! really.'

'On one condition, though.'

'What is it ?'

'That your Majesty has tables spread, and music and ladies. *Ma foi !* we will dance all night.'

'Saint-Luc !' was the exclamation of the terrified King.

'I feel frolicsome to-night. Will your Majesty drink and dance ?'

The King returned no answer. His usually bright and lively spirits were clouding more and more, as if struggling against some secret thought oppressing them, like a leaden weight attached to the feet of a bird which vainly stretches his wings to fly.

'Saint-Luc !' at last remarked the King, in a gloomy voice, 'do you believe in dreams ?'

'Reason compels me.'

'Why ?'

'The page came forward blushing.'

'Well, dreams console one for realities. Last night I had a charming dream. I dreamed that my wife——'

'You still think of your wife?'

'More than ever.'

'Ah!' said the King, sighing, and looking upward.

'I dreamed, that my wife, preserving her charming face—for she *is* pretty, your Majesty——'

'Yes, alas! Eve, too, was pretty, and she brought ruin on us all.'

'Ah! that is why you are spiteful? But, to continue my dream——'

'I, too, had a dream——'

'My wife, preserving her pretty face, had taken the form and wings of a bird, and, defying doors and railings, flew over the Louvre, and landed at my window, crying in at the panes, "Open to me, Saint-Luc; open, my husband."'

'You opened the window?'

'Of course I did,' answered Saint-Luc eagerly.

'Worldling!'

'Worldling if you like, your Majesty.'

'You woke up, then?'

'Not at all, I took care of that; the dream was too delightful.'

'So you went on dreaming?'

'As long as I could.'

'To-night you hope——'

'To dream again, yes, if your Majesty has no objection; that is why I refused the kind offer to read prayers to your Majesty. If I stay up, I should like to find, at least, the equivalent of my dream. If your Majesty would prepare a banquet and have musicians——'

'That is enough, Saint-Luc,' said the King, rising. 'You are going to destruction, and would drag me with you. Adieu, I hope Heaven may send you a salutory dream to encourage you to repentance, and to save us both.'

'I doubt that, your Majesty. Indeed, I feel so certain of it, that my advice is to turn this rascal Saint-Luc out of the Louvre immediately, for he is determined to die impenitent.'

'No,' said Henri, 'I hope to-morrow grace will touch your heart as it has touched mine. Good-night, Saint-Luc, I will pray for you.'

'Good-night, your Majesty, I will dream for you.'
With that Saint-Luc hummed the first verse of a most
frivolous song, sung by the King in good-humoured
moments. Henri hastened his steps, murmuring as he
retired, 'Lord, my God! True and just is Thy wrath,
for the world goes from bad to worse.'

CHAPTER VIII

SHOWS HOW THE KING WAS AFRAID OF HAVING SHOWN FEAR

On leaving Saint-Luc, the King found all the court
assembled, according to orders, in the great gallery. He
thereupon distributed favours to his friends, despatched
d'O, D'Épernon, and Schomberg to the provinces, threatened Maugiron and Quélus should they again quarrel
with Bussy, gave the latter his hand to kiss, and clasped
his brother François for a long time to his heart. Upon
the Queen he showered praises and marks of friendship
to such a degree that the onlookers conceived the happiest
auguries for the succession to the throne.

As the usual hour for retiring approached, Henri seemed
anxious to delay it as much as possible. At length the
clock struck ten. He glanced around as if seeking a
friend to entrust with the duties of reader, which Saint-
Luc had refused. Chicot watched him.

'You are looking very sweetly at me to-night, Henri,'
he remarked, with his usual boldness. 'Perhaps you seek
an occupant for some fine abbey, with ten thousand a
year? Zounds! what a prior I should make! Give me
the post, my son.'

'Come with me, Chicot,' was the King's answer. 'Good-
night, gentlemen.'

Chicot, turning to the courtiers, curled his moustache
and glanced tenderly round as he said, imitating Henri's
tones, 'Good-night, gentlemen, we are going to bed.'
The courtiers bit their lips, while the King reddened.

'Now, my barber, my hairdresser, my valet, and, above
all, my cream,' continued the jester.

'No,' said the King, 'not to-night; we are in Lent, and
I am doing penance.'

'I regret the cream,' said Chicot.

Then the King and his jester entered the room with which we are familiar.

'So I am the favourite !' was Chicot's comment. 'I am indispensable surely? Am I handsomer even than that Cupid Quélus ?'

'Silence, fool, and you, sirs, leave the room.'

The valets obeyed, the door was shut, Chicot and Henri remained alone; the former looked at the King in astonishment.

'Why have you sent them away?' he asked; 'they have not anointed us yet. Are you to do my toilet with your royal hand ? That is penance with a vengeance !'

'Let us pray,' said Henri presently.

'No, thank you,' exclaimed Chicot; 'it is not amusing enough. If you brought me for that purpose, I would rather rejoin the naughty company I was in. So, goodnight, my son.'

'Stay,' said the King.

'Oh ! it is a case of tyranny. You are a despot, a Phalaris, a Denys. I am loved here; the whole day you forced me to lash my friends' shoulders with a scourge, and you seem inclined to begin again to-night. The deuce ! Do not let us begin. There are only two of us, and every blow would tell.'

'Silence, wretched babbler, and think of repenting.'

'Good ! now we have begun. Repent ! Of what would I repent ? Of making myself a monk's jester ? *Confiteor*, I repent; *Mea culpa*, it is my fault, my most grievous fault !'

'No sacrilege, wretched man !'

'Ah, now ! I would rather be shut up with lions or monkeys than in the room of a mad king. Farewell, I am going.'

The King removed the key.

'Henri,' observed Chicot, 'you are looking sinister, and if you do not let me go, I will shout; I will break the door and the windows. Ah, good gracious !'

'Chicot,' said the King in gloomy tones, 'you take advantage of melancholy.'

'Ah ! I understand; you are afraid of being alone ; tyrants always are. Have twelve rooms built like Denys, or twelve palaces like Tiberius. Meanwhile, take my sword, and let me depart with the sheath.'

At the word 'afraid' Henri's eyes lit up; then, shivering strangely, he rose and walked about the room. His body was so shaken, his face so pale that Chicot began to think him really ill, and, after watching him cross the room a few times, he said : 'Come, my son, tell friend Chicot your grief.'

The King, stopping in front of his jester, said,—

'Yes, you are my friend, my only friend.'

'The Abbey of Valencey is vacant.'

'Listen, Chicot, you are discreet.'

'Pitheviers is vacant too, where they eat such fine lark pies.'

'In spite of your foolery,' the King continued, 'you are a brave man.'

'Then give me a regiment, not an abbey.'

'You have even good advice to offer.'

'In that case, make me a councillor. Ah ! no, when I think of it, I would rather have a regiment or an abbey. I do not wish to be a councillor; I should be compelled to agree with the King.'

'Silence, silence—the awful hour approaches. Chicot, you are brave ?'

'I boast of it; but I do not expose my bravery to the test in this fashion. When the King of France and Poland calls out at night and scandalises the Louvre, the wretched Chicot only brings discredit upon him. Farewell, Henri, call the Captain of the Guard, the Swiss troops, the lackeys, and let me go; the deuce take the unseen peril, the unknown danger.'

'I command you to remain,' the King said, in a tone of authority.

'An amusing master, upon my word, who wishes to command by fear; I am afraid, I tell you; help ! help ! fire !'

Chicot stood up on a table.

'Come, you rascal, I will reveal everything, if it is necessary to keep you quiet.'

'Ah !' said Chicot, rubbing his hands, stepping carefully from the table and drawing his immense sword; 'once warned, it is all right; we will make short work of it; tell me about it. It was a crocodile, eh ? Never mind, my blade is good, since I cut my corns with it every week, and they are hard. You said it was a crocodile, Henri.'

Chicot settled himself in an arm-chair, placing his bare

sword between his knees, and twining his legs round the blade, as the serpents, symbols of peace, clasp Mercury's wand.

'Last night, I was sleeping——'

'So was I,' remarked Chicot.

'Suddenly a breath fanned my cheek.'

'The beast was hungry, and tried to lick your cream.'

'Half awakened, I felt my beard bristling with terror, under my mask.'

'You make me thrill delightfully,' said Chicot, huddling up in his chair and leaning his chin on his sword-hilt.

'Then,' the King continued, in such weak, trembling tones that his words hardly reached Chicot, 'a voice resounded in the room, with such gloomy vibration, that my whole brain was shaken.'

'The voice of the crocodile, yes. I read in Marco Polo's *Journeys* that it has a terrible voice, like children crying; but calm yourself, if it comes, we will kill it.'

'Listen carefully.'

'*Pardieu!* I *am* listening,' and Chicot unbent like a spring. 'I am motionless as a block and dumb as a carp with listening.'

The King resumed in a still more gloomy, mournful voice :—' "Miserable sinner," ' said the voice.

'Bah! the voice spoke; it was *not* a crocodile ?'

' "Miserable sinner," it said, "I am the voice of the Lord thy God." '

With one bound, Chicot was cowering in his chair again.

'The voice of God ?' he asked.

'Ah! Chicot, it is a terrifying voice.'

'Is it a pretty voice ? Does it resemble the sound of a trumpet, as the Scriptures say ?'

' " Art thou there ? Hearest thou ? " asked the voice; "hearest thou, hardened sinner ? hast thou decided to continue in thine evil courses ?" '

'Ah! truly,' remarked Chicot, 'the voice of God is like his people's, it seems to me.'

'Then followed numerous other reproaches which were exceedingly cruel, I tell you, Chicot.'

'But, now, continue a little, tell me what the voice said, that I may know if God was well instructed.'

'Impious man! if you doubt, I will have you thrashed.'

'I am not doubting; it only surprises me that God should have waited till this hour to reproach you. He has been very patient since the Flood. So, my son, you were horribly frightened.'

'Oh, yes!'

'You had reason to be.'

'Perspiration poured down my brow, and the marrow seemed congealed in my bones.'

'As in Jeremiah; it is quite natural; on the word of a gentleman, I do not know what *I* should have done; then you called?'

'Yes.'

'And people came?'

'Yes.'

'Did they search well?'

'Everywhere.'

'There was no God?'

'All had vanished.'

'King Henri, too, had swooned. It is dreadful.'

'So dreadful that I sent for my confessor.'

'Ah! he came? What did your confessor think of this revelation?'

'He shuddered.'

'I should suppose so.'

'He crossed himself and commanded me to repent, as God had ordered.'

'Very good! He has never anything to repent of. But what did he say of the vision itself, the voice?'

'That it was providential, a miracle; that I ought to consider the safety of the state. So, this morning I——'

'What did you do this morning?'

'I gave a hundred thousand pounds to the Jesuits.'

'Very good!'

'And lacerated my skin and my young noblemen's with scourging.'

'Splendid! But, what then?'

'Well, what then—what is your opinion, Chicot? I address the friend, the sober-minded man, not the scoffer.'

'Ah! your Majesty, I think you had a nightmare.'

'You think?'

'It was a bad dream, your Majesty, and will not recur, unless your Majesty gives way to depression.'

'A dream?' answered Henri, shaking his head. 'No, no; I was wide awake, I assure you.'

'You were sleeping.'

'So little that my eyes were wide open.'

'I sleep like that.'

'Yes, but I saw with my eyes; that does not happen if one is really asleep.'

'What did you see?'

'The moon through the window and the amethyst in my sword-hilt shining there, where you sit, Chicot, with a dull glow.'

'What had become of the lamp?'

'It had gone out.'

'Purely a dream, my son.'

'Why do you not believe, Chicot? Is it not said that the Lord speaks to kings when he wishes to make a great change upon the earth?'

'Yes, He speaks to them, but so low that they never hear Him.'

'What makes you so incredulous?'

'You heard so well.'

'You understand why I made you stay?'

' *Parbleu!* ' was Chicot's answer.

'It was that you yourself might hear the voice.'

'So that people will think I am jesting if I repeat what I hear. Chicot is so insignificant, so puny, such a fool that nobody will believe him. Not a bad trick, my son.'

'Why not rather believe, friend, that I am confiding this secret because of your fidelity?'

'Do not lie, Henri; for the voice will reproach you, and your sins are numerous enough already. But, no matter what happens, I accept the trust. I shall not be sorry to hear the Lord's voice; perhaps it will say something to me as well.'

'What must we do?'

'Go to bed.'

'But if, on the contrary——'

'No buts.'

'However——'

'Do you think by chance that your remaining standing will hinder the voice of God? It is only a king's crown that makes him bigger than other men. When he is bareheaded, believe me, he is the same height, sometimes smaller.'

'All right, you are to stay?'

'It is arranged.'

'You will not sleep?'

'Ah! I cannot promise anything; sleep, like fear, is apart from our wills.'

'You will do what you can, at least.'

'I shall pinch myself, you may be assured; moreover, the voice will waken me.'

'Do not jest about the voice,' said Henri, getting out of bed again.

'Come, come,' said Chicot, 'must I put you to bed?'

The King sighing, and having glanced anxiously at every nook and cranny of the room, slipped, with a shudder, into his bed.

'Ha,' remarked the jester, 'now it is my turn.' Stretching himself upon the arm-chair, he arranged the cushions and pillows.

'How do you feel, your Majesty?'

'Fairly comfortable, and how are you?'

'Very well; good-night, Henri.'

'Good-night, Chicot, do not sleep.'

'The deuce! I have no wish to sleep,' and Chicot yawned till he almost broke his jaws.

Both closed their eyes, the King to feign sleep, Chicot to sleep in reality.

CHAPTER IX

HOW THE VOICE WAS DECEIVED

FOR ten minutes the King and Chicot had remained silent, when suddenly the King sat up with a start. Chicot, roused by the noise out of that sweet slumber which anticipates sleep, did the same. They looked at each other with startled eyes.

'What is it?' asked Chicot, in a low voice.

'The breath,' the King answered, in still lower tones.

Just then one of the candles held by the satyr went out, then a second, a third, finally the fourth.

'Oh!' gasped Chicot, 'what a breath!'

Hardly had he spoken the last word when the lamp, too, was extinguished, leaving the room lit by the dying gleams from the fire.

'Heavens!' said Chicot, starting up.

'He is going to speak,' said the King, bending down.

'Then, listen,' said Chicot.

At that moment a hollow, hissing voice was heard at the bedside :—

'Hardened sinner, art thou there ?'

'Yes, Lord,' the King answered, his teeth chattering.

' Oh !' cried Chicot, ' what a hoarse voice to come from Heaven ! anyhow, it is terrifying.'

'Dost thou hear ?' asked the voice.

'Yes, Lord,' stammered Henri, 'I listen, bending under Thy wrath.'

'Thinkest thou to have obeyed me, in performing all these external mummeries yesterday, while thine inmost heart remained untouched ?'

'Well said,' exclaimed Chicot.

The King's hands shook as he clasped them. Chicot approached him.

'Well,' asked the King, 'do you believe now, wretched man ?'

'Wait,' was the reply.

'What do you mean ?'

'Silence ! Listen : come here quietly, and let me take your place.'

'Why?'

'That the wrath of the Lord may light first on me.'

'Do you think He will spare me on that account ?'

'Try, anyhow.'

With a tender insistence, Chicot pushed the King away and took his place.

'Now,' he said, 'sit in my chair and let me act.' Henri obeyed; he began to guess what was going on.

'Thou answerest not ; art thou then hardened in sin ?'

'Oh ! pardon, Lord !' cried Chicot, in nasal tones like the King.

Bending towards Henri, he remarked, 'It is curious, is it not, the Lord does not recognise Chicot ?'

'Bless my soul ! what does it mean ?'

'Wait, you will see other things as strange.'

'Wretched man ?' said the voice.

'Yes, Lord, I am a hardened sinner, a dreadful sinner.'

'Then, confess your crimes and repent.'

'I confess to have acted treacherously towards my cousin de Condé, whose wife I seduced, and I repent.'

'What are you saying ?' whispered Henri. '*Will* you be quiet ? That is an old story now.'

'Ah! really, let us pass to other matters,' observed Chicot.

'Speak!' commanded the voice.

'I confess to have robbed the people of Poland, who had chosen me King; I left them one day, carrying off the crown diamonds, and I repent.'

'Eh! rascal!' said Henri again, 'what are you recalling? That's all forgotten.'

'Still I must keep on deceiving him; leave me alone.'

'Speak!'

'I confess to taking the throne of France from my brother d'Alençon, to whom it rightfully belonged, since I had formally renounced it, when accepting the throne of Poland, and I repent.'

'Scoundrel!' muttered the King.

'That is not the chief thing yet,' the voice resumed.

'I confess to have conspired with my good mother, Catherine de Médicis, to drive my brother-in-law, the King of Navarre, from France, first destroying all his friends and the lovers of my sister, Queen Margaret, whom I also banished, for which I sincerely repent.'

'Ah! rogue!' the King muttered, clenching his teeth in rage.

'Your Majesty, let us not offend God by hiding what He knows as well as us.'

'It is not a question of politics,' resumed the voice.

'Ah! now we have it,' said Chicot sadly, 'it is a question of my manners and morals, I suppose?'

'Well and good.'

'It is true, Lord, that I am very effeminate, lazy, weak, silly, and a hypocrite.'

'That is true,' came in cavernous tones.

'I have ill-treated women, my wife especially, who is a most worthy person.'

'One should love one's wife as oneself, preferring her above all things,' the voice declared angrily.

'Ah!' cried Chicot, in despair, 'I have indeed sinned.'

'Thou hast made others sin by thy example.'

'True, still true.'

'Thou hast nearly damned poor Saint-Luc.'

'Bah! art thou sure, Lord, that I have not utterly damned him?'

'No; but such a thing may happen, unless thou sendest him back to-morrow to his family.'

'Ah!' Chicot remarked to the King, 'the voice appears friendly to the Cossé family.'

'And unless you make him a duc and his wife a duchesse, to indemnify her for her premature widowhood.'

'If I do not obey?' asked Chicot, with some defiance in his tones.

'Then'—here the voice grew terrifyingly loud—'thou shall burn throughout eternity in that great furnace where Sardanapalus, Nebuchadnezzar, and Maréchal Retz await thee.'

Henri groaned. At this threat, fear again assailed him.

'The deuce, Henri, do you notice how interested God is in Saint-Luc,' exclaimed Chicot; 'one would say he enjoyed the Almighty's special favour.'

The King apparently was oblivious to Chicot's jests, or found no comfort in them.

'I am lost,' he cried wildly, 'lost! and this voice from on high will kill me.'

'From on high!' retorted Chicot; 'you are mistaken this time. Voice from at hand, rather.'

'What! from near at hand?'

'Yes! don't you hear it coming from the wall? Henri, God stays in the Louvre. Probably, like the Emperor Charles V., he descends to hell by way of France.'

'Atheist! blasphemer!'

'What an honour for you, Henri. I congratulate you. I confess, though, you take it very coolly. What! God is in the Louvre, separated by a wall merely, and you do not pay him a visit? Come, Valois, I do not recognise you when you lack this politeness.'

A branch in a corner of the chimney blazed, and, in lighting up the room, lit up Chicot's face, just then beaming with mirth and gaiety, so as to astonish the King.

'What!' said he, 'you are inclined to jest? you dare——'

'Yes, I dare, and so will you, presently, or may I die of the plague. Use your reason, my son, and do what I counsel.'

'To go and see——'

'If God is really and truly in the adjoining room.'

'But if the voice speaks again?'

'*I* will be here to answer. The voice will imagine you are still here; it is nobly credulous, the divine voice, and hardly knows its creatures. Imagine! I have brayed for a quarter of an hour, and it does not recognise me ? What humiliation for a supreme intellect !'

Henri frowned; his incredible credulity began to be shaken.

'I believe you are right, Chicot; I should like——'

'Go, then !' cried Chicot, pushing him.

Henri softly opened the door of the corridor leading into the next room. Scarcely had he advanced a few yards when the voice redoubled its reproaches, and was answered by the most mournful laments from Chicot.

'Yes,' the voice was saying, 'thou art fickle as a woman, soft as a sybarite, corrupt as a pagan.'

'Hey ! hey !' whimpered Chicot, 'is it my fault, Lord ? Thou hast given me such a tender skin, such white hands, a fine nose, and a changeable disposition ! But from to-day I shall wear nothing but sackcloth. I shall hide myself in the ashes, like Job, and eat cow's dung like Ezekiel.'

Henri noted that, as Chicot's voice died away, his questioner's grew louder, and seemed really to come from Saint-Luc's room. He was about to knock at the door, when he saw a ray of light shining through the carved keyhole. Bending down, he looked through. Suddenly, from being very pale, he reddened with anger, and stood up, rubbing his eyes as though to see better what he could not at first sight believe.

'*Par la mordieu !*' he muttered, 'do they really dare to play me a trick like that ?'

This is what he actually saw : Saint-Luc, in a corner, his dressing-gown on, was speaking into an air-cane the threatening words which the King had taken for divine; beside him, leaning on his shoulder, was a young woman in white, who, at times, seized the cane and spoke into it, deepening her tones, uttering any madness which arose first in her wicked eyes and on her laughing lips. Mad outbursts of joy succeeded each fresh saying, while Chicot wept and lamented with such a natural, nasal intonation that the King almost believed it was he himself weeping and lamenting.

'Jeanne de Cossé in Saint-Luc's room, a hole in the wall, a hoax for me ! wretches !—they shall pay dearly for this !'

As madame uttered an even more insulting remark, Henri burst open the door. Jeanne, in her scanty raiment, hid herself in the curtains with a shriek. Saint-Luc, clasping the cane in his hand, pale with terror, sank on his knees before the King, who was pale with rage.

'Ah!' cried Chicot from the royal room,—'ah! mercy! I appeal to the Virgin Mary, to all the saints. I am becoming weak, I——'

None of the actors in the burlesque scene had yet strength to speak, so rapidly had the situation become tragic. Henri broke the silence by speech, the stillness by a gesture.

'Go,' said he, extending his arm.

Yielding to passion, unworthy of a king, he tore the cane from Saint-Luc's hands, and raised it to strike. Saint Luc drew himself up as though raised by a spring.

'Your Majesty, you have no right to strike me, except on the head. I am a gentleman.'

Henri threw the cane violently on the floor. It was picked up by Chicot, who, hearing the noise, and thinking a mediator might be useful, had rushed in. Leaving the King and Saint-Luc to settle their affairs, he ran straight to the curtain, where he guessed some one was hidden, and drew forth the poor woman.

'Hallo!' he cried, 'Adam and Eve after the transgression! You are expelling them?' he continued, questioning the King.

'Yes,' answered the King.

'Wait, I will be the exterminating angel.'

Throwing himself between the King and Saint-Luc, he held the cane like a flaming sword over the two culprits' heads, and said,—

'This is my paradise, which you have lost through your disobedience. I forbid you to enter it.'

Leaning towards Saint-Luc, who was clasping his wife, to protect her, if necessary, against the King's wrath, he whispered: 'If you have a good horse, kill it if you please, but ride fifty miles before to-morrow.'

CHAPTER X

HOW BUSSY SOUGHT FOR HIS DREAM

Bussy and the Duc d'Anjou left the Louvre reflecting deeply—the Duc because he feared the consequences of the vigorous action which Bussy had, in some way, compelled him to make; Bussy, because his thoughts remained completely engrossed by the incidents of the last evening.

'In short,' he soliloquised, as he reached his dwelling, after complimenting the Duc upon his energy—'in short, the one thing certain is that I was attacked and wounded. Now, while fighting, I saw the cross of the Petits-Champs, the wall of the Hôtel des Tournelles, and the battlemented towers of the Bastille. I was attacked at the Place de la Bastille, a little in front of the Hôtel des Tournelles, between Rue Sainte-Catherine and Rue Saint-Paul, while I was proceeding to the Faubourg Saint-Antoine, to fetch the Queen of Navarre's letter. Close by was a door with an opening, through which, afterwards, I saw the pale cheeks and the flashing eyes of Quélus. I found myself in an alley, at the end of which was a staircase. I stumbled against the first step. Then I fainted; after which my dream began. Later I found myself on the slope of the Temple moat, surrounded by a monk, a butcher, and an old woman. How is it that my other dreams vanish so quickly and so completely from my memory, whilst this one engraves itself more as time passes? Ah! there's a mystery.'

He stopped at his house, and, leaning against the wall, closed his eyes.

'Mordieu! it is impossible a dream should leave such an impression. I see the room with the tapestry and figures, the painted ceiling, the bedstead of carved oak, its curtains of white and gold damask; I see the portrait; the fair lady; I am now less confident that they were not one and the same thing; finally, I see the honest, joyful face of the young doctor who was led with bandaged eyes to my bedside. To sum up: tapestry, ceiling, carved bed, white and gold damask curtains, a portrait, a lady, and a doctor. I must begin a search for these things, and, unless I am the stupidest man alive, I shall find them. And first, I will dress as befits a night-rover, and then, to the Bastille !'

Carrying out this rather unreasonable resolve, Bussy entered the house, had his bandage fixed by a valet possessing some surgical skill, put on long boots reaching beyond his knees, took his strongest sword, threw on his cloak, stepped into his litter; stopping at the end of Rue du Roi-de-Sicile, he descended, and telling his servants to wait, he passed along the High Street of Saint-Antoine, and proceeded to the Place de la Bastille.

It was nearly nine o'clock; curfew had sounded; the streets were becoming deserted. Thanks to the thaw, produced by the sun and the warmer air during the day, the pools of frozen water and muddy ruts had made of the Place de la Bastille a piece of land, intersected with lakes and precipices, surrounded by the trodden track to which we have already referred. Bussy first sought the place where his horse had fallen, and believing he had found it, retreated and advanced just as he had done before; retiring to the wall, he examined every door, searching for the corner against which he had leaned, the wicket through which he had seen Quélus. But every door possessed recesses and wickets. However, there was an alley behind the door. By some fatality, not extraordinary when we reflect that the 'concierge' was unknown then in middle-class houses, three-fourths of the doors had alleys.

'*Pardieu !*' said Bussy, with profound vexation, 'when I have knocked at all these doors, questioned all the tenants, spent a thousand crowns in coaxing the servants and old women to speak, I shall know what I wish to learn. Fifty houses; doing ten houses a night, will waste five nights; only I will wait till the roads are drier.'

Bussy was ending this monologue, when he saw a small light approach, reflected in the pools as signal lights shine in the sea. It advanced slowly and unevenly towards him, stopping at times, bending now to the left, now to the right, suddenly wavering and dancing like a will o' the wisp, then resuming its calm advance, and again straying hither and thither.

'Decidedly,' remarked Bussy, 'the Place de la Bastille is a remarkable place; it may be worth while to await events.'

To watch more at his ease, Bussy wrapped himself in his cloak and crouched in the corner of the door. The night was extremely dark, and one could not see more than a yard in front. The lantern advanced, describing the wildest evolutions, but not being superstitious, Bussy concluded this was no wandering fire like those which so terrified travellers in the Middle Ages, but simply a lantern suspended from a hand forming part of a human body. After waiting a few seconds the conjecture was confirmed. Almost thirty paces away Bussy perceived a tall, dark, thin figure, which gradually became defined as a living being, bearing a lantern in its left hand, holding it sometimes in front, sometimes at the side, now resting it close to its person. This being apparently belonged to the brotherhood of drunkards, for to this cause alone could one attribute its strange circuits, and the philosophy with which it stumbled into muddy ruts and splashed into the pools. Once it even slipped upon a half-thawed layer of ice, and a dull thud, accompanied by an involuntary movement of the lantern, told Bussy that the night-roamer, none too steady on his legs, had settled into a safer position. Bussy began to feel sympathy for this belated drunkard, and was preparing to help this minister of Bacchus, when the lantern was raised up so quickly as to show that the person using it so clumsily was more sober than might have been argued from his appearance.

'Ah! here's an adventure,' murmured Bussy.

As the lantern advanced, he retreated more into the corner of the door. The lantern moved on another ten steps, and Bussy became aware that the man who carried it wore a bandage over his eyes.

'*Pardieu!* a curious idea, surely, to play the blind man with a lantern, especially in weather and on ground like this. I am perhaps dreaming again.'

The man with the bandage continued to advance.

'God forgive me, I believe he talks to himself. He is neither a fool nor a drunkard, but a mathematician trying to solve a problem.'

This was suggested by the words of the lantern-bearer, which had reached Bussy's ear.

'Four hundred and eighty-eight, four hundred and eighty-nine, four hundred and ninety; it must be very near here.'

Raising the bandage, he walked up to the door of the house in front, and carefully examined it.

'No,' he observed, 'that is not it,' and, replacing the bandage, he resumed his walk and his counting.

'Four hundred and ninety-one, four hundred and ninety-two, four hundred and ninety-three, four; I must be very close.'

Raising the bandage again, he approached the house next to Bussy's hiding place, and examined it as carefully as the first.

'Hum! hum! that might well be the one; no—yes; these wretched doors are all alike.'

'I have already remarked that,' said Bussy to himself, 'which makes me respect this mathematician.'

The latter resumed his bandage and walked on.

'Four hundred and ninety-five, ninety-six, ninety-seven, ninety-eight, ninety-nine. If there is a door in front, it must be the one.'

There was actually a door, the one where Bussy was hiding; so when the supposed mathematician lifted his bandage, he and Bussy were face to face.

'Hallo!'

'It is not possible.'

'It is, but it's extraordinary. You are the doctor?'

'And you are the gentleman?'

'Exactly.'

'Heavens! what luck!'

'The doctor who, last night, attended to a gentleman with a sword-cut in his side?'

'Quite right.'

'Yes, I recognised you immediately; you had such a light, soft touch, but such a skilful one.'

'Ah! monsieur, I did not expect to find you here.'

'What were you seeking then?'

'The house.'

'You do not know it?'

'How can you expect it; I was taken there with my eyes bandaged.'

'You were taken with your eyes bandaged!'

'Without a doubt.'

'Then you really came to this house?'

'To this or the one adjoining it; I cannot say which.'

'Then I was not dreaming?'

'You were not dreaming.'

'I must confess that I regarded the whole adventure, all but the sword-cut naturally, as a dream.'

'Well! you do not astonish me, monsieur. I suspected some mystery underneath it.'

'Yes, a mystery I should like cleared up; you will assist me, will you not ?'

'Very willingly.'

'Good; first of all, two words. What is your name ?'

'Monsieur, I will answer without reserve. According to the most approved methods, at such a question, I should draw myself up proudly and say, "And pray what may *your* name be, sir ?" But you have a long sword, and I only my lancet; you look like a distinguished nobleman, and I must appear a sorry rascal, being wet through and half covered with mud. I therefore reply frankly to your question: "I am Rémy le Haudouin"'

'Very good, monsieur, a thousand thanks. I am Comte Louis de Clermont, Lord Bussy.'

'Bussy d'Amboise, Bussy the hero !' exclaimed the young doctor, with evident joy. 'What ! monsieur, your are that famous Bussy, the colonel who—— Oh !'

'I am, monsieur. Now that we are both enlightened, please satisfy my curiosity, drenched and bespattered as you are.'

'The fact is,' answered the young man, looking at his instrument case, spotted with mud, 'like Epaminondas of Thebes, I shall be obliged to remain indoors three days, since I possess only one suit. But, excuse me, you were asking a question, I believe ?'

'I was about to inquire how you came to the house.'

'It is at once very simple and very complicated, as you will see.'

'Come, now.'

'Monsieur le Comte, excuse me, I was so confused that I forgot your title.'

'No matter, proceed.'

'Monsieur le Comte, this is what happened : I live in the Rue Beautreillis, five hundred paces off, and am a surgeon, though not without skill.'

'I can vouch for your skill.'

'I have studied hard,' the young man continued, 'without obtaining any patients. I am called Rémy le Haudouin; Rémy, my Christian name, and Le Haudouin, because I was born at Nanteuil le Haudouin. Seven or

eight days ago, behind the Arsenal, a man received
a nasty stab with a dagger, and I sewed up his stomach.
That gave me a certain reputation in the district, and to
this I owe the good fortune of being awakened the other
night by a small, flute-like voice.'

'A woman's voice!'

'Yes, but notice this, Comte; rustic as I am, I am sure
it was a servant's voice. I am a competent judge, having
heard more servants' than mistresses' voices.'

'What did you do?'

'Getting up, I opened the door, and was barely on the
threshold when two little hands, not too gently nor too
harshly, placed a bandage over my eyes.'

'Without saying anything?' asked Bussy.

'With these words : "Do not try to discover where you
are going; be discreet; here is your reward."'

'And this reward was——'

'A purse full of pistoles, which she put into my hand.'

'Ah! and what was your reply?'

'That I would willingly follow my charming leader.
I had no idea whether she was charming or not, but the
compliment could do no harm.'

'You followed without making any remarks or requiring
any guarantee?'

'I have often heard of similar stories, and noticed that
something pleasant always occurs for the doctor. I
followed, then, and was led along a hard pathway. It
was freezing, and I counted four hundred, four hundred
and fifty, five hundred, finally five hundred and two
paces.'

'Very good; it was ingenious; this must be the door.'

'It cannot be far from it, at least, since I have counted
up to four hundred and ninety-nine; unless the artful
woman, as I suspect she was, made me take some detours.'

'Even if she thought of that precaution, surely she
gave some clue, or told some name?'

'None.'

'But you surely noticed something?'

'I noticed a door, studded with nails ; behind this door
a passage, and a stair at the end of the passage.'

'On the left?'

'Yes. I even counted the steps.'

'How many?'

'Twelve.'

'And it opened straight into——?'

'A corridor, I fancy, as three doors were opened.'

'Good.'

'Then I heard a voice—ah! that was the voice of a mistress, if you like, sweet and pleasant.'

'Yes, yes, it was her voice.'

'Good; it was hers.'

'I am certain.'

'Good. Then I was led into the apartment where you lay in bed, and was ordered to remove my bandage.'

'Quite so.'

'Then I observed you.'

'Where was I?'

'Lying in bed.'

'Of white damask, sewn with gold flowers?'

'Yes.'

'In a room, hung with tapestry?'

'Precisely.'

'A ceiling with figures?'

'Yes; moreover, between the windows——'

'A portrait?'

'Precisely.'

'Representing a girl of eighteen to twenty years old.'

'Yes.'

'Fair.'

'Very good.'

'Beautiful as the angels?'

'More beautiful.'

'Bravo! What did you do next?'

'I dressed your wound.'

'Very skilfully, too, on my honour.'

'As well as I could.'

'Admirably, my dear sir, admirably; this morning the wound was almost closed and quite pink.'

'Thanks to my balsam, which appears to be a sovereign remedy; often having no one on whom to experiment I cut myself in different places, and, faith! the wounds closed up in two or three days.'

'My dear Monsieur Rémy,' exclaimed Bussy, 'you are a charming person, and I feel a great liking for you.— But, afterwards? Come, tell me.'

'Afterwards? you fainted again. The voice asked me how you were.'

'Where did the voice come from?'

'From an adjoining room.'

'So you did not see the lady ?'

'I did not see her.'

'And you replied ?'

'That the wound was not dangerous, and that, in twenty-four hours, there would be no trace of it.'

'She seemed satisfied ?'

'Charmed; for she exclaimed: ''Ah! how fortunate!'' '

'She said: ''How fortunate!'' My dear Monsieur Rémy, I will make your fortune. Afterwards ?'

' I had nothing further to do,' the voice said to me, ''Monsieur Rémy——'' '

'The voice knew your name ?'

'Surely, through the incident of the dagger thrust of which I told you.'

'Of course; well, the voice said : '' Monsieur Rémy''—'

' Be a man of honour; do not compromise a poor woman, carried away by kindly feelings; replace your bandage and permit yourself to be taken home.'

'You promised ?'

'I gave my word.'

'You kept it ?'

'You see that,' was the simple answer, 'since I am looking for the door.'

'That is a splendid trait, which shows a gentleman; though at heart I am furious, I cannot help saying, ''Shake hands, Monsieur Rémy.'' '

Full of enthusiasm, Bussy extended his hand to the young doctor.

'Monsieur !' said Rémy, embarrassed.

'Shake hands, you deserve to be a nobleman.'

'Monsieur, it will be an everlasting glory merely to have touched the hand of the brave Bussy d'Amboise; meanwhile, I have a scruple.'

'What is it ?'

'There were ten pistoles in the purse.'

'Well ?'

'It is far too much for a man who charges five sous a visit, and often nothing at all; and I was seeking the house——'

'To return the purse ?'

'Exactly.'

'My dear Monsieur Rémy, you are too scrupulous,

I protest; you earned the money honourably, and it belongs to you.'

'You think so ?' said Rémy, internally satisfied.

'I assure you; only the lady should not have paid, since we do not know each other.'

'Another reason for my returning it.'

'I simply meant that I, too, am in your debt.'

'In my debt ?'

'Yes, and I will discharge it. What are you doing in Paris ? Confide in me, my dear M. Rémy.'

'What am I doing in Paris ? Nothing at all, Comte; but I would do something if I had a practice.'

'Well ! you meet me at the proper moment; I will give you one. What do you say to me ? I am a practice in myself, believe me. Not a day passes, but I wound some one, or am wounded myself. Come, will you undertake to mend the holes made in my skin and those I make in others ?'

'Ah ! Monsieur le Comte,' said Rémy, 'my merits are too slight——'

'On the contrary, you are the man I want, or may the devil take me ! You have a hand as light as a woman's, and the balsam worthy of Ferragus——'

'Monsieur !'

'You shall come with me. You shall have your own apartments and your own servants; accept, or, upon my word, you will break my heart. Moreover, your task is not completed : another dressing is necessary, dear Monsieur Rémy.'

'Monsieur le Comte,' replied the young doctor, 'I am so enchanted that I cannot express my delight. I will work; I will have patients !'

'No, since I engage you for myself—including my friends, naturally. Now, there is nothing else you recall ?'

'Nothing.'

'Ah ! well, assist me to solve the mystery, then, if that is possible.'

'How ?'

'Come, you, a man of observation, who count steps and grope along walls, you who distinguish voices, how came it that, after your departure, I found myself lying on the edge of the Temple moat ?'

'You ?'

'Yes, I. Did you help in that ?'

'No! I should have opposed it strongly, had I been consulted. The cold might have proved fatal.'

'Then, I am quite at a loss. Will you not search a little longer with me?'

'I am ready to do anything you wish, monsieur, but fear it is useless; all the houses are alike.'

'Ah! well, we must see them in daylight.'

'Yes; but we shall be seen in the daylight.'

'Then, we must make inquiries.'

'We will do so, my lord.'

'And succeed. We have something to work upon, which is a great advantage.'

CHAPTER XI

DESCRIBES BRYAN DE MONSOREAU

Bussy, both on the way to his hotel and afterwards, talked incessantly of the unknown lady; but at length, Rémy, entering upon his duties as doctor, ordered him to sleep, or at least, to go to bed. First of all, however, Bussy installed his new guest in the three rooms which formed part of the third story of the hotel. Then, feeling sure that the young doctor, contented with his new prospects, would not wish to leave the house, he returned to his own magnificent apartments on the first floor. Next day, on awaking, he found Rémy standing near his bed. The young man had spent the night in doubting the reality of his good fortune, and he waited till Bussy woke, to assure himself that it was no dream.

'Well!' he asked, 'how do you feel?'

'Wonderfully well, my dear Æsculapius; are you content?'

'So much so that I would not change my lot for King Henri's, although he must have advanced considerably towards heaven yesterday. But that is not the question; can I see your wound?'

'Look!' Bussy turned on his side, so that the young surgeon could raise the dressing. The edges of the wound were pink, and had closed together. Bussy, being happy, had slept well, and sleep and happiness had aided the doctor, who had hardly anything more to do.

'Well!' asked Bussy, 'what is your opinion of that, Master Ambroise Paré?'

'I dare not admit that you are nearly cured, lest you send me back to the Rue Beautreillis, five hundred and two steps from the famous house.'

'Which we will find again?'

'I believe so.'

'Now, I wish you to consider yourself one of the household, and permit me, while you are bringing your things here, to be present when the First Huntsman receives the estortuaire.'[1]

'Ah! now we are beginning to commit indiscretions.'

'No! I promise to be very reasonable.'

'But you will have to ride on horseback.'

'Of course, it is absolutely necessary.'

'Have you a quiet horse with easy action?'

'I have a choice of four.'

'Take the one you would choose for the lady of the portrait.'

'Ah! Rémy, you touch my heart; I was horribly afraid you would keep me from going to this mock-hunt. You understand the lady of the portrait must belong to the court or the town, for she does not belong to the middle class: these tapestries, the fine enamels, the painted ceiling, the bed with white and gold damask— all that refined luxury reveals a lady of quality, or at least a rich lady; suppose I meet her at the hunt!'

'All things are possible,' was the philosophic rejoinder.

'Except to find the house.'

'And to get inside when we find it!'

'I do not think of that till I am there; besides, once there, I have a plan.'

'What is it?'

'To get wounded again.'

'Good; then I may hope you will keep me.'

'Rest assured of that; I seem to have known you for twenty years; on my honour, I could not manage without you.'

The young doctor's charming face lit up with pleasure.

'It is settled, then; you go to the hunt to look for the lady, while I return to the Rue Beautreillis to look for the house.'

[1] The estortuaire was the stick handed over by the First Huntsman, to the King, and used by the latter to thrust aside the branches when he was riding at full gallop.

'It will be a queer thing,' observed Bussy, 'if we are both successful in our quest.'

Thereupon Bussy and Le Haudouin parted, more like friends than master and servant.

A grand hunt was arranged in the Forest of Vincennes for the inauguration of M. Bryan de Monsoreau, who had been appointed First Huntsman some weeks before. Owing to the procession and the King's penance, every one thought Henri would not be present; for at times his fits of devotion kept him in the Louvre for weeks together, when his austerity did not compel him to retire to a convent. But, to the astonishment of the court, towards nine o'clock in the morning, news arrived that the King had left for Vincennes with his brother, the Duc d'Anjou. The meeting-place was at the Cross-ways of Saint-Louis. Here, legend had it, was the famous oak-tree where the martyr-king administered justice. Everybody was assembled at nine o'clock when the new officer, who being practically a stranger, was the object of general curiosity, appeared on a magnificent black horse. He was a tall man of about thirty-five; his face, pitted with small-pox and covered with spots, did not impress the beholder favourably. M. de Monsoreau was clad in a tunic of green cloth, braided with silver, with a silver shoulder-belt, embroidered with the King's arms, and his cap was adorned with a long feather. Brandishing in his left hand a boar-spear, and in his right the estortuaire intended for the King, M. de Monsoreau might appear a formidable warrior, but he certainly was not a handsome gentleman.

'Fie! what an ugly face you have brought us, my lord,' remarked Bussy to the Duc d'Anjou; 'are those the gentlemen your Highness exalts from the provinces? It would surprise me if the like could be found in Paris, which is a big enough town, and contains plenty of ugly men. It is whispered—though I refused to believe the rumour—that you insisted on presenting the First Huntsman to His Majesty.'

'M. de Monsoreau has done me good service, and I reward him,' observed the Duc laconically.

'Well said, my lord; it is as rare as it is agreeable to find princes showing gratitude; but, if that is the only qualification, I have served you well, and should certainly wear the Huntsman's coat with more grace than that

Phantom. He has a red beard; I did not notice it at first;
that is still another charm.'

'I was not aware that one needed to be modelled like
Apollo or Antinous in order to discharge court functions.'

'How astonishing,' said Bussy, with his usual coolness.

'I regard the heart, not the appearance,' answered the
Prince—'services rendered and not those promised.'

'Your Highness will consider me extremely curious, but
I search in vain for the service Monsoreau can have
rendered.'

'Ah ! Bussy, you are even too curious.'

'That is the way of princes ! They are always asking
questions; but if you question them they give you no
answer.'

'If you want the information, go and ask M. de Monsoreau himself.'

'You are right, my lord, and, should he refuse to
answer, there is, at least, one thing left for me to do.'

'What is that ?'

'To tell him he is an impertinent fellow.'

Turning his back on the Prince, without further reflection, and in sight of his friends, Bussy, hat in hand,
approached M. de Monsoreau. The latter, on horseback,
in the middle of the group, waited with wonderful calmness
the arrival of the King. On seeing Bussy's gay, smiling
face, he unbent a little.

' Excuse me, monsieur,' said Bussy, 'you seem to be
all alone. Can it be that your appointment has changed
all your friends into enemies ?'

'Faith, Monsieur le Comte, it may be so; but to what
do I owe the honour of your having addressed me ?'

'To the strong admiration which the Duc d'Anjou has
caused me to feel for you.'

'How was that ?'

'He told me why you were appointed First Huntsman.'

M. de Monsoreau paled in such a horrible way that the
marks of the small-pox appeared so many black spots
on his yellow skin, and he looked at Bussy with vehement
passion. Bussy realised he had made a false step, but was
not the man to draw back; rather, he made good an
indiscretion with an insult.

'His Lordship told you the reason for my appointment ?' asked the First Huntsman.

'Yes, monsieur, at length; it aroused in me a strong desire to hear the story from yourself.'

M. de Monsoreau grasped the boar-spear in his clenched hand, as if eager to use it against Bussy.

'Indeed, monsieur, I was inclined to acknowledge your courtesy by granting your request, but here is the King; we must defer the explanation till later.'

The King approached the rendezvous at a rapid rate, mounted on his favourite charger, a Spanish dun-coloured jennet. Bussy, glancing half round, met the Duc d'Anjou's eyes; the Prince was smiling in his most sinister manner. 'Master and servant,' thought Bussy, ' make a horrible grimace when they laugh; what must it be when they weep ?'

The King, who liked handsome countenances, had been little impressed by M. de Monsoreau's the first time he saw him, and was no more satisfied now. However, he accepted, good-humouredly enough, the estortuaire which the huntsman, according to custom, bent to offer him. Directly afterwards, the Masters of the Hunt announced that the stag was turned aside, and the hunt began. Bussy could see every one file past; he examined them all to find the original of the portrait, but in vain; pretty, handsome, and attractive ladies were present, but not the charming person he sought. He was reduced to the company and conversation of his usual friends. Antraguet, a laughing chatterbox, was a diversion from his annoyance.

'We have a frightful First Huntsman,' he remarked to Bussy; ' what do you think ?'

'I think he is hideous; if his relatives resemble him, they make a fine collection ! Which is his wife ?'

'He is unmarried.'

'Who told you ?'

'Madame de Vendron; she considers him very handsome, and would willingly make him her fourth husband, as Lucrèce Borgia did with Count d'Este. Observe how she urges on her bay behind M. de Monsoreau's black charger.'

'What estate does he own ?'

'Several, near Anjou.'

'He is rich, then ?'

'So it is reported; but that is all. He belongs to the inferior nobility.'

'Who is his mistress ?'

'He has none; he wishes to be unique; but the Duc is beckoning to you.'

'Ah! the Duc must wait. That man arouses my curiosity. I don't know why. One has such ideas on meeting some people for the first time; but I feel that I will have to break a lance with him. And then his name, Monsoreau!'

'Mons Soricis, that is the derivation.'

'As good a derivation as I want.'

'Bah! wait a moment. Livarot knows this Mons Soricis; they are neighbours.'

'Let us hear about it at once. Here! Livarot, come, tell me about Monsoreau.'

'Willingly.'

'Will the story be long?'

'No, short. I will give it you in three words. I fear him.'

'Ah! now tell us what you *know* about him.'

'I was returning one evening, about six months ago, through the forest of Méridor, from my uncle's house, when suddenly I heard a fearful cry, and saw passing into the thicket a white horse. At the end of a long alley, darkening with the shades of night, I spied a man on a black horse. He was not riding; he was flying. The same stifled cry was heard again, and I perceived before him on the saddle a woman, over whose mouth his hand was pressed. I had my fowling-piece; you know that I am a fairly good shot; I aimed at him, and upon my honour would have killed him had not the gun missed fire.'

'Well!' asked Bussy, 'afterwards?'

'I asked a wood-cutter who was the gentleman on the black horse, and he told me it was M. de Monsoreau.'

'But such things are done, are they not, Bussy? Women are carried off?' asked Antraguet.

'At least, they are allowed to cry out.'

'Who was the woman?' asked Antraguet.

'I did not discover that.'

'Decidedly, he is a remarkable man, and he interests me,' said Bussy.

'Indeed,' said Livarot, 'he has an abominable reputation, though he has never even done any great wrong openly. He is, moreover, kind enough to his tenants; but, in spite of this, in his district he is feared like fire.

The King will never have had such a First Huntsman, a hunter like Nimrod, not before God, true, but before the devil. He is better fitted for the duties than Saint-Luc, who was set aside through the Duc d'Anjou's influence.'

'He is still calling you ?' said Antraguet.

'Let him call; do you know what is said of Saint-Luc ?'

'No; is he still the King's prisoner ?' was Livarot's laughing question.

'Evidently, seeing he is not here,' said Antraguet.

'Not at all, dear friends, he departed at one this morning to visit his wife's property.'

'Banished ?'

'It looks to me like that.'

'Saint-Luc banished ! impossible.'

'It is the gospel, my dear fellow.'

'According to St Luke ?'

'No, according to Maréchal de Brissac, who informed me this morning.'

'Ah ! this is something new and strange; really this will harm Monsoreau.'

'I have found it,' exclaimed Bussy.

'Found what ?'

'The service he did the Duc d'Anjou.'

'Saint-Luc ?'

'No, Monsoreau.'

'Really ?'

'Yes, or I am much mistaken; you will see, too, come with me.'

Bussy, followed by his friends, galloped after the Duc, who, tired of signalling, was riding some distance in front.

'Ah ! my lord,' he cried, on overtaking him, 'what a precious man is this Monsoreau ! It is incredible.'

'You spoke to him ?' asked the Prince banteringly.

'Certainly.'

'And you asked him what he did for me ?'

'Of course, it was for that purpose I accosted him.'

'And he replied ?' went on the Duc, gayer than ever.

'Immediately, with a politeness which I took kindly of him. He courteously confessed, my lord, that he was a provider to your Highness.'

'Of game ?'

'No, of women.'

'Excuse me, what does this jesting mean ?' asked the Duc, with darkening brow.

'It means, my lord, that for you he carries off women on his black horse, and, as they are unaware of the honour destined for them, he puts his hand over their mouths to prevent their crying.'

The Duc knit his brows, clenched his hands angrily, paled, and set his horse to gallop so furiously that Bussy and his friends were left behind.

'It seems to be a good joke,' observed Antraguet.

'Everybody does not regard it as a joke,' said Livarot.

'The deuce !' said Bussy, 'I seem to have used the poor Duc badly.'

A minute later, the Duc d'Anjou was heard crying,—
'Eh ! Bussy, where are you ?'

'Here I am, my lord,' said Bussy, approaching. He found the Prince, laughing heartily.

'Ah ! my lord, you appear to have found my remarks comical.'

'No, Bussy, I am not laughing at what you said.'

'I am sorry; I should have liked to make a prince laugh who rarely does so.'

'I laugh, Bussy, because you state what is false in order to find out what is true.'

'Indeed, my lord, I told you the truth.'

'Good. Then, now we are alone, tell me the story; where did you get your information ?'

'In the forest of Méridor.'

This time the Duc paled again, but said nothing.

'It is clear the Duc is mixed up in the business,' thought Bussy.

Aloud, he said, 'If I can serve you in any way, tell me.'

The Duc drew him aside. 'Listen,' he said, 'at church I accidentally met a charming woman; her features, half hidden under a veil, reminded me of a deeply loved friend, so I followed her home. Her servant is won over, and I have a key to the house.'

'So far, things go well.'

'Although young, free, and beautiful, she is said to be very austere.'

'My lord, we are becoming romantic.'

'Listen, you are brave, and pretend to be fond of me ?'

'I have my days.'

'For being brave ?'

'No, for being fond of you.'

'Good; is this one of them?'

'To serve your Highness, I will make it one.'

'It means doing for me what one usually does only for oneself.'

'Ah! does it mean paying court to your mistress that your Highness may be sure she is as virtuous as beautiful?'

'I want you to find out what man visits the house.'

'There is a man, then.'

'I am afraid so.'

'A lover, a husband?'

'Somebody jealous, at least, and I wish to learn who he is.'

'Am I commissioned to find out?'

'Yes, and if you agree to do me this favour——'

'You will make me First Huntsman, when the post is vacant?'

'Upon my word, Bussy, I would promise to do so all the more readily that I have never done anything for you.'

'Your lordship realises that?'

'I have said so to myself for a long time.'

'Very low, as princes say these things.'

'Do you agree?'

'To spy on the lady?'

'Yes.'

'My lord, I confess the commission is scarcely flattering, and I should prefer another.'

'You offered to serve me, Bussy, and you draw back already!'

'The deuce! You wish me to act the spy.'

'No! it is a friend's business; moreover, it is no sinecure: you may need to use your sword.'

Bussy shook his head.

'My lord, some things are best done by oneself; so one ought to do them, even if one is a prince.'

'Then you refuse?'

'Indeed I do, my lord.'

The Duc knit his brows.

'I will take your advice, then; if I am killed or wounded, I will say I begged my friend Bussy to help me, and that, 'for the first time in his life, he was prudent.'

'My lord,' answered Bussy, 'you said the other evening: 'Bussy, I hate all those King's minions who jeer at and insult us on every occasion; you ought to attend Saint-Luc's wedding and stir up some quarrel to rid us of them.'' My lord, I went; they were five; I was alone; I challenged them; they laid a trap and attacked me in a body; they killed my horse, and yet I wounded two of them and overpowered a third. To-day you ask me to injure a woman. Excuse me, my lord, that is not a service a prince can demand from a man of honour, and I refuse.'

'Very well, I will go alone or with Aurilly, as I have already done.'

'Excuse me,' observed Bussy, feeling as if a veil had been lifted from his mind.

'What is it?'

'Were you on that errand, the other night, when you saw the minions lying in wait for me?'

'Exactly so.'

'The lady lives near the Bastille?'

'Opposite Sainte-Catherine, where one is easily butchered, as you ought to know.'

'Has your Highness watched since that night?'

'Yesterday. There was another man peering about. In all probability he saw me, and persisted in standing before the door.'

'Was this man alone?' asked Bussy.

'Yes, for half an hour or so. Afterwards another man with a lantern in his hand joined him. Then the man in the cloak——'

'The first one had a cloak?' interrupted Bussy.

'Yes. The man in the cloak and he of the lantern began to talk, and as they did not appear inclined to leave their post that night, I left it to them, and returned home.'

'Disgusted that your suspicions were thus doubly confirmed?'

'Upon my word I confess it. So that, before intruding into that house, which may probably be a den of cut-throats——'

'You would prefer one of your friends to risk his life first.'

'Rather that this friend, not being a prince, and, moreover, being accustomed to such adventures, should ascertain the risks, and give me an account of them.'

'In your place, my lord, I would abandon this enterprise.'

"'Madame,' answered Bussy, 'I am the
man whose life you preserved.'"

CHICOT THE JESTER

'Not at all.'

'Why?'

'The woman is too beautiful.'

'You say you scarcely saw her.'

'I saw enough to notice her wonderful fair hair, magnificent eyes, splendid complexion, wonderful figure. You understand one does not readily relinquish such a woman.'

'Yes, my lord, I understand; the situation moves me.'

The Duc cast a sidelong glance at Bussy.

'I give you my word of honour.'

'You are joking?'

'No; and for proof, I will watch to-night, if you give me instructions, and describe the situation of the house.'

'Then you recant?'

'Eh! my lord, only our Holy Father Gregory XIII. is infallible; tell what is to be done.'

'You must hide yourself, and if a man enters the house, follow to see who he is.'

'Suppose he shuts the door when he goes in?'

'I have a key.'

'Ah! true; there is only one point more to fear. I may follow some other man into another house.'

'You cannot make a mistake; this door is the door of a passage; at the end of the passage, on the left, is a stair; you go up twelve steps, and find yourself in the corridor.'

'How can you know, my lord, as you have never entered the house?'

'Did I not remark that the servant has been won over. She explained the whole thing.'

'Zounds! how convenient to be a prince; your work is all done for you. I should have had to find out the house, explore the passage, count the steps, search the corridor. That would have taken endless time, and who knows whether I might have succeeded?'

'You agree, then?'

'Can I refuse your Highness anything? Only you will come to point out the door.'

'It is unnecessary; on returning from the hunt, we will make a detour by the Porte Saint-Antoine, and I can show you the house.'

'What must I do to the man, should he appear?'

'Simply follow, till you learn who he is.'

'It is a delicate matter; for instance, suppose he is

so cautious as to stop half-way and put an end to my investigations?'

'I leave you the responsibility of continuing the adventure as you think fit.'

'Then, your Highness entrusts me to act as for myself.'

'Entirely. No word of this to our young noblemen.'

'On the word of a gentleman.'

'Nobody accompanies you?'

'I go alone, I assure you.'

'Well! that is agreed, we return by the Bastille. I point out the door—you come home with me—I give you the key—and to-night——'

'I take your lordship's place.'

Bussy and the Prince returned to the hunt, which M. de Monsoreau was conducting like a man of genius. The King was delighted with the exact way in which the consummate hunter had arranged the halts and disposed the relays. After being hunted two hours, after being turned in an enclosure of four or five leagues, and viewed twenty times, the animal returned to be captured exactly where it had been started. M. de Monsoreau received the congratulations of the King and the Duc d'Anjou.

'My lord,' said he, 'I am extremely happy to have merited your compliments, since it is to you I owe my position.'

'To continue to merit them,' said the Duc, 'you must leave for Fontainebleau to-night; the King hunts there to-morrow and the next few days, and a day is not too long to gain acquaintance with the forest.'

'I am aware of it, my lord, and my equipage is already prepared. I will set out to-night.'

'Ah! M. de Monsoreau,' said Bussy, 'henceforth no more rest for you. You wished to become First Huntsman; well, there are fifty good nights' sleep the less for you in this post than for other men; lucky thing you are not married.'

Bussy laughed as he spoke. The Duc glanced piercingly at the Huntsman; then, turning to the other side, he went to congratulate the King upon the improvement on his health since the preceding day. As to Monsoreau, he had, at Bussy's joke, paled in that dreadful manner which made him look so sinister.

CHAPTER XII

HOW BUSSY FOUND BOTH THE PORTRAIT AND THE ORIGINAL

THE hunt was over by about four o'clock : at five o'clock, as if the King had anticipated the Duc d'Anjou's desires, all the court returned to Paris by the Faubourg Saint-Antoine. M. de Monsoreau, under the pretext of setting out immediately, had taken leave of the Princes, and was proceeding towards Fontainebleau. As the procession passed the Bastille, the King commented on its majestic and gloomy appearance, thus reminding his courtiers of what might happen should they incur his displeasure. Many understood his meaning, and became doubly deferential towards His Majesty. Meanwhile, the Duc whispered to Bussy, who rode alongside, 'Look carefully to the right, to the wooden house with the little statue of the Virgin under the gable; follow the same line, and count four houses, inclusive of the one with the Virgin.'

'Good,' replied Bussy.

'It is the fifth, the one exactly opposite the Rue Sainte-Catherine.'

'I see it, my lord; watch how the sound of the trumpets announcing the King fills all the windows with curious people.'

'Except those of the house I pointed out; they remain closed.'

'A corner of the curtain is drawn aside,' said Bussy, his heart beating at a dreadful rate.

'One can see nothing, though. The lady is well guarded, or guards herself well. However, that is the house, and, at the hotel, I will give you the key.'

On arriving at the Hôtel d'Anjou, the Duc gave Bussy the key, bidding him be vigilant; and Bussy, promising to do his utmost, returned home.

'Well ?' he said to Rémy, 'have you discovered anything?'

'The house is as unapproachable by day as by night. I cannot decide between five or six houses which stand together.'

'Then I have enjoyed more luck than you.'

'How can that be, my lord; have you been searching too ?'

'No, I passed along the street simply.'

'And recognised the door ?'

'Providence, dear friend, has indirect ways and mysterious combinations.'

'When shall I learn the result of your visit ?'

'To-morrow morning.'

'Meanwhile, have you any need of me ?'

'None at all, my dear Rémy.'

'Be cautious at least, my lord.'

'Ah ! the advice is useless ; I am noted for my caution.'

Bussy dined as a man who does not know where or how he will sup ; then, when eight struck, he chose his best sword, and, having put a pair of pistols in his belt, in spite of the edict which the King had just issued, he had himself carried in his litter to the end of the Rue Saint-Paul. There, he looked for the house with the statue of the Virgin, counted the next four, assured himself that the fifth was the one, and putting on a dark cloak, hid at the corner of the Rue Sainte-Catherine, resolved to wait for two hours, and if no one came by that time, to act for himself.

Nine o'clock was ringing at Saint-Paul when Bussy went into hiding. Ten minutes later, he saw two horsemen approach by the gate of the Bastille, and stopped on reaching the Hôtel des Tournelles. One of them dismounted, throwing the reins to the other, probably a servant, and, after watching him take the horses away, he advanced towards the house over which Bussy kept vigil. A few paces away, he wheeled round, as if wishing to explore the neighbourhood ; then, convinced that he was not observed, he approached the door, and disappeared.

Bussy waited a moment, and then advanced in his turn, crossed the pavement, opened the door, and, taught by experience, shut it noiselessly. The wicket was on a level with his eyes, and was, in all probability the one through which he had looked at Quélus. *That was not all.* He went on slowly, groping at both sides of the passage, at the end of which he found, on the left, the first step of the stair. There he stopped, for two reasons : first, because of the stress of his emotions ; secondly, because he heard a voice saying, 'Gertrude, tell your mistress that I wish to enter.'

The request was made in too imperative a tone to admit of refusal; an instant passed, and then Bussy heard a servant's voice replying : 'Go into the drawing-room, monsieur; madame will join you there.'

Remembering the twelve steps that Rémy had counted, Bussy counted twelve, and found himself in the landing. He remembered the corridor and the three doors, and advanced a few steps, holding in his breath and stretching out his hand. He touched the first door, by which the stranger had entered. Continuing his way, he encountered a second door, which he opened noiselessly. The apartment would have been in complete darkness but for one portion which received, through a side door, a reflection of the light in the drawing-room. This reflected light shone upon a window, hung with tapestry curtains, the sight of which caused the young man a thrill of joy. His eyes travelled to the part of the ceiling illuminated by the same light, and he recognised the mythological design; stretching out his hand, he felt the carved bed. There was no longer any doubt; he was in the very room of his dream. Bussy hid in the bed-curtains and listened. From the adjoining room sounded the impatient step of the stranger, who from time to time stopped, muttering between his teeth, 'Will she come ?'

Presently a door, parallel to the one already ajar, opened into the drawing-room. The rustling of a silk dress reached Bussy's ears, and he heard a woman's voice exclaim disdainfully,—

'Here I am, monsieur; what are your wishes ?'

'Oh ! oh !' thought Bussy, 'if this man is the lover, I heartily congratulate the husband.'

'Madame,' said the visitor, 'I have the honour to inform you that, as I am obliged to leave for Fontainebleau to-morrow morning, I come to spend the night beside you.'

'Do you bring me news of my father ?'

'Madame, listen to me.'

'Monsieur, you know what we agreed yesterday, when I consented to become your wife, that, before anything else, either my father should come to Paris, or I should go to him.'

'Madame, immediately on my return from Fontainebleau, we will set out, I give you my word of honour; but, meanwhile——'

'Oh, monsieur, do not shut the door, it is useless;

I will not pass a night under the same roof as you, until reassured about my father's fate.'

The woman blew a little silver whistle, which emitted a sharp, prolonged sound. Immediately the door by which Bussy had entered opened again, to admit the servant, a tall, strong girl of Anjou, who seemed to have been waiting for the signal. She entered the drawing-room. A ray of light penetrating into the room where Bussy was, he recognised the portrait.

'Gertrude,' said the lady, 'do not go to bed, but keep within call.'

The maid withdrew without answering, and retraced her steps, leaving the drawing-room door wide open, so that the wonderful portrait was in full view. Bussy had no longer any doubt; this was really the one he had seen. He moved softly toward the opening, but in spite of his caution the floor creaked. At the noise, the woman turned; she was the original of the portrait, the fairy of his dream. The man, though hearing nothing, moved at the same time. He was Monsieur de Monsoreau.

'Ah!' said Bussy, 'the white horse—the woman carried away!' He wiped his face, which was covered with perspiration. He could see the two : the woman standing pale and scornful; the man, livid, moving his foot impatiently and biting his nails.

'Madame,' said de Monsoreau at last, 'do not expect to keep up the rôle of a persecuted and victimised woman; you are in Paris, in my house. Moreover, you are now Comtesse de Monsoreau, that is to say, my wife.'

'If I am your wife, why do you refuse to take me to my father ? why continue to hide me from the eyes of the world ?'

'You have forgotten the Duc d'Anjou, madame.'

'You assured me that, once your wife, I had no more to fear from him.'

'I must take precautions, madame.'

'Well! monsieur, take them, and come to see me when you have done so.'

'Diane,' said the Comte, whose anger was visibly rising, 'do not treat lightly the holy bond of marriage.'

'Remove my distrust in the husband, and I will respect the ceremony.'

'I believed my actions ensured your entire confidence.'

'Monsieur, I think my interest has not been your

only guide, or, at least, if so, chance has served you well.'

'Oh! this is too much,' exclaimed the Comte; 'I am in my own house, you are my wife, and though all the powers of hell rose against me, you shall be mine to-night.'

Bussy, placing his hand on the guard of his sword, advanced a step; but Diane gave him no time to appear.

'Look!' said she, drawing a dagger from her belt; 'this is my answer.'

Bounding toward the apartment in which Bussy watched, she shut the door, and drew the double bolt, leaving Monsoreau to tire himself out with threats, and to knock with his fists on the wood.

'If you burst one single plank,' exclaimed Diane, 'you will find me dead on the threshold.'

'Be assured, madame,' said Bussy, clasping her in his arms, 'you will have an avenger.'

Diane nearly cried out; but fortunately she realised that the only danger came from her husband. She remained, therefore, in an attitude of defence, but dumb and motionless. M. de Monsoreau kicked the door violently; but, convinced that Diane would carry our her threat, he finally left the drawing-room. They heard his steps retreating into the corridor, until the noise died away on the stair.

'But you, monsieur,' said Diane, leaving Bussy's arms and stepping back, 'who are you, and how did you come here?'

'Madame,' answered Bussy, reopening the door and kneeling in front of Diane, 'I am the man whose life you preserved. How can you imagine I entered the house with evil intentions, or that I plot against your honour?'

Thanks to the flood of light which illumined the young man's noble face, Diane recognised him.

'Oh! you here, monsieur,' she exclaimed, clasping her hands. 'You were there; you heard everything?'

'Alas! yes, madame.'

'But, who are you? what is your name, monsieur?'

'Madame, I am Louis de Clermont, Comte Bussy.'

'Bussy, you are the brave Bussy!' cried Diane simply, little suspecting what joy the exclamation caused.

'Ah! Gertrude,' she continued, speaking to her servant, who had come in terrified at hearing her mistress speaking to some one; 'I have nothing more to fear, for, from this moment, I put my honour under the safeguard of the noblest and most loyal gentleman of France.'

Holding out her hand to Bussy, she observed,—

'Rise, monsieur, I know who you are; you must be told who I am.'

CHAPTER XIII

WHO DIANE DE MERIDOR WAS

Bussy, intoxicated with his happiness, entered, with Diane, into the drawing-room. He looked at Diane with wondering admiration; he had not dared to think that the actual woman could bear comparison with the one of his dream, and behold the reality surpassed his imagination. Diane was eighteen or nineteen; in the first flush of youth and beauty, when the flower has its purest colour and the fruit its most charming bloom.

'Monsieur,' she said, 'you answered one of my questions, but not the other. How came you here?'

'Madame, from your conversation with M. de Monsoreau, I am sure the cause of my presence will be understood after the story you have kindly promised to tell.'

'I will tell you all, monsieur. I am the daughter of the Baron de Méridor, that is to say the sole heiress of one of the noblest and oldest names of Anjou.'

'There was a Baron de Méridor,' said Bussy, 'who might have won his freedom at Pavia, but who gave up his sword to the Spaniards on hearing that the King was a prisoner. Having begged to accompany François I. to Madrid, he shared his captivity, only leaving him to return to France, to arrange his ransom.'

'That was my father, and if ever you come to Méridor, you will see the portrait of King François, painted by Leonardo da Vinci. On his return from Spain, my father married. His first children, two sons, died. This was a terrible grief to him. Then the King died, and the Baron's grief became despair. A few years later he left the court to settle in the country, where I was born, ten years after my brothers' death. All the Baron's love was given to the child of his old age; his affection for me became idolatry. When I was three, my mother died. This was, of course, fresh anguish for the Baron, but I, being too young to understand my loss, still smiled, and helped to console him for my mother's death. As I was all to him, so he was all to me. I reached my sixteenth birthday without suspecting there was another world beyond that of my sheep, my peacocks, my swans, and my turtle-doves; without thinking this life should ever finish, and without wishing it to finish. The Château de Méridor was surrounded by vast forests, belonging to M. the Duc d'Anjou. They were filled with deer, roe-buck, and stags, which nobody dreamed of disturbing, and who, in consequence, became tame; all were more or less known to me, some recognised my voice so well as to come at my call; a hind, my special favourite, Daphne, ate out of my hand. One spring, not seeing her for a month, I thought her lost, and mourned as for a friend. Suddenly she returned with two fawns.

'About this time a report spread that the Duc d'Anjou had just sent a lieutenant-governor to the capital of the province. In a few days we learned of his arrival, and that he was called Comte de Monsoreau. Why did this name affect me so strongly? I can only explain the painful sensation as a presentiment. A week passed. Many and varied were the opinions held throughout the countryside in regard to the Comte. One morning the forest resounded with the sound of horns and the barking of dogs; running to the park gate, I saw Daphne pass, with her two fawns, pursued by a pack of hounds. A moment later a man passed like a vision, riding a black horse which seemed to have wings; it was M. de Monsoreau. I wished to cry out, to demand grace for my poor protégée, but either he did not hear my voice or paid no attention.

'Not thinking of the anxiety my absence would cause my father, I ran in the direction of the hunters, hoping to meet the Comte, and to beg him to stop the pursuit, which was breaking my heart. I ran for half a league, and had long since lost sight of hind, pack, and huntsmen. Sinking at the foot of a tree, I began to weep. Presently the hunt again approached, and my poor Daphne rushed, panting, into the thicket. Only one fawn accompanied her; the other had succumbed to fatigue, and had doubtless been torn by the dogs. Daphne was becoming exhausted, and the distance between her and the dogs was less than at first.

'I again endeavoured to attract attention. M. de

Monsoreau saw nothing but the deer; he passed more quickly than before, blowing a hunting horn furiously. Behind him, three or four prickers urged on the dogs with cries and horn-blasts. This confusion of barks, fanfares, and voices passed like a tempest, disappeared into the thickness of the forest, and was lost in the distance. I was in despair; I said to myself, if I had been only fifty paces farther on, at the edge of the glade, he would have seen me, and, at my pleading, might even have stopped. At this thought my courage revived; the hunters might pass a third time. I walked through an avenue, which led to the Château de Beaugé. This château, owned by the Duc d'Anjou, was almost three leagues distant from my father's home. Only then did I realise that I had walked three leagues, and that I was alone.

'A vague terror seized me, and I thought of the rashness and even impropriety of my conduct. I walked by the edge of the pond, resolving to ask the gardener to show me home, when suddenly the noise of the chase was heard. I stood motionless, listening. I forgot everything. The hind rushed out of the wood from the other side of the pond, closely pursued. She was alone, her second fawn also having succumbed. The sight of the water redoubled her strength; she snuffed the fresh air and dashed into the pond as though wishing to come to me. I looked at her, with tears in my eyes, my arms stretched out and nearly as breathless as herself. Her strength now became gradually weaker, while the dogs, animated by the nearness of their quarry, grew more fierce. Soon the swiftest reached her, and she stopped swimming. Just then M. de Monsoreau appeared on the edge of the forest, rushed to the pond, and dismounted.

'Gathering all my strength, I shouted, with clasped hands, "Mercy!" I thought he noticed me: I called again, louder than the first time. Running to a boat, he loosed the moorings and rowed quickly towards the animal, still struggling in the midst of the pack. I never doubted but that M. de Monsoreau, moved by my appeal, was hastening to help the hind, when, as he came within reach, I saw him draw out a hunting-knife; a ray of sunlight shone upon it; then the sparkle died away; I uttered a cry; the whole blade was plunged into the poor animal's throat. The blood gushed out, tingeing the waters red. The hind, belling in a mournful, deathly manner, struck the water with her feet, nearly stood upright, and fell back dead. I cried almost as mournfully, and fell, fainting, at the edge of the pond.

'On recovering consciousness, I was in bed in the Château de Beaugé, and my father, who had been sent for, was weeping at the head of my bed. As it was only an attack of nerves, brought on by over-exertion, I returned home the next day. Still, I stayed in my room for three or four days. On the fourth, my father informed me that M. de Monsoreau had come to inquire for me; it had grieved him to learn that he was the unwitting cause of the accident, and he wished to offer his excuses, saying that he would be happy only on receiving my forgiveness. Feeling it would be ridiculous to refuse, in spite of my repugnance, I yielded. Next day he made his appearance. Having learned how absurd my action had been, I explained it by my tenderness for Daphne.

'The Comte assumed the rôle of a man in despair, asserting on his honour that, had he guessed my interest, he would have been most happy to spare the deer. However, his protestations failed to convince me, and he departed without effacing the painful impression from my mind. On leaving, he asked my father's permission to return. He had been born in Spain and brought up in Madrid, and the Baron was delighted to speak of a country where he had stayed so long. Moreover, the Comte was of high birth, lieutenant-governor of the province, a favourite, it was said, of the Duc d'Anjou. Alas! from that moment, my happiness, or, at least my peace of mind, vanished. I quickly perceived the impression I had made on the Comte. At first he came only once a week, then twice, at last every day. He was attentive to my father, who took the keenest pleasure in his conversation. The Comte treated me with politeness and respect. One morning my father came into my room, looking graver than usual, and yet joyful in his gravity.

'"My child," said he, "you have always declared that you would be happy to stay with me always."

'"Oh! dear father," I exclaimed, "you know it is my dearest wish."

'"Well! my Diane," he continued, stooping to kiss my brow, "it rests only with you to have your wish realised."

'Suspecting his meaning, I became so pale that he stopped.

'"Diane, my child!" he cried, "oh! good gracious, what is wrong?"

'"Monsieur de Monsoreau is it?" I stammered.

'"Well!" he asked, in astonishment.

'"Oh! never, my father, if you have any pity for your daughter, never!"

'"Diane, dearest, it is not pity I feel for you; I idolise you, as you know; take a week to decide, and if, in a week——"

'"Oh! no, no; it is useless; not a week, not a day, not a moment. No, no, no!" and I burst into tears.

'It was the first time my father had ever seen me weep. Taking me in his arms, he reassured me, pledging his word that he would say no more about the matter. A month passed before I saw M. de Monsoreau again. One morning we received an invitation to a grand fête which M. de Monsoreau was giving in honour of the King's brother. This fête was held in the Town Hall of Angers. A personal invitation was enclosed from the Prince, who said he remembered having met my father at court, and would be pleased to see him again.

'My first impulse was to beg my father to refuse; and, indeed, I would have insisted had the invitation been solely from M. de Monsoreau; but as it came partly in the Duc's name, my father feared to offend him. We went to this fête, M. de Monsoreau receiving us as if nothing had happened; his behaviour was neither indifferent nor affected, and I felt happy at not being distinguished by him in any way. With the Duc d'Anjou, the case was different. When I was introduced, he fixed his eyes upon me, and never looked away again. I felt uneasy under his glance, and without disclosing the reason, I insisted in such a way on leaving the ball that we were the first to go.

'Three days later, M. de Monsoreau came to Méridor. Seeing him in the avenue, I withdrew to my room. I was afraid that my father would send for me, but nothing happened. In half an hour, M. de Monsoreau left before anybody had informed me of his visit. More than that, my father never mentioned it; only he seemed graver than usual. Some days passed, when on returning from a walk, I was told that M. de Monsoreau was with my father. The Baron had asked for me, and had left orders to be told of my return. Hardly had I entered my room than he hastened to me.

' "My child," said he, "an event, which it is useless for you to know, compels me to separate myself from you for some days; do not ask questions; only be assured that the motive must be very urgent to force me to part with you for a week, a fortnight, a month perhaps."

'I trembled, though unconscious of the danger to which I was exposed. But this double visit of M. de Monsoreau could presage nothing good.

' "Where shall I go, father ?" I asked.

' "To the Château de Lude, to my sister, where you will remain hidden. Your arrival there must be in the night."

' "Will you not accompany me ?"

' "I must stay here to avert suspicion; the servants themselves will not learn where you are going."

' "Who will accompany me, then ?"

' "Two men, on whom I rely."

' "Oh, *mon Dieu !* father !"

' The Baron embraced me.

' "My child," said he, "it must be so."

'Knowing the depth of my father's love, I did not insist further, and asked no more explanations. Only it was agreed that Gertrude, my nurse's daughter, should attend me. At eight o'clock my father came for me. I was ready, and going down noiselessly we crossed the garden. He opened a little gate, leading to the forest, where we found a litter all ready, and two men. I mounted the litter, and Gertrude got in also. The Baron embraced me a last time, and we set out. It was very dark and cold, the season being the middle of winter.

'I was ignorant of the danger that compelled me to leave the Château de Méridor. I asked Gertrude, but she was equally ignorant. I dared not address our conductors, whom I did not know. We proceeded, therefore, silently and along bypaths, when, after two hours' journeying, as I was being lulled by the regular and monotonous movement, in spite of my uneasiness, into sleep, I was aroused by Gertrude, who seized my arm, and still more by the litter stopping.

' "Oh ! mademoiselle," said the poor girl, "what is happening ?"

'Thrusting my head through the curtains, I saw that we were surrounded by six masked horsemen. Our own men were disarmed and secured. I was too terrified to call for help; besides, who would have come at our cries ? The leader of the masked men advanced to the door.

'"Be easy, mademoiselle," said he; "no evil can come to you; but you must follow us."

'"Where ?" I asked.

'"To a place where, far from having anything to fear, you will be treated like a queen."

'This promise terrified me more than a threat would have done.

'"Oh ! my father ! my father !" I murmured.

'"Listen, mademoiselle," said Gertrude, "I know the district; I am devoted to you; I am strong; we shall be extremely unlucky if we do not manage to escape."

'This assurance was far from making me easy, yet it is so pleasant to feel oneself not entirely deserted, that I regained some strength.

'"Do with us what you will, gentlemen," I answered; "we are two poor women who cannot defend ourselves."

'One man dismounted, took our conductor's place, and turned the litter in another direction.'

Bussy listened with the greatest attention to Diane's story. The first emotions of a great love produces almost a religious feeling in one's heart. The woman chosen is raised above other women; she becomes great, pure, divine; her every motion is a favour granted you, her every word a boon accorded; if she look at you, you rejoice; you are overwhelmed by her smile. The young man, therefore, had listened without interruption; each detail interested him deeply, and he listened to Diane's words dumb and breathless. Now, as the young girl paused, being no doubt overcome by her two-fold emotion, Bussy, unable to bear the anxiety, clasped his hands, saying,—

'Oh ! go on, madame, go on !'

Diane understood the nature of his emotion; everything in his voice, gestures, expression, bore out the entreaty in his tones. She smiled sadly and resumed,—

'After proceeding for nearly three hours, the litter stopped. A door creaked, some words were spoken, and the litter went on again. Peeping out, I saw we were in the courtyard of a castle. What castle was it ? Neither of us had any idea. Often, during the journey, we had tried to ascertain our bearings, but had seen only an endless forest. The door of the litter opened, and the man who had already spoken told us to descend. I obeyed in silence. Two men, carrying torches, received us with every mark of respect. We followed them to a bedroom, richly ornamented and decorated in the style of François the First's reign. A splendidly served repast awaited us.

' "You have arrived at your destination, madame," said one of our conductors; "and as you require the services of a chamber-maid, yours will not leave you; her room is next door."

'Gertrude and I looked at one another joyfully.

' "You have only to knock on the door," he continued, "and a person constantly on duty in the ante-room will attend immediately."

'The masked man bowed and left the room; the door was double-locked, and we found ourselves alone. For a moment we stood motionless, looking at one another, by the light of two candelabra, which lit up the supper-table. Gertrude wished to speak, but I motioned to her to keep quiet, as some one might be listening. The door of Gertrude's room stood open; so, taking a candle, we tiptoed in. The apartment was fairly large, and there was a door parallel to that through which we had entered. This second door also had a small knocker of wrought copper. Both doors opened into the same ante-room. Gertrude held the light close; the door was doubly bolted. We were prisoners.

' "Mademoiselle," said Gertrude, in low tones, "did you notice that we only came up five steps on leaving the courtyard ?"

' "Yes," I answered.

' "We are on the ground floor, then ?"

' "Without doubt."

' "So that——" she continued in lower tones, looking at the outer shutters.

' "If the windows were not barred with iron——" I interrupted.

' "If mademoiselle had courage——"

' "Courage," I exclaimed; "oh ! rest assured of that; I will have courage."

'Gertrude now motioned to me to be quiet, and carried the candle back to the bedroom table. I had already divined her intention, so, approaching the window, I looked for the clasps. Gertrude, who had rejoined me found them. The shutter opened. I cried out joyfully;

the window was not barred. But Gertrude had already
noticed the cause of this apparent neglect. A large lake
washed the foot of the wall : ten feet of water guarded us
as effectively as iron bars could have done.

'Presently I recognised a familiar landscape; we were
prisoners in the Château de Beaugé, where, a month ago,
I had been received, on the day my poor Daphne died.
This château belonged to the Duc d'Anjou. By a lightning
flash, I understood everything. I regarded the lake with
gloomy satisfaction; it represented a last resource against
violence, a supreme refuge from dishonour. We closed
the shutters. I threw myself, still dressed, on the bed.
Gertrude slept at my feet, in an arm-chair. Twenty times
that night I awoke with a start, a prey to unheard of
terrors; but nothing justified these fears; all seemed to
sleep in the castle; only the cry of the birds from the fens
broke the silence.

'Day came. The light confirmed my apprehensions :
all attempt at flight was impossible without help from the
outside, and whence could this help come ? Towards
nine o'clock, some one knocked at our door, and going into
Gertrude's room I told her to open. Our attendants of
the previous night had come to clear away the supper,
which we had not touched, and to bring our breakfast.
Gertrude put some questions to them, but they did not
reply. The fact, however, of our being in the Château de
Beaugé, treated with feigned respect, made all clear.
The Duc d'Anjou had fallen in love with me, and my
father, wishing to keep me safe, had sent me away from
Méridor. His precautions, no doubt, had been rendered
useless through an unfaithful servant or an unlucky
accident, and I had fallen into the Duc's hands.

'At Gerturde's entreaty, I drank a cup of milk and ate
some bread. The forenoon was spent in making wild
plans for flight. Yet, before us was a boat with oars,
fastened amid the reeds. If it had been within reach,
my strength, increased by terror, added to Gertrude's
ordinary force, would have sufficed to end our captivity.
Dinner was served in the same manner as breakfast, and
Gertrude waited upon me, for our attendants had retired.
Suddenly, on breaking my bread, I found a little note,
which I hastily opened,—

'"A friend watches over you," it ran; "to-morrow
you will hear from him and from your father."

'You can understand how glad I was; my heart beat wildly. I gave the note to Gertrude, and spent the rest of the day watching and hoping. The second night was as calm as the first; then breakfast-time arrived, which I awaited impatiently, fully expecting to find another note. I was not disappointed,—

'"He who carried you off arrives at the Château de Beaugé to-night at ten o'clock; but at nine the friend who watches over you will be under your windows. He will bring a letter from your father, urging upon you that confidence you might not otherwise grant. Burn this note."

'Having read and re-read the letter, I obeyed instructions, and burned it. The writing was unfamiliar, and I had no idea who could have sent the note. An hour after dinner, a knock came to our door; we admitted the man who had spoken to us at the litter and in the court-yard; I recognised his voice. He gave me a letter.

'"From whom is this, monsieur ?" I asked.

'"If mademoiselle will read it, she will see."

'"But I do not want to read it."

'"Mademoiselle may do as she pleases. I was ordered to hand her the letter; I lay it at her feet; if mademoiselle deign, she will pick it up."

'Placing the missive on my footstool, the servant went out.

'"What shall I do ?" I asked Gertrude.

'"If I dare advise mademoiselle, I should say read the letter. It may warn us of some danger."

'This advice was so reasonable that I changed my mind and opened the letter.'

Diane paused, and, getting up, took the letter out of a silk portfolio. Bussy glanced at the address.

'This is written by the Duc d'Anjou,' he said.

'Ah !' she replied, with a sigh; 'he had not deceived me, then. Read it; chance has made you acquainted with the most intimate details of my life; I must have no secrets from you.'

Bussy, obeying her, read,—

'An unhappy Prince, deeply moved by your divine beauty, will come to-night at ten o'clock to excuse his conduct towards you—conduct which, he realises, has no other excuse than his unconquerable love.—FRANÇOIS.'

'So this is really from the Duc d'Anjou ?' asked Diane.

'Alas ! yes, it is his writing and his signature.'

'Is he less guilty than I thought ?' murmured Diane.

'Who, the Prince ?' asked Bussy.

'No, the Comte de Monsoreau.'

'Continue, madame, and we will judge both Prince and Comte.'

'This letter, as Gertrude had foreseen, showed the danger to which I was exposed, and made the intervention of my unknown friend all the more precious. My only hope was in him. We now began to look from the windows, but nothing appeared to support our hopes. Night came; four or five hours only separated us from the decisive moment; we waited anxiously. Having nothing by which to mark the flight of time, we were uncertain of the hour, when we saw some shadows moving on the edge of the wood. They walked cautiously, keeping close to the trees for protection. The neighing of a horse reached our ears.

' "It is our friends," whispered Gertrude.

' "Or the Prince."

' "Oh ! the Prince would not be hiding."

'This simple observation dispelled my suspicions. We paid double attention to the shadows. One man advanced, leaving a group of men in the shelter of a clump of trees. Walking straight to the boat, he loosed its moorings, got in and came towards us. At first I seemed to recognise the tall figure, then the gloomy and strongly marked features of the Comte de Monsoreau; finally, I could not doubt it. I now feared help almost as much as danger. On reaching the foot of the wall, he fastened his boat to a ring, and soon his head appeared on a level with our window-sill. I could not restrain a faint cry.

' "Ah ! excuse me," said the Comte, "I thought you were expecting me."

' "I was expecting some one, monsieur, but I did not know it was you."

'A bitter smile crossed his face.

' "Who, then, but your father and I, watches over Diane de Méridor's honour ?"

' "You told me, monsieur, in your letter, that you came in my father's name."

' "Yes, mademoiselle, foreseeing that you might doubt the honesty of my purpose, I have brought a note from the Baron."

'As we had no candles, I passed from Gertrude's room into my own, and, kneeling in front of the fire, read the following :—

'"MY DEAR DIANE,—Monsieur le Comte de Monsoreau can alone rescue you from the fearful danger that you run. Trust yourself, therefore, to him as the best friend Heaven can send us. He will tell you later what I most earnestly wish you to do, in order to discharge the debt we owe him. Your father, who begs you to have pity on yourself and on him,

'"BARON DE MÉRIDOR."

'There was nothing to influence me against the Comte; the repulsion with which he inspired was rather intuitive than the result of reflection.

'"Well ?" he asked, on my return.

'"Monsieur, I have read my father's letter; he states you are ready to take me away, but he does not say where."

'"I take you to where the Baron is waiting."

'"And where is that ?"

'"In the Château de Méridor."

'"So I am going to see my father ?"

'"In two hours."

'"Oh ! monsieur, if you speak the truth——"

'I stopped; the Comte seemed waiting for the end of my sentence.

'"Count upon my entire gratitude," I added in a trembling voice.

'"Then, mademoiselle, you are prepared to accompany me ?"

'I looked at Gertrude uneasily; the Comte's gloomy presence reassured her no more than it did me.

'"Consider that each moment is precious," said he; "I am nearly half an hour late; it is almost ten o'clock, and the Prince will be here. Then I can only risk my life without hope, which I do now, knowing I can save you."

'"Why has my father not come ?"

'"Do you imagine that he can go a step without its being known ?"

'"But yourself ?"

'"That is another matter; I am the confidential friend of the Duc."

'"But, if you are his friend, his confidant, then——"

' "Then I betray him for your sake! I have told you
that I am risking my life to save your honour."

'He spoke in such a tone of conviction that my distrust
began to lessen.

' "See," said M. de Monsoreau, "if you still doubt."

'He pointed to a troop of horsemen skirting the other
side of the lake, and informed me they were the Duc
d'Anjou and his suite.

' "Mademoiselle," exclaimed Gertrude, "we have no
time to lose."

' "There has been too much lost already," said the Comte;
"in Heaven's name, make up your mind."

' "Oh, *mon Dieu!* what should I do?" I murmured.

' "Listen; they are knocking at the door. In five
minutes there will be no time."

' "Gertrude!" I stammered, "help!"

' "Mademoiselle, do you hear the door opening? Do
you hear the horses stamping in the courtyard?"

' "Yes, yes," I answered; "but my strength fails me."

'Lifting me as though I were a child, Gertrude placed
me in the Comte's arms. I shivered violently, but he
carried me to the boat, and Gertrude followed. Seeing
that my veil had become loose, and was floating on the
water, I fancied it might show our traces.

' "My veil! catch it," I cried.

'The Comte, glancing at it, answered,—

' "No, better to let it stay there."

'Seizing the oars, he rowed quickly to the opposite
bank. Just then the windows of my room were lit up:
servants had entered with lights.

' "Did I deceive you?" asked M. de Monsoreau; "was
it time?"

' "Yes, monsieur, you are indeed my saviour."

'Suddenly a man, approaching the open window of my
room, leaned out, and, seeing the veil floating on the water,
uttered a cry.

' "The Prince will think you have thrown yourself into
the lake, and, while he searches for your body, we will
escape," said M. de Monsoreau.

CHAPTER XIV

THERE was a moment's silence. Diane's voice failed. Bussy, listening attentively, vowed an eternal hatred to her enemies, whoever they might be. Presently Diane continued :—

'Hardly had we landed than seven or eight men rode up. They were the Comte's men; a groom held two horses— one the Comte's, the other a white horse intended for me. The Comte helped me to mount, and then jumped into his own saddle. Gertrude sat behind one of the servants, and we galloped off. The Comte held my horse by the reins, and we rode like this for ten minutes, when I heard Gertrude calling. Turning round I saw that our troop had divided; four men had taken a side path into the forest, while the Comte and the other four kept on in the same direction as at first.

' "Why does not Gertrude come with us ?" I exclaimed.

' "It is an indispensable precaution," said the Comte; "we must leave double traces, in case of pursuit. Thus the Duc may follow your maid instead of yourself."

'This specious answer did not satisfy me; but what could I say or do ? Moreover, we were actually on the way to Méridor. At our rate of travelling, we should reach it in a quarter of an hour. Suddenly, where the roads forked, the Comte, swerving from the path, followed one to the left. I was preparing to dismount, despite our rapid pace, when the Comte, leaning over and lifting me from my horse, placed me on his saddle-bow. My horse immediately fled, neighing through the forest. All had been done so quickly that I had only time to cry out once, when he placed his hand over my mouth.

' "Mademoiselle," said he, "I swear to you that I obey your father's orders. When next we halt I will give you ample proof, and if this does not satisfy you, on my honour, mademoiselle, you shall be free."

' "But, monsieur, you said you were taking me to my father," I cried, thrusting away his hand.

' "You hesitated to follow me, and a minute more

meant our ruin. Do you want to kill the Baron ? do you desire your own dishonour ? Say one word, and I lead you to Méridor."

' "You spoke of a proof that you acted in my father's name ?"

' "There is the proof: take this letter and read it at our first resting-place. Afterwards, you shall be free to return to the château. But if you respect the Baron's orders, you will not return !"

' "Let us hasten, then, monsieur, for I am anxious to satisfy myself."

' "Remember, you accompany me freely."

' "In so far as a young girl is free when, on the one hand she sees her father's death and her dishonour, and on the other is obliged to trust a man whom she scarcely knows."

'The Comte ordered one of his men to dismount, and to give me his horse.

' "The other cannot be far away," said the Comte; "get it, and join us at La Châtre."

'I shuddered in spite of myself, for this place was ten leagues from Méridor, on the road to Paris.

' "Monsieur," I said, "at La Châtre, we will come to terms."

' "That is to say, mademoiselle, at La Châtre you will give me your orders."

'This feigned obedience did not reassure me; but, as this was the only means of escaping the Duc d'Anjou, I rode on in silence. At daybreak we reached La Châtre. Instead of entering the village, we struck across country towards an isolated house.

' "Where are we going ?" I asked, coming to a halt.

' "Consider, mademoiselle. Could we put up at an ordinary inn, in a village, where the first peasant might betray us ?"

'In all the Comte's replies there was a logic, or at least a speciousness, which struck me.

' "Very well, let us go," I replied; and we proceeded.

'Unknown to me, a man had gone on to prepare for us. A fire burned in a barely clean room, and a bed was prepared.

' "Here is your room, mademoiselle," said the Comte; "I shall await your orders."

'Bowing, he left me alone. My first act was to approach

the lamp and read my father's letter. Here it is,
Monsieur de Bussy. I leave you to judge of it.'

Taking the letter, Bussy read :—

'MY BELOVED DIANE,—If, as I doubt not, you have
obeyed my entreaty, M. de Monsoreau must have explained that you were unfortunate enough to please the
Duc d'Anjou, who had you carried to the Château de
Beaugé. By this violence you can judge of what he is
capable. Your only chance of safety lies in marrying our
noble friend. As his wife, the Comte will protect you
by all the means in his power. My wish is that this
marriage shall take place as soon as possible, and if you
agree, I add to my ready consent, my fatherly blessing,
and I pray God to grant you all the happiness He reserves
for hearts like yours.

'Your father, who does not command, but entreats.
'BARON DE MÉRIDOR.'

'There was no doubt of its being my father's letter.
Nevertheless, I read it three times before deciding anything.
Then I called the Comte.

'"You have read it ?" he said. "Do you still doubt
my devotion ?"

'"This letter compels me to believe in it, monsieur.
Suppose I agree to my father's wishes, what do you intend
to do ?"

'"To take you to Paris, the easiest place in which to
hide."

'"But my father ?"

'"When the danger is past, the Baron will rejoin us."

'"Well, monsieur, I am ready to accept this means
of safety, on three conditions."

'"Speak, mademoiselle."

'"The first is that Gertrude be restored to me."

'"She is here."

'"The second, that we travel apart, as far as Paris."

'"I intended proposing this, in order to reassure
you."

'"The third, that our marriage takes place in my
father's presence."

'"It is my own wish."

'I was stupefied. I had expected opposition, not
agreement.

' "Now, mademoiselle, may I give you some advice. Travel only at night, and trust to me implicitly."

' "Monsieur, if you love me as you assert, our interests are the same, and I cannot oppose your wishes."

' "Finally, I desire you to live in a quiet, retired house, which I have now got ready."

' "To remain hidden is all I ask, monsieur."

' "Then we understand one another. I go to send your maid and to plan your route."

' "Monsieur, keep your promises, and I will keep mine."

' "I ask nothing better; your promise assures me that shortly I shall be the happiest of men."

'With a low bow the Comte departed, and five minutes later Gertrude came in. Her joy was great, and she listened eagerly to my account of what had passed. Presently we heard the Comte depart by the very road we had just come. Why he was doing this instead of going on ahead I did not understand. His departure, however, reassured me. We spent the whole day in the little house, and at night, the chief of our escort came to ask my orders. I answered that I was ready; and five minutes later he brought me my white horse, which had been caught without trouble. We rode all night and stopped at daybreak, having gone about fifteen leagues.

'All our night journeys were similar. Always we were treated with consideration, and received courteous attention; somebody had evidently preceded us to prepare the lodging. Towards evening of the seventh day, I perceived a great collection of houses. It was Paris. We waited till nightfall before proceeding, when we passed through a gateway, where I saw an immense building which looked like a monastery; then we crossed the river twice. After ten minutes' riding, we reached the Place de la Bastille. A man, apparently waiting for us, approaching our conductor, said,—"Here it is."

'The door was open; a lamp lit up the staircase.

' "Madame," said our head guide, "you are now at home, and our mission is ended. May I hope that we have accomplished it to your satisfaction?"

' "Yes, monsieur," I answered, "I have nothing but thanks for you and those who have accompanied me."

'Gertrude's first care was to shut the door, and then we went up the staircase into the corridor. The three doors were open, and we entered the drawing-room. I passed through a large dressing-room into the bedroom. To my great astonishment, I perceived my portrait from my father's room at Méridor. There was a fire in every room, and a table set for supper in the dining-room. Only one cover was laid, so I was reassured.

'After supper we inspected the house again, but found no one. Gertrude slept in my room. The next day, on going out, she discovered that our house stood at the end of the Rue Saint-Antoine, opposite the Hôtel des Tournelles. The fortress to our right was the Bastille. I was not much wiser, being quite unacquainted with Paris. Just as we were beginning supper, a knock was heard at the door, and Gertrude went down.

'"It is Monsieur le Comte, madame," she reported.

'"Show him in," I replied.

'The Comte appeared on the threshold.

'"Well, madame," he asked, "have I kept the agreement?"

'"Yes, monsieur, and I thank you."

'"Will you permit me to enter?" he added, smiling ironically.

'"Come in, monsieur."

'He remained standing till I motioned him to sit down.

'"First of all, monsieur, have you any news of my father and Méridor?"

'"I have not been to Méridor."

'"Then of Beaugé and the Duc d'Anjou?"

'"That is another affair. I have spoken to the Duc, who seems doubtful if you are actually dead."

'"Where is he?"

'"In Paris since last night. He has promised to have me appointed as First Huntsman."

'"Ah! I remember you are a formidable hunter, and you have some right to the post."

'"I shall be appointed as a servant of the Prince, not as hunter, and because the Duc d'Anjou will not dare to prove ungrateful."

'Something in his speech terrified me: it seemed to express an implacable will.

'"Shall I be permitted to write to my father?" I asked.

'"Certainly; but your letters may be intercepted."

'"Am I forbidden to go out?"

' "Nothing is forbidden you, madame ; only, observe that you may be recognised."

' "But I may at least hear mass on Sunday?"

' "It would be much better not to do so; but if you must, at least attend service in the church of Sainte-Catherine, opposite your house."

' "Thank you, monsieur."

'Presently I asked when I should see him again.

' "I await your permission to return," he answered.

' "You have not a key?"

' "Your husband alone has that privilege."

' "Monsieur," I answered, terrified by such subdued answers more than by authoritative ones, "you may come when you wish, or when you have anything important to tell me."

' "Thank you, madame, I will not abuse your permission," and he stood up.

' "You are leaving me ?" I asked, more and more astonished at this unexpected behaviour.

' "Madame, you have no liking for me, and I cannot take advantage of your present situation which obliges you to receive my attentions. I sincerely hope that you will gradually become reconciled to me."

' "Monsieur," I answered, also rising, "I see how delicate is your behaviour, and I appreciate your remarks, although somewhat harsh. I will use the same frankness; I entertain some prejudices against you which, I hope, time will cure."

' "Permit me to share the hope, madame, and to live in expectation of that happy time."

' Bowing with all the respect that might be shown by my humblest servants, and beckoning to Gertrude, who had heard all the conversation, to light him downstairs, the Comte withdrew.'

CHAPTER XV

THE CONSENT

'A STRANGE man that, upon my soul,' said Bussy.

'Yes, monsieur. His love showed itself with all the harshness of hate. This chilling consideration, this ironical obedience, this restrained passion, frightened me more than if he had clearly defined his wishes, for then I could have opposed them. The next day was Sunday, and putting on a thick veil, I went to the church. I chose a retired corner, and Gertrude watched like a sentinel. It was needless, as no one heeded us. Two days later the Comte returned with the news of his appointment as First Huntsman, hoping this new dignity would hasten my consent to the marriage. The following Sunday I again went to church, and occupied the same seat. In the midst of the prayers my veil became loosened, and I felt Gertrude touch my arm. Raising my head I saw, with horror, the Duc d'Anjou. A man who seemed his confidant was near him.'

'That was Aurilly, his lute player.'

'I drew down my veil sharply, but he had seen me, and had been deeply affected by my resemblance to the woman he believed dead. Uneasy under his glance, I rose to go, but found him at the door, where he offered me the holy water in which he had dipped his fingers. I feigned not to see him. Without turning round, I realised we were being followed, but I was helpless.'

'Oh ! *mon Dieu !*' murmured Bussy, 'why did not chance lead me to you sooner.'

'The same evening, M. de Monsoreau came. His first words made it clear that he had heard of my adventure.

'"I warned you that it would be better not to go out, but you did not believe me. This morning you heard mass at Sainte-Catherine; the Prince, by some fatality, was there and saw you."

'"It is true, monsieur, though I am not certain that the Prince really recognised me."

'"He followed you and made inquiries, but without success."

'"He will forget me, I hope."

'"Those who have seen you do not forget you. I have tried, and failed."

'The first gleam of passion I had remarked in M. de Monsoreau, shone in his eyes. It terrified me more than the sight of the Duc had done. I remained speechless.

'"What do you intend to do ?" asked the Comte.

'"Can I not change my abode; go to the other end of Paris, or return to Anjou ?"

'" Quite useless, the Duc will not now abandon the search."

' " Then I ask you the same question. What do you mean to do, monsieur ?"

' " Alas ! I have little imagination. I know only of one way, and that does not suit you."

' " Perhaps the danger is less than you think."

' " Time will show. However, I repeat, Madame de Monsoreau will have less to fear; my new duty places me near the King, and my wife and I will enjoy his protection."

' I sighed. The suggestion was reasonable. After waiting a moment, the Comte smiled bitterly, bowed, and went out. I called Gertrude, and we stood at the window for nearly an hour, but no one appeared. The next day Gertrude was accosted by the Prince's companion, but to all his questions she remained silent. This meeting terrified me greatly, and fearing I might be attacked during the night, I sent for M. de Monsoreau, who came at once. I told him everything and described the man.

' " It is Aurilly," he said; " what did Gertrude answer ?"

' " Nothing."

' " She was wrong; we must gain time. To-day I am dependent upon the Duc d'Anjou : in a fortnight, a week, perhaps, he will be dependent upon me. We must play with him, or he may do some desperate act."

' " Monsieur, let my father seek audience of the King, who will have pity for an old man."

' " That depends on the King's mood, and whether for the moment he wishes to be a friend or an enemy to the Duc d'Anjou. Besides, it takes six days for a messenger to reach your father, who will take six days to come. In twelve days, unless we stop him, the Duc will have triumphed."

' " How are we to stop him ?"

' M. de Monsoreau returned no answer, and I understood his silence.

' Presently he said, " Madame, I may be seen leaving here; may I stay till dark ?"

' I motioned to him to sit down. I marvelled at the entire self-control the Comte possessed; he succeeded in relieving the strain of our position, and began a conversation on varied topics. He had travelled widely, and had observed and thought much. After his departure Gertrude and I returned to our point of observation. We distinctly saw two men examining the house, but as all our lights were out, they could not see us, and about eleven o'clock they went away.

'Next day Gertrude met the Duc's companion, and exchanged a few words with him. The day after she was more communicative, explaining that I was the widow of a counsellor, and, having no fortune, lived quietly. Later he seemed to doubt the truth of her statements, and spoke of Anjou, Beaugé, and Méridor. Gertrude said that the names were perfectly strange to her. Then he admitted being employed by the Duc, who had fallen in love with me; then followed splendid offers for us both; for Gertrude, if she would let the Prince in, for me, if I would receive him.

'Every evening I informed M. de Monsoreau of what had happened. On the Saturday night he looked paler and more agitated than usual.

'"Listen," he said, "you must marry me by Tuesday or Wednesday."

'"Why?" I exclaimed.

'"Because the Duc is determined not to wait, and as he is on good terms with his brother, we can expect nothing from His Majesty."

'"By Wednesday, something may occur to help us."

'"Perhaps. Any day now I may be able to force the Duc to do as I wish. To-morrow I must go to Monsoreau, with that very object."

'"But if you fail?"

'"I can do nothing, madam, where I have no right."

'"Oh! my father," I cried.

'The Comte looked at me keenly.

'"With what do you reproach me? Have I not been devoted as a friend, considerate as a brother? Did you not give me your promise, and have I ever reminded you of it?"

'"No."

'"Yet you prefer rather to be the Duc's mistress than the Comte de Monsoreau's wife."

'"That is unfair, monsieur."

'"Decide, then."

'"I have decided."

'"To be the Comtesse de Monsoreau?"

'"Rather than mistress to the Duc d'Anjou."

'"The alternative is flattering; never mind, let Gertrude cajole Aurilly until Tuesday, and then we will see."

'The next day Gertrude did not see him, and his absence made us uneasy. We were alone, and in our weakness I realised how unjust I had been to the Comte. Evening came; I had determined to kill myself rather than fall into the Duc's power alive. We barricaded our rooms, and shading the lamp, kept watch at the window. At eleven o'clock five men, emerging from the Rue de Saint-Antoine, hid at the corner of the Hôtel des Tournelles. In a quarter of an hour, two more men appeared at the corner of the Rue Saint-Paul, and Gertrude recognised one as Aurilly.

' " They will have to break down the door," she whispered, " and the noise will arouse our neighbours."

' " Why should they risk their lives in defending us. Indeed, Gertrude, we have no true protector but the Comte."

' " Yet you refuse to become Comtesse !"

'I sighed.

CHAPTER XVI

THE MARRIAGE

' MEANWHILE the two men creeping past the house stood below our windows. We opened the casement softly.

' " Are you sure this is it ?" asked a voice.

' " Yes, monseigneur, perfectly sure."

' " Will the key fit ?"

' " I took an impression of the lock."

' " And once we are inside ?"

' " The servant will open to us. Your Highness has a gold key in his pocket which is well worth this one."

' Suddenly the men in hiding rushed out upon the Duc, crying, " Die ! die !" I fell on my knees and thanked God, guessing only that some unexpected, unheard of help had arrived. But, on the Prince revealing his identity, the voices quietened, swords were sheathed, the aggressors fell back. The interruption, however, caused the Prince to withdraw, and the five men returned to their hiding-place. Being too uneasy to rest, we remained at the window.

'Presently a horseman appeared, apparently the one expected by the assassins, for crying out, "To swords! to swords!" they rushed at him. I need not tell you,' said Diana, blushing slightly, ' what an interest we took in this unequal combat, which was so bravely sustained. We shuddered, cried out, prayed by turns. We saw your horse fall, and believed you to be lost. Finally, surrounded on every side, you retreated, facing your opponents, and leaned against the door. We were coming down to let you in, when on reaching the landing-place we heard the street door close. Then a man, tottering and holding out his arms, fell on the steps with a dull moan. He had been wounded dangerously, mortally, perhaps, and needed help.

' "Bring the lamp," I said to Gertrude. Recognising you as the cavalier who had defended himself so bravely, we carried you into my room, and placed you on the bed. A doctor's care seemed necessary. Gertrude remembered hearing of some wonderful cure effected by a young doctor of the Rue Beautreillis. She knew his address, and offered to fetch him. She went away, taking money, a key, and my dagger, while I remained alone to pray for you. In a quarter of an hour the doctor appeared with Gertrude; he had obeyed her instructions, and accompanied her with his eyes bandaged.

' Having dressed your wound, he poured a few drops of a red liquid on your lips. He described it as an elixir which would make you sleep, and lessen the fever. A moment after swallowing this, you fell into a kind of faint. Gertrude covering the doctor's eyes with a handkerchief, led him back to the Rue Beautreillis. She noticed that he counted his steps, which frightened me, for he might betray us. We decided to efface all traces of what had happened. It was two in the morning, and the streets were deserted. Gertrude succeeded in lifting you, and, together, we carried you to the slope of the Temple moats. We returned, dismayed at our boldness in going out at an hour when men do not venture alone. On coming in, my emotion caused me to faint.'

' Oh, madame!' cried Bussy, clasping his hands, ' when shall I ever understand what you have done for me?'

A silence fell, during which Bussy looked ardently at Diane. Her head had fallen forward on her hand, and she rested her elbow on the table. The clock of Sainte-Catherine was heard striking.

'Two o'clock!' said Diane, starting, 'and you still here.'

'Oh, madame!' begged Bussy, 'Do not send me away until you explain how I can help you. Imagine that you have a brother, and tell this brother what he can do for his sister.'

'Alas! nothing now, it is too late!'

'What happened next day?' asked Bussy.

'Gertrude met Aurilly, who was more insistent than ever; he said nothing of what had passed the night before, but begged an interview in his master's name. Gertrude appeared to consent, asking him to wait till to-day on my decision. He promised that his master would wait. We had three days before us. In the evening M. de Monsoreau returned, and I described what had occurred, save that which concerned you. I said the Duc had opened the door with a false key, and I repeated the names of d'Épernon and Quélus, the two I had heard.'

'"Yes," he replied, "I heard of that; I suspected he had a false key."

'"Could the lock not be changed?"

'"He would have another key made."

'"Place bolts at the door."

'"He will come with his men and knock in doors and bolts."

'"What of the affair which was to place him in your power?"

'"It is put off indefinitely."

'I could not conceal from myself that the sole means of escaping the Duc was to marry the Comte.

'"Monsieur," I said, "the Duc has promised to wait till Wednesday night; give me until Tuesday."

'"I will be here on Tuesday at this hour, madame," said the Comte.

'Instead of going straight away, he stationed himself in a corner near the Hôtel des Tournelles, to watch over me during the night. Each proof of his devotion was a fresh blow to my heart. The two days passed quickly; when night came at the end of the second, I was overwhelmed; all feeling left me. I was cold and dumb, my heart alone beat. Gertrude, who stood at the window, held out her hand.

' " Madame !" she said, "four men are outside—they are opening the door—they are entering."

' " Let them enter," I answered, without moving.

' It is likely to be the Duc d'Anjou, Aurilly, and two attendants."

'Instead of replying, I drew out my dagger and put it on the table.

' Oh ! let me make sure, at least," said Gertrude, rushing to the door.

'In a moment she returned.

' " Mademoiselle, it is the Comte."

' Hiding the dagger, I turned round to the Comte, who was alarmed at my pallor.

' " Gertrude says you took me for the Duc, and were about to kill yourself."

'It was the first time I had seen him affected. Was his emotion real or assumed ?

' " Do you know that I am not alone ?" he asked.

' " Gertrude saw four men."

' " Do you suspect who they are ?"

' " I suppose one is a priest and the other two are witnesses."

' " Then you are prepared to be my wife ?"

' " Was, it not agreed upon ? Only, unless forced by necessity, I was not to marry save in my father's presence."

' " I recall the condition, madame, do you think there is such a necessity?"

' " I believe so, but remember, I will be your wife only in name, until I meet my father."

'Frowning, the Comte bit his lips.

' " Mademoiselle, I have no wish to force you; I give you back your word, you are free; only——"

'Approaching the window, and glancing at the street, " Look," said he.

'There was a man in a cloak under the window, seeking how to enter the house.

' That was yesterday ?' asked Bussy.'

' Yes, about nine o'clock; a moment later, a man with a lantern joined the first.

' " What do you think of it ?" the Comte asked.

' " It must be the Duc with his confederate," I said.

C.J.   E

' " Must I stay, or go : command me," continued the Comte.

'I wavered for a moment : in spite of my father's letter, my pledged word, the present danger, palpable, threatening, I hesitated; and had these two men not been there——'

' Oh! unhappy that I am !' cried Bussy, ' I was the man in the cloak, and the lantern-bearer was the young doctor. I was eager to find the house again: the room, the woman, the angel who had appeared to me.'

Bussy seemed overwhelmed by the fatality, which had made Diane accept the Comte.

' So you are his wife ?'

' Since yesterday; but how did you get here ?'

Bussy showed her the key. 'Did not Gertrude promise to let the Prince in to-night ? The Prince, having seen M. de Monsoreau and me, feared a trap and sent me instead.'

' You accepted the mission ?' asked Diane reproachfully.

' It was the only way of getting near you. Do not be angry. God has led me here to unravel this plot, of which you are the victim. I have dedicated my life to you. You asked for news of your father ? Well, I take it upon myself to gratify your wish. Keep kind memories of him who, henceforth, lives by you and for you."

' But this key ?'

' I give it to you, being willing to accept it only at your hands. But I swear that never will sister have trusted the key of her house to a more devoted and respectful brother.'

' I trust the word of brave Bussy,' said Diane; 'take the key, monsieur.'

' Madame, in a fortnight we shall know what sort of man Monsieur de Monsoreau really is.'

Having bowed respectfully to Diane, Bussy departed, and long after his footsteps died away Diane sat listening with heart beating fast, and eyes filled with tears.

CHAPTER XVII

HOW KING HENRI III. TRAVELLED

THE day following these events witnessed the King's
departure for Fontainebleau, where a great hunt had been
arranged. This, like all the King's acts, was the occasion
of much noise and bustle. Towards eight o'clock in the
morning, on the quay of the Louvre, a great crowd
gathered, noblemen in attendance, on horseback and
wrapped in fur cloaks, a great number of pages, lackeys, and
lastly, a company of Swiss, immediately preceding the
royal litter. This was drawn by eight mules richly caparisoned, and was fifteen feet long by eight wide.

It contained Henri, his physician, Marc Miron, his
chaplain, Chicot, four or five of the King's favourites,
a pair of greyhounds, and a collection of little English
dogs. A copper-wire cage, containing some fine turtle-
doves, with white plumage and double black rings, hung
from the roof. A Notre-Dame de Chartres, sculptured by
Jean Goujon, was placed in a gilded niche. In all the
pamphlets and satirical verses of the day, the litter was
frequently referred to as Noah's Ark.

The King sat on the floor just below the statue; Quélus
and Maugiron at his feet plaited ribbons, one of the
favourite diversions of the period; Schomberg, in a corner,
was embroidering tapestry; in another corner the chaplain
and doctor were chatting; d'O and d'Épernon, having
been wakened too early, yawned like the greyhounds;
Chicot, sitting on one of the doors, his legs hanging out,
that he might easily descend if he wished, made anagrams,
which were then fashionable, on the courtiers' names,
breaking up their character into many disagreeable
traits. Presently he broke into impromptu song, cleverly
satirising first the King, and then the Duc d'Anjou, to the
undisguised merriment of the courtiers. Henri laughed
louder than any one, which brought upon him another
burst of satire from the witty jester, who, amidst the
laughter of the company, proceeded to show how the name
Henri de Valois was identical with Vilain Herodes.

A few minutes later they saw him rush from the litter,

and, thrusting aside the guards, kneel down at the corner of a respectable looking house with a carved wooden balcony.

'Good and just God,' he exclaimed, 'here is the house where Chicot suffered for one of Thy creatures; Chicot never asked Thee to send misfortune to M. de Mayenne, author of his martyrdom, nor to Maître Nicolas David, the instrument of his torture. No, Chicot has waited, and for six long years the interest of the little account opened with them has accumulated; now, at ten per cent. in seven years, the interest doubles the capital. Cause Chicot's patience to last another year, so that the fifty blows which drew a pint of blood from Chicot become a hundred and the one pint two; so that M. de Mayenne, fat as he is, and Nicolas David, for all his length, will not be able to pay their debts, but become bankrupts, expiring at the eightieth or eighty-fifth blow. In the name of the Father, the Son, and the Holy Ghost, so be it.'

'Amen!' added the King.

To the amazement of the spectators, Chicot kissed the ground before returning to the litter.

'Ah! Chicot, what means this long, peculiar litany? Why all those blows on the chest?'

'Your Majesty, in this house lived a young and charming girl whom Chicot loved; one night a certain jealous prince had Chicot seized and beaten so roughly that he jumped from the window into the street. Now, as it was a miracle that Chicot was not killed, each time he passes the house he kneels to thank God for his escape.'

It was three o'clock when they reached Juvisy, and saw the large hostelry of Cour-de-France. Chicot, leaning out of the litter, saw in the distance some men wrapped in cloaks standing at the door. In the middle was a short, fat man, whose wide brimmed hat entirely covered his face. As the procession approached, the men suddenly retired inside. But the little fat man had been noticed by Chicot, who leaped down from the litter, and, asking for his horse, hid in a corner of a wall till the *corlège* had disappeared in the direction of Essonnes, where the King intended to sleep. Then, leaving his hiding place, Chicot rode behind the castle, thus reaching the hotel, as if coming from Fontainebleau. The men were still there, and Chicot, not wishing to be noticed, ordered a bottle of wine to be

served in the room opposite, and sitting so that nobody
could go out without being seen, he gazed in at the
company.

'I must have scented this man's return when I prayed
at the house in Rue des Noyers. But why does he come
back thus secretly into the capital of our friend Herod, or
why hide when he passes? Ah ! it looks as if the repayment
will come sooner than I thought.'

Finding that he could hear as well as see, Chicot began
to listen with great attention.

'Gentlemen,' he heard the stout man saying, 'it is time
to start. The last lackey of the retinue has long since
passed, and the road is now safe.'

'Perfectly safe, monseigneur,' rejoined a voice that
made Chicot jump. Its owner was as long as monseigneur
was short, as pale as he was ruddy, as obsequious as he
was haughty.

'Ah ! Maître Nicolas,' said Chicot, laughing noiselessly,
' it will be unlucky indeed if we separate without a few
words.'

Emptying his glass, Chicot paid his host just as the
seven travellers, taking their horses, rode off towards Paris.

'Good,' said Chicot, 'he goes to Paris; then I return
too,' and Chicot rode off, always keeping within the sound
of the horses' hoofs. Striking across country, the travellers crossed the Seine at the Pont de Charenton, and entering Paris by Saint-Antoine, disappeared into the Hôtel
de Guise.

'Very good,' observed Chicot, hiding at the corner of
the Rue Quatre-Fils, 'so de Guise as well as de Mayenne
is concerned. This becomes interesting. Let us wait.'

He waited fully an hour, in spite of cold and hunger.
Then the door opened to let out, not seven cloaked
horsemen, but seven monks of Sainte-Geneviève, in
hoods, and carrying great rosaries.

'What an unexpected event. Has the Hôtel de Guise
such an odour of sanctity that wolves are changed into
lambs merely by touching the threshold ? It is more
and more interesting.'

Chicot followed the monks, never doubting but that
the frocks covered the same bodies as the cloaks. They
stopped at the abbey of Sainte-Geneviève, where inside
the porch stood another monk, attentively examining
the hands of the newcomers.

'Zounds ! one must have clean hands to be admitted to the abbey to-night. Decidedly something unusual is happening,' and Chicot, puzzling as to what he could do, noticed monks of Sainte-Geneviève by ones or twos streaming from all directions towards the abbey.

'Ah ! so there is a general meeting of Chapter at the abbey, to which all the order is summoned ? I confess I have a great desire to be present. I might enter with them, but for two essentials—the respectable robe and the token. Ah ! Brother Gorenflot, if I had you at hand, my worthy friend.'

This exclamation was forced from him at the remembrance of one of the most worthy monks of the Order of Sainte-Geneviève.

'Come,' soliloquised Chicot, 'there is something strange to-night. It is half-past seven; the collection will be over. I ought to find Brother Gorenflot at the Corne d'Abondance; it is his supper-time,' and, leaving the monks circulating round the abbey, Chicot galloped off to the Grande Rue Saint-Jacques, where, near the cloister of Saint Benoît, rose the inn of the Corne d'Abondance, the haunt of monks and scholars. Chicot was known as a visitor who occasionally left a gold crown and a piece of his mind in the establishment of Maître Claude Bonhomet.

CHAPTER XVIII

INTRODUCES BROTHER GORENFLOT

It was a cold evening, and the frosty weather made the red lights of the hostelry look doubly attractive. Entering the hall, and looking round without finding the person he sought, Chicot passed into the kitchen. Maître Bonhomet, busy reading a pious book while superintending cookery operations, raised his head.

'Ah ! it is you, my dear sir. I wish you good-evening and a good appetite.'

'Thanks for the double wish, though part will benefit you as much as me. But that will depend.'

' How is that ?'

'You know I cannot bear to sup alone.'

'If need be, monsieur, I will bear you company.'

'Thanks, but I am looking for Gorenflot. Has he began supper?'

'Not yet, though in five minutes he will have finished.'

Chicot shook his head to express his incredulity.

'Decidedly something has gone wrong with this sub-lunary universe when five minutes suffices for Brother Gorenflot's supper! I am fated to see wonderful things to-day,' said he, advancing towards a sort of private room where, in the light of a smoky candle, sat the worthy monk toying with a little spinach, with which he was mixing some Surènes cheese.

Brother Gorenflot was about thirty-eight years old, and five feet high. This small stature was redeemed by wonderful harmony of proportion, for he made up in breadth what he lost in height, measuring nearly three feet from shoulder to shoulder. From the centre of these Herculean shoulders rose a thick neck, with powerful muscles, that stood out like whipcord.

'Eh! friend, what are you doing there?' cried the Gascon.

'You see, brother, I sup,' answered Gorenflot, in a voice as powerful as his abbey bell.

'We are in the first Wednesday of Lent; let us effect our salvation,' and he raised his eyes devoutly to heaven.

'Our salvation!' repeated Chicot, stupefied, 'what have vegetables and water to do with that?'

'We are forbidden to eat meat on Wednesdays and Fridays,' said Gorenflot.

'When did you breakfast?'

'I have not breakfasted, brother; I composed a discourse.'

'Bah! why did you do that?'

'To pronounce it to-night at the abbey.'

'This is queer,' thought Chicot.

'It is time I was there; the audience will become impatient.'

Remembering that M. de Mayenne would be one of this audience, Chicot wondered why Gorenflot, distinguished for other things than eloquence, had been chosen by Joseph Toulon, the abbot, to preach before the Prince de Lorraine and such a large gathering.

'When do you preach?' he asked.

'From nine o'clock till half-past.'

'It is a quarter to nine. You can easily spare five
minutes. It is more than a week since we dined together.
It seems to me we should be glad to meet again.'

'I am exceedingly glad,' replied Gorenflot, looking
most miserable; 'nevertheless, I must leave you.'

'Finish your vegetables, at least,' said Chicot, pushing
him down in his chair.

Looking at the spinach, Gorenflot sighed, and after a
glance at the water, he turned his head away. Chicot saw
that the moment for attack had come.

'Do you remember when we ate a teal with crab sauce,
and drank that fine Burgundy wine—what is it called ?'

'It is a wine of my own country, La Romanée.'

'The other night our host claimed to have fifty bottles
in his cellar in comparison with which that other is worth-
less stuff.'

'It is quite true,' observed Gorenflot.

'And you drink this awful stuff when you can drink
such wine. Pooh !' and Chicot emptied the goblet on
the floor.

'When one has to pronounce a discourse, water is
preferable.'

'Bah ! wine is better, and I, who have also an address
to deliver, am going to order a bottle of that wine from
La Romanée; what do you advise me to take with it ?'

'Not these vegetables; nothing could be worse.'

'Master Claude, bring me two bottles of La Romanée
wine.'

'Two bottles,' said Gorenflot. 'Why two, when I do
not drink ?'

'If you did, I should order four bottles, six, all the cellar-
ful. But I am an indifferent drinker myself, so two
bottles suffice.' Going towards the larder, Chicot brought
out a fine capon.

'What are you doing there, brother ?' asked Gorenflot,
following with involuntary interest the Gascon's
movements.

'I am making sure of this carp. During Lent there is
a great run on fish.'

'Since when has a carp a beak ?' asked the monk.

'A beak ! a nose is all I see.'

'Wings?'

'Fins.'

'Feathers ?'

'Scales, my dear Gorenflot, you are drunk.'

'Drunk! It is likely when I have eaten nothing but spinach and drunk water.'

'Evidently the spinach has not agreed with you, and the water has gone to your head.'

Maître Claude, returning, uncorked a bottle of wine and half filled Chicot's glass. The latter drank it, remarking, 'Ah! I am not an experienced taster, and cannot say if it is worse or better than the Porte Montmartre wine. It may be the same even.'

Gorenflot's eyes sparkled at the ruddy drops in Chicot's glass.

'Help me, said Chicot, emptying a thimbleful of wine into the monk's glass. The latter, swallowing it slowly, observed :—

'It is the same growth, but——'

'What ?'

'There was too little to judge whether it was better or worse.'

'But for your discourse, I would ask you to sample it again.'

'It would be to please you.'

Chicot filled the glass half full. Gorenflot swallowed it carefully.

'It is better, I maintain.'

'Bah! you agree with our host.'

'A good judge should recognise the growth at the first sip, the quality at the second, the year at the third.'

'I should like to know the year of this wine,' said Chicot.

'That is quite simple, pour me out a few drops, and I will tell you.'

Chicot filled the glass three-quarters full, and the monk slowly swallowed it.

'1561,' said he, putting down the glass.

'It is exactly that,' cried Claude Bonhomet.

'Brother Gorenflot,' observed Chicot, taking off his hat, 'people have been canonised at Rome who deserved it less than you.'

'It is merely practice,' said Gorenflot modestly.

'And natural aptitude, habit alone could not do it. What are you doing ?'

'I am going to my meeting.'

'Without tasting my carp ?'

'Ah! true; obviously you know less about food than about wine. Maître Bonhomet, what animal is this?'

'*Parbleu!* it is a capon,' exclaimed the innkeeper amazed at the question.

'Well!' said Chicot, 'I must be wrong, but as I should like to taste this capon without sinning my soul, pray, brother, christen it a carp.'

'Agreed!' said Gorenflot, whose naturally sociable nature was asserting itself under the influence of the wine, 'only there is no water.'

'It is the intention alone that matters; christen it with wine, brother.'

Chicot filled the monk's glass to the brim.

'In the name of Bacchus, Momus, and Comus, trinity of the great Saint Pantagruel, I christen thee carp,' said Gorenflot, sprinkling a few drops upon the bird.

'Maître Claude,' ordered Chicot, 'roast this carp at once; cover it with fresh butter and finely chopped shalots, and when it begins to brown, toast some bread in the dripping, and serve hot. Now, bring some sardines and tunny fish. As we are in Lent, my dinner must be in keeping. And you may bring two more bottles of that excellent wine of 1561.'

The smell of the cookery insensibly rose to the monk's brain. His mouth watered, his eyes glistened; but he restrained his desires, and even attempted to rise.

'Are you leaving me?' asked Chicot.

'I must, brother.'

'It is very rash to pronounce a discourse fasting; you will not have enough lung power, brother. Gallien said: "Pulmo hominis facile deficit" (Man's lungs are weak and easily become exhausted.)'

'Alas! I have often experienced that; if I had stronger lungs I should be a splendid orator; fortunately my zeal makes up for my weakness.'

'Zeal is not sufficient; if I were you, I would taste these sardines and try a little wine.'

'Only one sardine and one glass,' answered Gorenflot.

'Well?' asked Chicot, 'how do you feel now?'

'Indeed I feel a little stronger.'

'*Ventre de biche!* it is not enough to feel better, one must be perfectly well to deliver a discourse; you should try the two fins of this carp; unless you eat more, the odour of the wine will cling to you.'

'Ah! you are right, I did not think of that.'

Just then the capon was brought from the spit, and Chicot, cutting off a leg, made the monk eat the whole of it, and then a second leg, whilst he delicately picked a wing.

'Some of this famous wine,' said he, uncorking the third bottle.

Once started and his prodigious appetite stimulated, Gorenflot could no longer contain himself; having devoured the wing and demolished the carcass, he called to Bonhomet,—

'Maître Claude, I am hungry, did you not offer me an omelette a while ago?'

'Exactly,' said Chicot, 'and it is ready, is it not, Bonhomet?'

'Well, bring it, bring it,' cried the monk.

'In five minutes,' answered Bonhomet, hastening out at a sign from Chicot.

'Ah! that is better,' exclaimed Gorenflot, letting his fist fall heavily on the table; 'were the omelette here, I would eat it at a bite just as I swallowed this wine at a gulp.' With his eyes sparkling greedily, the monk consumed a quarter of the third bottle.

'So you were ill, were you?' asked Chicot.

'I was stupid, friend; this wretched discourse weighed upon me, so that for three days I have thought of nothing else.'

'It ought to be a good one; tell me some of it while we wait for the omelette.'

'No, no, a sermon at table! when do you have that, Master Jester, at your King's court?'

'Very fine speeches are delivered at the court of King Henri, whom Heaven preserve,' said Chicot, raising his hat.

'Upon what subjects?'

'Upon virtue.'

'Ah! yes, and Henri is a most virtuous specimen.'

'I can't certify as to his virtue, but I have never seen anything to blush at.'

'I quite believe that; it is long since you blushed, you rake.'

'Oh! rake! I, who am abstinence itself, the embodiment of temperance! I, who practise all kinds of processions and fastings!'

'Yes, such as your Sardanapalus, your Nebuchadnezzar, your Herod favours ! Interested processions, calculated fastings. Luckily people are beginning to see through your King Henri, devil take him !'

Gorenflot, instead of repeating the discourse, began bawling out a song filled with allusions to the King's greediness. Presently Maître Bonhomet entered with the famous omelette and two fresh bottles of wine.

'Bring it here,' cried the monk, all his teeth showing in a broad grin.

'But, friend, I understood you had to deliver a discourse.'

'It is here,' answered the monk, touching his brow, now almost as flushed as his cheeks.

'At half-past nine ?'

'I was lying, it was at ten o'clock.'

'The abbey shuts at nine.'

'Let it shut,' said Gorenflot, gazing through his glass at the candle; 'I have the key.'

'The key of the abbey ?' repeated Chicot, in amazement.

'There, in my pocket.'

'Not possible; I know something of the rules of a monastery, having done penance in three of them; the key of the abbey is not entrusted to a simple monk.'

'There it is, then, said Gorenflot, throwing himself back in his chair, and gleefully showing Chicot a coin.

'Hallo ! money, I understand. You bribe the doorkeeper to let you in, you miserable sinner !'

Gorenflot grinned from ear to ear in a fatuous way, and prepared to put the coin back in his pocket.

'Wait a minute, what a queer coin !'

'With the heretic's effigy,' said Gorenflot, 'pierced through the heart.'

'Indeed, it is a coin struck by the King of Béarn, and here is the hole as you describe.'

'Death to the heretic ! Whoever kills him is blessed in advance, and gets my share of paradise.'

'Ah !' Chicot reflected, 'things are becoming clear, but the rascal is not drunk enough yet,' and he replenished the monk's glass.

'Long live the mass !' cried Gorenflot, gulping down the wine.

'So,' said Chicot, recalling how the doorkeeper had examined all the monks' hands, 'so you show this coin to the porter, and——'

'And I go in,' said Gorenflot.

'Without any trouble ?'

'As this glass of wine goes down my throat,' said the monk, swallowing a fresh dose.

'If the comparison holds good, you will simply dash in.'

'That is to say, that for Brother Gorenflot the doors are thrown wide,' stammered the monk.

'And you deliver your discourse ?'

'And I deliver my discourse. This is what happens : I arrive, you hear, Chicot——'

'I should think so; I am all ears.'

'I arrive, then. The gathering is large but select; there are barons; there are counts; there are dukes.'

'And even princes.'

'Even princes, no less. I enter humbly among the faithful of the Union.'

'What Union is that ?'

'I enter amongst the faithful of the Union; Brother Gorenflot is called for, and I advance,' continued Gorenflot, rising and striving to suit the action to the word. No sooner had he walked a step than, stumbling against the corner of the table, he rolled on the floor.

'Bravo !' cried the Gascon, lifting him to a chair, 'you advance, you bow to the congregation and say——?'

'No, I say nothing; the friends say, "Brother Gorenflot ! Brother Gorenflot's speech !" A fine name that for a Leaguer,' and the monk repeated his name, in caressing tones.

'A good name for a Leaguer; what truths are we to hear from this wine-bibber ?'

'Then I begin.' The monk, getting up, shut his dazed eyes, and leant drunkenly against the wall. Chicot supported him. 'I begin, "My brothers, it is a good day for the faith; it is a splendid day for the faith; it is a glorious day for the faith ?" '

Seeing there was no more to be extracted from the monk, Chicot released his hold, and Brother Gorenflot, losing his balance, slipped along the wall, striking the table with his feet, and knocking down some empty bottles.

'Amen !' said Chicot. The same moment, a snoring, loud as thunder, made the windows rattle.

'Good, the capon's legs are taking effect. Our friend is likely to sleep for a dozen hours, and I can undress him without trouble or risk.'

Chicot, feeling that time was precious, untied the monk's gown, drawing his arms out, and turning him over like a bag of nuts; then, wrapping him in the tablecloth, and setting a napkin on his head, he hid the monk's robe under his cloak, and passed into the kitchen.

'Maître Bonhomet,' he said, giving the innkeeper a rose noble, 'this is for our supper and for my horse's, which I entrust to you, and, above all, let nobody wake worthy Brother Gorenflot, who is sleeping like one of the elect.'

'Very well, Monsieur Chicot, be quite easy about that,' replied the innkeeper, well pleased with his payment.

Thus assured, Chicot went out, and, light as a deer and cunning as a fox, reached the corner of the Rue Saint-Étienne, where he placed the coin with the effigy carefully in his right palm, and slipped on the monk's gown. At a quarter to ten, he presented himself, his heart beating a little faster than usual, at the door of the Abbey of Sainte-Geneviève.

CHAPTER XIX

CHICOT ENTERS THE ABBEY OF SAINTE-GENEVIÈVE

WHEN Chicot slipped on the monk's cloak he had taken the important precaution to double the breadth of his shoulder by skilfully arranging his cloak and other parts of his discarded dress; his beard resembled Gorenflot's in colour, and he had so often amused himself by imitating his friend's voice that he now did it to the life. Everybody knows that the beard and the voice are all that come forth from the depths of a monk's hood. The door was about to close when Chicot arrived; the porter awaited only a few late-comers. Showing his pierced coin, the Gascon was immediately admitted. Following two monks, he entered the convent chapel, where he had often come with the King, who had ever given special support to the Abbey of Saint-Geneviève.

The chapel was Roman in style, dating from the eleventh century, and, like all chapels of that period, possessed a crypt beneath the centre. The centre was eight or ten feet higher than the nave, so that the choir was reached by two side stairs, between which an iron door led to the crypt. Passing through the crypt one descended as many steps as were in the choir stairs. In the choir on either side of the altar, above which was a picture of Sainte-Catherine attributed to Rosso, were statues of Clovis and Clotilde. Three lamps alone lit up the chapel, one hung in the middle of the choir, the other two at equal distances in the nave. This insufficient light rendered the church more solemn; the proportions were doubled, since the imagination extended the parts lying in shadow into infinite space.

Chicot needed first to grow accustomed to the darkness; to exercise his eyes he counted the monks to the number of one hundred and twenty in the nave, and in the choir twelve, sitting in a row before the altar like sentinels defending the tabernacle. It relieved him to notice that he was not the last to join the brothers of the Union, for presently three monks in wide gray robes entered, and placed themselves in front of the row of sentinels.

A minor monk, evidently a choir boy whom Chicot had not yet noticed, made a tour of the chapel to see if all were present, and then spoke to one of the three last comers, who announced in a loud voice : 'We are one hundred and thirty-six, our number is complete.' Immediately the hundred and twenty monks kneeling in the nave rose up to take chairs or stalls. A loud noise of bolts and hinges proclaimed the shutting of the ponderous doors, a noise which fluttered Chicot, brave though he was. To compose himself he sat down in the shadow of the pulpit, where he could easily see the three monks who were apparently the chief personages in this gathering. Footstools had been brought to them, and they sat like three judges. Behind them the twelve monks were standing. When the noise had subsided, a little bell rang three times. This was the signal for silence, and all sounds were quickly hushed.

'Brother Monsoreau,' said the monk who had already spoken, 'What news do you bring from the Province of Anjou to the Union ?'

Two things caused Chicot to listen attentively. The first was this voice, which seemed fitter to issue from the vizor of a helmet on a battle-field than from a monk's hood in a church. The second was the name of Monsoreau, only known for a few days at court, where, we have seen, it produced a mild sensation. A tall monk, whose robe fell stiffly round him, crossed over and mounted the pulpit steps with a firm, bold step. Chicot endeavoured to distinguish his face, but that was impossible.

'Good,' he reflected, 'if I cannot see their faces at least they will not see mine.'

'My brothers,' began a voice which Chicot recognised as the First Huntsman's, 'the news from the Province of Anjou is not satisfactory; not that our sympathy is wanting, but because we are short of representatives. Baron de Méridor was entrusted with our interests, but, in despair, at the recent death of his daughter, he has, in his sorrow, neglected the affairs of the League, and, until he has recovered from the shock, we cannot rely upon him. I myself bring the names of three fresh adherents to the association, and, according to rule, have placed them in the convent chest. The Council will judge if these candidates, for whose loyalty I answer as for my own, shall be admitted members of the Holy Union.'

A murmur of approval ran through the ranks, and had not subsided when Brother Monsoreau reached his seat.

'Brother la Hurière!' continued the monk, calling apparently on whom he fancied, 'tell us what you have accomplished in Paris.'

A man with hood lowered now appeared in the pulpit vacated by M. de Monsoreau.

'My brothers,' he began, 'you all know I am devoted to the Catholic faith, and that I proved this devotion on the great day of her triumph. At that time, I was a faithful follower of our glorious Henri de Guise, and from M. de Besme in person, whom God abundantly bless, I received orders which I followed so conscientiously that I desired to kill even my own guests. Now, this devotion to the holy cause was the reason of my being appointed a district officer, with, I venture to say, beneficial effects to our religion. I have thus been able to note all the heretics in the district of Saint-Germain-l'Auxerrois —where I still keep the hostelry of the Belle-Etoile, Rue de l'Arbre-Sec, at your service, brothers—and, having noted them, to name them to our friends. Of a truth, I do not thirst as formerly for the blood of the Huguenots, but I cannot hide from myself the true end of the Holy Union we are about to found.'

'Listen,' soliloquised Chicot, 'this La Huriére was, as

I well remember, a zealous slayer of heretics, and should have won the confidence of the League, if its members bestow it where it is deserved.'

'Speak! speak!' called several voices.

La Hurière, finding this a rare occasion for a display of the oratory he believed he possessed, collected himself, coughed, and resumed,—

'Unless I am mistaken, my brothers, the extinction of private heretics is not our sole aim; good Frenchmen require assurance that they will never be ruled over by a heretic. Now, what is the present state of affairs? François II., who promised to become zealous for the faith, died childless; Charles IX., who was zealous, died childless; King Henri III., whose belief I may not question, whose actions I may not criticise, will probably die childless; there remains the Duc d'Anjou, who likewise has no children, and whose devotion to the Holy League is but lukewarm.'

At this point several voices, that of the First Huntsman's among them, interrupted the orator.

'Why do you accuse the Prince of being lukewarm?' he asked.

'Because he has not yet joined the League, although he has given his promise.'

'Who told you he is not an adherent? There are new members being enrolled. It seems to me you should wait until the names are known.'

'True, I will wait; but after the Duc d'Anjou, who is but mortal and childless, and notice that the family is short-lived, to whom will the crown revert? To the most fanatical Huguenot that can be imagined, to a renegade, a heretic, a Nebuchadnezzar.'

Frenzied cheers drowned La Hurière's voice.

'To Henri de Béarn, in short, against whom this association was specially formed; the man the world hears of at Pau or Tarbes, engaged in gallantry, but whom we meet in Paris.'

'Paris! impossible!' cried several voices.

'He was here the night Madame de Sauves was murdered, and may be here still.'

'Down with the Béarnais!'

'Yes, death to him! and should he put up at the Belle Etoile, I will make short work of him; but a fox is not taken twice in the same hole; he will stay with one of his friends.

Now we wish the number of his friends to be known
and to be diminished. Our Union is holy, our League
is loyal, hallowed and blessed and encouraged by our
holy father, Pope Gregory III. I ask, then, that there
shall be no longer any mystery. Let lists be given to
the district superintendents, who will present them to
the citizens to sign. Those who sign are our friends,
those who refuse our enemies; and if a second Saint-
Bartholomew presents itself, which seems to the true
faithful most urgent—well! we shall do as we did once
before, spare God the trouble of dividing the good from
the evil.'

Thundering applause greeted this peroration, and as the
tumult slowly died away, the grave voice of the monk
who had already spoken, was heard saying,—

'The Holy Union thanks Brother la Hurière for his zeal,
and will consider his proposal; it will be discussed in a
higher assembly.'

The applause redoubled. La Hurière, after bowing to
express his thanks, left the pulpit and resumed his place
overcome by his triumph.

'Ah!' said Chicot to himself, 'I am beginning to see
daylight. They have less confidence in Henri's allegiance
to the faith than in his brother's and Messieurs de
Guise. It is probable, seeing Mayenne is concerned in
all this, Messieurs de Guise wish to be the heads of
a separate party in the State ; so the great Henri, who
is a general, will lead the armies ; the distinguished Cardinal
will rule the Church; one fine day the King will find himself
stripped of everything but his beads, with which he will
be asked to retire to a monastery. Powerfully reasoned !
Ah, well ! but—there is the Duc d'Anjou. The deuce !
what is to become of him ?'

'Brother Gorenflot !' called the presiding monk, but
Chicot, occupied with his reflections, or not accustomed
to his new name, made no answer.

'Brother Gorenflot !' repeated the monk, in a clear,
sharp voice which made Chicot start.

'Oh !' said he, 'it is like a woman's voice. Are sexes
as well as ranks confused in this honourable gathering ?'

'Brother Gorenflot, are you not here ?'

'That is myself,' observed Chicot, *sotto voce*. Aloud
he said,—

'Yes, here I am. The speech of Brother la Hurière

had plunged me into deep meditation, and I did not hear my name.'

Chicot did not hesitate an instant. Rising, he mounted the pulpit steps, making himself appear as broad as possible, and drawing his hood down.

'My brothers,' he began, imitating the monk's voice, 'this day which brings us together is a glorious one. Let us speak freely since we are in the Lord's house. What is the kingdom of France ? A body. Saint Augustine has said so : *omnis civitas corpus est.* What is the condition for safety in a body ? Good health. How is this maintained ? By judicious letting of blood when there is too much energy. Now the enemies of the Catholic religion are too strong, since we are afraid of them; we must then bleed this great body, called Society. That is what the faithful assert every day when I collect their offerings of eggs, ham, and money.' This first part of Chicot's speech produced a deep impression on the audience. When the applause had subsided, he resumed,—

'People will perhaps say that the Church hates bloodshed : *Ecclesia abhorret a sanguine.* But notice, my dear brothers, the theologian does not specify what blood, and I would wager an ox to an egg that it is not heretics' blood he refers to. Then, another argument, brothers : I said the Church, but we do not belong solely to the Church. Brother Monsoreau, who has spoken so eloquently, has, I feel sure, his Grand Huntsman's knife hid in his belt ; Brother la Hurière handles the spit with ease; I myself, Jacques-Népomucène Gorenflot, have borne a musket in Champagne, and burned Huguenots in their meeting-houses.

This part of the speech was equally applauded.

Chicot, bowing modestly, resumed,—'We have still to speak of our appointed leaders, and it seems to me, a humble monk of Sainte-Geneviève, that there is something to say. Verily it is a fine, above all a prudent, thing to come at night, in a gown, to hear Brother Gorenflot preach, but the duty of the great leaders should not stop there. Such extreme prudence may make these accursed Huguenots laugh, for they are desperate enough when it comes to an attack. I ask, therefore, that our behaviour be more in keeping with our real selves, courageous as we are, or rather as we wish to appear. What is it we wish ?

The extinction of heresy. Well! but that can be proclaimed abroad, it seems to me. Why should we not march through the streets of Paris like a holy procession, to show off our noble bearing and our fine halberds; but not like night robbers looking round at each step in fear of meeting the night watch! Who will set the example, you ask? Well! I will; I, Jacques-Népomucène Gorenflot, unworthy brother of the order, humble alms-collector of this convent, will march, with cuirass on back, sallet on head, and musket on shoulder, if necessary, at the head of the good Catholics who are willing to follow. That I will do were it only to shame the leaders, who hide themselves, as though defending the Church were a question of maintaining some ribald quarrel.'

Chicot's peroration corresponded with the feelings of many members of the League, who saw no necessity of attaining their ends by other means than those put into practice, six years before, on Saint Bartholomew's Eve, and who were annoyed at their leaders' slowness. Consequently, enthusiasm was kindled in every heart, and, with the exception of the three monks, who kept silence, the assembly cried: 'Long live the mass! Hurrah for Brother Gorenflot! the procession! the procession!'

The enthusiasm was the more keenly aroused because this was the first occasion on which the zeal of the worthy brother had shown itself. Until now, his most intimate friends had classed him as zealous, no doubt, but one whom the instinct of self-preservation prevented from ever being carried away. From this obscurity Brother Gorenflot had stepped, fully equipped, into the open arena; it was a great surprise, and some in their admiration elevated Brother Gorenflot, who had preached the first procession, to the same plane as Peter the Hermit, who had preached the first crusade. Unfortunately, or fortunately, for him, their leaders had no intention of letting him carry out this plan. One of the three silent monks whispered to the young one, and the latter's fluty voice re-echoed through the building three times,—

'Brothers, it is time to retire, the meeting is over.'

The monks chattering, and resolving to demand the proposed procession at the next assembly, slowly streamed out. Many had gone near the pulpit to congratulate the preacher on his success; but Chicot, reflecting that his voice, heard near at hand, might betray him, that his height—he was six or eight inches taller than Gorenflot —might cause some astonishment, had thrown himself on his knees as if in prayer. Respecting this religious ecstasy, they had hurried out quickly, to the great joy of Chicot, who watched them out of the holes he had contrived in his hood.

Yet he had nearly failed to achieve his purpose. The sight of the Duc de Mayenne had made him leave the King without asking leave. The sight of Nicolas David had caused him to return to Paris. Chicot had sworn a double vow of revenge; but he was too insignificant to attack a Prince of Lorraine openly, and would have to await patiently a favourable opportunity of doing so. The case was different with Nicolas David, a plain Norman lawyer—a cunning fellow, certainly, who had been a soldier before he was a lawyer and a fencing-master at the same time. Though not a fencing master, Chicot claimed to use the rapier well enough; his great anxiety, therefore, was to meet his enemy, and after that he relied upon his just cause and his sword. Chicot, then, watched the monks retiring, and looked for the long, lanky figure of Maître Nicolas. Presently he noticed that the monks were being examined as they had been on entering, and were producing some token to obtain their *exeant*. At first Chicot thought he was mistaken, but his momentary doubt was changed into a certainty which caused an icy perspiration. Brother Gorenflot had certainly shown him the way to go *in*, but he had forgotten to explain how he might get *out*.

CHAPTER XX

WHAT CHICOT SAW AND HEARD IN THE ABBEY

JOINING the last of the monks, and glancing over their shoulders, Chicot saw that the token was a farthing, cut in the shape of a star. Our Gascon had many such coins in his pocket, but, unfortunately, none of this particular shape. Chicot quickly surveyed the situation. If he could not produce his coin at the door, he would be recognised as a false brother. Rapidly surveying the situation, he concluded that his best policy was to hide;

so gaining the shadow of a pillar, he stood back, near the edge of a confessional box. Presently he heard the chorister crying,—

'Is there any one else ? We are going to shut the doors.' Nobody answered. Chicot could see that but for the three monks in the stalls in the middle of the choir, the chapel was empty. 'As long as they do not shut the windows, I don't care,' Chicot thought.

'Let us look round the church,' the chorister said, addressing the porter.

'Bother that youngster!' said Chicot.

The porter lit a taper, and the two began a tour of inspection. Not a minute could be lost, Chicot opened the door of the confessional, and slipping into the oblong box, shut the door softly. Through the carved wooden grating he perceived the light of the taper reflected on his robe.

'The deuce ! they cannot stay in the church for ever; when they go, I will pile up chairs on benches and escape by the window. Ah, yes! the window, but, once outside, I shall find myself in the courtyard, which is not the street. I believe it will be better to stay here all night. Gorenflot's robe is warm; it would be spending the night in a less heathenish manner than I might have done, and may help to save my soul.'

'Extinguish the lamps,' the chorister commanded, and the porter immediately put out the two lamps in the nave, plunging it in total darkness. Then the lamp in the choir was extinguished, leaving the church faintly lighted by wan moonbeams. The clock struck twelve.

'Midnight in a church,' said Chicot! 'Zounds! my son Henriquet would be frightened to death. Happily, I am bolder. Now, Chicot, my son, good-night and sound sleep to you !' Chicot settled himself as comfortably as possible, drawing the bolt on the inside of the confessional. He had been half dozing for some ten minutes when a loud blow struck on a copper bell resounded through the church.

'Hallo ! what does this mean ?' said Chicot, opening his eyes and straining his ears. At the same time the lamp in the choir was relit, and shone on the three monks, who still sat motionless. Though Chicot was brave, he belonged to his own age, a period of wild traditions and fearful legends. Making the sign of the cross, he whispered, '*Vade retro Satanas!*' The lights, however, did not go out, and the monks paid no heed to his *vade retro*, so Chicot began to fancy the lights were natural ones after all, and the monks real flesh and blood personages.

Just then a stone in the choir was slowly raised, and placed on its narrow end. A gray hood appeared in the opening, then the figure of a monk stepped out, and set the stone back softly in position. At this sight Chicot's fears returned; his hair stood on end, and for an instant he imagined all the priors, abbots, deans of Sainte-Geneviève were rising from their tombs in the crypt, and forcing the stones up with their bony skulls. But this doubt was soon dispelled.

'Brother Monsoreau,' demanded one of the three monks to the new-comer, 'has the person whom we are expecting arrived?'

'Yes, messeigneurs, and he is waiting.'

'Open the door, and let him come to us.'

'The comedy has two acts, then, and I have seen only one of them,' thought Chicot, shivering as he joked. Meanwhile Brother Monsoreau, descending one of the stairs leading from the nave to the choir, opened the bronze gate into the crypt. Just then the monk in the centre lowered his hood, displaying a great scar, the sign by which Parisians recognised the Hero of the Catholics.

'Henri de Guise in person, whom His Most Imbecile Majesty believes busy at the siege of La Charité! Now I understand, the one on his right hand is the Cardinal Lorraine, and the other is Monseigneur de Mayenne; but where is Maître Nicolas David?'

Chicot's suppositions were confirmed as the two monks lowered their hoods, displaying the intelligent head, broad brow, and keen eye of the famous Cardinal, and the much more common features of the Duc de Mayenne.

'I recognise you,' said Chicot, 'and am all eyes and ears to see and to learn what is going forward.'

'Did you expect him to come?' Le Balafré, asked his brother.

'I felt so certain that I brought a substitute for the holy ampulla.'

Chicot perceived a silver gilt box, with relief carvings, shining in the lamp-light. Meanwhile, twenty monks, issuing from the crypt, sat down in the nave. One placed

himself next to the Guises in the choir stalls. The Duc
de Guise looked all round the assembly, and began,—

'Friends, time is precious, so I go straight to the business
in hand. You heard in the first assembly one of our
leaders accused of coldness and even of evil intentions.
The time has come to render to this Prince the respect
and justice due to him. You will hear him, and will
judge if the charges of coldness and indifference brought
against your leaders by Brother Gorenflot, whom we have
not deemed fit to share our secret, were merited.'

At these words Chicot could not help laughing noiselessly.

'My brothers, the Prince whose support was promised,
for whose consent we hardly dared hope, is with us.' All
eyes turned curiously to the monk on the right hand
of the three Princes of Lorraine. 'Monseigneur,'
said the Duc de Guise, addressing this person, 'the will
of God seems clear, for, since you have joined us, we cannot be wrong in what we are doing. Lower your hood,
your Highness, and let the faithful see that you have kept
your promise.' Chicot, expecting some Prince of Lorraine to appear, was astonished to see the Duc d'Anjou's
face, pale as a statue.

'Long live the Duc d'Anjou!' cried all the spectators.
François became paler than before.

'My brothers,' exclaimed the Comte de Monsoreau,'
'His Highness asks if he may address you.'

'Yes, let him speak; we listen.'

The Duc d'Anjou began in a trembling voice, which
was hardly audible : 'Messieurs, I believe that God has
His eyes upon us, and, though seemingly careless, is only
awaiting an occasion of remedying the disorders caused
by the foolish ambitions of human beings.' This beginning was as hazy as the Duc's own character; all waited
for some light to shine before giving their criticism or
applause. The Duc resumed, more re-assured : 'I, too,
have looked upon the earth, at France especially, and what
have I seen there ? Christ's holy religion shaken on its
venerable base, the true servants of God scattered and
exiled. I have sounded the depths of the abyss opened
twenty years ago by heretics, who destroyed all belief,
while pretending to reach God more surely, and my soul,
like the prophet's, has been overwhelmed by grief.
In the midst of my affliction, I heard that certain pious and

noble men, venerating the ways of our ancestors, were endeavouring to strengthen the falling religion. Looking around me, I seemed to be present at the Last Judgment. On one side were the reprobates, from whom I recoiled in horror; on the other the elect, into whose arms I have thrown myself.'

Applause and bravos rang through the chapel.

'You came among us of your own free-will?' asked the Cardinal, approaching the Duc.

'Yes, monsieur.'

'Who instructed you in the holy mystery?'

'My friend the Comte de Monsoreau.'

'Now,' said the Duc de Guise, 'explain what you intend doing for the Holy League?'

'I intend to serve the Catholic religion, Apostolic and Roman, in all her needs.'

'What stupid people to make all this secrecy about such a matter! Why not propose it frankly to King Henri III.? Processions, extirpation of heresy, stakes, would suit him perfectly. Continue, fool, continue,' said Chicot.

The Duc resumed: 'The cause of religion is not our only object. I see another which I will explain to you. When a man thinks of what he owes to God, he thinks also of his country, and wonders if it enjoys all the honour and prosperity it ought; for a true gentleman derives his advantages from God first, and next from his native country. I ask myself, therefore, if my country, that fair and good France, enjoys the peace and happiness she deserves, and I observe sorrowfully that she does not. The State is torn by conflicting wills of equal strength, owing to the weakness of the Sovereign will, which, forgetting that it should dominate all for the good of its subjects, remembers this royal principle at uncertain intervals, and then only to act in a misguided way. To the fatal destiny of France or to her Sovereign's blindness, we must attribute this misfortune. But the evil is not less real because we ignore its true cause, and I would blame for it either the crimes committed against the true religion or the sacrileges committed by certain false friends of the King. In any case, messieurs, I feel obliged, as a true servant of religion and of the crown, to join those who seek to extinguish heresy and destroy false counsellors. That is what I intend to do for the welfare of the League in thus allying myself with you.'

This rather long speech interested the audience so much that many crowded round the Duc in order not to miss a word. The spectacle was a curious one. Twenty-five or thirty monks, their eager faces lit up with curiosity, were grouped round the solitary lamp; the pale face of the Duc d'Anjou, its sunken eyes hidden by the heavy brow, was distinguished in the middle.

'Monseigneur,' exclaimed the Duc de Guise, 'I would thank your Highness, while informing you that only men devoted to the principles and the person of your Royal Highness surround you; the further proceedings of the assembly will offer a more convincing proof of this devotion than you imagine.' The Duc bowed, glancing uneasily over the audience.

'Oh !' remarked Chicot, 'all this fuss is but the prelude to something more important.'

'Monseigneur,' said the Cardinal, observing the Duc's expression, 'should you feel at all uneasy, the names of those present will suffice to reassure you. Here are M. le Gouverneur de Aunis, M. d'Entragues the younger, M. de Ribeirac, and M. de Livarot, as well as M. de Castillon and MM. Crucé and Leclerc, all convinced of your Highness's wisdom, and happy to follow you in your efforts to obtain the freedom of the holy religion, and of the throne. We would gratefully receive your orders.'

The Duc could not restrain a feeling of pride. These haughty and unbending Guises to talk of obeying ! The Duc de Mayenne spoke next,—

'By your birth and sagacity, you are the natural head of this Union, and we desire to learn what should be done to the false friends of whom you have spoken.'

'Nothing is simpler; when parasitic plants encumber the ground, they must be uprooted. The King's courtiers are creating constant scandal in France and throughout Christendom.'

'Moreover,' said the Cardinal, 'these courtiers prevent us from approaching His Majesty, as we have the right to do.'

'Let us leave the task of serving God,' interrupted the Duc de Mayenne brusquely, 'to ordinary members of the League. We have our own business to do. These men provoke and insult us, and show no respect to the Prince whom we honour most, our chief.'

The Duc d'Anjou reddened.

'Let us destroy ' continued Mayenne, 'this accursed brood, who are enriched with the remnants of our fortunes. Let each of us be answerable for one of them.'

'I will undertake Quélus,' cried d'Entragues.

'I Maugiron,' said Livarot.

'I Schomberg,' Ribeirac declared.

'Very good,' observed the Duc d'Anjou, ' my gallant Bussy will dispose of some.'

'So will we all,' cried the Leaguers.

M. de Monsoreau then advanced, holding up his hand for silence.

'Messieurs,' said he, 'we are determined men, yet we fear to speak frankly to each other. It is not a question of the King's favourites, nor of the difficulty we have in approaching His Majesty. What concerns us is the objectionable manner in which we are treated— a manner not to be borne by the French nobility: litanies, despotism, impotence, orgies, lavish fêtes which make all Europe laugh in pity, parsimony in everything relating to war and the arts. This is neither weakness nor ignorance, messieurs, it is madness. Must we live under a mad, idle King, when other countries are awaking from slumber and destroying old ideas? We remain sleeping. Excuse me for saying so before a powerful Prince, but for four years we have been governed not by a King but by a monk.'

At these words the explosion, carefully restrained for an hour by the caution of the leaders, burst out so violently that no one could have recognised in these demoniacs the cold, crafty schemers in the preceding scene.

'Down with Valois !' they cried, 'down with Brother Henri ! give us a gentleman King, a knight, a tyrant if need be, but not a monk.'

'Messieurs,' interposed the Duc d'Anjou hypocriti- cally, 'pray be considerate to my brother, who deceives himself, or is deceived. Let us hope that the efficacious intervention of the League's power may restore him to the right path.'

'Hiss, serpent, hiss,' murmured Chicot.

'Monseigneur,' answered the Duc de Guise, 'your Highness has heard the sincere expression of the thoughts of the League. The question for us is to rescue the nobility of France from its servile position. For too long have we, out of respect to your Highness, been compelled to conceal our intentions. Now all is revealed, and your Highness is about to assist at a real meeting of the League, of which all that has passed forms the prelude.'

'What do you mean, Monsieur le Duc?' asked the Prince, his heart beating fast with uneasiness and ambition.

'Monseigneur, we are met together to act in a practical and effective manner, not to consider old worn-out questions. To-day we choose a leader capable of honouring and enriching the nobility of France; as was the custom of the ancient Franks, we offer you a present worthy of you——'

All hearts beat fast, the Duc d'Anjou's faster than any. Yet he remained still and quiet, his pallor alone betraying his emotion.

'Messieurs,' continued the Duc, raising from the stall behind him a heavy object, 'this is the present I offer the Prince in the name of all.'

'A crown for me, messieurs!' exclaimed the Duc, nearly falling.

'Long live François III.!' cried the whole group of gentlemen in ringing tones, their swords flashing.

'My brother still lives, the anointed of the Lord,' stammered the Duc, trembling with joy and terror.

'We depose him,' declared the Duc de Guise, 'until this election is sanctioned by his death, either in God's time, or anticipated by poison or the dagger.'

'Monseigneur,' said the Cardinal, ' here is our answer to the noble scruples your Highness has expressed : Henri III. was the Lord's anointed, but we have deposed him and chosen you; in this holy church, opposite the statue of the true founder of the French monarchy, I, one of the princes of the Church, declare it to you, there is a holy oil sent by Pope Gregory XIII., to replace the chrism. Monseigneur, nominate your Archbishop of Rheims and your Constable, and in an instant you will be our anointed King, and your brother Henri a usurper. Boy, light up the altar.'

The chorister appeared from the sacristy, and in an instant fifty lights sparkled on the altar and in the choir. Then Chicot perceived a mitre, shining with precious

stones, and a large sword ornamented with fleurs-de-lis :
these were the archepiscopal mitre and the Constable's
sword. In the midst of the darkness the organ pealed
forth the *Veni Creator*. This sudden and unexpected
turn of events produced a strong impression upon all
present. Raising his head and walking with a firmer step
than might have been expected straight to the altar, the Duc
d'Anjou took the sword and the mitre, one in each hand;
then he placed the mitre on the Cardinal's head, and girt
the Duc with the sword. This decisive action was applauded all the more because the Duc's irresolute character
was well known.

'Messieurs,' he exclaimed, 'hand in your names to
the Duc de Mayenne, Grand Master of France, that, on
the day I am King, you may be nominated Knights of the
Order.'

'To think that I must forgo this unique opportunity
of receiving the decoration,' said Chicot.

'Now, sire, let us approach the altar,' said the Cardinal
de Guise.

Each took the place which would have been his at a
proper coronation ceremony. The Cardinal, appearing in
pontifical attire, placed the holy ampulla on the altar.
The chorister brought the Bible and cross. The cross
was placed on the Bible, and the Duc, laying his hand
upon it, exclaimed : 'In the presence of God, I promise
to maintain our holy religion as befits the Most
Christian King, and pray God and His Word to help
me.'

'Amen !' answered all present. The Cardinal then laid
the Constable's sword on the altar, afterwards holding it
out to the King.

'Sire,' said the Cardinal, 'receive this sword that by
the grace of the Holy Spirit, it may enable you to resist
all your enemies, to protect and defend the Holy Church
and the kingdom entrusted to you. Receive it that you
may, with its assistance, dispense justice, protect widows
and orphans, and heal all disorders, so that, finally, you
may reign with Him whom you represent on the earth,
who reigneth with the Father and Holy Spirit, for ever
and ever.'

The Duc lowered the sword to the ground to offer it to
God, and then returned it to the Duc de Guise. Next,
with a gold needle, the Cardinal placed some holy oil on

the paten, and dipping his thumb in the oil, and tracing a cross on the Duc's head, said :—

'*Ungo te in regem de oleo sanctificato, in nomine Patris et Filii et Spiritus sancti* (I anoint thee King with the blessed oil, in the name of the Father, the Son, and the Holy Ghost').

The Cardinal then lowered the crown till it almost touched the Duc's head, continuing,—'God crown you with the crown of Glory and Justice.' Placing it upon his head, he added,—'Receive this crown in the name of the Father, the Son, and the Holy Ghost.' The Duc, pale and trembling, instinctively touched the crown.

After kneeling for a short time, the audience rose, brandishing their swords and shouting :—'Long live King François III. !'

'Messieurs,' said the Duc, rising proudly, 'I shall never forget the thirty gentlemen who judged me worthy to reign over them; and now—farewell, may God have you in His holy keeping !'

The Cardinal and the Duc de Guise bowed, but Chicot noticed that the two Princes of Lorraine exchanged an ironical smile.

'Hallo !' said the Gascon, 'what is the meaning of that, and what can be the nature of the game where everybody cheats ?'

Meanwhile the Duc had disappeared below, followed by all the assembly, with the exception of the three brothers, who entered the sacristy. The chorister, closing the door of the crypt, extinguished all the lights but one in the choir, which seemed to speak to the elect of some mysterious initiation.

CHAPTER XXI

CHICOT LEARNS SOME GENEALOGY

CHICOT rose to stretch his legs, fully expecting the performance was finished, but, to his unbounded surprise, as soon as the door of the crypt was securely fastened, the three Princes, now in ordinary costume, emerged from the sacristy. On seeing them, the chorister laughed so freely and joyously that Chicot laughed too.

'Do not laugh so loudly, my sister; they may hear,' suggested the Duc de Mayenne.

'His *sister*,' thought Chicot, 'can the little monk be a woman ?'

Throwing back the hood, the novice displayed the most charming face of a woman ever painted by Da Vinci. Black eyes, sparkling with malice, a small rosy mouth, aquiline nose, and rounded chin, completed the perfect oval of a rather pale face. It was the face of Madame de Montpensier, sister of MM. de Guise, a dangerous siren, who cleverly concealed her ungraceful limp and her malformed shoulder under a monk's thick robe. The soul of a demon dwelt behind the face of an angel.

'Ah ! brother Cardinal,' cried the Duchesse, ' what a good holy man you make. For a moment I was frightened, thinking you took the matter seriously. And the man who was crowned ! How ugly he looked with his crown on !'

'At any rate, François cannot retract now. Monsoreau has arranged things, so that we are certain he will not desert us, as he did La Mole and Coconnas, half-way to the scaffold.'

'Oh !' said Mayenne, 'that is a road princes of our family are not easily made to tread.'

Chicot, realising that they had been fooling the Duc d'Anjou, whom he detested, could have embraced them, all but Mayenne.

'Let us return to business,' said the Cardinal. 'Mayenne, you say he is here; I did not see him.

'He is hidden in a confessional box.'

'Who the deuce is hidden in a confessional ? I see only myself,' said Chicot, moving nervously.

'Bring him to me, Mayenne.' Descending one of the stairs, Mayenne considered a moment, then made straight for the confessional which sheltered Chicot. The Gascon was brave, but now a cold perspiration broke over him as he endeavoured to draw out his sword, muttering, 'The deuce ! I won't die here like a rat. Now I have the chance, I will kill him before I die.'

At that moment the voice of the Duchesse was heard : 'Not in that one, Mayenne, in the other, at the end.'

'Ah ! very good,' replied the Duc, turning away.

'Ouf !' sighed Chicot, 'it is high time too; but who the deuce is in the other ?'

'Here I am, monseigneur; I have not lost a word of what has happened,' exclaimed a man, stepping out of the box.

'I looked for you everywhere, Maître Nicolas, and lo ! here you are,' said Chicot.

'My brother of Mayenne declares you have worked miracles for us. What have you done ?' asked the Duc, who, along with his brothers and sister, was standing close to the lawyer.

'I have discovered a means of giving you an incontestable right to the throne of France.'

'Everybody wants to be King,' laughed Chicot, whose gaiety had three causes : first, he had most unexpectedly escaped from danger; secondly, he had discovered a plot; and, lastly, in this plot he saw an opportunity of destroying his two enemies : the Duc de Mayenne and Maître David.

'I am not only skilled in fencing,' continued the lawyer, 'but, brought up on legal and theological studies, I have consulted annals and decrees which strengthen my assertion, and I have discovered that you are the legitimate heirs, and the Valois only a parasitical and usurping branch.'

'It is difficult to believe, though,' said the Duc de Guise, 'that the House of Lorraine, illustrious as it is, should take precedence over the Valois.'

'That is proved, however, monseigneur,' said Maître Nicolas, producing a roll of parchment, which he handed to the Duc.

'What is this ?'

'The genealogical tree of the House of Lorraine.'

'Whose founder was ?'

'Charlemagne, monseigneur.'

'Charlemagne ! impossible. The first Duc de Lorraine, who was called Ranier, was in no way related to the great emperor.'

'Wait a moment, monseigneur. This question cannot be dismissed by a simple contradiction. What you require is a protracted law-suit, which will occupy Parliament and the people, and give you time to win over the Parliament. Here you see, monseigneur : Ranier, first Duc de Lorraine; Guilbert, his son; Henri, son of Guilbert; Bonne, daughter of Ricin, Ranier's second son, married to Charles de Lorraine, son of Louis IV., King of France. Let us add, brother of Lothaire, deprived of the throne

'Diane appeared, smiling and more
beautiful than ever.'

by the usurper Hugues Capet. Now, Charles de Lorraine derived the rights of succession from his brother Lothaire. The race of Lothaire is now extinct, therefore you are the true and only heirs to the throne.'

'Unfortunately,' objected Le Balafré, 'there exists the Salic law to destroy our claims.'

'I was anticipating this objection,' cried David, with an air of satisfied pride; 'what was the first example of this law?'

'The accession of Philippe de Valois, rather than Edward of England.'

'And the date ?'

'1328.'

'That is three hundred and forty-one years after Hugues Capet's usurpation, two hundred and forty years after the House of Lothaire became extinct, so for that latter period your ancestors held the rights of succession before the Salic law was invented. Every one is aware that the law has no retrospective effect.'

'You are a clever man, Maître David,' said Le Balafré, eyeing the lawyer with admiration, combined with a certain contempt.

'It is decidedly ingenious,' observed the Cardinal.

'It is very fine,' said Mayenne.

'It is admirable,' declared the Duchesse; 'and as I am now Princess Royal, I shall be content only with an emperor for a husband.'

The Duc de Guise was reflecting amidst this enthusiasm.

'To think that such subterfuges are needed by a man like me,' he muttered. 'Must the people be instructed in such documents before obeying ? Cannot a man's nobility be read in the flashing of his eye or of his sword ?'

'You are perfectly correct, Henri. If appearance alone were considered, you would be a king among kings. Just now, however, it is essential to get up a good lawsuit. When we have reached the throne, as you declared yourself, our escutcheon will be a fitting one to place beside those of the other thrones of Europe.'

'Well, this pedigree is apparently correct,' said the Duc, 'so here are the two hundred gold crowns my brother promised you, Maître David.'

'Here are two hundred more,' said the Cardinal, 'for the new commission with which you are to be entrusted.'

'I am at your Eminence's service.'

C.J.　　　　　　　　　　　　　　　　　　　F

'We cannot ask you to carry this document to Rome for the Pope's approval. You are of too humble birth to enter the Vatican, so we are compelled to entrust Pierre de Gondy with this service.'

'My brother, permit me,' interposed the Duchesse, 'Gondy has only his ambition as guarantee, and that may be as well satisfied by the King as by ourselves.'

'My sister is right, Louis,' observed the Duc de Mayenne, with his accustomed frankness; 'we cannot trust Pierre de Gondy as we can Nicolas David, whom we may hang when we choose.'

The lawyer laughed convulsively at this brutal threat, thus betraying his great terror.

'Reassure yourselves, Charles and Catherine; all m· plans are made. Pierre de Gondy will carry this pedigree to Rome, with certain other documents. The Pope will approve or disapprove, and Gondy will bring the document back to France in total ignorance of its character. You, Nicolas David, will start at the same time as Gondy, and wait for him where you are instructed. You, alone, hold the true secret of this business, and are the only person in our confidence.'

'You are thoroughly aware of the conditions, dear friend,' muttered Chicot; 'make one false move and you are hanged. I swear by Sainte-Geneviève that you are between two gibbets, but the nearer one is that on which I shall hang you.'

The three brothers now embraced, and kissed their sister, who brought them the robes which had been left in the sacristy. Drawing her own hood over her eyes, she preceded them to the porch, through which they disappeared, followed by Nicolas David, jingling his gold crowns. The doorkeeper locked the door and extinguished the lamp, and five minutes passed without anything disturbing the silence and gloom.

'Very good,' said Chicot, 'the play really must be over, for the actors have gone away. Let us try to follow them.' He had abandoned his original intention of waiting in the church for daylight, and already was stepping from his box. He had noticed a ladder in a corner, which he quickly and cautiously placed against a window. Opening this he drew the ladder outside with that unusual strength which fear or joy usually produces. Once down, he hid the ladder in a yew-hedge and, gliding among the tombs, crossed the wall into the street, bringing down some stones with him. Chicot drew a long breath as he reflected that he had escaped with a few scratches from a danger in which he might easily have lost his life. Making for the Rue Saint-Jacques, he stopped at the inn of the Corne d'Abondance, and knocked without any hesitation. Maître Claude Bonhomet opened the door, and immediately recognised Chicot in his monk's disguise.

'Ah! welcome, good sire.'

'And Brother Gorenflot!' asked Chicot.

The innkeeper, smiling broadly, opened the door of the room, where Brother Gorenflot was snoring in exactly the same place as Chicot had left him.

'Ah! my worthy friend,' observed Chicot, 'without being conscious of it, you have had a fearful nightmare!'

CHAPTER XXII

THE JOURNEY OF MONSIEUR AND MADAME DE SAINT-LUC

NEXT morning, when Brother Gorenflot was waking, two horsemen, a nobleman, and his page passed along the road between Chartres and Nogent; their steeds were walking side by side, and neighing as honest animals do to express their thoughts. At nearly the same hour the day before, the two had arrived at Chartres, their horses covered with foam. The good people of Chartres, using their powers of observation, had noticed that the taller horseman had given a boy a crown to take them to an inn, and from this inn the two had emerged by a back door, half an hour later, mounted on fresh animals.

Once in the open country, the tall horseman, approaching his companion, held out his arms, saying:—'Dear little wife, kiss me, we have nothing now to fear.' Then Madame de Saint-Luc, for it was really she, bending forward gracefully, kissed her husband tenderly. The two had stopped that day at a little inn, situated four leagues from Chartres. There they remained all day and all night, mysteriously shut up in their room, having given orders to the innkeeper to waken them at daybreak. So we find them in the morning of the second day, travelling from Chartres to Nogent. Feeling more reassured, they were behaving like schoolboys, hunting for the first buds of spring, gathering flowers and mosses, and joyfully watching the hares scurry over the plain.

'Zounds!' exclaimed Saint-Luc suddenly, 'how good it is to be free! Were you ever free, Jeanne?'

'Never,' laughed the young woman; 'I do not remember running over the grassy lawns since I played, as a happy child, in the big woods of Méridor with my Diane, and challenged her to races till we were both exhausted. But you, being a man, were free, dear Saint-Luc.'

'Never. Brought up beside the Duc d'Anjou, condemned by etiquette never to leave him, ever pursued by that lamentable voice: "Saint-Luc, I am bored, my friend; come and be bored with me." Free with this corset cramping my chest, this starched collar scraping my neck, with hair frizzled and plastered with gum, and this cap fixed to my head with pins. No, my dear Jeanne, I was even less free than you. So you see, I am taking advantage of my liberty.'

'If we are caught, Saint-Luc, and caged in the Bastille?' asked his wife, glancing uneasily round.

'If we are together, it will not be so bad.'

'Oh, don't trust to that; I don't think they will let us stay together.'

'Then, let us hide ourselves carefully.'

'In that respect we have nothing to fear at Méridor, with its great oaks, its slow-winding rivers, its corn-fields, flower-beds, endless lawns, and little turrets, from which thousands of pigeons fly out, turning and cooing. And, in the midst of all is the queen of the little kingdom, the beautiful, incomparable Diane, a diamond encased in gold! You will love her, Saint-Luc. Think what a happy life we shall lead in this nest of flowers and moss! Diane has taken over the management of her father's, the Baron's, house. He has become as weak and inoffensive as he was formerly strong and courageous; he dwells in the past, on the victory at Marignan, the defeat at Pavie; and has but one affection in the present, one hope for the future— his beloved Diane. We can live at Méridor without his ever noticing us. Think of our life there, in the pavilion which Diane will give us for a lodging. Its architecture is charming, and, from its many windows, one has a view of the great woods, rising out of sight. From the other side one sees the gilded plains, the villages with red roofs, the Loire sparkling in the sunlight; we shall have a boat on the lake, three leagues away; horses and dogs, with which we shall hunt the stag in the woods.'

'Let us hasten, Jeanne; I long to be at Méridor already.'

So the pair journeyed from Chartres to Mans, where they stayed for a day. Determining to reach Méridor the next night, they set out the following morning across the sandy forest lands which then stretched from Guécelard to Ecomoy. Saint-Luc now considered they were out of danger, for he was aware that it depended on the King's mood whether he would send twenty couriers and a hundred guards to bring them back, alive or dead, or only murmur as he drew his arms out of bed: 'Oh! that traitor Saint-Luc, why did I not find him out sooner!' Now, as the fugitives had not been overtaken by guard or courier, the King had evidently been in a lazy mood. So Saint-Luc argued, as he gave an occasional backward glance at the deserted road.

Suddenly he felt his wife's hand on his arm. 'Look,' she said. Turning round he perceived a horseman pressing forward swiftly in their direction. Outlined against the sky, at the top of a hill, he appeared unnaturally tall. This seemed a bad omen to Saint-Luc, who perhaps feared some capricious act on the King's part. 'Yes, indeed, there *is* a horseman yonder,' said he, paling.

'Let us fly,' exclaimed Jeanne, urging on her horse.

'No, he is alone, and we must not fly before a single man. Let us step out of the way till he has passed, and afterwards resume our course.'

'But, if he stops?'

'In that case, we shall see who he is, and act accordingly.'

'You are right. I was wrong to be afraid when my Saint-Luc is here to defend me.'

'Let us fly, all the same,' said Saint-Luc, who had noticed that the stranger at sight of them galloped more swiftly. 'There is a feather in that hat, and a ruff beneath it, the fashion of which makes me uneasy.'

'Oh! *mon Dieu!* Why should you be afraid of a feather and a ruff?' asked Jeanne, as she followed her husband, who was dragging his horse into the wood.

'Because the feather is of a colour very popular at court, and the collar is of quite a new shape; now, these feathers and these ruffs are too extravagant for gentlemen of Le Mans. This horseman is probably an ambassador of the King, my august master.'

'Let us hurry,' cried Jeanne, trembling. But this was a difficult matter, for the branches closed round like a wall, and their horses sank into the sandy ground. Meanwhile the horseman advanced with lightning speed.

'He is dismounting, he has entered the wood. Ah! troth! though it were the devil himself, I will go to meet him.'

'Stop, he is calling,' said Jeanne, and, indeed, the stranger, after tying his horse to a branch, came forward, crying out : 'Eh! good sir! don't run away; I am bringing something you have lost.'

'Faith!' cried Saint-Luc, 'he says we have lost something.'

'Eh! monsieur, the little monsieur, you left your bracelet in the hotel at Courville. One must not lose a woman's portrait, especially that of the worthy Madame de Cossé.'

'I know that voice! It's Bussy!' exclaimed Saint-Luc, running eagerly to meet the nobleman.

'Saint-Luc! I was not mistaken,' said Bussy, in sonorous tones.

'Do you come to arrest us in the King's name ?' asked Jeanne, smiling.

'I should think not; I am not friendly enough with the King for that. I merely found your bracelet, and pushed on to overtake you.'

'So, chance brings you in our way ?' observed Saint-Luc, with a remnant of suspicion in his mind.

'Chance, or now I will say a good Providence.'

Saint-Luc's doubts vanished before the frank glance and smile of the handsome cavalier.

'So, you are journeying, but not like us,' said Jeanne.

'No, unfortunately.'

'Not because you are in disgrace, I meant.'

'Not far short of it.'

'Where are you going ?'

'Towards Angers. And you ?'

'The same way.'

'Yes, I understand. Brissac lies between Angers and Saumur; you are flying to your father's home. I would envy your happiness, only envy is such an ugly trait.'

'Well, Monsieur de Bussy, get married and you will be as happy as we are.'

'Such happiness is not for me,' said Bussy, sighing.

'Are you in love with some one you cannot marry, then?'

'Comte, pray tell Madame de Saint-Luc not to wound me in this manner.'

'Ah! take care, Bussy, or I shall imagine you are in love with my wife.'

'You will at least agree I show such delicacy that husbands could hardly be jealous of me.'

'Ah! true,' said Saint-Luc, remembering that Bussy had brought his wife to the Louvre. 'No matter, confess that your affections are engaged.'

'I confess it.'

'Is it love or mere fancy?' asked Jeanne.

'It is a passion, madame.'

'I undertake to cure you. I will get you married, and give you the happiness you deserve.'

'Alas! madame, my only happiness lies in being unhappy.'

'I am very obstinate, I warn you. You will yield.'

'Come, madame, let us travel as good friends: first leave this sand-pit, and, by sunset, we shall reach that charming little village shining in the sun.'

'Then you will accompany us?'

'As far as my destination, if it is convenient.'

'Better still, come all the way with us.'

'Where are you going?'

'To the Château de Méridor.'

The blood rose to Bussy's cheek, then ebbed away, leaving him so pale that Jeanne must have guessed his secret, had she not been smiling to her husband. However, he found time to recover, and paid back the young woman's archness by concealing his own intentions.

'To the Château de Méridor, madame; and what place is that?'

'The home of one of my dearest friends.'

'And—is she at home?'

'Doubtless,' answered Jeanne, ignorant of what had happened in the last two months; 'have you never heard of Baron de Méridor and his daughter, Diane, the most beautiful girl that ever lived.'

'No, madame,' said Bussy, whose emotion nearly overcame him.

Could this be a trap? It was almost impossible. Saint-Luc had left Paris when Madame de Monsoreau had informed him that her maiden name was Diane de Méridor.

'You will come with us?' asked Jeanne.

'Yes, madame.'

'Good; it is always one step nearer the happiness I offered you.'

'This Baron de Méridor, what is he like?'

'A perfect gentleman: a warrior of ancient days; a knight who would have sat at King Arthur's Round Table, had he lived then.'

'And to whom is his daughter married?'

'Diane is not married! I should have been the first to know.'

'Then, Mademoiselle de Méridor is at home with her father?'

'We sincerely hope so,' answered Saint-Luc, emphasising his reply to show his wife that he understood and shared her plans.

'Ah!' cried Jeanne, suddenly rising in her stirrups, 'there are the turrets of the château. Look, Monsieur de Bussy; don't you see the slate roof, in the midst of the woods?'

'Yes, yes,' exclaimed Bussy, feeling an emotion which surprised him, so unimpressionable had he always been. At the sight of this lordly dwelling, this beautiful country-side, his thoughts returned to the poor girl buried in the fogs of Paris, and shut up in the stuffy house in the Rue Saint-Antoine. This time he sighed, but not wholly in sadness. By promising happiness, Madame de Saint-Luc had at least given him hope.

CHAPTER XXIII

THE ORPHANED OLD MAN

MADAME DE SAINT-LUC was not mistaken, as two hours later they stood in front of the Château de Méridor. After their conversation, Bussy wondered whether he should inform his friends of the adventure which kept Diane far from her home. But, considering that once started he would have to reveal not only what everybody would soon know but what he alone knew, and was unwilling to tell, Bussy shrank from a confession, involving so many interpretations and questioning. He wished to enter Méridor a perfect stranger, to see M. de Méridor, to hear him speak of M. de Monsoreau and the Duc d'Anjou, without being prepared for the interview; he wished to convince himself, not that Diane's story was true (he did not suspect that angel of falsehood for an instant), but that she, herself, had not been deceived in any way.

So Madame de Saint-Luc, deceived by Bussy's self-control, was convinced that he had heard Diane's name for the first time, and that he expected to find at Méridor some awkward country girl who would be embarrassed at receiving her guests. So she prepared to enjoy his surprise. But one thing astonished her; the guard had blown his trumpet to announce their arrival, but no Diane had rushed, as was her custom, to the drawbridge. Instead of Diane, an old bent man, leaning on a stick, advanced through the principal gate. He was dressed in a green velvet coat, trimmed with fox's fur, and at his belt dangled a silver whistle near a small bunch of keys. The evening wind lifted his snow-white hair. Crossing the drawbridge, followed by two great dogs, who walked slowly, with heads bent, the old man reached the parapet, and inquired in a weak voice : 'Who is there?'

'It is I, Seigneur Augustin,' cried the laughing voice of the young woman. Jeanne addressed him thus to distinguish him from his younger brother, Guillaume, who had died three years before. But, instead of answering joyfully, the Baron, slowly raising his head, fixed vacant eyes upon them.

'You?' said he; 'I do not see. Who are you?'

'Oh! *mon Dieu!* do you not recognise me? But, I had forgotten my disguise.'

'Pardon me, but I can hardly see at all. Old men's eyes are not made for weeping, and tears destroy them.'

'Ah! dear Baron, your sight is weak, or you would have recognised me even in men's clothes. Must I tell you my name? I am Madame de Saint-Luc.'

'I do not know you.'

'But, before my marriage, I was Jeanne de Cossé-Brissac.'

'Ah! my God!' exclaimed the old man, trying with trembling hands to open the gate.

Jeanne, understanding nothing in this strange, un-expected reception, which she attributed to the Baron's age and declining faculties, leaped from her horse to throw herself into his arms; and, as she kissed him, she felt his cheeks wet with tears.

'It is with joy,' she thought; 'his heart is still young.'

'Come,' said the old man, and he walked towards the castle with equal, measured step, seemingly oblivious of Jeanne's two friends. The château had a strange, gloomy look; all the shutters were closed; the servants were dressed in black. Jeanne, eager to solve the mystery approached the Baron, saying, 'Diane, is she unfortunately not at home?'

He stopped, as though thunderstruck, and looked at her, almost in terror. 'Diane!' said he. At the name the two dogs, lifting their heads, howled dolefully. Bussy shuddered; Siant-Luc stopped, uncertain whether to advance farther or to retire. 'Diane! you have not heard, then?' The old man's trembling voice ended in a deep sob.

'What is wrong?' exclaimed Jeanne, clasping her hands.

'Diane is dead!' he wailed, raising his hands despair-ingly towards heaven and weeping violently.

'Dead!' cried Jeanne, turning pale as a ghost.

'Dead!' echoed Saint-Luc, with tender compassion for the unhappy father.

'Dead!' stammered Bussy. 'Monsoreau has allowed him, also, to believe the lie! Poor old man, what happi-ness I shall bring you, some day!'

'Ah! my dear seigneur,' sobbed Jeanne, finding refuge in tears and twining her arms round his neck.

The Baron rose stumbling. 'My house is desolate,' he said; 'but still hospitable; enter.'

Taking his arm, Jeanne crossed the dining-hall into the drawing-room. A servant, with sorrowful face and red eyes, opened the doors before them; Bussy and Saint-Luc followed. In the drawing-room, Diane's father sank into a carved wooden arm-chair. Jeanne was afraid to break silence, and re-open his wounds; yet, like all happy young people, she could not grasp the reality of the misfortune. The Baron himself resumed the conversation.

'You said you were married, dear Jeanne; is this gentle-man your husband?' he asked, indicating Bussy.

'No, Seigneur Augustin; here is M. de Saint-Luc.'

Saint-Luc bowed respectfully before his unhappy host, who, returning the compliment in a fatherly way, endeavoured to smile. Presently, turning with dull gaze to Bussy, he asked :—

'Is this gentleman your brother, your husband's brother, or a relative ?'

'No, dear Baron, monsieur is no relative, but our friend, M. Louis de Clermont, Comte de Bussy d'Amboise, one of the Duc d'Anjou's gentlemen.'

At these words the Baron, starting up, glanced wildly at Bussy, then, as if exhausted by this mute challenge, fell back in his chair groaning.

'Does the Baron know you, Seigneur de Bussy ?' asked Saint-Luc.

'It is the first time I have had the honour of meeting the Baron de Méridor,' answered Bussy, who alone understood the effect produced by the Duc's name.

'Ah ! you are in the service of the Duc d'Anjou, of that demon, that monster, and you dare to avow it, and have the audacity to come here !'

'Is he mad ?' asked Saint-Luc, in low tones, of his wife.

'Grief has unhinged his mind,' answered Jeanne, in terror.

'Yes, this monster,' resumed the Baron, 'this assassin who killed my daughter.'

'What *is* he saying ?' asked Jeanne.

'You have not heard, then,' said M. de Méridor, 'the Duc d'Anjou killed my Diane; my child, he killed her !'

'Seigneur, if it were so, you cannot blame M. de Bussy, the most generous gentleman in the world, for this misfortune. Look, he is ignorant of all this, and weeps with us. Dear Seigneur Augustin, explain how this dreadful catastrophe happened ?'

'Then you did not know ?' said the old man to Bussy, who bowed without replying.

'No one knew of this tragedy,' Jeanne declared.

'My Diane is dead, and her best friend remained in ignorance. Oh! true, I informed no one; I thought the world could not exist after my Diane's death; it seemed to me that the whole universe would be in mourning.'

'Speak, it will relieve you,' urged Jeanne.

'Ah, well ! this infamous Prince, seeing my Diane, and finding her so beautiful, had her carried off to his Château

de Beaugé, as he might have done with a serf's daughter.
But my noble Diane, preferring death to dishonour,
threw herself into the lake, and only her veil was found
floating on the water.' He could not finish without
crying and sobbing in such a manner that Bussy thought
it the saddest spectacle he had ever seen : Jeanne, nearly
fainting, gazed at the Comte in anguish.

'Oh ! Comte,' cried Saint-Luc; 'you must leave this
infamous prince; a nobleman like yourself cannot remain
the friend of an assassin and a ravisher.'

Their host, a little comforted by Saint-Luc's sympathetic words, awaited Bussy's reply in order to form an
opinion of him ; but Bussy, instead of answering Saint-
Luc, stepped towards M. de Méridor, saying, 'Monsieur
le Baron, will you grant me the honour of a private
interview ?'

'Speak, monsieur,' said the Baron, perceiving a strange
look in his visitor's eyes.

'You permit me ?' said Bussy, turning to Saint-Luc
and his wife with a glance full of friendship. The young
couple went out, appreciating their own happiness all the
more in the midst of such desolating sorrow.

'Monsieur le Baron,' began Bussy ; 'you have just
accused a prince whom I serve with a violence which
compels me to ask an explanation.'

His companion glanced up with a startled air.

'Oh ! do not misunderstand my meaning, which is most
respectful; it is with deepest sympathy I speak, and with
the keenest desire to alleviate your grief I say, "Monsieur
le Baron, tell me all about this terrible catastrophe, which
you have narrated to M. de Saint-Luc and his wife.
Is all hope really lost ?"'

'Monsieur, I had hope for a moment. A noble, loyal
gentleman, M. de Monsoreau, loved my poor daughter,
and acted in her interests.'

'And what was his conduct in this crisis ?'

'That of a loyal, worthy man, for Diane had refused his
offer. Yet he first informed me of the Duc's infamous
plots, and showed me how to defeat them, begging, as
a reward, my daughter's hand, that he might defend her
against a powerful prince. I joyfully consented; but alas !
he arrived at the château too late, and learned that my
poor Diane had escaped dishonour by death.'

'From that fatal moment, has he sent you no news ?'

'It is only a month since these things happened; no doubt the poor gentleman has felt ashamed to meet me, after the failure of his generous plan.'

All was explained to Bussy, who now understood how M. de Monsoreau had carried off Diane, and how fear of the Prince's discovering his treachery had induced him to allow the poor father even to believe her dead.

'Well, Monsieur le Baron,' said Bussy presently, 'I am commissioned by His Royal Highness the Duc d'Anjou to escort you to Paris, where he desires to speak to you.'

'To speak to *me*; what can *he* have to say to me—the murderer ?'

'Perhaps he may justify his conduct.'

'Even so, I would not go to Paris, Monsieur de Bussy; it is too much to drag me from the spot where my poor child lies dead.'

'Monsieur le Baron, permit me to insist; it is my duty to escort you to Paris, and the sole reason for my coming here.'

'Well ! I will go to Paris,' cried the old man, trembling with rage; 'but woe to those who have wronged me ! The King shall listen to me, and if he refuses, I will appeal to all the gentlemen of France. My grief caused me to forget that I have a weapon which I have never used. Yes, Monsieur de Bussy, I will accompany you.'

'I recommend you to be patient, calm, and dignified, as becomes a Christian gentleman, Monsieur le Baron. God has infinite pity for noble hearts, and you cannot say what He has in store for you. I beg you, until that time arrives, not to consider me an enemy, for at present you cannot judge of my actions. Good-bye until to-morrow, then; we will start at daybreak, with your permission.'

'I agree,' said the old man, deeply moved by Bussy's gentle tones; 'meanwhile, you are my guest, and I must show you to your room.' The Baron, lifting a silver candlestick, walked upstairs, attended by Bussy, and followed by two servants bearing other candles. On reaching his room, Bussy inquired what had become of M. and Madame de Saint-Luc.

'My old Germain will have attended to them,' answered the Baron. 'Good-night, Monsieur le Comte.'

CHAPTER XXIV

FATHER AND DAUGHTER

NEXT morning Monsieur and Madame de Saint-Luc were overwhelmed by astonishment at seeing Bussy sharing secrets with M. de Méridor and preparing to start with him for Paris, Bussy suddenly taking over the management of affairs of which he had seemed completely ignorant. As for the Baron, the magic of the title, 'Royal Highness' produced its usual effect upon him; a gentleman of the time of Henri III. could not fail to be impressed by names and armorial bearings. Bussy wished to explain his strange conduct to his friends, and seized an opportunity of whispering a few words into the eager ear of Madame de Saint-Luc. Jeanne's face lit up; her brow coloured and her coral lips parted in a smile; then, as her astonished husband gazed questioningly at her, she rushed off, placing a finger on her mouth.

The Baron had noticed nothing of this expressive pantomime : he was gazing at his home and caressing his two dogs. Issuing some orders to his servants, he mounted a favourite old piebald horse, and set off without speaking. It was a long journey from Méridor to Paris, especially for an old man, covered with scars, and for this worthy piebald horse Jarnac, who rolled a still proud eye and tossed his shaggy head when addressed.

Once on the way, Bussy strove to win the Baron's affections by care and attention, and doubtless he succeeded, for on reaching Paris in the morning of the sixth day, Méridor spoke to him after this manner,—

'It is strange, Comte, I am now nearer the source of my misfortune than ever, and yet am less uneasy than when I started.'

The travellers entered Paris by the Faubourg Saint-Marcel, and Bussy went straight to his hotel in the Rue de Grenelle-Saint-Honoré. The Comte's servants were no longer expecting him. His disappearance, the dangers he had run the week before, his adventurous habits, had led them to imagine that he had fallen into some trap, or had been stabbed to death. One person, alone, when asked

for news of Bussy, answered :—'Monsieur le Comte is
well.' This optimist was Maître Rémy le Haudouin, who
was constantly running hither and thither, disappearing
from the hotel, now by day, now by night, returning with
an extraordinary appetite, and ever brightening up the
house. After one of these mysterious absences, Le
Haudouin returned to find the valets eagerly surrounding
Bussy, who remained on horseback, in spite of their offers
of assistance.

'Come,' Bussy was saying, 'you are glad to see me alive.
I thank you. You ask if it is really myself; look at me,
touch me, but do it quickly. Now, help this gentleman to
alight, and notice that I treat him with greater respect
than I would a prince.' Bussy's warnings were needed,
as little attention had been paid to the old man with his
simple dress, rather out of fashion, and his piebald horse,
whose value was quickly appraised by those who daily
handled Bussy's animals. All now crowded round the
Baron, while Le Haudouin stood by smiling.

'Quick, a room for monseigneur—the best—my own,'
cried Bussy, and, giving his companion his arm, he led him
upstairs. The Comte's gold cup was brought, and Bussy
poured out wine for his guest.

'Thank you, monsieur, but are we going where we ought
to go ?'

'Yes, be reassured, Seigneur Augustin; it will be happiness
for me as well; I spoke to you of a Providence pitying
towards great hearts, and, in your name, I will presently
appeal to that Providence.' The Baron regarded Bussy
with surprise, but Bussy, smiling, left the room.

Le Haudouin was waiting at the door. Bussy drew him
into a small room, asking, 'Well ! my dear Hippocrate,
how are affairs in the Rue Saint-Antoine ?'

'There is nothing new, monseigneur.'

'Then the husband has not returned ?'

'Yes, but without success. There is a father, it seems,
who must appear one morning to solve the difficulties.'

'How have you learned that ?'

'Monseigneur, your absence made my position here
a sinecure. Wishing to utilise my leisure to your advantage, I carried some books, a sword, and money to
a small room which I had hired at the corner of Rue
Saint-Antoine and Rue Sainte-Catherine. From there
I could see the house in which you are interested, and,

once in possession, I settled myself at a window. But this excellent plan had its drawbacks. I could be seen as well as see, and people might object to a man always gazing at the same spot : I might have been mistaken for a thief, a lover, a spy, or a madman.'

'What did you do, then ?'

'Deciding that extreme means must be resorted to, I fell in love.'

'Eh !' exclaimed Bussy, who failed to see how this helped him.

'I fell violently, madly in love with Gertrude.'

'With Gertrude, Madame de Monsoreau's servant ?'

'Yes, with Gertrude. I am not a gentleman, monseigneur, to be in love with mistresses : I am merely a poor doctor with one patient, who, I hope, will employ me seldom.'

'Poor Rémy, believe me, I appreciate your devotion.'

'Monseigneur, I do not need much pity, after all; Gertrude is a fine, handsome girl, two inches taller than myself, and we never dispute; besides, she has a valuable talent—she tells stories wonderfully well.'

'Ah ! really !'

'Yes, so that from her I discover everything that is happening in the house.'

'How did you arrive at such happiness.'

'Two days after your departure, I waited till the lady of my thoughts went out shopping. Then I encountered her. She recognised me, and, crying out, ran away. Running after her, I caught her with great difficulty.'

' "The doctor !" she cried.

' "The charming housekeeper," I answered. She smiled, then she said : "You are making a mistake, monsieur, I do not know you."

' "But I know you; for three days I have done nothing but adore you; I have changed my apartments in order to see you going in and out; if you need my services again to dress the wounds of handsome gentlemen, you must come to my new lodgings !"'

'That is how our acquaintance was renewed. I am overflowing with happiness, since I have advanced your interests as I wished.'

'But perhaps she will suspect?'

'No; I have never mentioned you. I simply asked casually: "Is your young master better ?"'

' "What young master ?" she asked.

' "The horseman whom I attended."

' "He is not my master; *mon Dieu*, no, he was nothing to us; we have seen him only once since."

' "Then you don't even know his name ?"

' "Oh, yes, we do. Have you ever heard of Seigneur de Bussy ?"

' "*Parbleu !* the brave Bussy ?"

' "It is he."

' "Your mistress, then ?"

' "My mistress is married, monsieur."

' "Yes, but one may think sometimes of a handsome young man acquaintance."

' "I do not deny she thinks of him; we even speak of him when we are alone. I relate his brave deeds, and have even taught her a little song about him, which is very popular. My mistress sings nothing else." '

Bussy grasped the young doctor's hand. A feeling of happiness possessed him.

'Is that all ?' he asked.

'Oh ! I shall discover more later on; but, the deuce, one cannot know everything in a day—or in a night.'

This report of Rémy's cheered Bussy. He had learned two things : first, that M. de Monsoreau was detested as much as ever, and that he himself had gained more favour. He understood, too, that no time must be lost; each pang felt by the unhappy father was almost a sacrilege. He resolved to hurry things on, and M. de Méridor, on descending to the courtyard, found a fresh horse prepared for him; another awaited Bussy, and the two mounting, set out, accompanied by Rémy. They reached the Rue Saint-Antoine, and entered the Rue Saint-Paul, M. de Méridor being considerably astonished at the noise of the horses, the cries of lackeys, and the frequent passing of carriages. Rémy went on in front to prepare their reception, and having questioned Gertrude, returned with the information that the staircase and corridor were clear.

'Enter, monsieur,' said Bussy, with a smile which always bewitched the old gentleman. The Baron dismounted. Gertrude, who had run out to the door in amazement, gazed wildly at Le Haudouin, Bussy, and the old man, unable to fathom what had brought these three together.

'Go and inform Madame de Monsoreau that Monsieur de

Bussy has returned and wishes to speak to her,' said the
Comte.

While his companion mounted the stair with tottering
steps, Diane's voice was heard answering,—

'M. de Bussy, Gertrude ! Let him enter.'

'That voice,' cried the Baron, stopping suddenly; 'oh,
mon Dieu !'

At the same moment, Diane appeared, in a ray of sunlight at the head of the stair, smiling and more beautiful
than ever. The perplexed father, uttering a pitiful cry,
stretched out his arms to heaven, and presented such a
picture of terror and delirium that Diane, who had been
ready to rush into his arms, stopped, too, dismayed and
stupefied. The Baron leaned on Bussy's shoulder, murmuring : 'Diane living ! Diane whom they told me was
dead; *mon Dieu !*' This robust warrior, this athlete who
had struggled so powerfully against grief, crushed and
beaten, overcome with joy, tottered, and would have fallen
but for Bussy.

'*Mon Dieu !* Monsieur de Bussy,' cried Diane, hurriedly
descending the stair, 'what *is* wrong ?'

'M. le Baron thought you were dead, madame, and
mourned for you.'

'What ! did no one undeceive him ?'

'No one.'

'Oh ! no, not even M. de Bussy,' exclaimed the old man,
who had recovered from his temporary faintness. Then,
suddenly, as though some sad memory or new fear had
crept into his heart in spite of his joy, he asked : 'Did you
not tell me, Seigneur de Bussy, that I was about to see
Madame de Monsoreau ? Where is she ?'

'Before you,' answered Bussy; 'Comte de Monsoreau
is your son-in-law.'

'M. de Monsoreau my son-in-law ! and you, Diane,
himself, every one has left me in ignorance ?'

'I feared to write lest the Prince should intercept the
letter. Moreover, I understood you were acquainted with
everything.'

'But what is the meaning of these mysteries ?'

'Yes, father, how comes it that M. de Monsoreau permitted you to believe me dead ? why has he not informed
you that he is my husband ?'

'M. de Monsoreau my son-in-law !' stammered the
Baron.

'That cannot astonish you,' said Diane, with soft reproach; 'did you not beg me to marry him?'

'Yes, if he saved you from the Prince.'

'Well! he has saved me, not from unhappiness but from shame.'

'Then why did he leave me in despair, when a single word would have restored me.'

'Oh! there is some trap beneath it,' cried Diane. 'Father, you will not leave me; Monsieur de Bussy, you will protect me?'

'Alas! madame, I cannot pry any more into family secrets. I have brought a protector whom you can acknowledge. Now I withdraw.'

'He is right,' said the Baron; 'like Monsieur de Monsoreau, he fears the Duc d'Anjou.'

'Monsieur le Baron, will you excuse the strange question which I wish you to ask, and will you, too, excuse it, madame? Will you please ask Madame de Monsoreau if she is happy in the marriage to which she consented?'

Diane, clasping her hands, burst into sobs. It was her only answer, but no other could have been so conclusive. The Baron's eyes filled with tears as he began to suspect that his hasty friendship for M. de Monsoreau accounted for much of his daughter's unhappiness.

'A man of honour keeps his word, and you should know this better than most people, monsieur. M. de Monsoreau saved my daughter's life, therefore she is his.'

'Ah!' murmured Diane, 'why am I not dead?'

'Madame, you see I cannot interfere further. M. le Baron gives you to M. de Monsoreau, and you promised to marry him when you saw your father safe.'

'Ah! do not break my heart; my father does not know that I fear, that I hate this man, that he is my executioner.'

'Diane! he saved you!' cried the Baron.

'Yes,' exclaimed Bussy; 'but suppose the danger were a fictitious one? Baron, there is some mystery, which I will solve. I protest that, had I been in M. de Monsoreau's place, I would have saved your fair daughter from dishonour, without compelling this payment.'

'He loved her, and we must pardon love.'

'And I, then! do I——?' Bussy stopped; but his expression finished the sentence. Diane understood.

'Well! my friend, my brother,' said she, reddening, 'will you come to my assistance?'

'If you wish, Monsieur de Méridor, I will place you on such a footing with the Prince that he will protect you against M. de Monsoreau, from whom, believe me, comes the real danger—unknown, but certain, invisible, but perhaps inevitable.'

'All will be lost, if the Duc hears that Diane lives.'

'Come, I see you trust M. de Monsoreau rather than me. Reject my offer, Monsieur le Baron; throw yourself into the arms of the man who has so well justified your confidence; I have accomplished my task, there is nothing more to be done. Adieu, Seigneur Augustin; adieu, madame; you will see me no more.'

'Oh!' cried Diane, seizing Bussy's hand, ' I ask you on my knees, Monsieur de Bussy, do not desert me.'

As Bussy clasped her suppliant hands, his anger vanished as the snow melts in the warm May sunshine.

'Very well, madame; I accept the sacred mission you have charged me with, and, in three days (for I need that time to rejoin the Prince), you shall receive fresh light on the matter, or I lose my name of Bussy.'

Approaching Diane, he added in low tones :—

'We are allied against Monsoreau; remember that it is not he who has restored your father to you, and do not be unfaithful to me.' Then, pressing the Baron's hand, he rushed from the room.

CHAPTER XXV

HOW BROTHER GORENFLOT WAS RECEIVED AT HIS CONVENT

WE left Chicot admiring the profound sleep and wonderful snoring of Brother Gorenflot. Signing to the innkeeper to carry away the lights, he ordered him not to say a word to the worthy brother of his own going away and return. Maître Bonhomet promising, withdrew, and left the two friends in darkness. Gorenflot was snoring and speaking at the same time, and his words formed a fearful mixture of sacred eloquence and Bacchic maxims. Chicot concluded that, in the darkness, it would prove very difficult to restore the monk's clothes so that he might have no suspicion of the truth. He blew on the embers to light up the scene, and at the noise, Gorenflot stopped snoring to murmur : 'My brothers ! it is the breath of the Lord which inspires me.' Waiting till the monk was asleep again, Chicot began to unloose his coverings, finally succeeding in rolling him in his robe, and drawing the hood over his head. Then, making a pillow of some table-napkins and a sheet of the cloth, he fell asleep beside his companion. The daylight streaming in on his face dispersed the mists from Gorenflot's brain, and managing, with difficulty, to sit up, he contemplated the frightful confusion of the room. Chicot, lying in a position where he could see everything, pretended to snore.

'Full daylight ! Zounds ! it seems I have spent the night here.' Then, collecting his ideas, 'the abbey !' said he, drawing the cord of his robe tighter. 'Anyhow,' he resumed, 'I have had a strange dream; luckily it was a dream.'

His glance fell on Chicot, who, to avoid exciting suspicion, snored with double force. 'How fine he looks, to be a drunkard !' mused Gorenflot. 'How happy he is to sleep like this ! He is not in my shoes ! I shall have trouble enough to escape the dungeon, whatever falsehood I invent. Not the dungeon alone, but bread and water will be the result of this. If only I had some money with which to bribe the doorkeeper !'

Hearing this, Chicot skilfully drew out his purse and hid it under him. Gorenflot, more contrite than ever, approaching his friend, murmured : 'If he were awake, he would not refuse me a crown; his sleep is sacred to me— and I will take his consent for granted.' He felt softly in the sleeping man's jacket pocket, while Chicot, emptying his purse into his hands, replaced it in his trousers pocket.

'Strange, nothing in the pockets. Nothing in his hat ! My friend Chicot never goes out penniless. Ah ! I forgot the trousers.'

Slipping his hand into the pocket, he drew out an empty purse.

'*Mon Dieu !* who will pay the reckoning ?' The question produced such a deep impression on the monk that he rose, and with uncertain but rapid steps crossed the kitchen and fled. As he pursued his way, he conceived one of these splendid falsehoods common among monks in disgrace and late soldiers. In the distance, he saw the gates of the convent and several monks conversing on the door-step.

'They are speaking of me,' said he; 'my absence has created a scandal; I am ruined!' His head turned; he had the foolish idea of running away; then he advanced with head down towards his companions, who hesitated to address him. At last one ventured. 'Poor, dear brother,' said he. Gorenflot, sighing, raised his eyes to heaven.

'The prior awaits you.'

'Immediately on your return, you are to be taken to him.'

More dead than alive, Gorenflot entered the convent. The doorkeeper shut the door upon him. 'Ah! it is you. Come quickly, the Reverend Prior Joseph Toulon is asking for you.'

In the abbot's chamber, Gorenflot lowered his eyes.

'Ah! it is you at last,' said the Abbot; 'what anxiety you have caused us! You feared to enter after last night's scene, I suppose? Ah! dear brother, it was a very imprudent thing you did.'

'Let me explain, father.'

'I understand it perfectly. In a moment of exaltation, your enthusiasm carried you away. I am as good a Catholic as yourself, yet your boldness dismayed me.'

'Was I very bold?'

'More than bold—rash; I cannot help fearing the consequences of this outburst for you and for us. You were aware that more than a hundred laymen listened to your address. It was a good one, I admit, and the applause and approval must have turned your head; but when a procession through the streets is proposed, when you offer to dress in a cuirass and helmet and appeal to good Catholics, it is too much. Now, one means of conciliation remains. That religious enthusiasm is not to your advantage in Paris. I wish you to expend it in the provinces. In remaining here, you risk imprisonment, and even death You escape this danger by submitting to temporary banishment. Go then, quickly, Brother Gorenflot; it is perhaps too late; the archers may have received orders to arrest you.'

'Reverend Father, what do you say?' asked the monk, rolling startled eyes, for, as the prior spoke, he grew more astonished at the proportions which a seemingly venial sin had assumed. 'Have I been denounced, then ?'

'I would wager as much. Go, then; go.'

'It is easy to speak; but how shall I live ?'

'Nothing is simpler. You beg alms for the convent; there is your means of livelihood. Your action, rest assured, will procure you partisans in the provinces, so that you will want for nothing. Go instantly, and don't return before you are told.'

Tenderly embracing Brother Gorenflot, the prior gently, but persistently, pushed him outside. All the community awaited him.

'Adieu,' said one; 'do not forget me in your prayers.'

'Adieu, martyr !' exclaimed another, kissing the end of his girdle; 'blindness still reigns among us, but light will come.'

Gorenflot found himself at the street door, which closed behind him. He looked at this door with an indescribable expression, and left Paris, walking backwards, as if the exterminating angel pointed at him with his flaming sword. He would not speak except to say,—

'The devil take me ! they are all mad, or, if *they* are not, *mon Dieu*, then *I* must be !'

CHAPTER XXVI

HOW GORENFLOT DEPLORED HIS SLEEP-WALKING

HITHERTO Brother Gorenflot had led a contemplative life : that is to say, he went out early when he wanted the cool air, and late when he preferred to bask in the sun. Trusting in God and in the abbey kitchen, he never imagined obtaining more than the worldly extras of the Corne d'Abondance. These extras, being deducted from the alms he received, were subject to the caprice of the faithful. Then there was his friend Chicot, who delighted in good living. But Chicot was an oddity, whom he saw sometimes for three or four consecutive days, and then not for a month or six weeks.

Suddenly thrust out from his convent, Gorenflot felt lost and frightened. However, his first business was to take himself from the unknown danger that threatened him, and he set off at once, passing the Porte Bordelle with a rapid step. Once in the open country, when he saw the early verdure of spring, the sun on the horizon, the solitude right and left of him, and the murmuring town behind, he sat down on the roadside and began a reverie, to which he groaned an accompaniment. He groaned more than ever when nine o'clock came, for that was dinner-hour at the convent. As well try to count the grains of sand on the seashore after a tempestuous day as to reckon up the number of contradictory ideas that came, one after the other, into the head of the hungry Gorenflot. The first was to go back to the convent, to tell the abbot that he infinitely preferred the dungeon to exile; that he would submit to discipline, the whip, the double whip, and the *in pace*, so long as he might enjoy his meals, which he was willing to reduce to five a day. To this idea succeeded that of going to the Corne d'Abondance, asking to see Chicot, pointing out to him how he was placed, and endeavouring to obtain a pension through that generous friend. This plan held his mind for about a quarter of an hour, for he was a shrewd fellow, and the idea was not without merit. At last a plan which, was not wanting in audacity, struck him. He would return by the Porte Saint-Germain or the Tour de Nesle, and continue clandestinely his begging in Paris.

The last project pleased him best; but to carry out his intention he must remain in Paris, and risk meeting at every step archers, sergeants, church officials—a dangerous crowd for a vagabond monk. Again, the treasurer of the convent was far too careful to leave Paris without a begging friar. Gorenflot thus ran the risk of finding himself face to face with a colleague who would possess incontestable superiority over him, inasmuch as he would be exercising his legitimate functions. The very thought made Gorenflot groan.

In the midst of his communings, he perceived far in the distance, under the Porte Bordelle, a horseman, who soon made the dust rise under the hoofs of his mount. He alighted near a house standing about a hundred paces from the spot where Gorenflot sat. He knocked; the door opened, and horse and rider disappeared. Gorenflot noticed this, for he envied the good fortune of the cavalier who had a horse, and therefore could sell it. The next moment the horseman came out again, and hid himself

behind a clump of trees and some stones. Presently the
stranger caught sight of Gorenflot, and pulling himself
together he pretended to walk about with an air of
indifference.

'What a shape, what a figure,' said Gorenflot. 'I seem
to know him—but no, that is impossible.'

At this moment the unknown, who had turned his back
upon Gorenflot, collapsed suddenly, as if his legs had given
way beneath him. He had just heard the thud of horses'
hoofs, and very soon three men, two of whom looked like
lackeys, three good mules, and three great portmanteaus
came slowly from Paris by the Porte Bordelle. The cavalcade passed without seeing the watcher, who, as soon as the
coast was clear, re-entered the house.

'Good,' said Gorenflot; 'unless I am deceived, this is
something to my advantage. My secret is worth six
deniers, and I shall hold out for the price.'

Without waiting, Gorenflot made his way to the house.
Then he remembered the martial bearing of the cavalier,
the long rapier that swung against his calves, and the
terrible eye with which he had glared on the passing
cavalcade.

'I believe I am absolutely wrong,' he said; 'such a man
would never allow himself to be browbeaten.'

Suddenly his face brightened. 'An idea!' he cried,
'and a very ingenious one. I shall say to him, "Sir,
every man has his projects, his desires, his hopes. Give
me something and I shall pray for your success." If the
projects are evil, and I have no doubt on that score, he
doubly needs praying for. As to my share in the matter,
I can submit the question to the first divine I meet; if
he tells me that to pray for an unknown project which may
be evil is not wrong, the responsibility lies with him. If
I don't meet a divine, which is more than possible, I
shan't pray; but by then I shall have breakfasted with
the ill-intentioned man's alms; so it won't matter.'

Having thus decided, Gorenflot flattened himself
against the wall and waited. Five minutes later the
door opened, and horse and rider appeared. Gorenflot
approached.

'Monsieur,' said he, 'if five *paters* and five *aves* for the
success of your plans would be agreeable to you——'

The horseman, turning his head, exclaimed, 'Gorenflot!'

'Monsieur Chicot!' exclaimed the monk.

'Where the deuce are you going, my dear fellow?' asked Chicot.

'I don't know. And you?'

'That's different, I *do* know; I am going straight on.'

'Far?'

'Until I stop. But, since you cannot tell why you are here, I must suspect you are spying on me.'

'Spying on you! Lord preserve us, I saw you lying in wait for the passage of the mules; that's all.'

'You're a fool.'

'Ah, now! behind the stones with your very attentive eyes.'

'Listen, Gorenflot. I want to build a house outside the walls; these stones are mine, and I was making sure they were of good quality.'

'Oh, that's different,' said the monk, who did not believe a single word. 'I must have been deceived.'

'But yourself, my dear fellow; what are you doing outside the walls?'

'Alas! Monsieur Chicot, I am driven out,' answered Gorenflot, with an extraordinary sigh.

'Bah! And for what?'

'Listen, Monsieur Chicot,' said the monk, placing his hand on his heart; 'believe me if you like, but on the faith of a Gorenflot, I don't know.'

'But last night?'

'You know perfectly well what I did last night.'

'That is,' replied Chicot, 'yes, from eight to ten, but not from ten to three.'

'What? From ten to three?'

'Certainly; you were out at ten; you told me you were going to preach a sermon.'

'There must be something true in all this, surely,' muttered Gorenflot.

'So true that you told me part of your sermon. It was very long.'

'It was in three parts.'

'And contained such terrible things against King Henri III., that I should not be astonished if you were prosecuted as a fomenter of disturbance.'

'Monsieur Chicot, did I look awake as I spoke to you?'

'I ought to say, my dear fellow, that you looked very strange, indeed; you stared with a fixedness that frightened me. In fact, you seemed to be talking in your sleep.'

'Well,' replied Gorenflot, 'I am sure I was awake this morning in the Corne d'Abondance, or the very deuce was in it.'

'Why, what was astonishing in that ?'

'Astonishing—when you say I went out at ten o'clock ?'

'Yes; but you came back at three in the morning, and in confirmation, let me say you left the door open, and I felt very cold.'

'So did I,' said Gorenflot; 'I can recollect that.'

'I should say that you were choke-full of pride on your return—a bad thing, particularly in a monk.'

'Proud about what ?'

'About the success of your sermon, about the compliments paid you by the Duc de Guise, the Cardinal, and M. de Mayenne, whom God preserve,' added the Gascon, raising his hat.

'At length everything is clear to me,' said Gorenflot. 'I'm a somnambulist. I've thought so for a long time.'

'That's not natural,' replied Chicot; 'away Beelzebub, *vade retro*, *Satanas*.' And he turned away on his horse.

'Thus you, too, leave me, Monsieur Chicot. *Tu quoque, Brute !* I never could have believed it of you,' and the monk tried desperately to choke back a sob.

Chicot took pity on this terrible despair, and said : 'You spoke of travelling.'

'True; the prior told me to go where I pleased.'

'Where are you going ?'

'I don't know,' Gorenflot answered, raising his hands to heaven. 'For the love of God, Monsieur Chicot, lend me two *écus* to help me on my way.'

'I'll do better than that,' said Chicot; 'I'll take you with me, if you will behave yourself. Do you accept my proposal ?'

Gorenflot looked at Chicot like a man who dared not believe in such luck.

'Do I accept ?' said the monk; 'do I accept ! But what about money?'

Chicot showed his purse, and Gorenflot leaped for joy.

'When shall we dine ?'

'At once.'

'But on what shall I ride ?' asked Gorenflot.

'You have the body of Silenus; you are as drunken as he. Well, complete the resemblance, and ride on an ass.'

'You are my king, Monsieur Chicot. You are my sun. But get a strong ass. And now, where shall we dine ?'

'Here, even here,' replied Chicot. 'Look at that door and read, if you know how to read.'

Following the direction of Chicot's finger, Gorenflot read,—

'*Here bacon, eggs, eel pies, and white wine may be had.*'

'Well said,' cried Chicot; 'and that we may lose no time, get to the table, my dear brother. As for me, I shall serve you by looking for an ass.'

CHAPTER XXVII

HOW BROTHER GORENFLOT TRAVELLED ON AN ASS

CHICOT scoured the neighbourhood, seeking the ass demanded by his companion, and at length found one four years old, and worth twenty pounds. He paid twenty-two, and was blessed for his generosity. When Chicot returned with his prize, Gorenflot, running to the ass, gave him a long crust of bread, which made the animal bray with pleasure.

'Oh ! ho !' cried Gorenflot, 'since he possesses such a fine voice, we will sing together at times. Thanks, friend Chicot, thanks.' And he at once christened the ass Panurge.

Chicot cast a glance at the table and cried, 'Come along; let us set off, my friend, let us set off. We shall lunch at Melun.'

Chicot's voice was sharp, but in the midst of his command he had let slip so sweet a promise that Gorenflot could do nothing but repeat, 'To Melun, to Melun'; and, without wasting time, climbed to the back of the ass from a chair. As to Chicot, he mounted with the ease of a perfect horseman, and at a gentle trot the two riders set off for Melun. When they had travelled about four leagues, they halted for a short space, of which the monk made use to throw himself down and sleep, while Chicot calculated that at ten leagues a day a journey of a hundred and twenty leagues would take twelve days. And really ten leagues a day was all that could reasonably be expected from the combined forces of a monk and an ass. Chicot shook his head.

'It is not possible,' he muttered, as he glanced at Gorenflot. 'It is not possible. If the priestling is determined to
accompany me, he must do at least fifteen leagues a day.'

Chicot jogged the sleeper with his elbow, and when
Gorenflot was awake, told him what he had been thinking.
Gorenflot opened his eyes.

'Are we at Melun?' he asked; 'I'm famishing.'

'No, my dear fellow, not yet, and that's exactly why
I woke you. We really must get there soon. We are
travelling too slowly; yes, hang it all, far too slowly.'

'And is that troubling you, Monsieur Chicot. Are we
not making this journey, you for pleasure and I for the
propagation of the Faith? Well, the slower we go, the
better will the Faith be propagated, and the more highly
will you be amused. So my advice would be to spend
some days at Melun, for I earnestly desire to make a con-
scientious comparison between the eel pies of Melun and
those of other parts of the country. What do you say to
that, Monsieur Chicot?'

'I say,' replied the Gascon, 'that my advice, on the
contrary, is to hurry as quickly as possible, not to lunch
at Melun, and only to sup at Montereau, so that we may
make up for lost time.'

Gorenflot stared as if he hardly understood.

'Come, let us get on!' cried Chicot.

The monk sat up, puffing and groaning.

'Now, then,' continued Chicot, 'if you would prefer to
remain behind and travel at your own sweet will, you are
at liberty to do so.'

'No,' cried Gorenflot, dismayed at this prospect; 'no;
I shall accompany you, Monsieur Chicot. I love you too
well to leave you.'

'Well, into the saddle with you.' And Chicot set off
at a quick pace, followed by the braying ass.

From time to time Chicot cast wary glances all round
him, and, not perceiving what he sought, increased his
speed. Gorenflot permitted these first signs of impatience
to pass without asking the cause, but when he observed
that Chicot continued to act in the same strange manner,
he said, 'What are you looking for, Monsieur Chicot?'

'Nothing,' was the reply. 'I am merely looking to see
where we are going.'

'But we are going to Melun, it seems to me; you yourself have said so; you even——'

'We are not going to Melun, my dear fellow,' replied Chicot, pushing on.

'What! not going?' cried the monk.

'Quicker,' exclaimed the Gascon, increasing still further the speed of his mount.

The donkey followed the horse's example, and Gorenflot was almost choked.

'But—but, Monsieur Chicot,' he cried, as soon as he could speak; 'you described this as a pleasure excursion, though it is no pleasure to me.'

'Come along.'

'But Panurge is resolved to stop.'

'Then adieu!' cried Chicot.

Reviling Chicot's horse from the bottom of his heart, Gorenflot, inspired by the recollection that it bore the purse as well as its master, banged the donkey's sides with his sandals, and compelled it to gallop once more.

'I shall kill my donkey,' groaned Gorenflot.

'Kill him then, and we shall buy a mule.'

Suddenly Chicot, having arrived at the summit of the hill, drew rein; but Gorenflot, a much poorer horseman, continued on his way.

'Stop, you stupid, stop!' cried Chicot, 'or I shall send a bullet after you.'

'What the dickens has got into his head?' asked Gorenflot. And then, in fear of the promised bullet, slipped to the ground and glanced round for Chicot, who was hidden behind a rock, whence he continued to threaten Gorenflot. This caused the monk to understand that there must be some adventure afoot, and, looking in front, he perceived, at a distance of about five hundred paces, three men jogging along on their mules. The first glance satisfied him that they were the three travellers who had come out of Paris that morning by the Porte Bordelle, and whom Chicot, from his hiding-place, had scanned so closely.

When Chicot rejoined Gorenflot, the monk had already begun to lose patience. 'I wish you would explain, dear Monsieur Chicot, the business on which we are engaged. At first we must needs go as fast as we can, and now we stop short in this wretched place,' he complained.

'My dear sir,' answered Chicot, 'I wished to discover if I had been cheated in paying twenty-two pounds for the ass. Now that the experiment is completed, I am more than satisfied.'

The monk was not deceived by this reply, but contented himself by answering, with no attempt to hide his ill humour: 'It doesn't matter! I'm extremely tired and very hungry.'

'Ah,' replied Chicot, tapping the monk on the shoulder, 'I, too, am tired and hungry, and at the first hotel we reach we will have roast pork, one or two chickens, and a jug of the best wine in the cellar.'

'Really,' said Gorenflot, 'is it certain this time?'

'I promise you, my dear fellow.'

Chicot remounted his horse, Gorenflot led the ass by the bridle, and soon the much-desired inn appeared. To Gorenflot's great surprise, however, Chicot ordered the monk to mount the donkey, and make a detour by the left, so as to pass behind the house. But in an instant Gorenflot, whose understanding was making rapid progress, perceived the reason for this curious behaviour. The three mules that Chicot appeared to be following, had stopped before the door.

'So the events of our journey and the regulation of our meals lie at the will of these wretched travellers,' thought Gorenflot. ' 'Tis sad.' And he heaved a deep sigh.

Panurge, on his part, observing the deviation from the straight line, which even an ass knows to be the shortest distance between two points, came to a dead stop, standing stiff on his four legs, as if he meant to take root where he was.

'See,' cried Gorenflot, 'my ass refuses to proceed.'

'Ah! he won't go on,' said Chicot; 'watch, then!' Proceeding to the hedge, he selected a switch about five feet long, as thick as his thumb, at once solid and pliable. Panurge, noting Chicot's manœuvres, and guessing his intention, relaxed his legs and set off.

'He moves! he moves!' cried the monk.

'That's all right,' said Chicot. Travel in the company of an ass and a monk had taught that a stick is not always useless, and he finished cutting his.

CHAPTER XXVIII

HOW GORENFLOT TRADED HIS ASS FOR A MULE AND THE MULE FOR A HORSE

THE troubles of Gorenflot, however, had ended for that day at least. After this detour, they stopped at a rival inn three-quarters of a league farther on. Chicot took a room which overlooked the road, and ordered supper to be served ; but it was plain that eating was only a secondary matter with him. Indeed, he scarcely ate anything, but listened with all his might. This pre-occupation lasted until six o'clock. By that time, as he had neither seen nor heard anything, Chicot abandoned his vigil, and ordered his horse and the monk's ass to be ready at daybreak, and telling the host to see that they had double rations of oats and bran.

At this command, Gorenflot, who had been asleep, heaved a sigh and queried, 'At daybreak ?'

'You ought to be accustomed to getting up early ! Besides, man is made for work.'

'And the monk for rest,' protested the friar; 'the monk is the exception to the man.'

Very early in the morning, had Gorenflot not been asleep, he would have seen Chicot get up, go to the window and place himself behind the curtain, where he could see without being seen. Soon, although thus screened from observation, he stepped back quickly, and had Gorenflot been awake he would have heard the clatter of three mules' hoofs upon the road. Going to the monk, Chicot shook him by the arm till he opened his eyes.

'Can't I have a moment's peace,' grumbled the monk.

'Be sharp,' cried Chicot; 'dress and let us get on the way. Come along; I am going to pay our bill, and in five minutes, if you are not ready, I shall go without you.'

A monk's toilet does not take long, but Gorenflot took six minutes, and when he got down Chicot had vanished. The monk pressed Panurge, who, excited by the double portion of oats and hay, galloped of his own accord, and soon overtook Chicot. The Gascon was standing on his stirrups, and when the monk stood on his, he saw on the

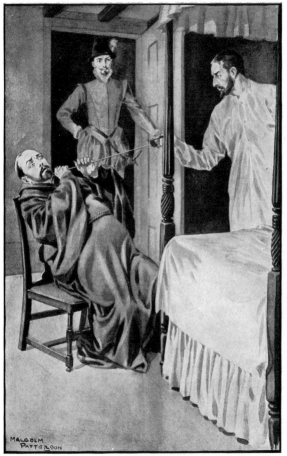

C.J.   Page 204.

'Chicot appeared at the door.'

horizon the three mules and their riders, who were just disappearing behind a hill. The monk sighed, thinking how sad it was that such an influence should settle his destiny. This time, however, Chicot decided not to hurry, and they breakfasted at Montereau.

For two days they proceeded in this manner, but on the second evening Chicot began to lose his lightheartedness. Since midday he had seen no sign of the three travellers; he supped in ill humour and slept badly. Gorenflot ate enough for two, and sang his best songs; Chicot remained impassive. The day had barely dawned when he was on foot shaking his companion. The monk dressed, and they started almost at a gallop. About midday ass and horse were famishing, and Chicot stopped at a tollhouse at a cross-road.

'Have you noticed three travellers, mounted on mules go past this morning?' he asked.

'This morning? No, my lord,' answered the tollkeeper, 'no. Yesterday, early; about seven o'clock.'

'Can you remember what they were like?'

'They looked like a master and two lackeys.'

'It is they,' said Chicot, giving the tollkeeper a crown. Speaking to himself, he continued: 'Yesterday, at seven. They are twelve hours in front. Come along; have courage.'

'Listen, Monsieur Chicot,' said the monk; 'for myself I have courage enough, but I have none for Panurge. And observe what a state your horse is in.'

In truth the poor ass, overdriven for two days, was staggering upon his feet, while the spirited horse was covered with flakes of foam; a hot smoke issued from his nostrils, and the blood seemed ready to spirt from his eyes.

Chicot, after rapidly examining the two animals, exclaimed, 'My horse can't do more, neither can your ass.'

'Well, what is to be done?'

'Leave them here and get them again on our return.'

'But what of us? Are you thinking of continuing the journey on foot?'

'We shall mount on mules, which we shall buy.'

'Good! Go for the mules.'

'Well done; you are certainly improving. See that Bayard and Panurge are properly tended, and I will arrange for the mules.'

Gorenflot accomplished his task, and soon Chicot returned with two mules, upon which they travelled twenty leagues that day, the result being that in the evening, from the door of a smithy, Chicot had the satisfaction of perceiving the three animals he had been following But the sharp eye of the Gascon recognised neither their harness, their master, nor the lackeys, for the mules had been despoiled of their trappings, whilst their master and the lackeys had disappeared. Still more, the animals were being examined by experts: first a horse-dealer, and then a shoeing smith with two Franciscans, who moved the mules about and looked carefully at their teeth, feet, and ears.

A shiver ran through Chicot's frame. 'Go forward,' he said to Gorenflot, 'take the Franciscan apart, and find out whence the mules came, the price paid for them, and who now owns them. Then come back as quickly as possible.'

Gorenflot, infected by his friend's impatience, set off in a hurry, and returned a few minutes later.

'Here is the tale,' said he. 'To begin with, do you know where we are?'

'Yes, confound it! we are on the road to Lyons,' said Chicot; 'that is the only thing it is not important to know.'

'So be it; but at least you desire to learn what has become of the riders.'

'Yes, go ahead.'

'The one who appeared a nobleman proceeded toward Avignon.'

'Alone?'

'With a lackey.'

'And the other lackey?'

'He went toward Lyons.'

'Wonderful! And why did the gentleman go to Avignon? I believe he is making for Rome. But,' continued Chicot, to himself, 'I am asking you questions that you cannot answer.'

'Well, but I can answer them,' replied Gorenflot. 'Ah, now you are astonished. He goes to Avignon because His Holiness Pope Gregory XIII. has sent to Avignon a legate, with plenary powers.'

'Good,' said Chicot, 'I understand. And the mules?'

'As they were tired out they were sold to a horse-dealer, who has resold them to the Franciscans, at fifteen pistoles apiece.'

'How did the men continue their journey?'

'On horses, which they bought from a captain of troopers.'

'My dear Gorenflot, you *are* worth something,' cried Chicot; 'it is only now that I appreciate you.'

Gorenflot tumbled heels over head.

'Now,' continued Chicot, 'finish what you have so well begun. Offer these two mules to the Franciscans for twenty pistoles. They should give you the preference.'

'They shall,' said Gorenflot, 'or I will denounce them to their superior.' And the monk advanced with firm step towards the Franciscans, while Chicot, by a cross street, gained the principal square of the little town.

In a short time he bought two horses for thirty-five pistoles, and was proceeding to bargain for the saddles, when he perceived Gorenflot advancing with a couple of saddles on his head, and the bridles in his hands.

'Oh, ho! What have you there? asked Chicot.

'Why, these are the saddles and bridles of our mules.'

'You have kept them?' asked Chicot, with a broad smile.

'To be sure,' replied the monk.

'And the mules?'

'Ten pistoles each.'

'You certainly are a great man.'

'Just what I am,' said Gorenflot, with modest self-conceit.

They mounted. 'So far so good,' cried Chicot, putting his mount to a gallop. Gorenflot, seeing supper in front of him, followed suit, but instead of holding the mane of his beast with one hand and the tail with the other, as formerly, he seized with both hands the pommel of the saddle, and with this sole support got ahead as fast as even Chicot desired. Their efforts were rewarded, for just before reaching Chalon, Chicot rediscovered Maître David disguised as a lackey, and kept him in sight till they reached Lyons on the eighth day after leaving Paris. Almost at this moment, traversing the opposite road, Bussy, Saint-Luc, and his wife arrived, as we have seen, at the castle of Méridor.

CHAPTER XXIX

AT THE CYGNE DE LA CROIX

MAÎTRE NICOLAS DAVID, still disguised as a lackey, proceeded to the Place des Terreaux, and put up at the chief hostelry in the town, the Cygne de la Croix. Chicot, watching closely, waited until he was sure his enemy had secured accommodation and would not go elsewhere.

'Have you any objections to the inn of the Cygne de la Croix ?' the Gascon asked his travelling companion.

'None in the least,' answered the latter.

'Go there and arrange for a private room; explain that you are expecting your brother, and wait for me at the entrance; I will come at nightfall, and you can show me to the room without our meeting any one I do not wish to see. Choose a room spacious, bright, and as near as possible to that of the traveller who has just arrived; see that it has windows facing the street; do not mention my name, and promise the landlord to pay lavishly.'

Gorenflot executed this commission wonderfully well. At night he led Chicot to the room, explaining that it was next to that of Nicolas David, being separated only by wood and plaster. Chicot asked for the host, who sent word that his new guest must wait a little, as he was attending a traveller who had arrived just before. Chicot guessed this was his friend the lawyer. 'What can they be saying ?' he asked Gorenflot.

'Do you think the landlord and your man are discussing secrets ?'

'Yes, otherwise why should the landlord be so considerate to a lackey ?'

'Ah ! he has changed his clothes, and is now wearing a suit of black.'

'All the more reason the landlord must be in the plot.'

'Shall I try to learn the secret from his wife ?'

'No, go and stroll in the town.' No sooner had Gorenflot gone than Chicot made a hole in the partition, and with his ear applied to this, heard the voices plainly enough; he saw the host distinctly as he talked to Nicolas David, and some words of their conversation reached him. David was boasting of his fidelity to the King, speaking even of a mission with which M. de Morvilliers had entrusted him. The landlord was listening with respect but with indifference, for he answered seldom. Chicot even noticed something like irony in his expression, or in his voice, every time he pronounced the King's name. 'Eh! perhaps our host is a Leaguer? I will find out.'

Presently the door of his own room opened; and the host entered, cap in hand, but with the same jeering expression which had struck Chicot already.

'Sit here, my dear sir, and listen to my story. You saw me with a monk.'

'Yes, monsieur.'

'Silence! say no more—this monk is outlawed.'

'Is he a Huguenot in disguise?'

'Huguenot? I would have you know that he is my relative, and I have no Huguenot relatives. You ought to blush to say these dreadful things.'

'Ah! monsieur, one does sometimes find such cases.'

'Never in my family. This monk is the most bitter enemy to the Huguenots. On that very account he is in disfavour with King Henri, who protects them, as you are aware.'

'Silence,' said the host warningly, and laying his finger on his lips.

'Have you any of the King's servants here?'

'I am afraid so; next door is a traveller——'

'Then we must go at once, my friend, and I, for proscribed——'

'Where will you go?'

'We have some addresses which a friend, Maître la Hurière gave us.'

'You know La Hurière?'

'Silence! do not mention it; we became acquainted on the eve of Saint-Bartholomew.'

'Then your relative and you are holy people; I, too, am acquainted with Hurière. So, you say, monsieur, that your friend——'

'Was rash enough to preach against the Huguenots; his success was enormous, and as His Most Christian Majesty sought to imprison him, I carried him off. M. de Guise offered to protect him, but I feared that might lead to civil war.'

'Then, if you are a friend of M. de Guise, you know this?'

asked the landlord, making a Masonic sign with his hand. Chicot, during the night he had passed in the convent of Sainte-Geneviève had noticed this sign and the answering one. '*Parbleu*,' said he, 'and you this ?' making the second sign.

'Then,' said the innkeeper, with the most complete abandon, 'you are at home here, my house is yours; regard me as a friend.'

'But you were speaking of a man next door there.'

'Yes; but he had better be careful, for, on the least suspicion, he will have to remove, or my name is not Bernouillet. Say one word and I will turn him out.'

'Why ? leave him rather,' Chicot advised. 'Better to have one's enemies near; then one can watch them.'

'You are right,' agreed Bernouillet.

'But what makes you fancy this traveller is our enemy ? I say *our* enemy, because it is certain we are brothers.'

'Because he arrived here dressed as a lackey, and then assumed a lawyer's garb. Now, he is no more a lawyer than a lackey, for, under his cloak, I caught sight of the point of a large rapier. Next, he spoke of the King as nobody speaks of him, and finally confessed that he was on a mission for M. de Morvilliers, who is, as you are aware, a servant of Nebuchadnezzar.'

'Of Herod, as I call him.'

'I see we understand one another.'

'So I say,' concluded Chicot; 'but mind, not a word about my relative or myself.'

'You can trust me. Silence, some one is coming.' Gorenflot appeared at the door.

'Oh ! it is he, worthy man !' cried the host, making the sign of the Leaguers to the monk. Gorenflot was struck with surprise and fear.

'Answer, brother,' exclaimed Chicot. 'Our host knows everything; he belongs to it.'

'To what ?'

'To the Holy Union,' said Bernouillet, lowering his tones.

'You see it is quite safe to answer.' Gorenflot answered the sign to the innkeeper's joy. 'But I was promised sherry,' said the monk, hastening to change the conversation.

'Sherry, Malaga, Abeaute; all the wines in my cellar are at your disposal, brother.' Gorenflot glanced from the host to Chicot, and from Chicot up into the sky. He understood nothing of what had happened, and it was evident that he recognised in his humility that his good fortune far exceeded his merits. For three days, then, Gorenflot drank heavily. Meanwhile Chicot kept his room and watched Nicolas David. The host, imagining Chicot's seclusion was due to his fear of the supposed Royalist, exerted himself to annoy the latter in every way, but apparently to no effect. Nicolas David, having arranged to meet Pierre de Gondy at the Cygne de la Croix, was unwilling to leave it lest he should miss him. He affected not to notice his host's impertinences, but when left alone he gave vent to outbursts of anger, much to Chicot's amusement. As the sixth day of his arrival at the inn approached, Nicolas David fell ill. The host insisted on his departure before his illness became serious : the lawyer begged to remain till the next day, declaring he would soon be better. The next day he was much worse.

The host announced the news to his friend the Leaguer.

'Bah !' said Chicot, 'you think he is going to die ?'

'He has a dreadful fever, dear brother; he tried to strangle me and to beat my servants; the doctors cannot understand it.'

'How is he looking ?'

'Pale, agitated, dishevelled, crying like one possessed.'

'What does he cry ?'

'"Take care of the King. Evil is intended to the King." Then he says he is waiting for a man from Avignon, whom he wishes to see before he dies. It would be queer if he died, would it not ?'

'Very queer; but I don't want him to die before the man from Avignon arrives.'

'Why ? the sooner he dies, the sooner we'll be rid of him.'

'Yes; but I do not hate him so much as to wish him to lose both soul and body; and since this man comes to confess him——'

'Eh ! you know this is merely some fancy of his sick brain, and really he expects nobody.'

'Who can say ?'

'It is certain at least that you are a good Christian.'

'Return good for evil, is the divine law,' Chicot said solemnly, and the landlord withdrew filled with wonder.

CHAPTER XXX

THE MONK CONFESSES THE LAWYER

At last the day arrived which was to rid the innkeeper of his guest. Maître Bernouillet rushed into Chicot's room laughing so immoderately that the latter had to wait some time before discovering the cause of this mirth.

'He is dying; he is expiring!' cried the charitable innkeeper.

'And that makes you laugh like this?'

'Yes; the trick is so good. Confess that you played it, monsieur.'

'I play a trick on an invalid. What is it? What has happened to him?'

'You remember how anxiously he has waited for his messenger from Avignon. He has come.'

'What is he like?'

'Small, thin, and high coloured.'

'That is he!' said Chicot, forgetting himself.

'Ah! You must have sent him, since you recognise him.'

'The messenger has arrived! tell me about it, dear Bernouillet.'

'An hour ago, a tall horse and a small man stopped before the door. "Is Maître Nicolas here?" asked the rider. "Yes, monsieur," I replied. "Tell him the person he expects from Avignon has come." "Willingly, but I must warn you that Maître Nicolas is dying of a malignant fever." "Then I must ask you to be quick, for I must see him." So I led the visitor to the dying man's room.'

'Is he there?' asked Chicot, motioning towards the room.

'Yes, it is funny, isn't it? What a pity one cannot hear them!'

'What hinders you from listening at the door?'

'You are right,' said the host, rushing away. Chicot immediately moved to the hole. Pierre de Gondy was seated at the sick man's bedside, and they spoke so low that Chicot could not hear a word of their conversation. In five minutes Pierre de Gondy rose, said farewell, and left. Chicot, running to the window, saw a lackey holding the tall horse; the ambassador from M. de Guise appeared, mounted and turned into the street leading to Paris.

'*Mordieu!*' said Chicot, 'if only he does not carry off the pedigree; in any case, I will overtake him though I kill ten horses in the chase. But no, these lawyers are cunning blades, ours especially, and I suspect—— I wonder where that rogue Gorenflot can be,' continued Chicot, no doubt linking this idea to some other in his mind. Just then the host entered. 'He has gone,' said he.

'And how is the patient?'

'He fainted after the meeting.'

'He is still in his room?'

'The deuce! He will leave it only to be carried to the cemetery.'

'Good; go, and send my brother to me as soon as he arrives.'

Chicot was uncertain whether to follow Gondy, or to enter David's room; if the lawyer was as ill as the innkeeper described, he had probably entrusted his despatches to Gondy. Chicot strode about like a madman, seeking to find a clear idea amid the confusion in his brain. Suddenly a voice sounded from the stair; it was the monk's. Gorenflot, propelled by the host, mounted the steps, singing in a thick voice. 'Silence, drunkard,' cried Chicot, opening the door and leading the monk to a chair. 'Now, let us talk seriously; you forget the calls of your profession; you are wallowing in debauchery and drunkenness; your robe is torn; you have been fighting, you have mud up to your knees; if this continues, I will abandon you. What a time you choose for such behaviour? when our neighbour is dying.'

'It is true,' said Gorenflot, with a deeply contrite air.

'Come, are you a Christian or not?'

'I a Christian! by the Pope's crown I am,' cried Gorenflot, rising and singing loudly.

'That will do,' said Chicot, 'if you are a Christian, do not leave your brother to die without confession.'

'That is true; where is my brother, and whom must I confess?'

'Our unhappy neighbour who is dying.'

'Do you think I am sufficiently prepared, Monsieur Chicot?' asked the monk timidly.

'Yes, I never saw you so full of unction. But it is not

only your duties, you must remember; you must also do my will. If you execute my wishes faithfully, I will let you drink or eat one hundred pistoles' worth at the Corne d'Abondance; you hear that? if you confess this dying man.'

'How must I confess him?'

'You will speak in the name of God and the King; you must, by your eloquence, force this man to hand you the papers that have been brought to him from Avignon.'

'And if he refuses?'

'You will refuse him absolution, and will anathematise him.'

'Or take them from him by force.'

'Agreed; but are you sober enough to follow my instructions?'

'You will see.' Gorenflot passed his hand across his face to efface the outer traces of drunkenness; his eyes became calm though dazed; his demeanour became sober. Then he advanced towards the door solemnly.

'A moment,' said Chicot; 'when he gives you the papers, clasp them in one hand and knock on the wall with the other.'

'And if he refuses?'

'Knock in any case.'

Ten minutes later, Chicot, hearing the floor creak, knew that Gorenflot had entered their neighbour's apartment, and soon saw him appear within his circle of vision. The lawyer, getting up in bed, watched the strange apparition.

'Good day, brother,' began Gorenflot.

'What have you come for, father?' murmured the sick man in a feeble voice.

'I am a monk; knowing you are in danger, I come to speak of your soul.'

'I thank you; but your care is useless. I am a little better, and have just confessed to a worthy priest from Avignon.'

Gorenflot shook his head. 'What! that was no priest! I know him,' speaking with such conviction that the lawyer became uneasy; 'now, since you are not better, and this man is no priest, you must confess.'

'I am ready to confess, but it must be to whom I please.'

'You have no time to send for another priest, my son, and since I am here——'

'Not have time? I assure you, father, I feel much stronger.'

'It is the last flicker of the lamp before going out. Now,' continued the monk, sitting near the bed, 'tell me your intrigues, your plottings, your scheming.'

'My intrigues, my plots, my scheming!' repeated Nicolas David, recoiling before this peculiar monk with whom he was unacquainted, yet who seemed to know him so well.

'Yes,' replied Gorenflot, 'when you have told me all, you shall give me the papers, and God may perhaps permit me to grant you absolution.'

'What papers?' cried the sick man.

'The papers that this supposed priest has brought you from Avignon.'

'Who told you he brought me papers?' asked the lawyer, getting partly out of bed. Gorenflot decided the time had come for vigorous action.

'My informant knows what he says; come, the papers or no absolution.'

'I laugh at your absolution, scoundrel,' cried David, leaping from bed and flying at Gorenflot's throat. Brother Gorenflot was robust, but he was, unfortunately, at the stage of reaction when drunkenness acts on the nervous system and paralyses it. Collecting all his strength, he could only rise in his chair, seize the lawyer by the shirt, and push him violently from him, so violently that the latter rolled into the middle of the room. Rising in a fury, and drawing his sword, he presented the point at the monk's neck. 'It is your turn to confess or to die,' said he. Gorenflot, completely sobered at the touch of cold steel, realised the gravity of the situation.

'Your name?' asked the lawyer.

'Brother Gorenflot.'

'You are a real monk, then?'

'Yes.'

'Why are you at Lyons?'

'Because I am exiled.'

'What led you to this hotel?'

'Chance.'

'Why have you been spying on me?'

'I have not been spying on you.'

'How did you know I had received papers?'

'Because I was told so.'

'Who told you ?'

'The one who sent me to you.'

'Who sent you to me ?'

'I cannot tell you.'

'You will tell me, however, or I will kill you.'

The monk cried out; a drop of blood appeared at the point of the lawyer's sword.

'His name ? The person who sent you ?'

'It was——' Gorenflot still hesitated; he would have to betray a friend.

'Finish your sentence,' said the lawyer, knocking him with his foot.

'It was Chicot.'

'The King's jester ? And where is he ?'

'Here I am !' said a voice, and Chicot appeared at the door, pale and grave, with his naked sword in his hand.

CHAPTER XXXI

THE DEATH OF NICOLAS DAVID

MAÎTRE NICOLAS DAVID, recognising his mortal enemy, could not restrain a movement of terror, and Gorenflot seized the opportunity of getting to a distance from the lawyer's sword. 'Help, good friend,' he cried, 'I am being throttled.'

'Ah ! dear Monsieur David, I am delighted to meet you,' said Chicot, and, turning to the monk, 'My good Gorenflot,' he added, 'since monsieur is now so well that he does not require a confessor, he will deal with a gentleman. Oblige me by standing on guard on the landing and preventing any one from interrupting my little talk with monsieur.' Gorenflot very carefully, and keeping close to the walls, reached the door, and rushed out. Closing the door behind him, Chicot drew the bolt.

'Dress yourself, monsieur,' said he, 'I have no wish to take any advantage. I know you are a splendid fencer, and handle the sword like Leclerc himself; but it is all one to me.'

David laughed.

'It is a good joke,' said he.

'Yes, it seems so to me, and will seem better to you

presently. Can you guess what I have come for, Maître Nicolas ?'

'The remainder of the blows I owed you, in the name of the Duc de Mayenne, the day you so lightly jumped through a window.'

'No, monsieur; I remember the number, and will return them to the person who had me thrashed. I am seeking a certain pedigree which M. Pierre de Gondy gave you a little ago. It is that of MM. de Guise, who descend, as you are aware, from Charlemagne in direct line.'

'Ah! so you are a spy, monsieur; I thought you only a jester ?'

'Dear monsieur, I will be both, if you wish : a spy to get you hanged, a jester to laugh at it.'

'How will you manage that ?'

'Oh! that will be very simple : I will tell the truth. I must explain, dear Monsieur David, that I was present last month at the conference held in the convent of Sainte-Geneviève, between their Highnesses MM. de Guise and Madame de Montpensier. I was in the confessional opposite yours; it is very uncomfortable, is it not ? I heard the speeches of M. de Monsoreau, of La Hurière, and of a certain monk whose name I have forgotten. I watched the coronation of M. d'Anjou, which was less amusing; but the little play was really funny; they acted ''The Pedigree of MM. de Lorraine,'' revised, augmented and corrected by Maître Nicolas David. It was remarkably ingenious, especially the passage about the Salic law. Only it is a great misfortune to be so clever : one gets hanged; so, feeling a tender interest in such an ingenious person, I said to myself, how can I let this brave M. David be hanged, this pleasant fencing master, a lawyer of foremost ability, one of my good friends—in short, when I can not only save him but make his fortune; no that will never do. Hearing you speak of travelling, I resolved to travel with you : that is, behind you. You left by the Porte Bordelle. Since then I have followed you—losing, overtaking you; at last we arrived at Lyons; I say *we*, for an hour after you I was installed in the same hotel, in the adjoining room, where I made a small hole through which I could watch you as much as I wished. Then you fell ill; the host wished to turn you out; you had arranged to meet M. de Gondy at the Cygne de la Croix; you were afraid he would not find you, or at least

not so quickly, elsewhere. I was only half deceived by it;
yet, as you might be really ill, I sent a monk to excite you
to repentance, but you, hardened sinner, endeavoured to
cut his throat with your rapier. Then, I came and said,
"Come, we are old friends, let us arrange the thing together;" now that you know all, will you settle the
affair with me ?'

'In what manner ?'

'Just as if you had really been ill, and my friend Gorenflot had confessed you, and obtained the papers. Then
I would have pardoned you. Not wishing to be harder on
the living than the dead, I say, Monsieur David, you are
an accomplished man in fencing, horsemanship, and
chicanery. It would be a pity that a man like you should
suddenly quit the world. Well ! dear Monsieur David,
make no more conspiracies, break with the Guises, trust
yourself to me, give me your papers, and on my honour
as a gentleman I will make your peace with the
King.'

'And if I refuse ?' asked Nicolas David.

'Ah ! that is another affair. I shall kill you ! Do you
still find it amusing, dear Monsieur David ?'

'More and more so,' answered the lawyer, caressing his
sword.

'If you surrender them, all will be forgotten; I hate you
—true; but I hate M. de Mayenne more; give me something with which I can destroy him, and I save you.
I will tell you something else; I love the King; simpleton,
corrupted as he is, he granted me protection against your
butcher de Mayenne. I wish him to reign in peace, my
poor King Henri, which is impossible with Mayenne, and
the pedigrees of Nicolas David. If you will give up the
pedigree, I will keep your name out of the affair, and
make your fortune.'

During this long exposition of his ideas, Chicot had
observed David intelligently, but he had not seen the
angry glare in his eyes soften, nor one good thought
lighten his gloomy expression, nor one kindly instinct
slacken the grasp on his sword.

'So, all this is but wasted eloquence. There is one way
left for me to punish you and to rid the earth of a man,
believing no longer in honesty or humanity. I will have
you hanged. Farewell,' and Chicot stepped backwards
towards the door. The lawyer rushed forward. 'You

think I will let you go ?' he cried; 'no, my fine spy, when one threatens Nicolas David, one dies ! When one behaves as you have done, one dies !'

'You put me perfectly at my ease,' answered Chicot calmly; 'I only hesitated because I am sure to kill you. Come, hand over the papers or I will cut your throat as you wished to do for my friend Gorenflot.'

Hardly had Chicot finished than David, with a wild laugh, rushed on him. The two adversaries were nearly the same height. Chicot, practising arms almost every day with the King, had become one of the best swordsmen in the kingdom, and Nicolas David discovered this as he continually met his adversary's weapon. He fell back a step. 'Ah ! you begin to understand !' said Chicot; 'once more, the papers.' For answer, David threw himself on the Gascon, and a second fight began, longer and keener than the first, finishing in the lawyer's retreat. Chicot then advanced, parried first, and, entangling his opponent's sword, thrust at him in the spot he had indicated, burying half of his rapier in his throat. David fell, spitting blood, and Chicot drew back a step. Wounded to death, the serpent can turn and bite. But David tried to drag himself to the bed, as though to defend his secret. 'Ah !' said Chicot, 'I was ignorant where you had hidden your papers, and you are showing me.' Whilst David rolled in a death-agony, he ran to the bed, drew down the mattress, and found a little roll of parchment. Just as he was unrolling it, David rose in a rage, then falling back, breathed his last. Chicot, rolling up the parchment, put it in his pocket, placed the lawyer's body on the bed, and called Gorenflot, who entered.

'How pale you are !' said the monk.

'Yes, the last moments of this poor man caused me some emotion.'

'He is dead, then ? He was so well a little ago.'

'Too well. He wished to eat things which are difficult to digest, and like Anacréon, he died through swallowing the wrong way.'

'Oh ! the rascal wished to strangle me, a churchman ! That has brought him ill luck.'

'You are a Christian, pardon him; light tapers and repeat some prayers beside his body.'

'Why ?' (That was Gorenflot's favourite word, you will remember.)

'Why ? That you may not be taken to prison as a murderer.'

'I, a murderer ! He wished to strangle me.'

'Yes, *mon Dieu !* As he could not, rage seized him, and he burst a blood vessel. You see, Gorenflot, you are the cause of his death. An innocent cause; but until your innocence is recognised you might be badly treated.'

'I believe you are right, Monsieur Chicot. What must I do ?'

'Install yourself here, recite all the prayers you know, and, when night comes, leave the hotel quietly. You know the farrier's place at the corner of the street ? Find your horse there; mount it, and at Villeneuve-le-Roi sell your horse and take Panurge again.'

'How can I exist till then ?'

'Here,' said Chicot, giving the monk a handful of crowns.

'Generous man ! let me stay with you at Lyons.'

'Stupid, I am leaving here, and so quickly that I do not invite you to come with me,' said Chicot, putting the monk near the bed, and descending to find the host.

'Maître Bernouillet,' said he, 'a great event has happened in your house. That enraged royalist, despiser of religion companion of the Huguenots, received this morning a messenger from Rome. Well ! our Holy Father the Pope sent him direct to the conspirator. Mount to his room, raise the coverlet, look at his neck, and you will see for what purpose the messenger was sent.'

'You terrify me.'

'The Pope has done you a great honour, to accomplish this act of justice in your house.' Chicot slipped ten crowns into the host's hand, and, reaching the stable, ordered his horses. The host meanwhile had climbed the stair to find Gorenflot praying. He approached the bed and drawing down the coverlet perceived the wound, still red.

'So perish all enemies of the holy religion,' said he. 'Amen !' answered the monk. These stirring events occurred almost at the same time as Bussy was restoring Diane de Méridor to the arms of the old Baron.

CHAPTER XXXII

THE PROMISE OF THE DUC D'ANJOU

THE last days of April had arrived. The great cathedral of Chartres was hung with white, whilst bunches of foliage were wreathed round the pillars. The King, barefooted, stood in the nave, looking to see if all his courtiers and friends were assembled. The religious ceremony, held for the purpose of praying for an heir to the throne of France, was nearly over; the two chemises of Notre-Dame, supposed to have miraculous power, had been taken from their gold shrines; the people crowded forward and bowed their heads when, in the midst of the general silence, Henri, hearing a strange noise like a stifled burst of laughter, turned round from force of habit to look for Chicot. Chicot, however, was absent, and the sound had come from a horseman with clothes and boots bespattered with mud, who stood in the midst of the courtiers dressed in their long penitents' robes, and all barefoot. Henri, annoyed at his arriving so late and making so much noise, glanced at him reproachfully. The new-comer, appearing not to notice the rebuke, knelt beside the velvet chair where the Duc d'Anjou sat, absorbed in thought. The latter turned round sharply, crying 'Bussy!'

'Good-morning, monseigneur.'

'But you are mad surely to leave wherever you were to come to Chartres.'

'Monseigneur, it is because I must speak to you?'

'Why did you not come sooner?'

'It was impossible.'

'What has happened in the three weeks since you disappeared?'

'That is precisely what I must tell you.'

'You must wait till we leave church. Here's the end; have patience, and we will soon return to my hotel.'

The King passed over his fine linen shirt the coarse chemise of Notre-Dame, the Queen doing likewise with the other. Then they knelt, praying earnestly, while the bystanders prostrated themselves, beating the ground.

After this the King, rising, took off the holy tunic, and bowing to the Archbishop and the Queen, advanced to the door of the cathedral. Recognising Bussy, he stopped. 'Ah! monsieur,' said he, 'it seems our devotions are not to your taste; you stick to your gold and silk, whilst the King wears drugget and serge?'

'Your Majesty,' answered Bussy, with dignity, 'nobody takes your Majesty's service more seriously than I do, even among those whose robes are humblest, whose feet are most torn; but I have had a long, tiring journey, and have only just heard of your Majesty's departure for Chartres. To rejoin your Majesty I have ridden twenty-two leagues in five hours: that is why I have not changed my dress.'

The King appeared satisfied with this answer, but noticing his friends shrug their shoulders at Bussy's words, he feared to offend them by being gracious to his brother's follower. So he passed on, and Bussy let him pass without emotion. The Duc took leave of his brother, who kindly allowed him to return to Paris when he chose, and accompanied by Bussy he returned to his hotel.

'Come,' said he, 'relate your adventures; I feared you were dead, and many people breathed freely for the first time since you could handle a sword; but enough of this; you left me to follow my fair stranger! Who was she and what may I expect?'

'You must reap what you have sown, monseigneur—much shame!'

'I beg your pardon?' said the Duc, more astonished at the strange words than at Bussy's cavalier tone.

'It is useless for me to repeat.'

'Who is this woman?'

'I thought Monsoreau had recognised her.'

'It was she, then?'

'Yes, monseigneur.'

'You saw her? she spoke to you?'

'Yes; only ghosts do not speak. Monseigneur, though you drove a young girl of noble race to ruin, she has escaped; but you are not absolved yet, for she has found misfortune greater than death. A man saved her honour and her life; but she has paid so dear for them that one regrets his services. Monseigneur, Mademoiselle de Méridor, to escape from M. le Duc d'Anjou, threw herself into the arms of a man whom she loathes.'

'What do you say?'

'I say that Diane de Méridor is called to-day Madame de Monsoreau.'

At these words, the Duc's pale face was suffused with red.

'Can this be true?' he cried.

'*Pardieu!* since I say it.'

'That is not what I mean; I do not suspect your loyalty, Bussy; I am amazed that one of my followers should dare to come between me and a woman I was honouring with my love. You know, I do not justify myself. I beg you to judge M. de Monsoreau, and advise me whether he is a traitor towards me, whose intentions he knew.'

'And the intentions of your Highness were?'

'To make Diane love me, but not to use violence.'

'Those were your intentions?' asked Bussy, smiling ironically.

'Which I kept to the last moment, although M. de Monsoreau fought against them with all the logic he was capable of.'

'Monseigneur! this man urged you to dishonour Diane? By his counsel?'

'By his letters. Would you like to see one? Wait a second,' and the Duc drew out from a little chest a letter which he handed to Bussy. The latter, taking it with trembling hands, read :—

'MONSEIGNEUR,—Your Highness may be reassured : the affair will be managed without risks, for the young person leaves to-night to spend a week with an aunt in the Château de Lude; I take it on myself, and you need have no uneasiness. As for the maiden's scruples, believe me they will vanish when she is in your Highness's presence; meanwhile, I act; and to-night she will be at the Château de Beaugé.

'Your Highness's most respectful servant,
'BRYAN DE MONSOREAU.'

'Well, what do you say about it, Bussy?' asked the Prince when Bussy had read the letter twice.'

'I say that you are well served, monseigneur.'

'I am betrayed, rather.'

'True! I forgot the sequel.'

'How would you act in my place? First, what has he done?'

'Induced the girl's father to believe you were seeking her dishonour. Offering himself as a saviour, he went to the Château de Beaugé with a letter from the Baron de Méridor, carried off the prisoner in a boat, shut her up in the house you know, and drove her, by sheer terror, to become his wife.'

'And that is not infamous disloyalty? Ah, Bussy! you shall see how I avenge myself!'

'No, monseigneur, princes do not avenge themselves; they punish. You will reproach this Monsoreau with his infamy, and punish him.'

'How?'

'By restoring Mademoiselle de Méridor to happiness and to liberty.'

'Explain yourself.'

'Nothing is simpler; the marriage, being forced, is null. Have this marriage annulled and you will have acted, monseigneur, as a worthy gentleman and a noble Prince.'

'Ah!' said the Prince suspiciously, 'what ardour! this interests you, Bussy?'

'Not in the least; I do not wish it said that Louis de Clermont serves a perfidious prince, and a man without honour.'

'You will see. How can this marriage be dissolved?'

'By getting the father to act.'

'But he is in the heart of Anjou.'

'He is here, monseigneur, in Paris; I mean, beside his daughter. Tell him he can count on you; that, instead of seeing in your Highness an enemy, he sees a protector, and, instead of cursing your name, he will adore you.'

'When can I see him?'

'On your return to Paris. It is agreed, monseigneur?'

'Yes.'

'When do you start?'

'To-night; will you await me?'

'No, I hasten in front. Where shall I find your Highness?'

'At the King's levée, to-morrow, towards midday.'

'I shall be there; farewell, monseigneur.'

Losing no time, Bussy returned to Paris in five hours, his heart filled with love and joy, to console the Baron, to whom he had promised assistance, and Diane, to whom he was bearing the half of her life.

CHAPTER XXXIII

ALL was quiet at the Louvre, for it was only eleven o'clock, and the King, tired with his pilgrimage, was still resting. Two men arrived at the same time at the principal entrance of the Palace, having come from opposite directions.

'Monsieur de Chicot,' exclaimed the younger one, bowing politely, 'how are you this morning ?'

'Ah ! it's the Seigneur de Bussy. I am wonderfully well, monsieur,' answered Chicot.

'You have come to see the King's levée, monsieur,' asked Bussy.

'And you too, I presume ?'

'No. I come to pay my respects to the Duc d'Anjou. Monsieur, will you be good enough to do me a service ? You are privileged to enter the Louvre; will you kindly inform the Duc that I await him.'

'Why not enter with me, monsieur ?'

'I fear the King. Up to now he has not smiled very graciously upon me.'

'That will soon change, be assured. Come, courage.' They both entered, one going towards the Duc's apartments, the other toward the King's. Henri had just awakened : already his chicken broth, spiced wine, and meat pâtés were served, when Chicot entering, began to eat and drink before saying 'Good-morning.'

'The deuce ! It's that rascal Chicot; my unhappiness has returned,' cried the King, delighted, yet feigning anger; 'I have been quiet enough, though, for three weeks.'

'Bah ! you are always complaining. What have you done in my absence, my little Henriquet ? Has this fair kingdom been ruled rather curiously ? Have you hanged any of these curled gentlemen ? Is there any money in your coffers or with the Jews?' asked Chicot, finishing the pâtés. The King laughed as usual.

'Come,' said he, 'what have you done during your long absence ?'

'I have thought out a little procession in three acts.

First, penitents, tearing their hair and striking one another, march from the Louvre to Montmartre; second, the same penitents, stripped to the waist, beating one another, descend from Montmartre to the Abbey of Sainte-Geneviève; third, the same penitents, naked, lacerating one another, return from Sainte-Geneviève to the Louvre.'

'But what became of you ? I searched the worst places of Paris, fancying one of your wicked friends had carried you off. I was wrong ?'

'Yes, quite wrong, as usual.'

'We shall discover you have been doing penance !'

'Exactly. I was trying the religious life, but have given it up. I have had enough of monks.' Just then M. de Monsoreau entered, bowing humbly.

'It is you, Monsieur the First Huntsman. When will you arrange another fine hunt for us ?'

'When your Majesty pleases. We have many wild boars at Saint-Germain-en-Laye.'

'It is a dangerous hunt, a boar-hunt. King Charles IX., I remember, was nearly killed at one; the boar spears are hard, too, and blister our little hands, don't they, my son?' said Chicot. M. de Monsoreau gave the latter a sidelong glance. 'Hallo,' said the Gascon to Henri; 'not long ago your First Huntsman evidently met a wolf, because, like the clouds of Aristophanes, he has retained its face, the eye especially; it is striking.'

M. de Monsoreau, paling, turned to Chicot. 'Monsieur Chicot,' said he, 'having rarely lived at court, I am little accustomed to buffoonery, and I warn you that, before my King, I do not care to be humiliated, especially when my services are in question.'

'Come, let us talk of other matters, gentlemen,' interposed Henri, foreseeing a quarrel. Presently M. de Monsoreau whispered to Chicot, 'Monsieur, would you kindly wait for me at the window?'

'With the greatest pleasure, monsieur.'

'Then, let us withdraw.'

'To the depths of a wood, if it suits you, monsieur.'

'Enough of joking; it is useless, now there is no one to laugh,' said Monsoreau, rejoining the jester at the window-recess. 'We are face to face, and should speak the truth; a gentleman forbids you to laugh at him; he invites you to reflect before arranging interviews in woods, for these

woods grow a collection of sticks worthy to succeed those
with which M. de Mayenne had you so rudely beaten.'

'Ah ! monsieur,' said Chicot, outwardly calm, but with
dark eyes flashing, 'You remind me of my debt to M. de
Mayenne; would you like me to become your debtor
also ?'

'It seems you are forgetting your principal creditor,
Maître Nicolas David.'

'Oh ! you are wrong. I owe him nothing now. He is
paid.'

A third person came to join in the conversation. It
was Bussy. 'Monsieur,' said he, addressing the Comte,
'I have the honour to tell you that M. le Duc d'Anjou
wishes to speak to you.' Monsoreau looked at the speaker
as if to penetrate to the depths of his soul, but he stopped
at the surface, Bussy's eyes and smile were so full of
serenity.

'Do you accompany me, monsieur ?' asked the First
Huntsman.

'No, monsieur, I hasten to inform His Highness that
you are obeying his orders, whilst you take leave of the
King.' Bussy returned as he had come, gliding among
the courtiers. The Duc d'Anjou was sitting re-reading
the letter we have already mentioned. Hearing a noise,
he thought it was Monsoreau, and hid the letter. Bussy
appeared.

'Here he is, monseigneur.'

'He suspects nothing ?'

'Though he did, is he not your creature ? Brought
from obscurity by you, can you not drop him into obscurity again ? Does he appear to you less guilty than
he was yesterday?'

'A hundred times more so; his crimes grow bigger
when one reflects upon them.'

'Moreover, all comes to this : he carried off, treacherously, a noble young girl, and married her by fraudulent
means unworthy of a gentleman; either he will ask that
this marriage be dissolved, or you will ask for him. I have
your word in the name of the father and the young
girl?'

'You have.'

'Think how anxiously they await the result of this
interview.'

'The girl shall be free, Bussy; I pledge my word.'

'If you do this, you will be truly a great Prince, monseigneur,' taking the Duc's hand, which had signed so many false promises, and kissing it respectfully. At that moment steps were heard in the vestibule.

'Let M. de Monsoreau enter,' cried François, with a severity which seemed to Bussy of good augury. The young nobleman could not help glancing with a certain irony at Monsoreau; the latter received his glance with a stony stare which served to conceal his feelings. Bussy waited in the corridor amid a crowd of noblemen, repressing the terrible agony he was experiencing. Suddenly the Prince's loud voice was heard, seemingly commanding; but to this outburst no other succeeded, and Bussy felt uneasy. Presently the door opened, and gay voices were heard issuing from the room. The voices approached, Monsoreau came out bowing. The Duc showed him to the threshold, saying, 'Farewell! my friend. It is settled.'

'So, monseigneur, that is your Highness's advice. Publicity is best at present.'

'Yes, all this mystery is but child's play.'

'Then, this evening, I can present her to the King.'

'Proceed without fear; I will have everything prepared.'

'Gentlemen,' said Monsoreau, 'allow me to announce some news. Monseigneur permits me to make public my marriage with Mademoiselle de Méridor, who has been my wife for over a month, and under his auspices I shall present her at court this evening.'

Bussy advanced towards the Duc, but the latter, anticipating him, drew the curtain, and shutting the door, locked it. Bussy felt the blood rush to his temples and his heart; mechanically he drew his dagger half out of its sheath; but love, which had driven him to this violence, paralysed his rage; bitter, deep sorrow stifled his anger; he understood that if he remained there, he would afford people the spectacle of his mad grief; gaining the secret stair, he descended into the courtyard, and galloped to the Rue Saint-Antoine. The Baron and Diane were awaiting the promised answer; they saw him approach, pale, his face discomposed, his eyes bloodshot. 'Madame,' he exclaimed, 'despise me, hate me; I thought I was of some consequence in the world, and I am only an atom. Madame, you are indeed the wife of M. de Monsoreau, his legitimate wife, to be presented to-night. But I am a poor fool, a wretched madman; or rather, yes, as you said,

Baron, M. le Duc d'Anjou is a coward and an infamous being.'

Leaving the father and daughter thunderstruck, Bussy, mad with sorrow, intoxicated with rage, retired, rushed down the steps, and rode off, spurring his horse, loosening the reins, without knowing whither he was riding, and pressing his clenched hand to his throbbing heart.

CHAPTER XXXIV.

THE INTERVIEW

WE must now explain this sudden change of action on the part of the Duc d'Anjou towards Bussy. The Duc, on receiving M. de Monsoreau after his follower's exhortations, was in a mood most favourable to the carrying out of the latter's projects. His easily aroused passions seethed in a heart wounded in its dominating emotions : his wounded self-love, and the fear of an outbreak with which Bussy threatened him, further increased the Duc's anger. M. d'Alençon, therefore, received the First Huntsman with a stern countenance.

'Your Highness summoned me ?' said Monsoreau, very calm, and glancing at the tapestry as though seeking to discover from the room its owner's projects.

'Fear nothing, monsieur, there is no one here; we can talk freely and, above all, frankly. You are a good servant, and are attached to my person ?'

'I believe so.'

'*I* am *sure* of it; many times you have warned me of plots; you have forwarded my schemes, often forgetting your own interests, exposing your life. More recently in this unfortunate adventure——'

'Which one, monseigneur ?'

'The carrying off of Mademoiselle de Méridor, poor young girl !'

'Alas !' murmured Monsoreau, in such a manner that his reply was not seriously applicable to the sense of François's words.

'You pity her, don't you ?' asked the latter.

'Would you not pity her, your Highness ?'

'I; you know how I regretted that evil fancy ! It has

taken all my friendship to make me forget that; without you, I should not have carried her off.' Monsoreau felt this blow.

'Monseigneur,' he replied, 'you have no more caused her death than I have; it is a misfortune, such as may happen any day.'

'And besides,' added the Duc, looking straight at Monsoreau, 'death has enveloped all in eternal silence.'

There was such vibration in the Prince's voice that Monsoreau said to himself : 'This is not remorse.' Aloud he asked : 'Monseigneur, do you wish me to speak frankly to your Highness ? With a Prince, eminent for his intelligence and nobility of heart, frankness should be henceforth the chief element in this conversation.'

'Henceforth ? What does that signify?'

'That your Highness has not been using that frankness towards me. Listen, monseigneur, I understand your meaning. You meant that perhaps Mademoiselle de Méridor was not dead, and in that case those who thought themselves her murderers need not feel so keen a remorse.'

'Oh ! how long you have taken to give me this consoling reflection. You are a faithful servant, upon my word; seeing me sad and gloomy, dreaming ghastly dreams, you have allowed me to live thus when with this doubt you could have spared me so much suffering ! What shall I call this conduct, monsieur ?' The Duc spoke in tones that presaged a burst of rage.

'Monseigneur,' answered Monsoreau, 'one would imagine your Highness was accusing me——'

'Traitor ! so I do accuse you. You have deceived me and taken away this woman whom I loved.'

'It is true.'

'Ah ! it is true, insolent knave !'

'Please speak softly, monseigneur. Your Highness forgets he is speaking to a gentleman, to a good servant of the King. This is my excuse : I loved Mademoiselle de Méridor fondly.'

'And I, too !' answered François, with inexpressible dignity.

'True, monseigneur; but Mademoiselle de Méridor did not love you. I loved her, and I am not one of your valets. My wife is mine as my estate is; nobody can take her from me, not even the King. I wished to have her, and I took her.'

'Really,' said François, springing to a silver bell which stood on the table; 'you took her, well! you will give her up.'

'You are mistaken, monseigneur,' cried Monsoreau, going towards the table to prevent the Prince from summoning any one; 'abandon your evil design, for if you do me public injury——'

'You will renounce this woman, I tell you.'

'How? She is my wife; I have wedded her before God.'

'If she is your wife before God, you will give her up to men.'

'He knows all,' murmured Monsoreau.

'Yes, I know all. You will dissolve this marriage; I will insist, though you are bound before all the gods that have reigned in heaven. To-morrow, Mademoiselle de Méridor will be restored to her father; you will go into banishment. In an hour, you will have sold your office of First Huntsman : these are my terms; if not, I will break you like this glass.' The Prince, seizing a crystal goblet, threw it furiously at Monsoreau, who was covered with the fragments.

'I will not renounce my wife, I will not abandon my office, and I will remain in France,' rejoined Monsoreau.

'Why?'

'Because I will ask a favour from the King of France, the King chosen in the Abbey of Sainte-Catherine, and this new Sovereign, so good, so noble, so happy in the divine favour still so recent, will not refuse to listen to the first suppliant who proffers a request.'

François paled, then, drawing the heavy door-curtain, he seized Monsoreau's hand, saying as though he were at the end of his strength,—

'It is well—Comte, this request, present it to me in lower tones—I am listening.'

'Do not crush me, monseigneur. I saw you rich, young, happy, the first Prince in the Christian world. For you are so,' whispered Monsoreau in the Duc's ear; 'between this rank and you there is but a shadow, easy to dissipate. I saw all the splendour of your future, and, comparing this immense fortune to my paltry ambitions, I said, "Leave the Prince to his brilliant dreams, his splendid projects; this is his purposed end. I seek mine in obscurity. He will scarcely notice my retirement, will

hardly miss one small pearl slipping from his royal chaplet.''
You will pardon me, monseigneur ?'

The Duc was dazed, in spite of himself, by the magic of
this picture. Just then, raising his eyes, he noticed
Bussy's portrait. The proud eye, the haughty expression,
made the Duc imagine he saw Bussy in person inciting him
to take courage.

'No,' said he, 'I cannot pardon you ; it is not for myself
I am harsh, God is my witness ; it is because a mourning
father reclaims his daughter, because a woman, coerced
into marrying you, cries for vengeance; because, in short,
the first duty of a Prince is justice.'

'If justice is the first duty of a prince, gratitude is the
first duty of a king. Now, monseigneur——'

'Well ?'

'You owe your crown to me, your Majesty !'

'Monsoreau !' cried the Duc, still more terrified than
by the first attack, 'you are a traitor towards the King
as you are towards the Prince ?'

'I am attached to whoever supports me, your Majesty.'

'I cannot ! You are a loyal gentleman. You will
understand that I cannot approve of your conduct.
Renounce this woman; my dear Comte, I will compensate
you in whatever way you wish——'

'Your Highness still loves Diane de Méridor ?'

'No, I swear to you.'

'Then, what can stop your Highness ? She is my wife;
can any one interfere with my private affairs ?'

'Do this for me, Monsoreau.'

'I cannot,' your Majesty.'

'You would denounce me ?'

'To the King dethroned for you, yes, your Majesty;
for if my new Prince wounds me in my honour, in my
happiness, I would return to the old one.'

'It is infamous ! It is cowardly !'

'Yes, your Majesty; but I love enough to be both
infamous and a coward.'

The Duc moved towards Monsoreau, but the latter
stopped him with one glance, one smile.

'You would gain nothing by killing me, monseigneur;
some secrets survive with the dead ! Come, my noble
lord, do some thing for the man who has best served you
in all things.'

François rose up. 'What do you ask ?'

'Monseigneur, you will pardon me; you will reconcile
M. de Méridor and myself ?'

'Yes.'

'You will sign my marriage contract with Mademoiselle
de Méridor ?'

'Yes.'

'You will honour my wife with a smile when she appears
in the Queen's circle on her presentation.'

'Yes; is that all ?'

'Absolutely all, monseigneur.'

'Go, you have my word.'

'And you will keep the throne I enabled you to mount.
Farewell, your Majesty.'

He added this so low that the harmony of the sound was
sweet to the Prince.

'There is nothing more to do,' soliloquised Monsoreau,
'except to ascertain how the Duc has been informed.'

CHAPTER XXXV

THE KING'S COUNCIL

THE same day M. de Monsoreau presented his wife to the
Queen-Mother and the Queen. Henri had gone to bed,
after M. de Morvilliers had mentioned that he desired an
audience the next day. Henri asked no questions : it was
late, and he wished to sleep. The worthy magistrate,
knowing his master perfectly, predicted that he would, on
waking, think of the requested audience, and would
regard it with curiosity, piqued by the gravity of the circumstance. All had happened as M. de Morvilliers had
anticipated. After a first sleep of three or four hours
Henri awoke; the Chancellor's demand returned to his
mind; sitting up in bed, he began to think, and, tired of
speculating alone, he made his way to Chicot's room.
The Gascon was sleeping heavily and snoring. Henri
pulled him by the arms three times without succeeding
in wakening him; then Chicot opened one eye. 'What
is it ?' he asked.

'Chicot, it is I—Henri.'

'Decidedly, friend, the snipes you ate are disagreeing
with you. I warned you, though.'

'No, I scarcely tasted them.'

'Then you have been poisoned. How pale you are!'

'It is my mask.'

'You are not ill? Why do you waken me?'

'Because I wish to talk to you; M. de Morvilliers last night requested an audience; what can he have to say to me, Chicot?'

'Is it for this you wakened me?'

'Chicot, you are aware that M. de Morvilliers is my police agent.'

'No, I did not know.'

'Chicot, I find he is always very well informed.'

'When I think that I might be sleeping instead of listening to such nonsense!'

'Do you doubt the Chancellor's supervision?'

'I do, and with reason. One night in the Rue Troidmentel, I beat you, thrashed you three times; Quélus and Schomberg were with you——'

'You beat me, why?'

'You had insulted my page, you were beaten, and M. de Morvilliers told you nothing about it; you sent for him next day; did you inform him of the distressing accident which had occurred the day before?'

'Yes.'

'Did he discover the culprit for you?'

'No.'

'Well, go to bed, Henri; there is sufficient proof that your police work is badly managed.' With this Chicot, turning over, began to snore, and Henri returned to his room sighing.

The next day the Council, composed of Quélus, Maugiron, d'Épernon, and Schomberg assembled, and M. de Morvilliers was announced. The statesman was wearing his darkest suit and his most gloomy expression. After bowing low he approached the King. 'I am in the presence of the King's Councillors?' he asked.

'Yes, speak.'

'It is a question of denouncing a very terrible plot to your Majesty.'

'Oh!' said the King, 'come, is it a Spanish plot?'

Just then the Duc d'Anjou, summoned to the Council, entered.

'You hear, my brother,' observed Henri, 'M. de Morvilliers informs us of a plot against the safety of the State!'

The Duc slowly glanced at the audience defiantly. 'Is it really possible ?' he murmured.

'Alas ! yes, monseigneur, a threatening plot,' replied M. de Morvilliers.

'Relate it to us,' said Chicot.

'Your Majesty,' began the Chancellor, assuming his most officious air, 'for a long time I have been watching the secret practices of certain malcontents—shop-keepers, tradesmen, small clergy, with here and there some monks and students. These malcontents always espouse two principal subjects : War and Religion. In the army, certain officers devoted to your Majesty kept me informed of everything; in the Church it was more difficult. At last I succeeded in inducing an official of the city to keep watch on the preachers who excite the people against your Majesty. These men receive their inspiration from a party extremely hostile to the Throne. For more than two months I have employed men of great courage in your Majesty's service. They are of insatiable greed, it is true, but this I was careful to turn to the King's profit, as by paying them well, I obtained still more information. The payment of a large sum of money brought me news of the first meeting of these conspirators.'

'Come, Chancellor, tell us the purpose of the plot,' cried Henri.

'Your Majesty, it is nothing less than a second Saint-Bartholomew against the Huguenots.'

Chicot turned to the King. 'If you like,' said he, 'for a thousand crowns, I will reveal this secret. It is the League pure and simple, the League begun ten years ago. M. de Morvilliers has discovered what any citizen of Paris knows like his paternoster. This is the actual truth, and I will prove it,' cried Chicot, like a lawyer.

'Tell me the place of the Leaguers' meetings ?'

'Willingly : firstly and secondly, the public square; thirdly, the public squares.'

'Monsieur Chicot is joking,' said the Chancellor; 'and what is their rallying sign ?'

'They are dressed as Parisians, and move their legs when they walk,' answered Chicot gravely.

A burst of general laughter greeted this explanation, and M. de Morvilliers, unbending for a moment, laughed too, but becoming grave again, he said : 'My spy was present at one of their meetings, in a place unknown to

M. Chicot.' The Duc d'Anjou paled. 'At the Abbey of Sainte-Geneviève,' finished the Chancellor.

'Impossible,' murmured the Duc.

'And what did they decide ?' asked the King.

'That the Leaguers should appoint leaders, that each member be armed, each province receive an envoy from the insurrectionary capital, that all the Huguenots dear to His Majesty be massacred on a given day.'

'Is that all ?' asked Henri.

'The deuce, one can be sure you are a Catholic,' said Chicot.

'Is that really all ?' asked the Duc.

'No, monseigneur.'

'Speak, Chancellor,' the King commanded.

'There are leaders : first, a preacher, a fanatic whose name I have bought for ten thousand pounds—Brother Gorenflot of Sainte-Geneviève !'

'Gorenflot,' said the King, noting the name; 'well, next——'

'That is all, your Majesty,' the Chancellor concluded, with a mysterious glance at the company, which implied. 'If your Majesty were alone, much more could be revealed.'

'Speak, Chancellor, I have only friends here.'

'Oh ! your Majesty, he whose name I hesitate to tell has extremely powerful friends everywhere.'

'Are they more powerful than I ?' cried Henri, pale with rage and uneasiness.

'Your Majesty, a secret is not spoken aloud. Excuse me, I am a statesman.'

'Monsieur,' observed the Duc d'Anjou, 'we will present our humblest respects to the King, if the communication cannot be made in our presence.'

M. de Morvilliers hesitated. The King motioned to the Chancellor to approach, to the Duc to remain, to Chicot to be quiet, to the three favourites to pay no attention. Immediately M. de Morvilliers prepared to speak into the King's ear; but he had only advanced half-way towards him when a loud clamour was heard in the courtyard. The King stood up; Quélus and d'Épernon ran to the window; Chicot, rising on tip-toe, looked into the courtyard, and was the first to exclaim : 'Hallo ! the Duc de Guise entering the Louvre.'

'The Duc de Guise ?' stammered M. d'Anjou.

'A strange thing, surely, that M. the Duc de Guise

should be in Paris,' remarked the King slowly; he had just read in M. de Morvilliers's stupefied glance the name the latter wished to whisper.

'Does your communication refer to the Duc de Guise ?' he asked in low tones.

'Yes, your Majesty, he presided at the meeting.'

'And the others ?'

'I do not know the others.'

The King glanced at Chicot.

'Let my cousin of Guise enter !' cried the latter, majestically; and bending towards Henri, he added : 'You know that name too well to be forced to write it down.'

The ushers opened the door noisily. 'One door, gentlemen,' cried Henri, 'one only ! the two are for the King !'

The Duc de Guise was near enough to hear the words; but that did not change the smile with which he had resolved to approach the King.

CHAPTER XXXVI.

THE DUC DE GUISE

'AH ! it is you, cousin,' said the King; 'what a clamour you make. Are the trumpets not sounding ? I fancied I heard them.'

'Your Majesty, the trumpets sound in Paris only for the King; in the provinces only for the General; and I am too well acquainted with the court and camp to make a mistake. Here the trumpets would be too loud for a subject; elsewhere, not loud enough for a prince.' Henri bit his lips.

'The deuce ! cousin, you are extremely brilliant; do you arrive from the siege of La Charité only to-day?'

'To-day only, your Majesty,' answered the Duc, reddening slightly.

'Faith, your visit does us too much honour, cousin, too much honour.' Henri kept on repeating his words in order to conceal his thoughts.

'Your Majesty is joking, doubtless; how could my visit honour him from whom all our honour is derived ?'

'I mean, Monsieur de Guise, that all good Catholics;

C.J.   H returning from a campaign, visit God first in His temple; the King comes after God. "Honour God, serve the King," you know, cousin; it is a maxim half religious, half political.' This time the Duc de Guise reddened visibly; the King, remarking it, turned instinctively to the Duc d'Anjou, and became aware that he was as pale as his cousin was red. This emotion struck him forcibly. Looking away affectedly and assuming an affable expression, he resumed : 'In any case, Duc, nothing exceeds my joy at seeing you safe from all the accidents of war, though I believe you sought danger in reckless fashion. I would beg you, cousin, not to be so ambitious of deadly peril, for it reflects little credit on idlers like ourselves, who sleep, eat, and hunt, and never do anything more than invent new fashions and new prayers.'

'Yes, your Majesty,' said the Duc, catching up the last word; 'we know that you are a pious Prince, never losing sight of the glory of God and the interests of the Church. That is why we approach your Majesty with so much confidence.'

'Do you not always approach us with confidence, cousin ?'

'Your Majesty, the confidence of which I speak refers to the proposal I intend making you.'

'Ah ! you have something to propose ? Then, speak with confidence. What have you to propose to us ?'

'The execution of one of the finest ideas which have ever moved the Christian world since crusades became impossible. Your Majesty, this title of Very Christian King is no vain one; it obliges one to be zealous in defence of religion. The eldest son of the Church ought always to be ready to defend his mother.'

'Hallo,' remarked Chicot, 'my cousin preaching with a rapier at his side and a helmet on his head; that's curious ! though not more astonishing than the monks who are eager to wage war. Henri, I crave a regiment for Gorenflot.'

The Duc feigned not to hear; Henri crossed his legs, leaned his elbow on his knee, sinking his chin in his hand. 'Is the Church threatened by Saracens, my dear Duc ?' he asked, 'or do you aspire to the title of King—of Jerusalem ?'

'Your Majesty, the people who follow me, blessing my name, do so only on account of my zeal in defence of the

Faith. I have already had the honour of speaking to your Majesty of a project of alliance amongst all true Catholics.'

'Yes, I remember, the League, Henri; you are very forgetful, my son, not to remember such a triumphant idea,' broke in Chicot.

The Duc, turning round, glanced in disdain at the speaker, ignorant what weight the words would carry with the King, recently enlightened by M. de Morvilliers. The Duc d'Anjou, much affected, looked hard at the Duc de Guise, placing a finger on his lips. This time the King did not notice the sign, but Chicot whispered : 'Look at your brother, Henri.' The Duc's finger was lowered, but Henri had seen and guessed the meaning.

'Your Majesty,' resumed the Duc de Guise, 'the Catholics have called this association the Holy League, and it is designed to fortify the Throne against the Huguenots, its mortal enemies. But it is a small matter to form a body; direction must be given to it. Now, in a kingdom like France, several millions of men cannot assemble without the King's approbation.'

'Several millions of men !' said Henri, making no effort to conceal his surprise; 'it is flattering for the Catholic religion; but how many Protestants are there in my kingdom ?'

The Duc appeared to search his memory.

'Four,' said Chicot. This sally made the King's friends laugh, while the Duc de Guise frowned, and the gentlemen of the ante-room murmured at the Gascon's audacity. Turning slowly towards the door, Henri quelled these murmurs. Then, glancing once more at the Duc, he resumed : 'Come, monsieur, what is your request ?'

'I beg your Majesty, for my King's popularity is dearer to me than my own, that your Majesty show your zeal clearly for the Catholic religion, and thus deprive the malcontents of all pretext for war.'

'Ah ! if it is only a question of war, cousin, I have some troops, whilst under your command, alone, there are nearly twenty-five thousand men.'

'Your Majesty, when I speak of war, I should perhaps explain myself. At the present time, kings are obliged to wage two kinds of war : war against ideas, and war against men. Men, being visible and mortal, are attacked, conquered, tried, hanged; but ideas slip by invisibly, hiding themselves from those who wish to destroy them; sheltered in the depths of minds, they send forth deep roots. An idea, your Majesty, is a giant dwarf which must be watched day and night; for the idea which crawled at your feet one day will rise above your head the next; that is why millions of watchers are necessary.'

'There are the four Huguenots done for,' cried Chicot; 'I pity them!'

'And in order to render this supervision of service, I suggest that your Majesty should appoint a leader to this Holy Union.'

'Well!' said the King, 'what do you think of that, gentlemen?'

Chicot, without replying, carried a lion's skin into a corner and lay down on it. 'What are you doing, Chicot?' asked Henri.

'Your Majesty, I am going to sleep, and to-morrow, with mind refreshed, I will answer my cousin de Guise.'

The Duc glanced angrily at the Gascon, who snored loudly for reply.

'Well! your Majesty, what is your opinion?'

'I think you are right, cousin; summon the chief of the Leaguers, come at their head, and I will select the leader.'

'When, your Majesty?'

'To-morrow.'

During this speech the King smiled, first at the Duc de Guise, then at the Duc d'Anjou. The latter was preparing to leave with the courtiers. 'Stay, my brother, I wish to speak to you,' said Henri.

The Duc de Guise departed with all his suite, and, as he left the Louvre, the crowd sent up a roar of cheering just as it had done on his arrival.

CHAPTER XXXVII.

CASTOR AND POLLUX

THE Duc d'Anjou, who had managed through the preceding scene to preserve the attitude of an indifferent person in the eyes of every one but Chicot and the Duc de Guise, betrayed no fear at Henri's invitation.

'Brother,' began Henri, 'I am a very fortunate prince;

when great ideas do not come to me, they come to those
who surround me. Now, it is a great idea which my
cousin de Guise has. To unite under one banner all the
Catholics, to arm all France, from Calais to the Languedoc,
from Brittany to Burgundy, so that I may always possess
an army ready to march against English, Flemish, or
Spanish, without alarming them, is a magnificent conception. I confess I am strongly disposed to reward the
author of so fine a project.'

Chicot opened both eyes, but shut them immediately;
he had just seen on the King's face a smile, visible only to
him, who knew his Henri better than any one.

'Yes,' continued the King,' 'such a project deserves
a reward; is the Duc de Guise really the originator of this
splendid scheme ?'

'No, your Majesty, the same notion occurred to the
Cardinal de Lorraine more than twenty years ago, but
the Saint-Bartholomew rendered its execution useless.'

'Ah ! how unfortunate that the Cardinal is dead !
I would have made him Pope at the death of His Holiness
Grégoire XIII.; but it is no less true that his nephew has
inherited the idea. Unfortunately I cannot make him
Pope; how can I reward him, François ?'

'Your Majesty, you exaggerate your cousin's merits;
the idea is but a heritage, and, besides, another person
has greatly helped him in working out the scheme.'

'His brother, the Cardinal.'

'The Cardinal is interested, but he is not the man.'

'It is Mayenne, then ?'

'Oh ! your Majesty, you do him too much honour.'

'True. How could such a butcher have part in this
magnificent conception. But to whom, then, must I be
grateful, François ?'

'To me, your Majesty.'

'What ! when everybody was arraigned against me,
preachers, poets, and lampooners; whilst my friends
laughed at my impotence; whilst trouble and anxiety
were making me visibly thinner and gray-haired, this
idea came to you ! François, I must confess (you know,
men are weak and kings are blind), I did not always regard
you even as my friend ! Ah ! François, what a culprit
I am !' Henri, almost moved to tears, stretched out
his hand to his brother. Chicot opened his eyes
again.

'The scheme is brilliant. I could not levy taxes or troops without causing an outcry; I could not walk, sleep, or show affection without being laughed at, and here an idea comes to M. de Guise, or rather to you, my brother, which gives me an army, money, friends, and peace. That this peace may endure, one thing alone is necessary. My cousin has spoken of giving a chief to the movement. This leader, you quite understand, cannot be one of my friends; not one of them is clever and brave enough for such a charge. To direct such a movement, a great prince is needed, a good captain, a skilful negotiator. François, does not this position suit M. de Guise in every way?'

'My brother, M. de Guise is extremely powerful already, commanding the army and the burghers; the Cardinal de Lorraine leads the Church; Mayenne is a tool in their hands; you are about to add considerable power to one family. If the Guises were even French, that might be comprehensible; their interest would be to ennoble the family of France.'

'Doubtless, but, on the contrary, they are Lorraine princes.'

'Belonging to a house always in rivalry with yours.'

'François, you have touched on the sore point; I did not imagine you were such a politician; yes, that is what troubles me, this elevation of the House of Lorraine. Not a day passes but one or other takes from me some scrap of my power, some bit of my prerogatives, and I, poor, weak, isolated, cannot act against them. Had this explanation come sooner, had I divined that you would support me, I would have resisted better; but now, it is too late. A struggle tires me; so I will appoint him Head of the League.'

'You will be wrong, brother.'

'Whom do you wish me to appoint? Who will accept this perilous position? The Duc's idea was that I should appoint him, and any one I appoint in his place will become his enemy.'

'Appoint a man who, by virtue of his own strength and yours, will have nothing to fear from the united power of the three Lorraines.'

'My good brother, I know no one in that position.'

'You do not understand, my brother.'

Henri regarded the Duc as if a veil had fallen from his

eyes. 'What!' he cried, and François motioned with his head.

'No, you will never consent to it, François. The task is too tremendous; one needs to be triple like M. de Guise, with a right arm called Charles, and a left arm called Louis. The Duc performed very well on the day of the Saint-Bartholomew, François?'

'Too well, your Majesty!'

'Yes, perhaps. But answer my questions. Would you really like to be mixed up in this bourgeois movement? to make yourself one of the populace—you, the highest lord in our court?'

'Not for myself, your Majesty, but certainly I would do it for you.'

'Good and excellent brother,' said Henri, wiping away a tear which had never existed.

'You are not displeased, Henri, that I charge myself with the task you intended to entrust to M. de Guise?'

'Displeased! I am enchanted. So you, too, thought of the League. So much the better. You had a small share in the idea—the biggest share, I should say. I am surrounded only by superior minds, whilst I am the stupidest person in my kingdom. I speak frankly François; you extricate me from an embarrassing situation, all the more so since my faculties are declining, as Miron often explains. But, to be serious; we say, therefore, that you shall be appointed 'Head of the League.''

François trembled with joy. 'Oh!' said he, 'if your Majesty judged me worthy of this trust!'

'Trust; ah! François; as the Duc de Guise is not to be the leader, of whom should I be afraid? Of the League itself? Would the League imperil me? How stupid! In that case my brother would not be its chief; or, better still, as soon as my brother became the leader, there would be no more danger. That is logic; no, I have no distrust. Besides, there are sufficient swordsmen in France to combat the League when it begins to annoy me.'

'It is true, your Majesty,' answered the Duc, whose frankness was nearly as well assumed as his brother's, 'the King is always the King.' Chicot opened one eye.

'Pardieu,' said Henri. 'I have an idea, too; strange how many ideas are springing up to-day. Our cousin de Guise, the author (or who supposes himself the author) of this scheme, has probably taken a fancy to be the leader. He will expect some command, too. He has put forward his plan only that it may benefit himself. It is true, of course, that you assisted him. Take care, François. I wager he expects it. He knows I am so thoughtless !'

'Yes, but as soon as you make your wishes plain, he will yield.'

'Or pretend to. Be cautious; he has a long arm, our cousin. I will say more: he has long arms, and not one in the kingdom, even the King, could touch Spain with one hand and England with the other—Juan d'Autriche and Elizabeth.'

'If your Majesty considers him so dangerous, that is a further reason for giving me command. We place him between my power and yours, and at the first sign of treachery, we can bring him to trial.' Chicot opened his other eye.

'His trial ? it suited Louis XI., who was rich and powerful, to arrange trials and erect scaffolds; but I have not sufficient money even to buy all the black velvet I should need.' In spite of his self-control, Henri gazed at the Duc with a look which the latter could not support with equanimity. Chicot shut both his eyes. Silence reigned for an instant, and was broken by the King.

'All must be arranged, my dear François; no civil war, no quarrels between my subjects. I am a son of Henri the fighter and Catherine the clever ; I have some of the astuteness of my good mother; I will recall the Duc de Guise and make him such fine promises that the business will be settled amicably.'

'Your Majesty will grant me the command ?'

'I hope so; but we must not displease the Duc de Guise too much, however.'

'Be reassured; if this is the only hindrance to my nomination, I undertake to pacify the Duc.'

'You are going to visit him. Oh ! my brother, the honour is indeed great !'

'No, your Majesty, I am not going to seek him; he awaits me in my apartments.'

'I heard the shouts which greeted his exit from the Louvre.'

'Yes, but after leaving by the principal entrance, he re-entered by the postern. The King had the right to his first visit; but I have a right to his second.'

'Go, then, François, and come to terms.' Taking his

brother's hand, the Duc bowed to kiss it. 'What are you doing, François; your true place is on my heart,' cried Henri, and the two brothers embraced several times. At last the Duc, released, left the room, and quickly traversed the galleries. His heart almost needed to be encircled with oak and steel not to burst with joy. The King, growling with rage, rushed to the secret corridor leading to the room of Marguerite de Navarre, where he could easily hear the conversation between the Ducs de Guise and d'Anjou.

'*Ventre de Biche!*' said Chicot, opening both eyes and sitting up, 'how touching these family scenes! For a moment I thought I was in Olympus, watching the reunion of Castor and Pollux, after their six months' separation.'

Henri III. reached his observatory when his brother entered the room, so that none of the conversation escaped him.

'Well! monseigneur?' asked the Duc de Guise sharply.

'Well! Duc, the meeting is over; the King noticed nothing.'

'Nothing, I believe; His Majesty detained your Highness; it was, doubtless, to speak of my proposal.'

'Yes, monsieur.' An embarrassing silence ensued, the meaning of which Henri understood. 'And what did His Majesty say?'

'The King approved of the plan; but seems to consider it dangerous to place you in command.'

'Then we shall fail?'

'I am afraid, dear Duc, that the League will be suppressed.'

'They have as much cunning, the one as the other,' said a deep voice in Henri's ear. Henri, turning sharply, perceived Chicot bent in a listening attitude. 'You followed me, rogue!'

'Be quiet, my son, you prevent me hearing.'

The Duc de Guise resumed: 'Monseigneur, in that case, the King should have announced his refusal at once; he received me with sufficiently ill grace. Does he wish, perchance, to get rid of me?'

'I believe so. He would ruin the enterprise.'

'Assuredly. However, I did my best, and in a way the fate of the League lies in my hands. If, instead of expelling you and dissolving the League, he were to

name a leader favourable to the enterprise; if, instead of
raising the Duc de Guise to this post, he were to place the
Duc d'Anjou in it ?'

'Ah !' said the Duc, the blood mantling in his cheek.
Then, to the surprise of Chicot and the King, he suddenly
began to speak in a calm and almost joyful voice : 'You
are a skilful politician, monseigneur, if you have managed
that.'

'Yes; circumstances aided me; however, nothing is
settled, and I wished to sound you first.'

'Why?'

'Because I am uncertain as to what that will lead us.'

'Well ! I will inform you, monseigneur, not where it
will lead us (God alone knows that), but how it can help
us; the League is a second army, and as I command the
first, as my brother the Cardinal holds the Church, nothing
can resist us, as long as we remain united.'

'Without counting that I am the Heir-Apparent to
the Throne.'

'Then, monseigneur, Heir-Apparent as you are, calculate the chances you run. First, the King of Navarre
does not lose sight of you or of your brother; he hungers
for your throne. Wait till some accident happens to the
King, and you will see if the cat will not jump from Pau
to Paris. Yes, an accident, monseigneur. Such things
are not rare in your family. A certain prince is in good
health and suddenly falls into decline; another reckons
on long life, who has only a few hours to live.'

'Yes, it is true; the princes of my house are born
under fatal influences; but my brother Henri III. is,
God be thanked ! strong and healthy ; he has borne the
fatigues of warfare, and will not break down now that his
life is only a series of recreations.'

'Yes, but remember, monseigneur, the recreations in
which the kings of France indulge are not without danger.
How did your father Henri II. die, for instance, he who
so miraculously escaped the dangers of war. Your
brother, the late King François, too, died in an unfortunate manner. Yes, for some time the name of king
has brought misfortune on its possessor. It is worth
while recounting the accident which befell King Charles IX.
It happened to him through the mouth; these hunting
books are dangerous things when the pages are stuck
together and have to be turned by wetting one's fingers;

the saliva becomes poisoned by these old books, and a man, even a king, cannot do much when his saliva is poisoned.'

'Duc! Duc! I believe you are inventing crimes.'

'Crimes! monseigneur, I am speaking of accidents, do you hear? Was that adventure of King Charles IX. at the hunt not also an accident. You comprehend, monseigneur, to what hunt I refer? The one when, intending to kill the boar which was charging your brother, you fired so hastily that, instead of hitting the animal, you hit the person you had not aimed at. Every one knows your skill. Your Highness rarely misses his aim, and you must have been considerably astonished to miss it then.'

'What is your advice, Duc?' asked Anjou, wishing to put an end to this interview, in which the Duc de Guise so clearly revealed his discontent.

'Monseigneur, I repeat that every king meets with some accident. Now, you are the destined accident for King Henri III., especially if you become Head of the League, considering that makes you almost King over the King.'

'Then I will accept; that is your advice?'

'I beg you to accept, monseigneur.'

'And you, this evening?'

'Oh! be reassured, my men have been in the field since morning, and to-night Paris will be a strange sight.'

'What is to be done in Paris to-night?' asked Henri.

'You cannot guess? You are stupid, my son; to-night the League is to be signed publicly; only your approval was needed, you gave it this morning, and the people sign this evening, *ventre de biche!*'

'It is well,' said the Duc d'Anjou; 'farewell till to-night, Duc.'

'Yes, till this evening,' observed Henri.

'What, will you risk the streets of the capital, Henri? you are wrong.'

'I shall be guarded strongly, never fear; moreover, come with me.'

'You take me for a Huguenot, my son. I am a good Catholic, and wish to sign the League.'

'One word more, what do you think of this?' asked the King.

'That your predecessors did not foresee their accidents. You have a great advantage over them, Henri, for you know your brother.'

'Yes, and zounds, before long he will discover that.'

CHAPTER XXXVIII

THE EVENING OF THE LEAGUE

AT eight o'clock, a crowd of citizens, clad in their best attire, and with their finest arms, were making for the churches, their faces both joyful and threatening, especially when they passed a troop of Swiss or Light Horse. This expression, and notably the cries, hootings, and bravadoes accompanying it, would no doubt have alarmed M. de Morvilliers had the magistrate not known his good Parisians—scoffers and inciters, but incapable of doing evil unless urged by some wicked friend, or provoked by an imprudent enemy. To add further to the noise and variety, many women followed their husbands, some even bringing a string of children, and it was a curious sight to see them clinging to the unwieldy muskets, sabres, and halberds of their fathers. Occasionally a group would draw old swords from their scabbards crying, 'To the flames with the heretics!' At the Rue de l'Arbre-Sec the throng was greatest. The street was blocked, and the noisy crowd pressed towards a brilliant light hung below a sign which many of our readers will recognise, when we say it represented a chicken on a background of azure, with this inscription : 'A la Belle Etoile.' On the threshold a man stood, declaiming and arguing. In one hand he brandished a sword, and in the other held a register half filled with signatures. 'Come, brave Catholics,' he was crying, 'come to the Belle Etoile, you will find good wine and welcome; come, you who know how to write and you who do not, give your names to me or to my assistant, M. Croquentin. It is for the holy religion; long live the holy religion!' Many people animated by the same zeal, signed the register, or gave their names to Croquentin. Directly these registers were full, La Hurière immediately asked for others, that there might be no interruption.

While the signers were thus displaying their zeal, a man arrived, making his way through the crowd by dint of blows and kicks. Having got to the register, he took a pen and traced his name in letters half an inch long upon a spotless white page, adding a flourish embellished with blots. 'Chicot!' read the next to sign. Chicot, not wishing to accompany the King, was watching the proceedings on his own account. After signing in M. Croquentin's register, Chicot passed to Maître la Hurière's, and was received warmly. After signing more magnificently than the first time, he asked for a third register. La Hurière could not take a joke; he glanced sideways at Chicot, but the latter looked him straight in the face. La Hurière murmured the word 'Heretic!' Chicot muttered, 'Eating-house keeper!' La Hurière left his register to finger his sword; Chicot put down his pen to draw his from the scabbard: in all probability the scene would have finished with some thrusts, of which the host of the Belle-Etoile would, no doubt, have received the larger share, when Chicot, feeling a pinch in his arm, turned round. It was the King, disguised as an ordinary citizen, with Quélus and Maugiron alongside, also disguised, and carrying an arquebuse in addition to a rapier.

'Well, well! what is this? good Catholics disputing! Zounds! that is a bad example to set,' remarked the King.

'My gentleman,' said Chicot, pretending not to recognise Henri, 'scold the right person; here's a rascal who bawls after the passers-by to sign his register, and when they sign, bawls still more loudly.'

La Hurière had his attention diverted by some fresh adherents, and in the bustle the King, with his minions and Chicot, became separated from the innkeeper. They were on a door-step, overlooking the whole gathering.

'What enthusiasm!' observed Henri; 'religion is in favour to-night in the streets of my good city!'

'Yes, your Majesty, but the heretics are not in favour, and your Majesty is supposed to support them. Look to the left; what do you see?'

'Ah! the broad face of M. de Mayenne, and the Cardinal's pointed beak.'

'Long live the mass!' cried a crowd of people, emerging from the market-places, and sweeping on like a rising tide into the Rue de l'Arbre-Sec.

'Long live M. de Guise ! long live the Cardinal ! long live M. de Mayenne !' replied the crowd stationed at the inn, recognising the two Lorraine princes.

'What are these cries ?' asked Henri, frowning.

'They show that each is in his proper place and should stay there; M. de Guise in the streets and you in the Louvre; return to the Louvre, your Majesty.'

'Do you come with me ?'

'No, I want to see the end of this performance. I am going to sign the other registers, for I wish a thousand signatures to be displayed to-morrow. Here we are on the quay; good-night, my son; I am off to Saint-Méry to hear a famous preacher.'

'Oh ! oh ! what is this noise, and why are the people rushing towards the Pont-Neuf ?' cried the King suddenly. Chicot, rising on his toes, could see nothing but a mass of people, crying and yelling, seemingly bearing somebody or something in triumph. Suddenly, the waves of the crowd opening, a man was driven almost to the King's feet. It was a monk, seated on an ass, speaking and gesticulating while the ass brayed.

'I was speaking of a famous preacher at Saint-Méry; no need to go so far, listen to this one,' said Chicot, pointing to the man. People crowded round the monk, who began his discourse thus : 'My brothers, Paris is a splendid city, the pride of the kingdom of France, and the Parisians are a race of intelligent people, as the song says.' Here the monk began to sing lustily, but the ass accompanied in such a high key that the words were drowned. 'Silence, Panurge; let me speak first,' cried the monk. 'Brethren, the world is a vale of sorrow where man has to quench his thirst with his tears. I return from exile, like the Hebrews, and for a week Panurge and I have lived on alms. It is Hérodès who has occasioned this misfortune. You know which Hérodès I refer to.' ('And you, too, my son, I explained the anagram,' said Chicot). 'Brethren, Panurge and I have come to participate in the solemn proceedings to-night; but we do not understand what is happening. Is it to-day we depose Hérodès, and put Frère Henri in a convent ? Gentlemen, I left Paris with two companions : Panurge, my ass, and Chicot, the King's jester. Can you tell me where my friend Chicot is ?'

'So that is your friend; he is handsome and, above all, respectable. What is his name ?' asked the King.

'Gorenflot, Henri; that dear Gorenflot of whom M. de Morvilliers spoke to you.'

'The incendiary of Sainte-Geneviève ?'

'The same.'

'Then I will have him hanged.'

'Brethren,' continued Gorenflot, 'you see in me a true martyr. I defend my cause at this time, or rather the cause of all good Catholics. You do not know what is happening in the provinces and what the Huguenots are plotting. As long as a single batch of them remains in France, good people, 'twill not be safe. Let us exterminate the Huguenots. To arms, brethren !'

'*Par la mordieu !*' cried Henri, 'silence this drunkard, or he will start a second Saint-Bartholomew.'

'Wait a bit,' said Chicot, taking a cane and giving the monk a resounding blow on his shoulders from behind. Then passing his head under the monk's arm, 'Hallo ! it is you ! how are you, priestling ?' he asked.

'Help, Monsieur Chicot,' cried Gorenflot, 'the enemies of the Faith wish to assassinate me. To the fire with the Huguenots ! To the flames with the Béarnais !'

'Will you be quiet, rascal ?'

'To the deuce with the Gascons !'

Just then a second blow from a stick landed on Gorenflot's shoulder, making him cry with pain. Chicot, glancing round in astonishment, perceived nothing but the stick. The wielder of it had disappeared in the crowd. Chicot immediately ran after this man, who slipped along the quay with one companion.

CHAPTER XXXIX

LA RUE DE LA FERRONNERIE

SOMETHING peculiar in the bearing of the two strangers caused Chicot to doubt the wisdom of seeking to recognise them. They, indeed, obviously endeavoured to be lost in the crowd, turning only at corners to discover if they were followed. Chicot, concluding that his best plan was to go straight ahead, passed them at the corner of the Rue Tirechappe. At the corner of Rue de la Ferronnerie the two men stopped again to look round. Meanwhile

Chicot had reached the middle of this street, where a
litter, drawn by two massive horses was stationed, and
he could see a woman anxiously peering through the
blinds. Imagining that this litter awaited the fugitives,
Chicot, slipping behind it, dropped under a wide stone
bench used by the vegetable sellers on market-days.
Presently the men approached, the taller one taking the
white hand which the woman extended to him in both
his, and placing his foot on the step.

'Well! my treasure, my dear heart, how are you?'

The lady shook her head sadly, and produced her
smelling-salts.

'Why the deuce do you bring Madame to Paris?' asked
the other man, rudely enough; 'did you come here to
make love, then? It seems to me Béarn is big enough
for your sentimental promenades without continuing
them in Babylon. Here, *mordioux*, carry on only political
intrigues, my master.'

Chicot wished to raise his head, but dared not risk it.
'At least get into the litter to carry on your love-making.
You risk being recognised if you stay outside.'

'You are right, Agrippa,' said the amorous lover;
'make room for me, my heart, if you permit me to sit
at your side.'

'Not only permit, your Majesty, but I warmly wish it.'

'Your Majesty!' said Chicot, rising without thinking,
and knocking his head on the stone seat, 'whatever is
she saying? Let us wait; all comes to those who wait.'

'Oh! how happy I am!' resumed the person addressed
as "your Majesty," 'here are my good Parisians, who
loathe me and would gladly cut off my head, doing their
best to smooth my path to the throne, while I hold in my
arms the woman I love. Where are we, d'Aubigné?
When I am King I will have a statue erected here to the
genius of the Béarnais.'

'We are in the Rue de la Ferronnerie, your Majesty,
and it does not seem a nice place.'

'It seems to me,' continued Henri, for our readers have
no doubt recognised the King of Navarre, 'that I see my
whole life, myself King, strong and powerful, but perhaps
not so much loved as now. My love, say again that you
love me, for at your voice my heart melts.'

'In truth, your Majesty, I cannot understand why you
sign yourself Henri de Navarre, instead of Rousard or

Clément Marot. *Cordioux!* why do you not agree better with Madame Margot, being both so fond of poetry?'

'Ah! d'Aubigné! for pity's sake, do not speak of my wife: if we should meet her? Mount, and let us be off.'

'Lavarenne!' said Henri, addressing the coachman, 'you know where to go.' The litter moved away slowly, relieving Chicot from a terrible fear, for after such a conversation with Henri, d'Aubigné was not the man to let any who had heard it live.

'Valois must know what has happened,' thought Chicot, stretching his legs, which were stiff with cramp. 'Yet, why should he know it? No, I will say nothing; besides, if I know, that's the main thing, since it is I who reign. Now I come to think, if Henri de Navarre is a serious claimant, if he really aspires to the throne, he should think a little of destroying his enemy Le Balafré, his enemy the Cardinal, and his enemy the Duc de Mayenne. I like this Béarnais, and am sure that some day he will play a nasty trick on that fearful Lorraine butcher. Decidedly, I won't breathe a word of this. Come, let us sum up,' continued Chicot, making his way to the church of Saint-Germain-l'Auxerrois, 'I have seen the Cardinal, the Duc de Mayenne, Henri de Valois, and Henri de Navarre; where is my François III.? I long to see him.'

Chicot was not the only person searching for the Duc d'Anjou; the Guises, too, were looking for him, but with as little success as Chicot. For a minute the latter thought he had found him; a group had gathered round a wine merchant's shop, and Chicot recognised in it Monsoreau and Le Balafré. 'Here are the suck-fish: the shark cannot be far away,' said he; but he was mistaken. M. de Monsoreau and Le Balafré were busy pouring out bumpers to an orator whose stammering eloquence they thus excited. The orator was Gorenflot, absolutely drunk, relating his journey to Lyons and his duel in an inn with a fearful follower of Calvin. M. de Guise gave keen attention to this tale, finding in it something to coincide with Nicolas David's silence. Chicot, listening, foresaw the moment when Gorenflot would divulge his name and throw a light upon the mystery. Losing no time, he untied the bridles of the horses at the tavern windows, and striking some of them with a stirrup-leather, launched them into the crowd, who broke away hurriedly. Passing into the group, Chicot approached Gorenflot with glaring

eyes, seized Panurge, and turned his back on the crowd,
so that soon a considerable space was left between Gorenflot and the Duc de Guise. Then, dragging the monk into
the *cul-de-sac* formed by the apse of Saint-Germain-
l'Auxerrois—'Ah! drunkard,' said he, 'traitor! renegade! you prefer a pot of wine to your friend! I nourish
you, I fill your pockets and your stomach, and you betray
me! You tell my secrets! You deserve punishment.'
The monk, thick-set, powerful as a bull, but overcome with
repentance and wine, shook in Chicot's grasp helplessly.
The Gascon's stick fell on the broad shoulders of the monk.

'A punishment to me, your friend! dear Monsieur
Chicot! Oh! if I were fasting,' he added, with an angry
gesture.

'You would beat me, your friend, ungrateful one!'

'My friend, and you thrash me!'

'He who loves punishes,' and Chicot redoubled these
proofs of his affection till the wretched monk howled
aloud.

'Now, we will go quietly to bed in the Corne d'Abondance,' continued Chicot, leading the ass by the bridle up
the Rue Saint-Jacques. Two young men helped the monk
down, and led him into the room with which our readers
are acquainted.

'That is done; he is snoring,' said Maître Bonhomet,
re-entering.

'Capital! but remember he will waken up some day,
and he must not know how he came here; let him think
he has never left here since the famous night when he
caused such a scandal in his convent, and imagine all that
has happened since is a dream.'

'That is all right, Seigneur Chicot; but what has
happened to this poor monk?'

'A great misfortune; it seems at Lyons he killed an
envoy of M. de Mayenne, so that the latter has sworn to
have him broken on the wheel.'

'Be easy, under no pretext will he leave here.'

'Very good! and now, I must really find the Duc
d'Anjou,' said Chicot, reassured, and setting off for the
latter's hotel

CHAPTER XL

THE PRINCE AND THE FRIEND

As we have seen, Chicot had vainly sought through the
streets for the Duc d'Anjou. The latter, though invited
to come out by the Duc de Guise, had displayed considerable hesitation to accept the invitation. Yet, since his
own interests required him to learn what was happening,
he decided to go abroad well and duly accompanied. The
Duc went for his sword, that is, Bussy d'Amboise. The
latter had scowled on him since his deception, and
François acknowledged that in Bussy's place he would
have shown more than scorn to the Prince who had so
cruelly betrayed him. Bussy was sleeping, so to speak,
in his grief. He had seen Diane received at Court as
Comtesse de Monsoreau, gazed at by all, in her matchless
beauty. All the evening, he too had gazed ardently at
her, but she never raised her weary eyes. 'Oh!' said
Bussy to himself, 'Diane should say frankly : "I thank
you, Monsieur de Bussy, for your services; but I do not
love you !" I should either have died or been cured by
the blow. She prefers, however, to let me love her vainly;
she gains nothing, though, for I love her no longer, I despise
her,' and Bussy retired in anger. His was no longer that
noble face, loved by all women, feared by all men; his
brow was dull, his eyes heavy, his smile feeble. Looking
in a mirror, Bussy found himself odious to behold.

'I am mad to make myself distasteful to a hundred
who seek me, for the sake of one who despises me ! Why
does she disdain me, or for whom ? For that livid-faced
skeleton, who gazes at her, pretending not to see me ?
To think that I might have him dead at my feet in a
quarter of an hour; to think that, unable to gain her love,
I could at least secure her hatred : her hate ! rather than
her indifference. That would be commonplace. Better
to resemble the young Antiochus, dying of love without
complaining or confessing. I will stifle my sorrow in my
heart.' So saying, Bussy walked slowly to the door,
outwardly calm and smiling. Meeting the Duc d'Anjou,
he turned away his head, afraid that his firmness might

drive him to smile or bow to the Prince. Bussy went home and, taking off his cloak, sat dreaming in a chair, never noticing another man, who sat watching him. An icy shiver passed through Bussy's body, his teeth chattered, then his head fell forward. The man, who was observing him, rose, sighing.

'Monsieur le Comte,' said he, 'you are feverish.'

'Ah! it is you, Rémy.'

'Come, do you wish to remain like this, or do you wish to overcome this fever? go to bed and have some book read which will inspire and strengthen you.' The Comte could only obey. All next day Rémy stayed by his bedside, but the next one, on which M. de Guise arrived at the Louvre, Bussy looked for him in vain. Towards evening loud voices were heard in the ante-room; a servant came in: 'Monsiegneur le Duc d'Anjou,' said he.

'Let him enter,' replied Bussy. The Duc entered. Bussy's room was in darkness.

'It is too dark here, Bussy; that must annoy you,' said the Duc. Bussy made no answer. 'You are seriously ill, since you do not reply?'

'I am very ill, monseigneur,' murmured Bussy.

'Speak to me, then, Bussy, are you angry with me?' asked the Duc, after some rebuffs.

'*I* angry! about what? people are not angry with princes. What good would it do? But we lose time. Let us get to business, monseigneur. You need me?'

'Ah! Monsieur de Bussy.'

'Yes, you need me; do you think I imagine your visit is out of pity? what do you require? When one belongs to a prince who dissembles to the point of calling you friend, well! one must favour this dissimulation, even sacrifice one's life to it. Speak.'

'I wished nothing from you, Bussy, and you are mistaken in thinking my visit interested. I simply desired, considering what good weather it is, and how all Paris is in an uproar over the signing of the League, that you should accompany me through the streets.'

'Have you not Aurilly? besides, you have ten ot twelve gentlemen, whose swords I hear clanking in my ante-room.'

Slowly the door-curtain was raised, and Le Haudouin entered in no way embarrassed. 'It is I—Rémy,' said he, in answer to an exclamation of the Duc.

'Who is Rémy ?' asked the latter.

'The doctor, monseigneur.'

'Rémy is more than the doctor, monseigneur, he is the friend,' said Bussy.

'You heard what monseigneur wishes,' he continued, getting out of bed.

'Yes, that you should accompany him, but you will not; monseigneur, it is too cold outside.'

'Too cold ?' said the Duc, surprised at any one daring to thwart him.

'Yes, too cold. Consequently, I, who am responsible to M. de Bussy's friends, and, above all, to myself, for his health, forbid him to go out.' Rémy pressed Bussy's hand significantly.

'Very good,' said the Duc, 'since he runs such risks in going out, he will stay. So you have decided; you will not risk it ?' he continued, approaching the bed.

'You see, monseigneur, the doctor forbids it.'

'Farewell, then.'

'Farewell, monseigneur !'

The Duc retired with great din and bustle. Hardly was he outside than Rémy, who had followed his movements, ran to his patient.

'Monseigneur, rise at once, if you please, and take a stroll with me. It is too hot in here.'

'But you told the Duc it was too cold outside !'

'Since he left the temperature has changed, so that now I am convinced the air would do you good. Come ! get up : have you no confidence in me ? then you must dismiss me.'

'Well, since you wish it,' said Bussy, rising, pale and trembling, 'but where are we going ?'

'To a district of which I have analysed the air, to-day even. It is excellent for your illness, monseigneur.'

Bussy dressed, took his sword, and both went out.

Rémy, taking his patient's arm, turned to the left, following the Rue Coquillière right to the ramparts.

'It is strange,' said Bussy, 'you lead me near the marshes of the Grange-Batelière, and pretend that this is a healthy district.'

'A little patience, monsieur, we are returning to the Rue Monmartre, and you know what a fine street that is.'

After walking some yards along this street, Rémy turned to the right.

'This is Rue de la Gypecienne, or Rue de l'Egyptienne, already called Rue de la Gyssienne, and which will end in being named Rue de la Jussienne, being softer.'

'Very true; but where are we going?'

'To that little church. I wager you have never noticed it before.'

'Indeed I do not recognise it.'

Bussy was not the only nobleman who had never entered the church of Sainte-Marie-l'Egyptienne, a very popular church, known to the faithful frequenters as the Chapelle Quoqhéron.

'Well! now that you know its name, monseigneur, and have examined the outside, let us enter to see the windows of the nave. They are curious.'

There were other things to be seen inside the church, especially some naïve paintings of the sixteenth century, frescoes of the life of Sainte-Marie-l'Egyptienne. In the most conspicuous part of the church was one picture in this series, which many people judged as being too crudely treated. Bussy watched Le Haudouin pay considerable attention to this picture.

'Come,' said he, 'you had some other end in bringing me here than to show me the knees of Sainte-Marie-l'Egyptienne!'

'No.'

'Then, I have seen them; let us go.'

'Patience, wait till the service is finished,' said Rémy, holding Bussy gently by the arm. 'No, everybody is retiring.'

'Well, we will do the same; but you are forgetting the holy water.'

Bussy, obeying like a child, proceeded to the pillar where the holy water basin was stationed. Le Haudouin beckoned to a woman who walked towards the same pillar. As the Comte stretched out his hand to the basin, a woman's hand, rather rough and red, touched his own. Bussy, looking from the hand to the face, paled and drew back; he had recognised Gertrude, half hidden by a black veil. Bowing to him, Gertrude passed into the porch. Two steps behind her followed a woman wrapped in a silk mantle; her elegant form and charming foot made Bussy think they could belong to only one person. Now he understood why Rémy had brought him there. He followed this woman and Rémy followed him; so the four figures walked on with equal step, Gertrude keeping in front. Presently, turning to the right into an alley, she opened a door, and let her mistress pass in. Le Haudouin let Bussy pass, then followed with Gertrude. Bussy found himself in a small garden, surrounded by high walls covered with ivy. Lilac gave forth its perfume to the warm air, the herald of spring, the leaves were beginning to unfold. The young man asked himself whether this perfume, warmth, and life did not come from the presence of a woman so tenderly loved. Diane sat down under a bower of jasmine and clematis, on a little wooden bench; her hands hung at her sides, while she aimlessly pulled a flower to pieces, scattering the petals on the ground. Rémy and Gertrude remained at a distance; Bussy approached Diane, who raised her head : 'Monsieur le Comte,' said she, 'if you were at the church by chance, it was not chance which led you here.'

'No, madame, Le Haudouin made me come out without explaining why, and I assure you I was not aware——'

'You mistake my meaning, monsieur. I am aware that M. Rémy led you to the church, by force, perhaps ?'

'Not by force, madame. I was ignorant of whom I was to see.'

'That is a cruel saying, monsieur. Do you mean me to understand that, had you been told Rémy's secret, you would not have accompanied him ? It is natural; monsieur, you rendered me signal service, and I have not yet thanked you. Pardon me. I wished to show that I am not ungrateful or forgetful, and therefore begged M. Rémy to arrange this interview; excuse me if I have displeased you.'

'Madame,' said Bussy, 'you cannot imagine that.' Ideas seemed to be returning to his mind, and a cloud was lifted from his eyes.

'I am aware how much trouble you experienced in doing my behest. I recognise what delicacy you displayed. I appreciate your efforts, be assured. Judge, then, my sufferings, knowing that you were ignorant of my feelings. I thank you for your attention, and vow an eternal gratitude to you.'

'Madame, those who profess friendship for one, show it as they can : I was near you in the Palace, and yet you never cast your eyes upon me; perhaps you failed to recognise me; you had only seen me twice.'

Diane looked with sad reproach at Bussy, who was deeply moved.

'Excuse me, madame; you are unlike the usual type of woman, yet your action in this marriage——'

'I was forced into it !'

'Yes, but it was easily broken off.'

'Impossible; on the contrary.'

'Nothing whispered that near you watched a man devoted to your interests ?'

'That, above all, made me afraid.'

'And to these considerations you sacrificed me. Think what my life has been since you belonged to another. Finally, madame, behold me become what I was before, a stranger to you. Your silence says so sufficiently. It is the continuation of your behaviour at the Louvre.'

'There I was in the presence of M. de Monsoreau. He was watching me, and he is jealous. For some days he has seen some one prowling around our new dwelling.'

'You have left the Rue Saint-Antoine ?'

'What ! it was not you ?' cried Diane; 'if you really had some desire to see me, thank this unknown man, for, knowing M. de Monsoreau as I do, I trembled for you, and wished to say : "Do not expose yourself thus, Monsieur le Comte." '

'Madame, I repeat, it was not I.'

'Now, let me finish my explanation. Owing to this man, who is perhaps known to M. de Monsoreau, I am obliged to leave Paris; so you may regard this as our last meeting. To-morrow I leave for Méridor. My father accompanies me. There I shall rejoin Monsieur and Madame Saint-Luc. Farewell, Monsieur de Bussy.'

'All is over for me,' said Bussy, hiding his face in his hands; 'this man who banishes you, and extinguishes my sole hope of breathing the same air as you, is my mortal enemy, and, though I perish, I will destroy him. Wretch ! is it not enough to have you for his wife ? must he be jealous ? Monster ! he would absorb the world.'

'Oh ! calm yourself, Count; perhaps he is excusable.'

'You defend him, madame.'

'Oh ! if you knew !'

'If I knew ? Madame, I know one thing, one is wrong to think of the rest of the world when one is your husband.'

'But, if you were mistaken, if he were not !'

The young woman rose with these words, and fled into the depths of the garden, before Bussy, mad, radiant with happiness, could raise his arms to hold her back. Uttering a cry, he rose totteringly, and Rémy arrived in time to place him on the bench which Diane had quitted.

CHAPTER XLI

THE ADVENTURES OF D'ÉPERNON AND SCHOMBERG

WHILE Maître la Hurière was heaping signature upon signature, while Chicot was depositing Gorenflot at the Corne d'Abondance, while Bussy was returning to consciousness in the little garden, Henri, gloomy at what he had seen in the town, annoyed at the preaching he had heard in the churches, furious at the mysterious greetings bestowed on his brother, whom he had seen in the Rue Saint-Honoré with M. de Guise, and M. de Mayenne, and a whole troop of noblemen, returned to the Louvre with Maugiron and Quélus. Schomberg and d'Épernon had disappeared to seek for adventures, and had not gone far when they found them. D'Épernon, tripping up a citizen, sent him flying, and Schomberg knocked off the bonnet of a woman whom he had imagined to be old and ugly, but who proved to be young and pretty. They had chosen the wrong day to attack these good citizens, who were now in a fever of revolt. The man, picking himself up, cried 'Down with the heretic!' and rushed on d'Épernon; the woman cried, 'Down with the minion!' which was worse; her husband, a dyer, had set his apprentices on Schomberg. The latter, being brave, tried to speak, and put his hand on his sword; d'Épernon, being prudent, ran away. Meanwhile, the King sat in his fencing-room, trying to find an opportunity of breaking out in anger.

'Their plot is progressing,' he declared; 'now tigers, now serpents; when they are not bounding, they crawl.'

'Eh! your Majesty, there are always plots in a kingdom. What the deuce would kings' sons, brothers, or cousins do, if they did not plot?' said Quélus.

'Come, Quélus,' resumed the King, 'don't try to smooth me over with stuff like that, as though I were a common king!'

'Your Majesty,' said Maugiron, 'if you are not a common king, prove it by acting as a great one. There's Narcisse, he is a good dog, but if any one pulls his ears he growls, and if one tramps on his paws he bites.'

'Good ! there's the other comparing me to my dog.'

'Not at all,' declared Maugiron, 'I put Narcisse far above you, since he can defend himself, and your Majesty does not know how.'

'I am left alone, then; very good, abandon me, insult me, slaughter me; I am surrounded by executioners. Ah ! my poor Chicot ! where are you ?'

'He calls for Chicot now, that is the climax,' exclaimed Quélus.

'It is quite explainable,' declared Maugiron, muttering, 'A man is known by the company he keeps.'

Henri frowned and darted a true kingly glance at his rash friends; and, exhausted with rage, fell back in his chair. Just then a rapid step was heard, and d'Épernon appeared with his doublet torn, and without hat or cloak.

'Your Majesty, look at me; this is how the friends of your Majesty are treated. All your people, or rather M. d'Anjou's, who were shouting "Long live the League ! Long live François !" recognised me as your friend, and that was sufficient.'

'Did Schomberg not defend you ?'

'Schomberg had his own affairs to look after. I left him in the hands of a dyer, whose wife's bonnet he had knocked off, and five or six young men were preparing to give him a bad quarter of an hour.'

'My poor Schomberg,' said Henri, rising; 'I will go to his aid.'

'Thank you, your Majesty,' said a voice behind Henri; 'I escaped, but not without difficulty.'

'It is Schomberg's voice !' cried the minions. 'But where is he ?'

A shadow advanced from the depths of the room. It was indeed Schomberg, but from head to foot he was of the finest royal blue colour.

'The wretches ! they put me in a vat, the rogues; I thought it was filled with water, but it was a vat of indigo.'

'How did you escape from them ?'

'I was courageous enough to be cowardly, your Majesty. I cried "Long live the League !" But that is not all;

when I was crying "Long live the Duc d'Anjou!" Bussy passed.'

'He did not help you? that is the duty one gentleman owes to another.'

'He seemed to be thinking of something else; he hardly touched the ground, and only needed wings to fly.'

'Then he would not recognise you. Were you already dyed?'

'Ah! true. No matter, we shall meet one day when I am not in a vat.'

'Oh! I don't bear the valet a grudge, it is the master,' said d'Épernon.

'Yes, Monseigneur le Duc d'Anjou, who wishes to kill us with ridicule before killing us with the sword.'

'He is master in Paris now, and not the King; let us go out a little and see if you will be respected more than us.'

'Ah! brother! brother!' murmured Henri threateningly.

'Yes, your Majesty, you repeat that often, without taking any stand against this brother. Yet I warn you, he is at the head of a conspiracy,' said Schomberg.

'Isn't that what I was saying to these gentlemen; but they shrugged their shoulders and turned away.'

'Now we turn to you to say, "Save us, or rather, save yourself, for, at our fall, you are dead; to-morrow the Duc de Guise is coming to the Louvre; you will appoint the Duc d'Anjou as you promised, and, once Head of the League, that is, of a hundred thousand Parisians, excited by to-night's doings, the Duc d'Anjou will do with you what he pleases.'

'In the case of an extreme resolution, you would second me?'

'Yes, your Majesty,' answered the young men.

Signing for silence, Henri seemed to reflect deeply. Presently he said: 'Quélus, find out if the Duc d'Anjou has returned.'

'Your Majesty,' asked Maugiron, 'you are then to take action?'

'You will see,' was the response.

Quélus, returning, announced: 'M. le Duc is not yet in.'

'Very good. D'Épernon, change your clothes; Schomberg, change your colour; Quélus and Maugiron, keep guard till my brother comes, and when he enters have all the doors shut.'

'Your Majesty is to remain alone ?' asked Maugiron.

'No, I remain with God, whose protection I will implore for our enterprise.'

Left alone, the King knelt to pray.

CHAPTER XLII

CHICOT IS MORE AND MORE KING OF FRANCE

ᴛHE doors of the Louvre were usually shut at midnight, but Henri, wisely calculating that the Duc d'Anjou would certainly sleep that night in the Louvre, in order to allay any suspicions which the tumult of the evening might have raised, had ordered the doors to be kept open till one o'clock. At a quarter past twelve Quélus remounted the stairs.

'Your Majesty, the Duc has entered,' he announced.

'Let him retire to rest quietly. Who is with him ?'

'M. de Monsoreau and his usual noblemen. M. de Bussy is absent. What are the King's orders ?'

'Tell d'Épernon and Schomberg to hurry, and inform M. de Monsoreau that I wish to speak to him.'

Five minutes later d'Épernon and Schomberg entered, freshly attired, and after them M. de Monsoreau appeared.

'The Captain of the Guard announces that your Majesty honours me by summoning me here,' said he, bowing.

'Yes, monsieur; during my walk to-night I noticed that the stars were very bright and the moon beautiful, so I thought we might enjoy a splendid hunt to-morrow. It is only midnight, start for Vincennes immediately and rouse a stag for us.'

'Your Majesty, I understood that to-morrow you met Monseigneur d'Anjou and M. de Guise here, in order to appoint a Head for the League. Afterwards the time will be short, perhaps.'

'Time is never short to one who can employ it; you have time to start to-night, if you go immediately. You have time to rouse a stag to-night, and you will have time to get everything ready for to-morrow at ten o'clock. Quélus, Schomberg, have the doors opened for M. de

Monsoreau, in my name; and in the King's name, have them shut when he departs.'

The First Huntsman withdrew, thoroughly astonished. 'Oh! he muttered to himself, glancing towards the Duc's apartments, 'this does not augur well for His Royal Highness.' But he had no means of warning the Prince, surrounded as he was by Quélus and Schomberg. Ten minutes later his attendants returned to the King.

'Now, silence, and attend me, all four,' said Henri. The minions, buckling on their swords, followed the King, who, torch in hand, led them by the secret corridor to the Duc d'Anjou's apartments. The Duc had just lain down, lulled by dreams of ambition; he had heard his name exalted and the King's name abased; never in his long career of dark dealings and timid plottings had he been so popular, and, consequently, so hopeful. He had just placed on the table a letter from the Duc de Guise bidding him not to fail to be present next day at the King's levée. The Duc d'Anjou had no need of such reminder; he had determined not to miss his hour of triumph. But his surprise was great when the door of the corridor opened, and his terror was at its height when he saw the King's hand on the door. Henri advanced, grave and frowning, to the bed.

'Your Majesty,' stammered the Duc, 'the honour is so unforeseen——'

'That it frightens you? I understand; no, stay my brother, do not rise; you were reading?'

'Yes, your Majesty. Did your Majesty wish to speak to me in private?' asked the Duc, noticing that the four noblemen were listening and enjoying the scene.

'What I have to say to you is best said before witnesses, monsieur. Gentlemen, listen; the King permits you.'

'Your Majesty,' interposed the Duc, looking up with a glance of hatred, 'before insulting a man of my rank, you should have refused me hospitality in the Louvre; in the Hôtel d'Anjou, at least, I should have been able to reply.'

'Indeed, you forget that you are my subject anywhere, and my subjects are under me wherever they are; *Dieu merci*, I am the King! Let us abridge matters, monsieur: give me the paper you were reading, and which you hid on seeing me.'

'Your Majesty, consider that your request is unworthy

of a true gentleman, though suitable, perhaps, to a police officer.'

'This letter, monsieur, or it shall be taken from you by four Swiss!' exclaimed the King, stamping his foot.

The Duc, leaping out of bed, crushed the letter in his hand, intending to throw it into the fire. 'You would do that to your brother?' he cried.

The King placed himself between the Duc and the chimney.

'Not to my brother, but to my most deadly enemy. To the Duc d'Anjou, who ran through the streets all the evening after M. de Guise! My brother who endeavours to conceal a letter from his accomplices, the Princes of Lorraine. I tell you I saw on the seal the three famous martlets of Lorraine, who wish to swallow the Fleur-de-lis of France. Give me it or——' Henri, stepping towards his brother, laid a hand on his shoulder. No sooner did François feel the weight of this royal hand, and see the threatening looks of the minions than, falling on his knees across the bed, he cried: 'Help! help! my brother wishes to kill me.'

These words extinguished the King's wrath, for he thought that François might indeed fear him as an assassin. He remembered that in his family brothers assassinated brothers by tradition.

'No,' said he, 'you are wrong, my brother. The King wishes you no ill of that sort; at least you have struggled, confess yourself beaten. You are aware that the King is the master; repeat it, not only softly, but aloud.'

'Oh! I repeat it, I proclaim it, brother,' cried the Duc.

'Very good. The King orders you to give him that letter.'

The Duc dropped the paper; the King, picking it up, folded it and put it in a bag.

'Monsieur, you will now keep your room until my suspicions have been dispelled. You will have good company, for these four gentlemen will guard you to-night.'

'May I not see my friends, M. de Monsoreau, for instance, M. de Ribeirac, M. de Bussy.'

'Ah! speak of that one again.'

'Has he had the misfortune to displease your Majesty?'

'Yes.'

'When?'

'Always, and to-night particularly. He insulted me,
or my friends, which amounts to the same, in the streets
of Paris.'

'You must be mistaken, your Majesty; M. de Bussy
has not been outside for two days! He is in bed, ill,
tossing in fever.'

The King turned to Schomberg.

'Though ill with fever, he was not at home, at least, but
in the Rue Coquillière ?' said he.

'Who informed you that Bussy was in the Rue
Coquillière ?' the Duc asked, sitting up.

'I saw him, fresh, well, bright, and seemingly the
happiest man in the world, accompanied by his usual
acolyte, Rémy.'

'Then I do not understand; I saw M. de Bussy in the
evening in bed; he must have deceived me.'

'Very good,' said the King, 'M. de Bussy will be punished
like the others, and with them, and the matter can be
cleared up.'

The Duc, thinking one way of diverting the King's
anger from himself, was to direct it upon Bussy, no longer
tried to defend his follower.

'If M. de Bussy has done that,' said he, 'if, after refusing
to accompany me, he went out alone, he must, indeed,
have had some projects which he could not confess to me,
conscious of my devotion to your Majesty.'

'Gentlemen, I entrust my brother to you; show him
the respect due to a Prince of the blood, the first in the
kingdom after me,' exclaimed the King. 'Farewell,
gentlemen.'

'Your Majesty!' cried the Duc, more terrified at the
King's absence than he had been at his presence, 'I am
really a prisoner! My friends cannot visit me! I cannot
go out! Let me at least appear beside your Majesty
to-morrow; that is my place, and I can be a prisoner
there as well as elsewhere. Your Majesty, grant me the
favour of remaining near you.'

The King was on the point of agreeing, when his attention was diverted by a very long, agile body motioning
with head, neck, arms, in every possible way, to imply
negation. It was Chicot saying 'No.'

'No,' said Henri, 'you are quite comfortable here,
monsieur, and it suits me that you stay. When it is the
King's good pleasure, it appears to me that is sufficient

for you, monsieur,' added Henri, with a haughty air which overwhelmed the Duc.

'And I boasted that I was the real King of France!' murmured Chicot.

CHAPTER XLIII

CHICOT VISITS BUSSY

THE next morning Bussy was breakfasting quietly with Rémy, and discussing the events of the previous night.

'Tell me, Rémy,' asked Bussy, 'did you not seem to recognise the gentleman who was being dipped in a tub as we passed the end of Rue Coquillière?'

'Yes, Monsieur le Comte; I have been trying to remember his name.'

'I should have rescued him, Rémy; but was too absorbed in my own affairs.'

'He recognised us, though, for he rolled his eyes wildly, and I heard him swear. He said, "*Gott verdamme!*"'

'Then it was Schomberg. My dear Rémy, prepare your balsams.'

'You are not so foolish as to get killed, when you are so well and happy.'

'On the contrary, Rémy, you cannot imagine what pleasure there is in risking one's life, when one is happy. I should fight splendidly to-day, for, thanks to you, I am wonderfully happy!'

'One day you will forgo that pleasure. A fair lady of my acquaintance has recommended you to my care, and has made me promise to keep you in safety.'

'Good Rémy,' said Bussy, becoming lost in a sweet reverie.

'You call me good Rémy, because I brought you to Madame de Monsoreau again, but what will you say when you are separated from her? Are you aware she is leaving for Anjou?'

'Rémy, when do we start?'

'As late as possible, Monsieur le Comte. Monseigneur d'Anjou, who got into such a pickle last night, will need our services; and M. de Monsoreau, who at present suspects nothing, might become suspicious if you left Paris at the same time as his wife.'

'What does that matter to me?'

'It matters a great deal to me, my dear seigneur. I am not commissioned to dress dagger wounds, inflicted by jealous husbands; these people can strike very hard; think of poor Monsieur de Saint-Mégrin, so shockingly slaughtered by our friend Monsieur de Guise.'

'Dear friend, if it is my fate to be killed by Monsoreau, I shall be killed.'

'In that case, Madame de Monsoreau will marry her husband, and your poor soul, looking on from above, or from below, will be greatly annoyed.'

'You are right, Rémy; I wish to live.'

'It is not sufficient merely to live, you must be charming to Monsoreau. Talk to him nicely, but do not ask him what has become of his wife.'

'I believe you are right, Rémy. I am not jealous of the bear, so I will tame him.'

Just then a knock came to the door. 'Who is there?' asked Bussy.

'Monseigneur,' answered a page, 'a gentleman wishes to speak to you below, a tall gentleman dressed in black velvet, who seems a respectable person.'

'Let him enter.' The visitor appeared on the threshold, and Rémy discreetly withdrew.

'Monsieur Chicot!' exclaimed Bussy, looking questioningly at him.

'Monsieur,' began Chicot in serious tones, 'I come to propose a little bargain, for which I shall expect a recompense. Are you acquainted with the League?'

'I have heard it much spoken of.'

'Well, monsieur, it is an association of good Christians, united for the purpose of conscientiously slaying their neighbours, the Huguenots. Do you belong to it? I do.'

'Monsieur Chicot, I beg you to change the conversation, as I dislike questions the sense of which I do not understand. I will wait a few minutes, for politeness' sake but I do not like questioners either. Come, Monsieur Chicot, we have only a few minutes more.'

'Admirable, in a short time one can say much. I should not have questioned you, for though you do not belong to the Holy League, you will doubtless soon join it, since Monseigneur d'Anjou has become a member.'

'Who told you that?

'Himself; now, you understand that, Monsieur le Duc

C.J. I

being a member of the League, you, who are his right hand,
cannot help becoming one. Well! after that, or after
people think you must be one, as they certainly will do,
the same thing which happened to His Royal Highness
will happen to you.'

'What happened to His Royal Highness?' exclaimed
Bussy.

'Monsieur,' answered Chicot, imitating Bussy's attitude,
'I do not like questions, nor, if you permit me to say so,
questioners; I am strongly inclined to let events take
their course.'

'Monsieur Chicot, where is Monsieur le Duc?'

'Imprisoned in his room, with four of my good friends
guarding him.'

'So, monsieur, my liberty is, you imagine, in danger?'

'I suppose even at this moment they are coming to
arrest you. Are you fond of the Bastille, Monsieur
de Bussy? Faith! I have something like an order to
convey you there. Would you care to see it?' Chicot
drew from his pocket an order from the King, with instructions to seize the person of M. Louis de Clermont,
Seigneur de Bussy d'Amboise. It is copied by Monsieur
de Quélus, and very nicely written.'

'Monsieur, are you intending to do me a service?'

'Yes; are you not of that opinion?'

'Monsieur, treat me as an honourable man; is it to
injure me later that you save me to-day? for you are
attached to the King, and he does not love me.'

'Monsieur le Comte, I save you for the sake of saving
you; now think what you please of my action.'

'To what am I to attribute such kindness?'

'You forget that I asked for a reward. You will do
what I will ask you some day.'

'In so far as the thing can be accomplished.'

'That is sufficient for me; now mount your horse and
disappear, while I carry this warrant to the proper
person.'

'But I am deserting my master.'

'Have no remorse, he has already deserted you.'

Bussy called Le Haudouin, who entered immediately:
'Our horses! Rémy!' cried Bussy.

'They are saddled, monseigneur.'

Bussy picked up some piles of crowns, filled his own
pockets and Rémy's, and thanking Chicot again,

prepared to go downstairs. Chicot followed them to the stableyard.

'Where are we going?' asked Rémy, carelessly gathering the reins.

'But——' said Bussy, hesitating.

'I believe you would decide for Anjou, would you not?' said Rémy.

'Yes, let us go to Anjou.'

'Monsieur,' remarked Chicot, 'since you have made your choice, I will wish you good-bye; remember me in your prayers,' and the worthy gentleman walked off, gravely and majestically.

'It is fate, monsieur,' Rémy declared.

'Come quickly, perhaps we shall overtake her,' cried Bussy, and the two started.

CHAPTER XLIV

HOW CHICOT, QUÉLUS, AND SCHOMBERG AMUSED THEMSELVES

CHICOT, in spite of his apparent coldness, returned to the Louvre full of joy. It was for him a triple satisfaction to have done a service for a gallant man like Bussy, to have helped on an intrigue, and to have rendered possible for the King the strong political action which the circumstances demanded. Indeed, when one considered Bussy's impulses, and the spirit evinced by MM. de Guise, it seemed pretty certain that one day a storm would burst over Paris. All that the King had feared, all that Chicot had prophesied happened. M. de Guise, after receiving the principal Leaguers, had promised to give the League a chief, and each member had promised to recognise the Head nominated by the King. He conferred earnestly with the Cardinal and with M. de Mayenne, and then proceeded to call upon M. le Duc d'Anjou, of whom he had lost sight the previous night. Chicot, anticipating this visit, was loitering about near the Hôtel d'Alençon, and after waiting a quarter of an hour saw M. de Guise enter the building. The valet showed considerable uneasiness at his master's non-appearance, but Aurilly was less anxious. He had been separated from his patron the

night before, and ignorant of his resolution to sleep at the
Louvre, had returned to the hotel. He related to the
Prince of Lorraine how three messengers had been sent
to the Louvre, and each had returned with the answer
that the Prince was asleep.

'Asleep at eleven o'clock? Rubbish! You ought
really to go yourself, Aurilly.'

'I will go, then; but what shall I say?'

'Tell him that the Assembly in the Louvre is at two
o'clock, and that we must have a private meeting beforehand. You understand, Aurilly, one does not sleep at
such a critical moment as when the King chooses a Chief
for the League. Tell him I wait impatiently, and meanwhile I will seek M. de Bussy.'

'How am I to act if I do not find His Highness?'

'If you cannot find him, pretend not to be looking for
him. In any case, I shall be at the Louvre within two
hours.'

Observing Aurilly leave, Chicot guessed the reason, and
also foresaw that if Guise learned of the Duc d'Anjou's
imprisonment, all would be lost. Aurilly ascended the
Rue de la Huchette, while Chicot, descending Rue Saint-
André-des-Arts as fast as his long legs could carry him,
quickly reached the Louvre. Let us follow Aurilly to
the scene of the day's events. Passing the quays, thronged
with triumphant townspeople, he approached the palace,
which preserved its calm, hallowed appearance. Aurilly
chatted with an officer at the gate, and ascending the
grand staircase which led to the Duc's apartments, bowed
frequently to the various courtiers gathered here and
there. At the door of the Duc's room, he found Chicot
seated on a folding-chair, and deep in a chess problem.
Aurilly tapped him on the shoulder. 'Ah! it is you,
excuse me, Monsieur Aurilly,' exclaimed the Gascon.

'What are you doing, Monsieur Chicot?'

'I am playing at chess; I am studying a move.'

'It seems to be a serious one?'

'Yes, my King causes me anxiety; you know, Monsieur
Aurilly, in chess the king is a very weak, insignificant
person, with no will of his own, and always surrounded by
very sharp enemies—knights and pawns—who harass him.
True, he has his fool, who trots all over the board for him,
but he risks his life by his devotion, so that at present my
king and his fool are in a most perilous position.'

'But,' asked Aurilly, 'why are you studying these moves at the door of His Royal Highness?'

'I am waiting for M. de Quélus, who is inside.'

'What is he doing? I did not know they were such good friends.'

Chicot, describing a curve with his long body, brought his face to a level with Aurilly's ear.

'He is begging His Royal Highness's pardon for the quarrel they had last night. The King commanded it; you are aware on what excellent terms the two brothers are just now.'

Passing into the ante-room, Aurilly was politely greeted by Quélus, who was spinning in his hands a splendid ebony ball, encrusted with ivory.

'Bravo! Monsieur de Quélus, bravo!' cried Aurilly.

'Ah! my dear Aurilly, when shall I play at cup and ball as well as you play the lute?'

'When you have studied as many years as I have. But where is Monseigneur? I expected to find him with you.'

'I have arranged an interview, dear Aurilly, but Schomberg has preceded me.'

Aurilly, opening a second door, found Schomberg reclining on a large divan, and busy attempting to shoot through a gold ring, suspended from the ceiling, perfumed pellets of earth which he blew through an air-cane.

'A game like this in monseigneur's room! I am surprised, Monsieur de Schomberg!' cried Aurilly.

'Ah! good-morning! Monsieur Aurilly, I am killing time till monseigneur is ready to see me.'

'Where is monseigneur?' asked Aurilly.

'He is engaged at present pardoning d'Épernon and Maugiron. But will you not enter, you who are so intimate with him? you will find him in his painting-room,' and Schomberg pushed Aurilly into the next room, where, to his astonishment, he found d'Épernon standing before a mirror, stiffening his moustache with gum, and Maugiron sitting at the window cutting out pictures. The Duc, without his sword, sat in an arm-chair between these two, who watched his every movement, and spoke only to utter disagreeable things. On seeing Aurilly, the Duc jumped up.

'Softly, monseigneur, you are treading on my pictures,' observed Maugiron.

'*Mon Dieu*, what do I hear? My master insulted!' cried the musician.

'How, my dear Aurilly?' asked d'Épernon.

'Be so kind as to hand me your dagger, monsieur,' said Maugiron.

'You see that M. le Duc has none,' added d'Épernon.

'Aurilly,' broke in the Duc in tones full of grief and rage, 'can you not guess that I am a prisoner?'

'Whose prisoner?'

'The King's. Did you not understand when you perceived my jailers?'

'You should have brought your lute to amuse His Highness, dear Monsieur Aurilly,' said a laughing voice, 'but I have sent for it, and here it is.' Chicot held out a lute to the poor musician, while behind him Quélus and Schomberg yawned wearily.

'And that game of chess, Chicot?' asked d'Épernon.

'Messieurs, I think my fool will save his king, though not without some trouble. Monsieur Aurilly, exchange your dagger for this lute.'

The thunderstruck musician, obeying, sat down at his master's feet.

'That's a second in the trap; let us wait for the others,' said Quélus. His words explained the preceding scenes to Aurilly. Quélus, returning to his post in the ante-room, begged Schomberg to exchange his air-cane for the cup and ball.

'That's right,' exclaimed Chicot, 'one must vary one's pleasures; I will vary mine by signing the League.' With these words he shut the door, leaving His Royal Highness with the poor lute-player.

CHAPTER XLV

THE KING APPOINTS A HEAD TO THE LEAGUE

THE hour of the grand reception was arriving; since midday the principal leaders, interested people, and even the merely curious, had assembled at the Louvre. Paris had sent its deputations of Leaguers, its guilds of workmen, its sheriffs, its militia, and its ever-increasing crowds of spectators. There was, therefore, a considerable throng

of the populace, but it was yet too early to fear a tumult.
The King in his Throne-room was surrounded by officers,
friends, attendants, and members of his family, waiting
till all the guilds filed before him to their places under the
windows and in the courtyard. Their leaders remained
in the Palace. The King was able at a glance almost to
count his enemies, with the help of Chicot, who was
hidden behind the royal chair. Suddenly M. de Monsoreau
entered.

'Hallo! look at your First Huntsman, Henriquet; he
well merits the exertion, pale and bespattered as he is.'

Henri signed to M. de Monsoreau, who approached.

'How are you at the Louvre, monsieur? I understood
you were at Vincennes, busy rousing a stag for us.'

'The stag was, in fact, roused at seven o'clock this morning, your Majesty; but twelve came, and receiving no
news, and fearing something had happened, I hurried here.
If I have failed in my duty, attribute the fault to my
excessive devotion.'

'Yes, monsieur, and believe I appreciate it.'

'Now, as I am reassured, if your Majesty wishes, I will
return.'

'No, no, remain, our First Huntsman; that hunting-
party was a mere fancy, which has vanished as it came;
stay, and station yourself among those upon whose devotion I can depend.'

'Where does your Majesty wish me to go?'

'Give him to me for half an hour,' whispered Chicot,
in a low voice; 'I wish to torment him a little.'

'Go where you will. Behind my chair, for instance,
where I put my friends.'

'Come here, our First Huntsman, and scent out these
rascals for me. The shoemakers have passed, and now
come the tanners. If you lose the trace of the latter, I
will deprive you of your office, I declare.'

M. de Monsoreau pretended to listen, or listened without
hearing, for he gazed about him with a pre-occupied air,
to which Chicot called the King's attention.

'Eh!' said he, 'he is hunting your brother. Do you
wish him to remain ignorant of what has happened?'

'I should not be displeased if he were put on a false
track.'

'Well, then, simply ask him where the Countess is.'

'Monsieur le Comte,' asked Henri, 'what have you done

with Madame de Monsoreau ? I do not see her amongst these ladies.'

The Comte shuddered as though a serpent had bitten him.

'Your Majesty,' said he, 'Madame la Comtesse was ailing, and has gone away with her father, Baron de Méridor.'

'To what part of France has she gone ?'

'To Anjou, her home, your Majesty.'

'The poor Comtesse,' said Chicot, 'she will be bored to death on the journey.'

'I informed the King that she travelled with her father.'

'A worthy escort, a father, but not an amusing one. Fortunately, some of our friends, witty ones, too, are travelling at present, and will entertain the Comtesse, should they meet her. As they are journeying in the same direction, it is probable. Oh ! I see them now. Do you see them, Henri ? Do you see them prancing on their horses and telling Madame la Comtesse stories which make her laugh, dear lady.'

This was a second and stronger blow to the Comte; yet he was unable to show his anger in the King's presence, and with forced affability he asked Chicot : 'Have you some friends who are travelling towards Anjou ?'

'You might say we have, Monsieur le Comte, for those friends are more yours than mine. They are even so dear to you these friends, that a little ago, from sheer force of habit (for you know perfectly well they are on their way to Anjou), you were looking for them in the crowd.'

'You saw me ?'

'Yes, you, the First Huntsman, the palest of all First Huntsmen, past, present, and future, from Nimrod to M. d'Autefort, your predecessor. Palest, I repeat : "*Veritas veritatum.*" That's a barbarism, for there is never more than one truth; if there were two, one would be false; but you are not a philologist, dear Monsieur Esau.'

'No, I am not; therefore I ask you to return to the subject of these friends, and to be kind enough to inform me of their real names.'

'Look around, First Huntsman, it is your profession to hunt down animals.' The eyes of Monsoreau glanced wildly round the company.

'What! M. le Duc d'Anjou?' he cried, observing an empty seat near the King.

'There is the beast started,' said Chicot.

'He has gone to-day!'

'It is possible that he went last night. But ask the King. When did your brother disappear, Henriquet?'

'Last night he disappeared, and his best friends are ignorant of his present whereabouts.'

'Oh!' said the Comte angrily, 'If I thought that!'

'Well! what would you do? Besides, he is doing no harm by saying pretty things to Madame de Monsoreau. Friend François is the gay gallant of the family. The deuce! I would give a good deal to be in your wife's place, were it only to see all day long a Prince with two noses, and to hear M. Aurilly, who plays the lute like Orpheus. What luck she has, your wife!' Monsoreau shook with rage.

'Gently, Monsieur the First Huntsman, conceal your joy and listen to the King's speech.' The First Huntsman was forced to remain in his place, motionless, and in a ceremonious attitude. Everybody was seated; the Duc de Guise had entered and knelt before the King, taking time to glance in surprise and uneasiness at the empty chair of M. le Duc d'Anjou. The King rose, and the heralds called for silence.

'Messieurs,' began the King, after ascertaining that d'Épernon, Schomberg, Maugiron, and Quélus had taken their places behind him, 'a King, placed as he is between heaven and earth, so to speak, hears with equal distinctness the voices from above and those from below, that is to say, the commands of God and of the people. I understand perfectly well that to defend the Catholic faith is a guarantee for all my subjects. So I approve of the advice given to you by my cousin de Guise. I declare, then, the Holy League to be well and duly authorised and instituted, and since such an important body needs a good and powerful head, as the leader called to uphold the Church must be one of the zealous sons of the Church, as this zeal must be imposed on him by his very nature and office, I take a Christian Prince to place at the head of the League, and declare that henceforth this leader shall be——' Henri paused intentionally, then repeated, amidst general silence, 'I declare that this leader shall be Henri de Valois, King of France and of Poland.' Henri,

in pronouncing these words, had raised his voice affectedly
in token of triumph—and to heighten the enthusiasm of
his friends, ready to burst out to crush the Leaguers, too
whose hoarse murmurs revealed discontent, surprise, and
affright.

The Duc de Guise was petrified; he exchanged glances
with the Duc de Mayenne and his brother the Cardinal,
who were standing in the midst of the chiefs. Monsoreau
began to be reassured, since the King's speech indicated
that he was not on friendly terms with his brother.
The Duc d'Anjou might, indeed, have disappeared without
having actually set forth to travel. Quitting his friends,
the Cardinal approached his brother and whispered in his
ear : 'François, unless I am greatly mistaken, we are no
longer safe here. Let us hasten to take leave, for the
populace is strange, and the King it execrated yesterday
will become its idol for a few days.'

'Very good,' replied Mayenne, 'let us go. Wait here
for our brother, whilst I arrange our departure.'

Meanwhile the King had signed the act, drawn up by
M. de Morvilliers, the only person, along with the Queen-
Mother, in possession of the secret. Then, passing the
pen to M. de Guise, he exclaimed, in hypocritical tones :
'Sign, my good cousin, below me. Now pass it to M. le
Cardinal and M. Duc de Mayenne.' But these two had
already disappeared, and this was noticed by the King.
'Then, pass it to M. the First Huntsman,' said he. The
Duc was preparing to go. 'Wait,' said the King; and
while all the nobility present and the leaders of corpora-
tions were signing, he began : 'Cousin, I believe you
suggested forming an army to guard Paris with all the
forces of the League ? The army is formed, and properly
so, since the King is the natural General of the Parisians.'

'Assuredly, your Majesty,' answered the Duc, without
understanding very well what he said.

'But I do not forget,' continued the King, 'that I have
another army to command, and that the direction of it
rightly belongs to the first warrior in the kingdom. Whilst
I command the League, therefore, do you command the
army, cousin.'

'When am I to start ?' asked the Duc.

'Immediately.'

'Henri, Henri,' said Chicot, prevented by etiquette
from stopping the King when he was speaking. But the

King did not hear, or did not understand, so Chicot, advancing respectfully with a huge pen in his hand, whispered : 'Be quiet, will you, simpleton.' It was too late. The King had already presented the Duc with his commission, signed beforehand, in spite of all Chicot's grimaces. The Duc withdrew, and, with the Cardinal and the Duc de Mayenne, mounted his horse, and was quickly out of Paris. The rest gradually withdrew, some crying, 'Long live the King !' others, 'Long live the League !'

'At least,' observed Henri, 'I have solved a great problem. In making all these rascals utter two cries, I have succeeded in forcing them to cry the same thing.'

'Oh ! your Majesty,' exclaimed the minions, crowding round the King, 'what wonderful imagination you displayed !'

Henri was led in triumph to his room; Chicot, in the midst of the procession played the part of the ancient detractor, pursuing his master with lamentations. This persistence in reminding the demi-god of the day that he was but a man impressed the King so much that he dismissed everybody but the Gascon.

'You are never content, Maître Chicot, and it becomes wearisome. The deuce ! I do not ask you to be agreeable, but simply to show common sense.'

'You are right, Henri, that is what you need most.'

'Agree, at least, that the stroke was well played.'

'That is exactly what I will not agree.'

'Come, am I, or am I not, King of the League ?'

'Certainly, it is incontestable. But—you are no longer King of France.'

'Who is, then ?'

'Every one but you; your brother the Duc d'Anjou, first.'

'Whom I hold as a prisoner ?'

'Yes, prisoner as he is, he is anointed, and you are not. Indeed, Henri, I advise you to speak to your police : a King is anointed by the Cardinal de Guise, before thirty-three people, in the church of Sainte-Geneviève, and you know nothing of it.'

'And how have *you* learned what *I* am ignorant of ?'

'Because you have your information obtained by M. de Morvilliers, and I obtain mine in person. We have, then, as King of France, without counting Henri de Valois,

François d'Anjou; in addition, we have the Duc de Guise, Henri de Guise, Henri le Balafré.'

'A fine King, in truth; Guise, whom I exile and send to the army.'

'As if you were not banished to Poland, yourself; as if it were not nearer from La Charité to the Louvre than from Cracovie to Paris! You send him to the army—that is, you put thirty thousand men under him, and what an army. Not like yours of the League, an army of burghers, good enough for Henri de Valois, King of the minions; but for Henri de Guise, an army of soldiers is needed, hardened warriors, able to destroy twenty armies of the League; so that, being King in fact, should Henri de Guise have the stupid notion to become so in name, he would need only to turn his trumpets towards the capital and to say: "Forward! let us swallow up Paris in a mouthful, Henri de Valois and the Louvre included." They would do it, the rogues; I know them.'

'You forget one thing in your argument, illustrious politician though you are,' said Henri.

'Ah! possibly, especially if it is a fourth king I have forgotten.'

'No,' said the King, with supreme contempt, 'you forget that to think of reigning over France, when a Valois wears the crown, one must look backwards a little and count one's ancestors. Should such an idea come to M. d'Anjou, one could expect it; *he* is of a descent to pre tend to the throne; his ancestors are mine, he can sustain an equally-balanced struggle against us. But M. de Guise —come Maître Chicot, go and study heraldry, my friend and tell us if the fleurs-de-lis of France are not of better origin than the martlets of Lorraine.'

'That is just where the mistake is, Henri. M. de Guise is of better descent than you imagine.'

'Of better origin than me, perhaps?' asked Henri, smiling.

'There is no "perhaps," my little Henriquet; read this,' and Chicot produced the parchment containing the pedigree written by Nicolas David, which had come back from Avignon with the Pope's approval, showing the descent of Henri de Guise from Charlemagne. Henri paled when he noticed the seal of Saint-Pierre.

'How have you procured this pedigree?'

'I don't bother with these things. It came to me.'

'But where was it before coming to you ?'

'Under a lawyer's pillow.'

'What is his name ?'

'Maître Nicolas David.'

'Where was he ?'

'At Lyons.'

'Who went to Lyons to take it from under his pillow?'

'One of my good friends.'

'What is his occupation ?'

'He preaches.'

'He is a monk, then; what is his name ?'

'Gorenflot.'

'What ? that abominable Leaguer who made the incendiary speech at Sainte-Geneviève, and who, yesterday, insulted me in the streets of Paris ?'

'Do you remember the story of Brutus who acted the fool——'

'He must be a deep politician, your monk of Sainte-Geneviève ?'

'Have you ever heard of Machiavelli? Your mother is his pupil.'

'Then, he stole this from the lawyer ?'

'He took it by force.'

'And, having performed this feat, he has not presented himself to receive payment ?'

'He has retired humbly to his convent, and wishes only to forget that he ever emerged from it.'

'Chicot, your friend shall have the first abbey that is vacant.'

'Thanks for him, Henri,' answered Chicot. Then to himself he added : 'There he is between Mayenne and Valois, between a rope and a prebendaryship; will he be hanged ? will he become abbot ? In any case, should he still be asleep, he must be having some queer dreams just now.'

CHAPTER XLVI

ETÉOCLE AND POLYNICE

THE day finished as noisily and brilliantly as it had begun. The King's friends rejoiced; the preachers in the League prepared to canonise Brother Henri. The favourites said : 'At last the lion has awakened.' The Leaguers said : 'At last the fox has detected the snare.' As the French object to leaders of an inferior intelligence, the conspirators themselves rejoiced at being duped by their King. It is true that the chief of them fled to shelter. The three Princes of Lorraine had departed at full speed, and their principal agent, M. de Monsoreau, was preparing to leave the Louvre in the hope of overtaking the Duc d'Anjou, when Chicot accosted him.

'Where are you hurrying, Monsieur the First Huntsman ?' he asked.

'To His Highness. I am uneasy about him. In these days Princes cannot travel without a suitable retinue.'

'If you are uneasy, so am I; it is rumoured that he is dead,' observed Chicot, in a low voice.

'Bah ! you declared he was travelling,' answered Monsoreau, with an accent of surprise, mingled with joy.

'So it was reported; but now I fully believe the poor Prince is travelling towards the other world.'

'Why have you such gloomy ideas ?'

'He entered the Louvre yesterday, you know, and he has never been seen to leave it !'

'It is a joke, Monsieur Chicot, is it not ?'

'Ask the King.'

'I cannot remain in such doubt,' protested the Comte, walking towards the King's apartments. The King had just gone out. 'Where has the King gone ?' asked the Comte.

'To M. le Duc d'Anjou's room.' The ideas of the First Huntsman were now sadly mixed; it was becoming certain that M. d'Anjou had not left the Louvre. Certain sounds, certain movements in the palace, confirmed the truth. Being ignorant of the real truth, the Prince's absence at so decisive a moment surprised him exceedingly.

The King had, indeed, gone to the Duc's room, and the First Huntsman being unable to follow, was obliged to wait in the corridor. The four minions, in order to be present at the meeting, had been replaced by Swiss guards; but as soon as the assembly was dissolved, they had returned to their posts. François was dreadfully bored, and the conversation of the four gentlemen was not calculated to cheer him.

'Do you know, Maugiron,' said Quélus, 'it was only an hour ago that I began to appreciate our friend Valois; truly he is a capable politician.'

'Do explain yourself,' said Maugiron.

'The King spoke out plainly about the conspiracy, therefore he fears it no longer. As he no longer fears it, he will punish it. Now, if he does that, it will be by means of the law, and we shall have a second presentation of the Amboise affair.'

'A fine sight, upon my word.'

'Unless (it is possible) one puts aside these formalities, on account of the position of the accused, and arranges matters at home privately.'

'I believe that is how family matters are treated, and this last conspiracy is really a family affair,' remarked Maugiron.

Aurilly glanced uneasily at the Prince.

'If I were in the King's place I would not spare the noble conspirators. I would make a thorough example of one or two, one especially, and would drown all the small fry.'

'In that case, it would be feasible to revive the famous invention of the sacks. Of course it would not apply to the leaders; they have the right to claim execution in a public place, or assassination in some corner. But, as you say, the small fry, and by that term I mean favourites, lute-players——'

'Gentlemen,' stammered Aurilly, pale with terror.

'Do not answer, Aurilly; their remarks cannot apply to me or my followers: royal princes are not mocked at in France.'

'No, they cut their heads off,' said Quélus. At this point in the conversation, steps were heard, the door of the room opened, and the King appeared.

François rose. 'Your Majesty,' said he, 'I appeal to your justice on the point of the infamous treatment to which I am subjected by your followers.' But Henri appeared neither to have seen nor heard his brother.

'Your Majesty, is it your intention that your brother be insulted like this ?'

'Silence, monsieur; I object to my prisoners complaining.'

'Prisoner, if you please, but none the less your——'

'The relationship to which you would appeal is fatal to you, in my opinion. My brother guilty is guilty twice over.'

'Of what crime is he guilty ?'

'Of having displeased me.'

'Your Majesty, have our family quarrels need of witnesses ?'

'You are right. Permit me, gentlemen, to talk a moment with monsieur my brother.' The noblemen carried off Aurilly.

'Now, we are alone then,' the King observed.

'I was impatiently awaiting this moment, your Majesty.'

'And I, too: ah! so you are aiming at my crown, worthy Etéocle; you make the League a means and the throne an end. You are anointed in a corner of Paris, in a deserted church, to show yourself presently to the Parisians, all glistening with holy oil !'

'Alas ! your Majesty does not allow me to speak.'

'Why should I ? That you may lie, or repeat what I already know ? You would speak falsely, and that is a shame I would spare you.'

'My brother, is it really your intention to insult me thus ?'

'If my words are insulting, it is I who speak falsely. Come, prove, if it be possible, that you are not disloyal, and a bungler into the bargain.'

'I do not understand your Majesty's meaning.'

'Then I will explain my words; you have conspired against me, as you did previously against my brother Charles. It is true that formerly you crawled like a serpent, now you aspire to bite like a lion; after perfidy, open violence; after poison, the sword.'

'Poison ! What do you mean, monsieur ?' cried François, pale with rage.

'The poison with which you assassinated our brother Charles, and intended also for Henri de Navarre. It has become quite well known, this fatal poison. No doubt that is why you abandoned it in my case, and assumed the airs of a captain. But look at me, François, and convince yourself that a man of your stamp will never kill a man of mine. The sword! I should like to see you in this room, alone with me, with a sword. I have already outdone you in cunning; if you wish to be a knave, at least imitate my methods. My intrigues were royal, my knavery worthy of a captain; from now I will be a King, a despot; I will pursue you in your dark dealings, and at the least suspicion I will hand you over to my executioner. That is what I had to say concerning our family affairs, my brother; that is why I ordered my friends to leave you alone to-night, that, in solitude, you might meditate on my words.'

'At least, your Majesty, fix a term to my captivity, that I may know what to expect.'

'When your sentence is pronounced, you will know. Gentlemen,' continued the King, opening the door, 'M. le Duc d'Anjou has asked permission to reflect to-night upon a reply he is to make to me to-morrow. You will leave him alone, therefore, and only visit his room occasionally as a precaution. You may find your prisoner a little excited by his recent conversation, but remember that in conspiring against me, M. le Duc has renounced his title of brother, so that there is only a captive here : no ceremonies; if the prisoner causes trouble, report to me; the Bastille is under my control, and Maître Laurent Lestu is the finest hand in the world for quelling rebellious spirits.'

'Your Majesty! remember that I am your——'

'You were also the brother of King Charles IX., I believe.'

'At least, restore my servants, my friends.'

'I am depriving myself of mine to give them to you,' and Henri shut the door, leaving his brother to stumble to his chair.

CHAPTER XLVII

WHAT WAS FOUND IN AN EMPTY CUPBOARD

THE stormy interview the Duc d'Anjou had just had with the King had made the former consider his position. The courtiers had not left him in ignorance of what had happened in the Louvre, but had depicted the defeat of MM. de Guise and the triumph of Henri as even greater than they really were; he had heard the mob crying, 'Long live the King' and 'Long live the League!' He saw himself abandoned by the principal leaders, who were desirous of safeguarding their own interests. As he recalled the past he sighed, reflecting that in his struggle against Charles IX. he had two devoted helpers for dupes—Coconnas and La Mole. For the first time, M. d'Anjou felt some remorse at having sacrificed his two associates. His sister Marguerite, too, had loved and consoled him : how had he rewarded her ? Queen Catherine remained, but she had never loved him. She had used him simply as an instrument; once in her hands he had no longer belonged to himself. Then he reflected that recently he had near him one loyal heart equal to all the rest—Bussy, the brave Bussy. In order to please Monsoreau, who knew his secret, he had treated Bussy badly. Now, behold ! the King shared the secret, so that Monsoreau's enmity was no longer to be feared. How passionately he wished that Bussy, grateful and faithful, invincible and loyal, watched over him : it would mean probable liberty, certain revenge. But Bussy, keenly wounded, had retired, and the prisoner remained with fifty feet to traverse before reaching the moats, and four courtiers to disable before arriving in the corridor. The courtyard, moreover, was filled with soldiers. From time to time he glanced from the window; such a height was calculated to turn the bravest giddy. Besides, one of his warders entered every hour, opened doors and windows, hunted in presses, looked under beds and tables, ascertained that the curtains were in their place, and that the sheets were not cut in strips. Occasionally they leaned out of the balcony, and the forty-five feet reassured them.

The favourites were perfectly right; the Duc d'Anjou would never risk a perilous or difficult escape. At times the Prince's pale face was pressed against the window-panes, and he followed the sunset through all its phases, the wonderful sight of old Paris with its roofs gilded by the last sun-rays, silvered by the first moonbeams; gradually terror seized upon him as he saw huge clouds piled up in the sky, above the Louvre, announcing an imminent storm. Among his weaknesses, the Duc numbered that of trembling at the sound of thunder. He threw himself on his bed, but could not sleep; he tried to read, and the letters danced before his eyes; he drank, but the wine seemed bitter; he swept the strings of Aurilly's lute, but the vibration acted on his nerves, increasing his misery. Then he began to swear and to break everything within reach. It was a failing common to the family, and well known in the Louvre. The favourites entered on hearing the terrific din ; but recognising that the Prince was amusing himself, they closed the door.

He had just broken a chair, when a peculiar sound, not to be mistaken, was heard from the window, and M. d'Anjou experienced a sharp pain in his leg. His first idea was that he had been wounded by an arquebus, and that the shot was fired by an emissary of the King. 'Ah ! I am dead !' he cried, slipping down on the carpet. In falling, his hand encountered a hard object, more irregular and bigger than the ball of an arquebus. 'Oh ! a stone; it is a falconet shot, then ?' said he. Picking up the stone, he examined the window. The missile had been thrown so violently that it had pierced a hole through the pane instead of breaking it irregularly, and it appeared to be wrapped in paper. The Duc's ideas changed; had the missile come from a friend ? Perspiration covered his brow; hope, like terror, has its anguish. The Duc approached the window; a paper was indeed rolled round the stone, and fastened with silk thread. Without this wrapping, the missile would have caused the Prince greater pain. To break the thread, to unwind the paper was the work of a second; the Duc was completely restored. 'A letter,' he murmured, glancing furtively around him. Then he read the following :—

'Are you tired of staying in your apartment ? Do you wish for fresh air and freedom ? Enter the room where the Queen of Navarre concealed your poor friend, M. de la

Mole; open the press and, on moving the hammer-beam at the foot, you will find a double bottom; in it there is a silk ladder; fasten this to the balcony, two strong arms will stretch it out to the moat. A horse, swift as thought, will carry you to a place of safety.

'A FRIEND.'

'A friend! oh! I did not believe I possessed one. What friend thinks of me?' cried the Duc. After reflecting a moment, he looked from the window, but saw nobody. 'Is it a trap?' he murmured. 'But first, I can ascertain if this cupboard has a double bottom, and if there is a ladder in it.' Trusting to his hands, the Duc approached the room, the door of which he had so often opened with beating heart, expecting to find the Queen of Navarre in her dazzling beauty. Opening the cupboard, he explored the planks, and, feeling the bottom one yield, he slipped in his hand and drew out a silk ladder. Like a thief fleeing with his booty, the Duc carried the treasure into his own room. Ten o'clock rang, and the Duc, recollecting the hourly visit, hid his ladder under the cushion of his chair. In five minutes Maugiron appeared in a dressing-gown, speaking to his friends as he entered.

'The bear is in a fury,' exclaimed a voice; 'take care he doesn't eat you, Maugiron.' The latter approaching the bed, examined the sheets, then the window curtains; he perceived the broken pane, but thought the Duc had broken it in his angry outburst.

'Hallo! Maugiron,' cried Schomberg, 'are you already eaten that you say nothing? Sigh, at least, that we may avenge you.' The Duc snapped his fingers impatiently. 'Not at all,' answered Maugiron, 'my bear is extremely quiet, and quite tamed.' The Duc smiled in the darkness. Maugiron retired, locking the door with a double turn. The Prince murmured, as the sound ceased, 'Gentlemen, take care; a bear is an exceedingly cunning animal.'

Let alone, the Duc d'Anjou, certain of not being interrupted for at least another hour, drew out his ladder, unrolled it, examined each knot, sounded each rung with extreme care and prudence. Then he unwound it to its full length, counting thirty-eight rungs, each fifteen inches apart. 'It is long enough,' he concluded, 'there is no danger on that score.' Still he hesitated. 'Perhaps those accursed courtiers provided the ladder : when I fix it to the balcony to descend they will cut the cords, that is the trap. Eh ! no,' he pursued his thoughts, 'they are not so stupid as to imagine I would descend without first barricading the door, and in that case, I should have time to fly before they could get in. Yet, why should I trust to a ladder found in the Queen of Navarre's cupboard ? Indeed, who but my sister could be aware of its existence ? Which of my friends is so well acquainted with the bottom of presses in my room or my sister's ?' The Duc finishing this seemingly conclusive argument, read the note again, hoping to recognise the writing, when an idea struck him. 'Bussy!' he exclaimed. Indeed Bussy, a hero to the Queen of Navarre, discreet, thoroughly acquainted with the interior of the apartment, very probably was the sender of the note. The Duc's perplexity increased. He had not understood the reason of Bussy's ill-will, being ignorant of his love for Diane de Méridor, though his suspicions had been roused, for how could any one see the beautiful young woman without loving her ! But Bussy's loyalty would not permit him to remain idle while his patron was imprisoned; his vengeance would take the form of restoring him to liberty. Bussy had written, and was waiting for him.

Approaching the window, the Prince discerned through the mist three oblong forms, horses probably, and two posts, which might be two men—Bussy and Le Haudouin. Peeping through the keyhole into the withdrawing-room, he perceived his four warders—two sleeping, two playing at chess. Putting out the light, and opening the window, he leaned over the balcony. The gulf beneath was even more terrifying in the darkness. But air and space are so attractive to a prisoner that François, on drawing back again, felt almost stifled. So strong was the impression that a sort of disgust of life and indifference to death seized him, and he imagined that his courage had revived. Profiting by this moment of exaltation, he fixed the ladder to the balcony, barricaded the door, and returned to the window. He could no longer see anything. The darkness was complete; the first rumblings of the storm shook the sky; a huge cloud stretched across the river; for a minute it was pierced by a flash of lightning, and the Prince imagined that he saw the figures beneath him in the moat. A horse neighed; without a doubt he

was expected. Shaking the ladder to feel if it was securely
fastened, he climbed the railing, and placed his foot on
the top rung. Hardly had he done this than the ladder,
instead of swaying, became firm, and the second rung
met his foot without the ladder moving. Did a friend or
an enemy hold the lower end ? An irresistible terror
seized François; he clutched at the balcony and endeavoured to raise himself up. The invisible person below,
as if guessing his thoughts, gave a gentle and even tug
at the ladder. 'Courage,' said the Duc, 'it is held from
below; evidently they do not wish me to fall,' and he
resumed the descent, letting himself shoot down like an
arrow, slipping on the supports rather than the rungs.
Suddenly, instead of touching the ground, he was clasped
in a man's arms, and the words, 'You are saved!' sounded
in his ear.

Then he was carried to the edge of the moat, pushed
along a path between fallen earth and stones, until finally
the summit was reached. Here another man, seizing him
by the collar, hurried him to the river. The horses were
where François had first seen them. It was impossible
now to draw back, so running to one of the animals he
mounted. The same voice said, in the same brief, mysterious way, 'Ride fast,' and the three galloped off. 'That
goes very well so far,' thought the Prince; 'let us hope the
sequel will not spoil the beginning. Thank you, my
brave Bussy,' he continued, addressing his right hand
companion, who was enveloped in a great brown cloak.
They reached the great moat of the Bastille, and, crossing
by a bridge constructed the night before by the Leaguers,
made for Charenton. Suddenly the man on the right hand
side, leaping the moat, dashed into the Forest of Vincennes, saying to the Prince, 'Come.' The second rider
imitated his companion without speaking. The Prince
had no need to apply the spurs to his horse; the noble
animal leaped the moat as alertly as the others had done;
and responses to his neighing were heard from the depths
of the forest. The Prince, fearful that he might be led
into an ambuscade, wished to stop his horse, but the
animal no longer felt the bit. After a while, however,
his companions slackened speed, and François found
himself in a sort of glade where eight or ten mounted men
were ranged in military fashion, the moonlight shining
on their cuirasses.

'Oh !' exclaimed the Prince, 'what does this mean, monsieur ?'

'It means that you are saved,' was the answer.

'*You*, Henri, my liberator ?' asked the Duc in amazement.

'Why does that surprise you, are we not allies ?' Then, glancing round him, the Béarnais cried, 'Agrippa, where the devil are you ?'

'Here I am,' answered d'Aubigné.

'Get two fresh horses that can go a dozen leagues without resting,'

'But where are you taking me, cousin ?' François asked uneasily.

'Where you wish; only be quick, for, as d'Aubigné says, the King of France possesses better studs than I do, and is rich enough to kill twenty horses should he think of overtaking us.'

'So I am free to go where I will ? Then, let us go to Angers.'

'Very well; true, you are at home there.'

'But you, cousin ?'

'I leave you within sight of Angers to hurry towards Navarre, where my Margot awaits me.'

'Nobody knew you were here ?'

'I came to sell three of my wife's diamonds, and to discover if the League intended to ruin me.'

'You see that such is not the case.'

'Yes, thanks to you. If, instead of refusing to become Head of the League, when you learned it was directed against me, you had accepted, making common cause with my enemies, I should have been lost. So, hearing the King had imprisoned you on account of your refusal, I swore to liberate you, and have done it.'

'Always as simple as ever,' said the Duc to himself.

'Go, cousin, into Anjou. Ah ! Monsieur le Guise, you thought you had gained the town ! but I send you a rather annoying companion; take care !' The fresh steeds Henri had demanded were brought, both mounted and galloped off, followed by Agrippa d'Aubigné, grumbling as he went.

CHAPTER XLVIII

THE FRIENDS

WHILE Paris was thus raging and roaring like a furnace,
Madame de Monsoreau, escorted by her father and two
servants, were quietly travelling towards Méridor, by
stages of ten leagues a day. She began to enjoy that
freedom, so precious to those who have suffered. The
Baron appeared twenty years younger, and to see him
spurring on his old Jarnac, one might have taken him for
an elderly husband accompanying his young wife and
tenderly watching over her. Sometimes Diane, rising
impatiently when the moon shone on her window in the
inn chamber, would waken the Baron, and they would
travel a few leagues in the moonlight. When Diane
saw only scattered flocks in the the pasture lands, or the
bell-tower of some little town standing up in the distance,
she became more impatient than ever. Then her father
would say : 'Have no fear, Diane.'

'Fear of what, father ?'

'Are you not looking to see if M. de Monsoreau is
following ?'

'Ah, true ! I was looking,' the young woman would
answer, glancing round again. So they arrived, towards
the end of the eighth day, at the Château de Méridor,
and were received by Madame de Saint-Luc and her
husband. Then these four people began an existence such
as everybody has dreamed of in reading Virgil and
Theocritus. The Baron and Saint-Luc hunted from
morning to night. Diane and Jeanne, sitting on the moss
beneath the trees, would start at the sound of the chase,
and then resume their tender and mysterious conversation.

'Tell me, little sister, all that happened to you in the
tomb, for you were truly dead for us,' Jeanne would say.

'What can I tell you ?'

'You have nothing to tell. You are happy, then ? Yet
that shadow under your beautiful eyes, those pale cheeks,
that forced smile. Diane, you must have much to tell
me.'

'Nothing.'

'You are happy—with M. de Monsoreau?' Diane shuddered.

'Why do you say that name?' she asked; 'why evoke this phantom in the midst of our woods and our happiness.'

'I know now why there are deep shadows under your eyes, but not why you try to smile. You told me, I think, that M. de Bussy had shown a great interest in you.' Diane blushed furiously.

'M. de Bussy thinks no more of Diane de Méridor. Oh! I have been cowardly. No, it is not my fault, he did not wish it. I remember my position seemed terrible. My father offered me support, and I was afraid. He offered me protection, but not so as to convince me. The Duc d'Anjou was against him; the Duc d'Anjou was leagued with M. de Monsoreau, you will say. Well! what do the Duc d'Anjou and the Comte de Monsoreau matter! Jeanne, if I ever loved——'

'Calm yourself, dear friend.'

'I tell you we were cowardly.'

'We, Diane, of whom are you speaking?'

'I mean my father and I; my father is a nobleman who could have spoken to the King; I am proud, and do not fear a man whom I hate. But the secret of this cowardice is that I understood he did not love me.'

'You are false to yourself! if you believed that, you would reproach him with it. But you know the contrary, hypocrite.'

'Consider a little; I, whom this passionate young man claims to love, I was married publicly, I offered myself before all the court, and he did not look at me; I entrusted myself to him in the cloisters of La Gypecienne. Oh! I think of it now, he could have carried me off! I saw him suffering, with languishing eyes and parched lips. If he had asked me to die for him, I would have done it. Well! I left, and he did not think of restraining me. He knew I was leaving Paris, that M. de Monsoreau is not my husband; he knew that I was coming alone, and all along the road I turned round, expecting to hear his horse. You see, he thinks no more about me, and I am not worth a journey into Anjou, when there are so many beautiful ladies at court, whose smile equals a hundred confessions of the provincial, buried at Méridor. Do you understand, my poor Jeanne, that I am forgotten, despised?'

She had not finished, when moss and plaster fell in a shower from the old wall, and a man landed at Diane's feet. 'You see that I am here,' murmured Bussy, kissing the edge of Diane's robe. Jeanne having seen and recognised him, had withdrawn. Diane now recognised the Comte's voice and smile, and, carried out of herself, overcome by this unhoped-for happiness, she fell into the arms of the man she had just accused of indifference.

CHAPTER XLIX

THE LOVERS

SWOONS of joy are neither long nor dangerous : some have been fatal, but the cases are exceedingly rare. Before long Diane opened her eyes to find herself in Bussy's arms, for the young man would not grant Madame Saint-Luc the privilege of receiving Diane's first glance.

'Oh,' she murmured, as she came to herself, 'oh, Comte, it was terrible to surprise us like this.'

'Ah, madame,' asked Bussy, 'is it thus you receive me?'

'No,' replied Diane,' 'for truly, Monsieur de Bussy, what you were going to do was tender and affectionate, but——'

'For mercy's sake, no buts,' sighed Bussy, kneeling again before Diane.

'No, no, not thus, not on your knees, Monsieur de Bussy.'

'Oh, for one moment let me plead to you as I am,' said the Comte, clasping his hands. 'For long I have envied this place.'

'Yes; but to take it you have overleaped the wall. Not only is it not suitable for a lord of your rank, but it is most imprudent for one who should have care of my honour.'

'How so ?'

'If by chance any one had seen you.'

'Who, then ?'

'Our pursuers, who, hardly a quarter of an hour ago, passed into the thicket behind the wall.'

'Calm yourself, madame; I have hidden with too great care to be seen.

'Hidden! Truly? This is supremely romantic. Tell us how, Monsieur de Bussy.'

'To begin with, if I did not rejoin you on the way, it was not my fault. I took one road and you the other. Besides, it was not in the presence of your father or of your people that I wished to see you again. I took the road stage by stage, biting at the handle of my whip, which became my constant nourishment during those days.'

'Poor fellow!' said Jeanne, 'look how thin he is.'

'At last you came,' continued Bussy; 'I took lodgings in the outskirts of the town, and, hidden by a blind, saw you pass.'

'Oh, my goodness!' cried Diane, 'were you at Angers undisguised?'

'For what do you take me?' asked Bussy, with a smile. 'No, no; I was a merchant. Owing to my brown clothes, no one took any notice of me.'

'Bussy, handsome Bussy, two days on end in a provincial town without being noticed? They'll never believe that at the court.'

'Continue, Comte,' said the blushing Diane; 'how did you get here from the town?'

'I have two horses of fine breed. One of them I mounted, and rode slowly from the town. But as soon as I was out of sight, I proceeded at a gallop that covered the three and a half leagues in twenty minutes. Once in the Wood of Méridor, I turned to the east and found the wall. Then I saw you as you re-entered the house.'

'It seems a beautiful story,' said Jeanne; 'but had I been in your place I should have gone straight to the bridge of the château of Méridor and entered. The Baron would have clasped me in his arms, Madame de Monsoreau would have placed me near her at table, M. de Saint-Luc would have overwhelmed me with favours, and Madame de Saint-Luc would have made anagrams with me. It is the simplest thing in the world; though it is true that the simplest thing is just what lovers won't notice.'

'No,' said Bussy, shaking his head; 'I could not enter the château. Madame is married, and the Baron owes a strict guard on behalf of his daughter's husband.'

'Good,' said Jeanne, 'I am receiving a lesson in manners. Thanks, M. de Bussy, it will teach me to interfere in the concerns of fools.'

'Of fools!' repeated Diane.

'Fools or lovers,' answered Madame Saint-Luc; 'and as a result——'

She embraced Diane, made a curtsey to de Bussy, and fled. Diane looked at her plucking flowers at a distance, and then, with a blush, sat down, whilst Bussy threw himself at her feet.

'Have I done well, madame?' he asked; 'do you approve of my action?'

'I will make no pretence,' replied Diane, 'and besides, you know what I think. Yes, I approve, but there my indulgence calls a halt; in wishing for you, in calling you as I have done, I have been foolish and wicked.'

'What *are* you saying, Diane?'

'Alas, Comte! I speak the truth. I have the right to render M. Monsoreau unhappy, because he has driven me to this extremity, but no right to make another man happy. I may deny him my presence, my smiles, my love; but if I give these favours to another, I shall rob him who, despite myself, is my master.'

Bussy listened patiently to this moral speech. Then he asked,—

'Is it my turn to speak?'

'Speak,' answered Diane.

'With freedom?'

'Speak.'

'Well, not a single word of what you have said comes from your heart.'

Diane moved, and opened her mouth to reply, but Bussy stopped her by a sign.

'I know what you would say,' the young man continued. 'You would tell me that if I provoke M. de Monsoreau and kill him, you will never see me again. So be it. I shall die of grief at never seeing you, but you will be free and joyful, and will make happy some other man, who will sometimes bless my name. And you, yourself, Diane, who dare not thank me living, will thank me when I am dead.'

The young woman seized the Comte's hand and pressed it tenderly. 'You have never asked me, Bussy,' said she, 'yet you are threatening me.'

'Threatening you? God knows what I mean. I love you dearly, Diane, and I know you love me. I love you, and it is for my whole life. I swear before Heaven that

I would die for you, and die adoring you. Yet if you say "Go away; do not steal the happiness of another," I would rise without a sigh, without a sign, from this place where I am so happy and depart, and you would never see me more.'

Diane read in his looks the strength of his resolution, and as snow melts beneath an April shower, so her firmness disappeared in the fire of his glance.

'Will you love me till death, as you say ? Shall I not be your plaything, and will you not leave me one day with a hateful regret that I did not listen to M. de Monsoreau's love ? But, no; I am conquered, I am free, I am yours, Bussy. Remain then, dear one, and now that my life is yours, watch over us both.'

Saying these words, Diane placed one of her hands upon de Bussy's shoulder and offered him the other, which he took and carried to his lips. Diane thrilled under the kiss. Then they heard the approach of Jeanne, accompanied by a little warning cough. Instinctively the interlaced hands separated.

'Pardon, my good friends, for disturbing you,' said she, 'but we must return upon pain of their coming to search for us. Come along, Diane.' And Jeanne, taking her friend's arm, drew her away.

De Bussy looked at the two friends with a smile. Diane, turning towards him, held out her hand. He approached them.

'Ah,' he asked, 'is this all you have to say ?'

'Till to-morrow,' answered Diane.

'Only till to-morrow ?'

'To-morrow and always.'

Bussy could not restrain a cry of delight. He bent and kissed Diane's hand; then bidding a last adieu to the ladies, he walked off at a rapid pace.

CHAPTER L

BUSSY MEETS THE DUC D'ANJCU

NEXT day Bussy left Angers before the earliest risers
had broken their fast. He did not run; he flew upon the
road. Diane, having climbed upon a terrace of the château,
whence could be seen the white, winding highway, perceived this black speck advancing like a meteor, and leaving
behind it the road, stretched out like a ribbon. Diane's
heart was full of joy. She felt the exhilaration of youth,
beauty, and love, and it seemed to her that her soul
raised her body upon wings as if approaching the presence
of God. But the way from the house to the thicket was
long, her tiny feet grew tired with treading on the dried
grass, and several times she became breathless. She
arrived at the trysting-place at the very moment when
Bussy appeared on the top of the wall and threw himself
down. He saw her run. Uttering a cry of joy as he
advanced with extended arms, she threw herself towards
him, both hands pressed upon her heart. This morning
salute was a long, ardent embrace. What need they say ?
They loved each other. What need they think ? They
saw each other. What had they to wish for ? They were
seated side by side, hand in hand. The day passed like
an hour. When Diane awoke from that sweet torpor
which is the slumber of a soul exhausted with happiness,
Bussy pressed her to his heart, saying,—

'Diane, it appears to me that to-day my life really
begins; to-day I can see clearly the road that leads to
eternity, and you are the light which has revealed so
much happiness. I am ignorant of the world and of the
men in it; but I repeat to-day my assertion of yesterday.
Having gained life through you, I shall die with you.'

'And I,' she answered, 'I, who was ready to throw
myself into the arms of death—I tremble to-day lest
I should not live long enough to enjoy to the full the
treasures promised by your love. But why not come to the
château, Louis ? My father would be happy to welcome
you; M. de Saint-Luc is your friend, and he is discreet.'

'Alas, Diane, if I went for an hour to the château,

I should be there always. All the province would hear of it, and if the rumour reached the ears of your husband, he would hurry—— You have forbidden me to take you away.'

'What would be the use ?' asked she, with that inflection which one finds only in the voice of the woman one loves.

'Well, for our safety, that is to say, for the safety of our happiness, we must hide our secret from all the world. Madame Saint-Luc knows it already ; Saint-Luc will discover it, too.'

'Oh, why ?'

'I have written him this morning, asking for an interview at Angers. He will come, and I shall have his promise as a gentleman that never a word of this adventure will escape him. This is the more important, dear Diane, because they will certainly search for me. Matters were in a grave condition when we left Paris.'

'You are right; and since my father is so scrupulous, much as he loves me, he would be capable of denouncing me to M. de Monsoreau.'

'We must hide it well, and then, if God gives us over to our enemies, we can at least assert that to have acted differently was impossible.'

'God is good, Louis; not for a moment must we doubt Him.'

'I do not doubt God, but I fear the malice of some devil jealous of our joy.'

The two lovers exchanged a thousand pleasantries, intermingled with a thousand kisses. At length, sounds of the chase reached the château, and Bussy departed. As he approached the town, dreaming of this entrancing day and proud of being free, for the cares of riches and the favours of a prince of the blood had always held him in golden chains, he noticed that it was almost time for the town gates to be closed. Bussy prepared to spur his horse, to make up for lost time, when he heard behind him the galloping of horses. To a man in hiding, and to a lover, everything appears a menace, and Bussy asked himself whether it were better to gallop and thus keep in front, or to draw to one side and let the horsemen pass. But their pace was so rapid that they were upon him in a moment. They were two. Drawing to one side, Bussy perceived that one rider was spurring his mount and lashing it with a stirrup-leather.

'Good; here's the town,' cried this man, in a most pronounced Gascon accent; 'a hundred more cuts with the whip, a hundred more jogs with the spur, and we shall be there. Courage!'

'The brute can hardly breathe; she is shivering and losing strength, and will no longer move,' answered the one in front. 'I would give a hundred horses to be within my town.'

'Some belated Angevin,' said Bussy to himself. 'What fools fear makes of men. I thought I recognised the voice. But how the fellow's horse staggers.'

At this moment the riders were level with Bussy. 'Look out, sir,' he cried, 'the beast is going to fall.'

In truth the horse fell heavily upon its flank, and kicked convulsively with one leg as it struck the earth; the laboured breathing ceased, the froth suffocated it, and it expired.

'Monsieur,' cried the dismounted rider, 'three hundred pistoles for the horse that carries you.'

'Ah, *mon Dieu!*' cried Bussy, as he approached.

'Do you hear me? I am pressed.'

'Ah, Prince, take him for nothing,' said Bussy, trembling with deep emotion as he recognised the Duc d'Anjou.

At this very moment they heard the sharp click of a pistol, with which the Prince's companion was armed.

'Stop!' cried the Duc d'Anjou to this pitiless defender; 'stop! It is M. de Bussy, or the very deuce is in it.'

'Yes, Prince, it is I. But what in the world makes you kill your horses at this time of night, and upon this road?'

'Ah, it is M. de Bussy?' said d'Aubigné; 'then, my lord, you have no further need of me. Permit me to return to him who sent me, as saith the Holy Scripture.'

'Not without receiving my thanks and the promise of my friendship,' said the Prince.

'I accept all, my lord, and will one day bring your words back to remembrance.'

'M. d'Aubigné! My lord! I am quite bewildered.'

'Did you not know?' asked the Prince, with a defiant discontent which did not escape the nobleman. 'If you are here, were you not waiting for me?'

'The deuce,' said Bussy to himself, recognising what suspicions his secret stay in Anjou might raise in François's mind, 'I must be careful.' Aloud he said: 'I was doing

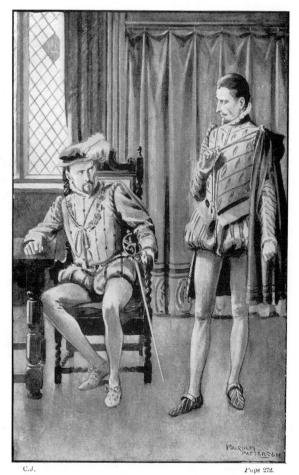

'" Poison! What do you mean?"
cried Francois.'

better than wait for you; and since you wish to enter the city before the gates are closed, mount, my lord.'

He offered his horse to the Prince, who was busily engaged taking out important papers hidden between the saddle and the saddle-cloth of his animal.

'Farewell, then, my lord,' said d'Aubigné, turning to the right-about; 'M. de Bussy, your servant.' And off he went.

Bussy leaped lightly on the animal behind his master, and guided the horse to the town, which they entered at the first sound of the trumpets.

'Where now, my lord ?'

'To the château; where my flag flies, where I am known, and where the nobility of the province gather together.'

'Nothing easier,' said Bussy, making up his mind that docility would gain time. Besides, he was too surprised to be anything but passive.

'Hallo ! trumpeters,' he cried.

They paid him little attention, for they saw only two dusty travellers with a poor enough equipage.

'Ho ! ho !' cried Bussy, going up to them; 'is the master not recognised in his own house ?'

This arrogant tone drew the heralds' attention, and one of them approached.

'Heavens !' he cried in affright, looking keenly at the Duc, 'it's our lord and master !'

'Well,' said Bussy, 'put breath into your trumpets, and let the whole town know in a quarter of an hour that monseigneur has come home. Now, my lord, let us go to the château. By the time we arrive, everything will be prepared for us.'

In truth a crowd soon gathered from all quarters. The sheriffs, the governor, the chief gentlemen all moved towards the palace, followed by a crowd which every moment became denser. As Bussy had predicted, the authorities were at the château before the Prince, that they might receive him worthily. They had trouble enough in their progress because of the crush; but Bussy found a trumpeter who, rapping the heads of those within reach of his trumpet, forced a way for the Prince.

'Gentlemen and faithful friends,' said the Prince, 'I have come to throw myself into my good town of Angers. At Paris, the most terrible dangers threatened my life. I even lost my liberty, but thanks to good friends, I succeeded in escaping.'

C.J.   K

Bussy bit his lips. He guessed the irony intended by this speech.

'Since I am within your town my peace and safety are assured.'

The magistrates, half-dazed, cried feebly, 'Long live our lord.' The people, in the hope of the usual alms, shouted with more spirit.

'Let us sup,' said the Prince; 'I have had nothing since morning.'

In a moment the Duc was surrounded by his retainers, and the reception lasted till midnight. The town was illuminated, musket shots rang in the streets and squares, the cathedral bells were rung, and the wind bore even to Méridor the joyful sounds raised by the good Angevins in honour of their ruler.

CHAPTER LI

THE DUC D'ANJOU'S DIPLOMACY

'LET us talk,' said the Duc, when the noise of the muskets and the clanging of bells had died down a little. The ante-chambers were empty, and he and Bussy were alone. Thanks to his acuteness, François felt that since their meeting Bussy had made many more advances than was his custom, and with his knowledge of the court, came to the conclusion that the nobleman was in an awkward fix. As a result, with a little tact the Duc might take advantage of this. But Bussy having had time to prepare himself, waited on the Prince with a bold front.

'Let us talk, my lord,' he replied.

'The last time I saw you, you were very ill, Bussy.'

'True, my lord,' answered the young man; 'I *was* ill, and was saved almost by a miracle.'

'That day there was near you a certain doctor much troubled about your health, for he seemed to me to fly at every one who approached.'

'True, again, Prince. Haudouin loves me well.'

'He kept you strictly to bed, did he not ?'

'At which I was mightily angry, as your Highness could see.'

'But,' continued the Duc, 'if you were so very angry,

you should have sent the Faculty to the deuce and attended me as I wished. In reality, you were afraid of compromising yourself.'

'What ?' said Bussy; 'you asserted, I believe, that I was afraid of compromising myself, Prince ?'

'I said so,' replied the Duc.

Bussy sprang from his seat and faced him.

'Then you lie, my lord,' cried he. 'You lie to yourself, do you hear, for you do not believe a word, not a single word of what you have just said. Upon my body there are twenty scars to prove that occasionally I compromise myself, but that I am never afraid. And by my faith I know many men who could not affirm so much, still less show the scars.'

'You always produce strong arguments, M. de Bussy,' replied the Duc, who was pale and agitated; 'when you are assured you shout very loudly, which makes you believe you are in the right.'

'Oh, I am not always right, my lord; I know that well enough. Indeed, I admit occasionally being in the wrong.'

'And when are you wrong, pray ?'

'When I serve ingrates.'

'Truly, sir, I think you forget yourself,' said the Prince, suddenly raising himself with a dignity, which under certain circumstances he could assume quite naturally.

'Ah ! I forget myself, do I ? Once in your life you did the same.' And he took two steps to go out. But the Prince was quicker, and the young man found the Duc before the door.

'Do you deny, monsieur,' said the Duc; 'do you deny that on the day you refused to accompany me you went out almost an instant after ?'

'I deny nothing, my lord, if that is all you are seeking to make me avow.'

'Tell me why you remained so obstinately in your house.'

'Because I had business to look after.'

'At home ?'

'And elsewhere.'

'When a gentleman is in the service of a prince is not his business chiefly that of his prince ?'

'And who looks after your business, my lord, if I do not ?'

'I don't say you do not,' said François, 'and, speaking generally, I find you faithful and devoted. I shall say more—I will excuse your bad temper.'

'Ah, you are very good.'

'I promise you the disgrace of M. de Monsoreau. It seems you dislike him.'

'Not at all. I think him ugly, and want him removed from court so that I need not see him. You, on the contrary, have a liking for him. We must not inquire too deeply into tastes.'

'Anyhow you were wrong not to accompany me, and then to set off on deeds of useless bravery.'

'Deeds of useless bravery? And a moment ago you reproached me with having—— Come, my lord, come, be consistent. What deeds of bravery I been doing?'

'Well, there are M. d'Épernon and M. de Schomberg.'

'What of them?' asked Bussy.

'Kill them, man; kill them both, but do not anger them, especially if you are going far off, for their anger falls upon me.'

'Why, what have I done to the worthy Gascon?'

'You attacked him.'

'I?'

'To such an extent that his doublet was in tatters, his cloak in rags, so that he was forced to enter the Louvre in trunk hose.'

'So much for one,' replied Bussy. 'Now, let us get on to the German. How have I treated him?'

'Do you deny that you dipped him in indigo? When I saw him three hours afterwards he was still of an azure hue; and you call that a good joke! Go along with you.'

The Prince laughed in spite of himself, while Bussy could not forbear joining in, as he recalled the figure Schomberg had cut in the vat.

'So the credit of this exploit is laid to me,' he said.

'Perhaps I did it?'

'And you have the courage, my lord, to reproach a man who has ideas like those? Did I not assert you are ungrateful?'

'Agreed. But, now, if you really went out for this purpose, I forgive you.'

'Are you quite sure?'

'Yes, on my word of honour. But you have not come to the end of my troubles.'

'Continue, my lord.'

'Let us speak of myself for a little.'

'I am listening.'

'What have you done to get me out of my awkward fix ?'

'You see well enough what I have done,' replied Bussy.

'No, I don't see.'

'Well, I have come to Anjou.'

'That is, you are saving yourself.'

'Yes, because at the same time I am saving you.'

'Instead of saving yourself so far off, it seems to me you would have been much more useful at Montmartre than at Angers.'

'That is where we differ : I chose to come to Angers.'

'That is a poor reason. Your caprice——'

'Not so; for this caprice had for its aim the recruiting of your retainers.'

'Come, that's a different story. Well, what have you done ?'

'Time enough to discuss that to-morrow, my lord, for we are now at the hour when we must part.'

'But why leave me ?'

'To confer with a very important person.'

'Ah, in that case, it is quite another thing. Go, Bussy, but be prudent.'

'Prudent ? What is the use ? We are the strongest here.'

'No matter : risk nothing. Have you already gone about very much ?'

'I have been here two days; what would you expect in that time ?'

'Where do you lodge ?'

'Ah, that is where my devotion proves itself. I live—I live in a hut near the rampart, with a bolt-hole to the river. But you, Prince, in your turn, why have you left the Louvre ? Why did I find you on the highway with a foundered horse between your knees and M. d'Aubigné at your heels ?'

'Because I had friends of whom you are ignorant.'

'Good. And who were they ?'

'The King of Navarre, and M. d'Aubigné, whom you have seen.'

'The King of Navarre . . . Ah, true. Haven't you conspired together ? But how did you get out of the Louvre ?'

'By my bedroom window.'

'Ah, then you are aware of the rope-ladder in the armoury?'

'Oh, so you know of it, too,' said the Prince, growing pale.

'Just so,' said Bussy; 'your Highness will remember that sometimes I had the honour of entering that room.'

'In the time of my sister Margot! And you came in by that window?'

'You came out by it, anyhow. But what astonishes me is that you should have found the rope-ladder.'

'The King of Navarre informed me.'

'So he knew of it! I should not have believed it. Well, here you are, my lord, safe and sound. We are going to set Anjou in a flame, and Angoumois and Bearn will follow. It will be a very pretty blaze.'

'But did you not say something about a rendezvous?'

'True; but this interesting conversation made me forget. Adieu, my lord.'

'Are you taking your horse?'

'If he is of service to you, your Highness may have him I have another.'

'Then I accept. Later on we will settle accounts.'

The Prince, who felt his need of Bussy, held out his hand, which Bussy shook, and the two parted.

CHAPTER LII

THE DIPLOMACY OF SAINT-LUC

Bussy returned home on foot, but instead of Saint-Luc, whom he expected, he found a note announcing that his friend would arrive on the morrow. About six o'clock Saint-Luc left Méridor and set out for Angers. He arrived on foot at the ramparts as the gates were being opened, and did not notice the strange excitement of the citizens as he threaded his way to Bussy's house. The two friends exchanged cordial greetings.

'Deign to accept the hospitality of my poor chamber,' said Bussy; 'I am camping at Angers.'

'Yes,' replied Saint-Luc, 'like a conqueror on the field of battle.'

'What do you mean, my dear fellow?'

'That my wife has no more secrets from me than I have from her, my dear Bussy, and that she has revealed everything. Receive my compliments, and permit me to offer a word of advice. Get rid quickly of Monsoreau. Nobody knows of your intrigue with his wife; this is a good moment, but don't let it slip. When later on you marry the widow, nobody will be able to say that in order to marry her you made her a widow.'

'There is one obstacle to this fine scheme, which occurred to me, as it has to you.'

'What is that?'

'I promised Diane to respect the life of her husband so long as he did not attack me.'

'You were wrong. Nobody pays any attention to such oaths. If you do not make haste, Monsoreau will discover you, and as he is chivalrous, will kill you.'

'That will happen which God determines,' replied Bussy, with a smile. 'But supposing I break my oath, the world will stone me, my dear fellow, and the man who is to-day a monster to every one will appear as an angel when he lies on his bier.'

'I did not advise you to kill him yourself.'

'Assassins! Ah, Saint-Luc, that is sad advice.'

'Don't be so hasty. Who spoke to you of assassins?'

'Of what did you speak, then?'

'Of nothing, my dear friend. There passed through my mind an idea which is not yet sufficiently developed to communicate. I don't like Monsoreau any more than you do, though I have not the same reasons for hating him. Let us speak of the wife instead of the husband.'

Bussy smiled.

'You are a good companion, Saint-Luc,' he said; 'and you can reckon on my friendship. Now, you know my friendship is composed of three parts—my purse, my sword, and my life. But what do you wish to say about Diane?'

'I wish to ask you if you cannot pay a short visit to Méridor.'

'My dear friend, thanks for your insistence, but you know my scruples.'

'I know everything. At Méridor you run the risk of meeting Monsoreau, although he is eighty leagues away; you may have to shake his hand, and it is hard to shake the hand of a man you would gladly strangle; lastly,

you might see him embrace Diane, and it is grievous
to see the woman one loves kissed by another.'

'Ah!' cried Bussy; 'how well you understand why
I do not got to Méridor. Now, my dear friend——'

'You are turning me off,' said Saint-Luc, misunder-
standing Bussy's intention.

'Not at all. On the contrary,' he replied, 'I beg you
to remain, for it is now my turn to question you.'

'Very well.'

'Did you not hear last night the clanging of bells and
the rattle of muskets?'

'Yes, and down there we wondered what had happened.'

'Did you not notice this morning a remarkable change
as you came through the town?'

'I was going to ask what it meant.'

'It means that the Duc d'Anjou arrived yesterday.'

Saint-Luc sprang from his chair as if his companion
had announced the presence of the devil.

'The Duc at Angers! It was reported he was in prison
at the Louvre.'

'It is just because he was in prison at the Louvre that
he is now at Angers. He managed to escape by a window,
and has come to seek refuge here.'

'Well?' queried Saint-Luc.

'Well, my dear friend, here is an excellent opportunity
of avenging yourself for His Majesty's little persecutions.
The Prince has already a party; he is about to gather
troops, and we shall stir up something like a pretty little
civil war.'

'Oh, oh!' exclaimed Saint-Luc.

'And I counted on you to draw the sword with us.'

'Against the King?' questioned Saint-Luc, with sudden
coldness.

'Not precisely against the King,' replied Bussy, 'I
mean against those who draw the sword against us.'

'My dear Bussy, I came to Angers for the country air,
and not to fight against His Majesty.'

'But let me present you to Monseigneur.'

''Twould be useless, my dear Bussy. I don't like
Angers, and mean to leave it soon. It is a tiresome place;
the stones are as soft as cheese, and the cheese as hard as
stones.'

'My dear Saint-Luc, you will do me a great service
if you join me. The Duc asked what I was doing here,

and not being able to answer truthfully, since he himself loves Diane and has come too near her, I pretended I had come to draw the gentlemen of the province to his side. I even added that this morning I had a rendezvous with one of them.'

'Well, tell him you have seen this gentleman, and that he asked six months to think it over.'

'You have the advantage just now,' said Bussy; 'I have need of your assistance.'

'Not at all. It is I, on the contrary, who claim your protection.'

'How so ?'

'Suppose the Angevins besiege and put Méridor to fire and sword.'

'The deuce ! you are right,' said Bussy; 'you do not wish the inhabitants to suffer the consequences of an assault.'

The two friends laughed, and as Bussy's servant announced that the Prince had called thrice for him, they swore fealty to their new comradeship, and separated, each charmed with the other. Bussy proceeded to the ducal palace, where already the nobles were gathering from all parts of the province. Hurriedly he arranged an official reception, a repast, speeches; and as these things would occupy the Prince for some time, he decided to see Diane, if it were only for an instant. When he had finished the Duc's business, he regained his house, mounted his second horse, and started at a gallop for Méridor. The Duc, left to himself, made some very fine speeches, and produced a wonderful effect in speaking of the League, touching with caution upon the points dealing with his alliance with the Guises, and representing himself as persecuted by the King because of the confidence the Parisians had manifested in him. During the replies and the hand-kissing, the Duc d'Anjou noted with care the gentlemen who were present, and with still greater care those who were away. When Bussy arrived, it was four o'clock in the afternoon. Leaping from his horse, he presented himself, covered with dust, before the Duc.

'Ah, my good Bussy,' said the Duc, 'you have been at work it seems. Take care you do not make yourself ill.'

'There is no danger.'

'And whence do you come ?'

'From the environs. Has your Highness had a full court?'

'Yes, pretty fair; but I miss your friend the Baron of Méridor. However, I have not neglected him, though he has neglected me. The Baron has influence in the province.'

'Do you think so?'

'I am sure of it. He has been appointed correspondent of the League in Angers. He was chosen by M. de Guise, and as a rule the Guises select good men. He must come, Bussy.'

'But if he refuses?'

'Then I shall go to him.'

'To Méridor?'

'Why not?'

Bussy could not restrain the devouringly jealous light that leaped to his eyes.

'Yes,' he said, 'why not? You are a prince, and all things are permitted to you.'

'Have you not seen him?'

'What!' exclaimed Bussy; 'I have not been so fortunate in the fulfilment of my promises to be in a great hurry to visit him.'

'Has he not had his desire gratified?'

'How so?'

'He wished his daughter to marry the Comte, and the Comte has married her.'

'Let us say no more about that, my lord,' remarked Bussy, turning his back upon the Prince.

At this moment some other gentlemen entered; the Prince went to greet them, and Bussy remained alone. Anjou's conversation made him extremely thoughtful. What could be the Duc's real intentions with regard to the Baron de Méridor? He examined the Prince's position, such as it was; he saw him at loggerheads with his brother, exiled from the Louvre, and heading an insurrection in the provinces. He threw into the balance his material interests as against his amorous fancies, and could pardon everything except the last. He passed the evening banqueting with his Royal Highness and his Angevin followers, and in bowing to the Angevin dames. Then, as violins were at hand, he taught them the latest dances. It goes without saying that he was the admiration of the ladies and the despair of their husbands; and directly any of the latter looked at him unpleasantly, Bussy pulled his moustache

eight or ten times, and asked if they would not like to
walk on the lawn with him in the moonlight.   But his
reputation has preceded him to Angers, and the
invitation was not accepted.

CHAPTER LIII

THE DIPLOMACY OF M. DE BUSSY

At the gate of the ducal palace, Bussy found a frank,
loyal, smiling figure whom he imagined to be eighty
leagues away.

'Ah!' he exclaimed joyfully, 'is it you, Rémy?'

'Why, yes, my lord.'

'I intended to write asking you to come.'

'In that case it is wonderful, for I feared you would
scold me.'

'Why?'

'Because I came without permission. But, my faith!
I heard that the Duc d'Anjou had escaped from the
Louvre, and that he had left for the province. Remembering that you were in the neighbourhood of Angers, and
believing civil war would arise, I feared you would get
several holes in your skin. Then, since I love my neighbour as myself, and better than myself, I came here.'

'You have done well, Rémy.'

'How is Gertrude, my lord?'

Bussy smiled. 'I promise to ask Diane the first time
I meet her,' he said. 'But you are a charming companion.
How did you manage to find me?'

'With little difficulty. I asked for the ducal palace,
and waited for you at the gate, after having seen my horse
stabled.'

'Well, then, come and see where I am lodged,' said
Bussy, conducting Rémy into the little house on the
ramparts. 'Behold the palace: put up where and as you
like.'

'That won't be very difficult; besides, I am tired enough
to sleep on my feet.' And the two friends parted for the
time.

Early in the morning Bussy went to the château to
see, if possible, His Highness as he awoke, hoping thus

to obtain some insight into the Duc's real designs. Like his brother, Anjou wore a mask at night. Bussy was prepared with a list of engagements for the morning, each more important than the other. First, a walk beyond the walls to view the fortifications; then a review of the citizens and their arms; a visit to the arsenal; a minute examination of the resources of the province, in order to obtain from the Prince's good and faithful vassals an extra tax to fill his coffers; last of all, correspondence. But Bussy did not lay too great stress on this last item; the Duc d'Anjou wrote very little, for in that age they paid serious attention to the saying, 'Writing remains to be seen.' In spite of the Duc's ill and gloomy thoughts, Bussy could gather nothing from his eyes.

'Ah,' said the Duc, 'are you here already?'

'Yes, my lord. Your Highness's interests gripped me so closely that I was unable to sleep. Now, what shall we do this morning? Shall we hunt?'

'What?' asked the Duc; 'you pretend to have been studying my interests all night, and the whole result is that you propose a hunt. That is good!'

'It is true,' replied Bussy; 'but, anyhow, we have no pack.'

'Nor a grand hunter,' said the Prince.

'My word! I find hunting more agreeable without him.'

'Ah! I differ from you.'

The Duc said this with a peculiar smile which Bussy did not fail to observe. 'I know that smile,' he reflected; 'it bodes no good.'

'You have a grudge against him?' asked the Prince.

'Against Monsoreau! What have I against him?'

'That he is my friend.'

'On the contrary, I pity him very much.'

'That is to say?'

'That the higher you raise him the greater will be the height from which he will fall when his time arrives.'

'Ah, you are in a merry mood.'

'Yes, it is only when you are in good humour that you say these things.'

'No matter; I hold to my opinion—Monsoreau could be useful here.'

'How so?'

'Because he has estates in the neighbourhood.'

Bussy bit his lips. 'Do you think so,' he asked.

'To be sure. Méridor is three leagues from Angers. You who brought the old Baron ought to know that.'

'I only brought him to you because he hung on to my mantle.'

'Listen,' said the Duc; 'I have an idea.'

'The deuce you have,' said Bussy, who always opposed the Prince's ideas. 'What do you mean, Prince?'

'It is very simple. You know me, Bussy?'

'I have that misfortune.'

'Do you think me the man to submit to insult and let it go unpunished?'

'That depends.'

The Duc's smile was more evil than his previous one, as he stood biting his lips and nodding his head.

'What do you mean, my lord?' Bussy asked.

'Well, the First Huntsman has stolen from me a young woman whom I loved, in order that he might marry her. In my turn I intend to steal his wife from him, in order to make her my mistress.'

Bussy made an effort to smile, but though he tried hard he only succeeded in making a grimace.

'Steal M. de Monsoreau's wife?' he stammered.

'Nothing is easier, it seems to me,' replied the Duc. 'The wife has come back to her estates; you tell me she hates her husband; then, without too much vanity, I can count on her preferring me to Monsoreau, especially if I promise her—what I shall promise.'

'And what will you promise, my lord?'

'To rid her of her husband.'

'Ah, why did you not do it at once?' Bussy was on the point of crying; but he had sufficient strength to control himself.

'Will you really do this?' he asked.

'You will see. I am going to pay a visit to Méridor.'

'Will you dare?'

'Why not?'

'You will present yourself before the old Baron whom you have abandoned——'

'I have an excellent excuse. I shall say to him, "I have not broken off this marriage because Monsoreau, aware that you were one of the chief agents of the League, and that I was its chief, threatened to sell us both to the King."'

'Ah! Did your Highness invent this?'

'Not altogether,' replied the Duc.

'Now I understand,' Bussy observed.

'You understand ?' queried the Duc, deceived by the nobleman's reply.

'It is splendid,' replied Bussy.

'Isn't it. But take a look out of the window, Bussy.'

'For what ?'

'Keep on looking. What kind of weather is it ?'

'Your Highness compels me to say it is fine.'

'Ah ! order the horses, and let us go to see how Baron Méridor is keeping.'

'Pardon, my lord,' cried Bussy, 'but how many horses do you desire ?'

'Four, six, as many as you like.'

'If you are guided by me, my lord, you will order a hundred.'

'Very well, a hundred,' said the Prince, somewhat surprised; 'but why?'

'To have at least twenty-five of whom I can be sure in case of attack.'

The Duc gave a start. 'In case of attack ?' he questioned.

'Yes; I hear there are numerous outlaws in the neighbourhood; and it would not be extraordinary if we fell into an ambuscade.'

'Ah, do you think so ?' asked the Duc.

'My lord knows that true courage does not exclude prudence.'

The Duc began to reflect.

'I shall order a hundred and fifty,' said Bussy, moving towards the door.

'One moment,' said the Prince.

'What is wrong, my lord ?'

'Do you consider I am safe at Angers, Bussy?'

'Well, the town is not very strong, but it is well defended——'

'Yes; well defended, but it may be ill defended. Brave as you are, you could not hold the place alone.'

'That is probable.'

'If I am not secure in the town, I must act promptly.'

'These are golden words, my lord.'

'Well, I shall visit the château, and entrench myself there.'

'You are right, my lord; good entrenchment, mark you.'

'Then I have another idea.'

'This is a fruitful morning, my lord.'

'I wish to make the Méridors visit me here.'

'My lord, you have a wonderful number of thoughts this morning. Let us visit the château.'

The Prince called his people, and Bussy, profiting by the opportunity, sought Rémy, whom he found in his room. Sending him to the Duc's apartment, he wrote a short note, entered a greenhouse, gathered a bunch of roses, rolled the note round the stems, passed to the stable, saddled Roland, put the bouquet into Rémy's hands, and invited him to mount. Then leading Rémy out of the town, he put him on a kind of track. 'There,' said he, 'let Roland go. At the end of the path is the forest, in the forest is a park, round the park a wall. At that part of the wall where Roland stops you will throw over this bouquet. The note says, "He who is expected is not coming, for he who was not expected has come. Take, with lips and heart, all that is invisible to the eyes, on this paper."'

Bussy let go the bridle, and Roland set off at a gallop for Méridor. Returning to the palace, Bussy found the Prince dressed. As to Rémy, for him it was a half-hour's business. Confident in his master's words, and carried like a cloud by the wind, he crossed meadows, fields, woods, streams, and hillocks, and stopped at the foot of a semi-ruined wall, the coping of which, covered with ivy, seemed united by it to the branches of the oak trees above. There, Rémy stood in his stirrups, and, fixing the note more firmly in its place, uttered a vigorous hem! at the same time throwing the bouquet over the wall. A slight cry from the other side told him that the message had reached its haven. Waiting for nothing more, as he had not been instructed to expect an answer, he turned his horse's head, and was home in forty minutes. Bussy visited the château with the Prince, and Rémy joined him as they were examining an underground passage to a postern.

'Well,' he demanded of his messenger, 'what have you seen ? What have you heard ? What have you done ?'

And with Spartan brevity Rémy replied, 'A wall, a cry, seven leagues.'

CHAPTER LIV

A FLOCK OF ANGEVINS

Bussy kept the Duc d'Anjou so busy with his preparations for war, that for two days he found no opportunity of visiting Méridor or of making the Baron come to Angers. Needless to say, Bussy, from time to time, on a pretext of visiting the outer fortifications, mounted Roland, and in forty minutes arrived at a certain wall, over which he climbed very easily. Towards evening of the third day an enormous store of provisions had arrived, and the Duc was tasting the soldiers' black bread and salted herrings when a loud noise was heard near one of the gates. A man on a white horse had presented himself at the barrier. Now, Bussy had become Captain-General in the province, and had established the strictest discipline; nobody could leave or enter the town without proper authority. All this was to prevent the Duc from sending a messenger to Diane, or Diane herself from coming without his being informed of it.

'I am Antraguet, and have a message for the Duc d'Anjou,' the horseman announced.

'We do not know Antraguet; but you can deliver your message, since we shall arrest you and convey you to His Highness,' said the captain of the militia.

'Wait, my good friends. My horse, which has only come ten leagues, will ride over you, unless you do stand aside.' Antraguet, drawing his sword, had beaten down the halberds nearest to him. The furious citizens rushed forward, raining blows upon him, which he parried with wonderful skill. They continued the attack, however, cutting and slashing at random until Antraguet began to feel tired.

'Come,' said he, 'you are brave as lions, I agree, and render you homage. But you have only the handles of your halberds, and are ignorant how to load your muskets. I abandon the idea of conquering you. Farewell! only, tell the Prince that I came from Paris on purpose to see him.'

'Die! die!' cried the militia; 'do not let him escape!'

'Ah! you are unwilling to let me go. Beware! that will change my tactics; take care of your fingers, I shall cut your hands!'

He was preparing to execute this threat when a second horseman appeared, galloping madly, and falling like a thunderbolt in the midst of the fray.

'Antraguet!' cried the new-comer, 'what the deuce are you doing with these citizens? I was sure of overtaking you; I have been following you for four hours. You are being massacred.'

'Yes, my friends the Angevins will neither let me in nor out.'

'Gentlemen, will you please stand on one side that we may pass.'

'They insult us! Die! die!' cried the citizens.

'That's what they're like at Angers,' said Livarot; 'bah! we three will soon make an end of them. Here is Ribeirac coming.'

Indeed, Ribeirac at that minute was endeavouring to enter the town like his companions.

'Hallo! what luck! you are fighting,' cried he.

'Ah! there's a regiment of them,' exclaimed the captain of the militia; 'gentlemen, I propose that we make a half-turn to the left.' The order was immediately obeyed; they saw the three horsemen ranging themselves with a martial air which made the bravest tremble.

'It is their advance guard,' cried the citizens.

'Fire!' cried some.

'The enemy!' shouted the majority.

'We are fathers of families. Each for himself!' commanded the captain.

A terrible noise was heard in the street, blows were rained upon the spectators, who were thronging round the terrified militia, and preventing them from fleeing. The sound of the scuffle reached the Place du Château, where the Prince was tasting his followers' black bread and salted herring. Bussy and he were informed that three men, or rather devils incarnate arrived from Paris, were creating all this din. The two set out to investigate, and Bussy, rising in his stirrups, recognised Livarot's long face.

' 'Zdeath!' he cried to the Prince, 'hurry, monseigneur, our Paris friends are besieging us.'

'Down with your arms! villains, these are friends,' cried the Duc.

'Friends! they should have given the countersign, then; for a good hour we have been treating them as Pagans,' grumbled the citizens, retreating.

Livarot, Antraguet, and Ribeirac advancing in triumph, kissed the Duc's hand, and threw themselves into Bussy's arms.

'It seems that we were taking a flock of Angevins for a flock of vultures,' remarked the captain philosophically.

'Monseigneur, count your militia,' whispered Bussy.

'There are at least a hundred and fifty; what do you mean?'

'I mean that you have not very famous soldiers, since three cavaliers could beat them. You cannot leave the town with men like that!'

'No; but I can leave with the three who beat them.'

'I had not thought of that. Trust the poltroon for being logical!'

CHAPTER LV

THE TIDINGS BROUGHT BY M. DE MONSOREAU

THANKS to the reinforcements which had arrived, the Duc d'Anjou could now reconnoitre at will round the neighbourhood. Accompanied by his friends he explored the ramparts, the adjoining gardens, the country beyond, finally the châteaux scattered about the countryside. The gentlemen of Anjou found at the Duc's court such liberty as they did not meet with in Henri's, and they did not fail to enjoy life in a town which, like all capitals, was full of pleasure and gaiety. Three days had not passed before Antraguet, Ribeirac, and Livarot were on good terms with the Angevin nobles, particularly those who possessed young and pretty wives. Joy was at its height, when there arrived one day in state the equipage of M. le Duc, consisting of twenty-five led horses, thirty draught horses, and forty mules, along with litters, chariots, and wagons. This entry produced a great effect in Angers. The reputation of the Duc's wealth was solidly established; and the province was convinced that he could wage war against all Europe if necessary. Bussy contrived that the Duc's reconnoitring was never extended to the Château de Méridor, reserving this treasure for himself, pillaging in his own way this little corner of the province. While M. d'Anjou reconnoitred and Bussy pillaged, M. de Monsoreau, mounted on his war-horse, arrived at the gates of Angers. It was four o'clock; he had come eighteen leagues that day; his horse, white with foam, was half dead. M. de Monsoreau came straight in, saying, 'To the palace of Monseigneur le Duc d'Anjou.' Stopping at the palace, 'Monseigneur le Duc!' cried the First Hunts-man.

'Monseigneur has gone out to reconnoitre,' answered the sentry; 'better stable your horse; the animal is nearly done.'

At that moment the major-domo approached M. de Monsoreau.

'Monsieur,' said he, 'pray enter and rest. It is hardly ten minutes since Monseigneur left; he will not return before eight o'clock.'

'Eight o'clock! I bring news which His Highness cannot know too soon. Have you a horse and a guide to lend me?'

'A horse! there are ten, monsieur. A guide is a different matter, for Monseigneur did not say where he was going; moreover, I cannot reduce the garrison. It is one of the strictest orders.'

'Ah! then you are not in safety here?'

'One is always safe with men like MM. de Bussy, de Livarot, de Ribeirac, d'Entragues, but you understand——'

'Yes, when they are absent, there is less security. I will borrow a fresh horse and try to overtake His Highness.'

'Enter the stable and choose: all belong to Monseigneur.'

In the stables, ten or twelve splendid horses were eating an ample meal. Monsoreau glanced at them with the air of a connoisseur.

'I will choose this bay; have him saddled.'

'Roland, it is the favourite mount of His Highness. He rides him every day; he was a present from M. de Bussy.'

M. de Monsoreau sprang lightly into the saddle, asking in what direction the others had gone.

'One would say Roland follows the scent,' said he, seeing the horse set out in the direction indicated.

'Oh! I heard M. de Bussy and his doctor say that Roland is a most intelligent animal; he will scent his companions and overtake them.'

Indeed, the horse started deliberately, making a detour to shorten the way to the city gate, and gradually increasing its speed. Monsoreau let the reins hang on Roland's neck. Arrived at the outer boulevard, the horse hesitated a minute, then turned to the left, just as a countryman passed.

'Have you seen a troop of horsemen?' asked Monsoreau.

'Yes, monsieur, I met them down yonder.' It was exactly in the direction Roland had taken. Suddenly turning to the right, Roland struck across country into a flowery lane; as he advanced he became brisker; the trot turned to a gallop, and in a quarter of an hour the town was lost to sight. The horseman, too, began to recognise the locality.

'One would fancy we were approaching Méridor; can His Highness have taken this direction?' queried Monsoreau, his brow clouding at the idea. 'Oh!' he murmured, 'I who came first to see the Prince, putting off till to-morrow the visit to my wife. Shall I have the good fortune to see them both at once?'

At that moment Roland neighed, and was answered from the depth of the park. The horse redoubled his speed, passing like lightning through the underwood. Suddenly Monsoreau noticed a wall and a horse tied up near it. This horse neighed, and was evidently the same one which had neighed previously.

'There is some one here!' Monsoreau said, paling.

M. de Monsoreau became more and more mystified: the wall of Méridor found as by magic, this horse caressing the horse he had brought as though it were an intimate acquaintance, there was surely enough there to make the least suspicious reflect. On approaching, he noticed the dilapidation of the wall; it was a regular ladder, threatening to become a breach; feet seemed to have constructed steps in the stone; the bramble bushes hung torn and trampled. Taking in all this at a glance, M. de Monsoreau passed to the details. The horse wore a saddle-cloth, sewn in silver with a double F, interlacing a double A. There was no doubt about it being from the Prince's stables, since the initials stood for François d'Anjou.

The Comte's suspicions became positive alarm.
The Duc had come here, and was in the habit of coming,
since one of his horses knew the way so well. Being led
by chance on this track, Monsoreau concluded that he
ought to follow it to the end. Attaching his horse near
the other, he began to climb the wall, finding it an easy
matter. No sooner was he settled in his post of observation than he saw at the foot of a tree a blue mantilla and
a black velvet cloak; the man and the woman who owned
them were walking fifty paces away, arm in arm, their
backs turned to the wall and hidden by the bushes.
Unluckily for M. de Monsoreau, a stone fell from the wall,
breaking the branches, and striking the ground. At this
noise the persons whose features were hidden turned,
and a woman's shrill cry rang out, followed by rapid
footsteps, which told the Comte that they were fleeing like
two startled deer. At the woman's cry, perspiration
bathed Monsoreau's brow; he had recognised Diane's
voice. With sword in hand, he rushed from the wall to
follow the fugitives, but they had disappeared; nothing
disturbed the silence of the park. What could he do in
this silence, this solitude ? The discovery was sufficient
for the moment; moreover, he felt himself too violently
moved to act with proper prudence in the presence of
such a formidable rival as François, for he doubted not
it was the Prince. In any case, he had a pressing commission to carry to the Duc, and would be able to form an
idea as to his guilt or innocence. Presently it occurred
to him to climb the wall at the same place and to carry
off the intruder's horse. Retracing his steps, he reached
the foot of the wall, but found on the other side no horses.
The idea had evidently come also to his enemy, who had
profited by it. M. de Monsoreau muttered angrily, but
possessing an indomitable will, he resolved to fight stub-
bornly against the fates which seemed conspiring to
overwhelm him. Finding his bearings in spite of the
darkness, he regained Angers by a cross road, familiar to
him from childhood. Two hours later he reached the
gate, dying of thirst, heat, and fatigue; one thought
sustained him; he would question the sentries, go from
gate to gate to learn where a man with two horses had
entered, and pay heavily for his description. Then,
whoever he was, sooner or later he should pay his debt.
He asked the sentry, who having been newly stationed,

could give no information; the guard, however, had noticed a horse enter without its master and go towards the palace.

Monsoreau proceeded to the château, where the windows were ablaze with light, and the kitchen, gleaming like furnaces, sent out the smell of venison and cloves. The gates were closed, and Monsoreau called the porter, who refused to admit him. 'Go and tell the major-domo,' said Monsoreau. The major-domo, recognising Monsoreau, asked, 'Where do you come from in such a state ?' and was answered by the ingenious explanation that his horse had shied, thrown him, and returned home itself.

'Indeed, we were terribly anxious at seeing the horse riderless; Monsiegneur especially, whom I had informed of your arrival.'

'What did he say ?'

'That you were to be brought to him immediately on your return.'

Without changing his attire, Monsoreau went to the dining-room, where all the noblemen were grouped round a table, magnificently served and splendidly lighted.

The court is complete,' Antraguet was saying.

'Not so, a First Huntsman is wanting. In truth, it is shameful that we should be eating His Highness's dinner which we did not procure ourselves,' said Ribeirac.

'I vote for any First Huntsman, no matter whom, even M. de Monsoreau,' Livarot remarked, when the door opened and the First Huntsman entered.

At sight of him the Duc exclaimed loudly, 'Here he is. Heaven favours us, gentlemen, by sending us our desire.'

Monsoreau, embarrassed at this cool reception, which did not usually characterise the Prince, bowed, turning his head away like an owl dazzled by the sun.

'Sit down and sup,' said the Duc.

'Monseigneur, I am very hungry, thirsty, and tired, but I must first deliver an important message to your Highness.'

'You come from Paris, I think ? Well, I am listening.'

'Monseigneur, Madame the Queen-Mother advances by rapid stages on her way to see your Highness.'

All eyes were fixed on the Duc, who exclaimed joyfully : 'Very good, I thank you, M. de Monsoreau; I find you, as ever, a faithful servant; continue, gentlemen.'

The supper recommenced; the First Huntsman,

becoming lost in gloomy reflections, returned to the park of Méridor, recalling the horse, the broken wall, the two shadows fleeing, Diane's startled cry. Indifferent to the sounds around him, he sat buried in thought, and uttered a deep groan, which drew the guests' attention.

'You are thoroughly tired, you ought to retire to rest,' said the Prince.

'Excuse me, monseigneur, I am indeed exhausted,' Monsoreau answered, raising his head.

'You will have to arrange a fine hunt for us, Comte, all the same; you know the country,' said Ribeirac. 'You have equipages, woods, even a wife, here.'

'Let us hunt a wild boar, Comte,' the Prince suggested.

'I will endeavour to arrange it, monseigneur.'

'Yes! to-morrow!' cried the young men in chorus.

'I am at your Highness's orders, but as monseigneur remarked, I am too tired to conduct a hunt to-morrow, and, moreover, I require to visit the neighbourhood.'

'Let him see his wife,' laughed the Duc, with a cordiality which convinced the poor husband of his treachery.

'Agreed! We give twenty-four hours to M. de Monsoreau to make all his preparations in the woods.'

'Now, our First Huntsman, I permit you to go to bed,' said the Duc.

M. de Monsoreau bowed and left the room, glad to be alone. People in affliction, even more than happy lovers, are fond of solitude.

CHAPTER LVI

HOW HENRI LEARNED OF HIS BROTHER'S FLIGHT

AFTER the First Huntsman retired, the party became gayer and freer than ever. The Prince resumed his tranquil expression.

'Come,' said he to Livarot, 'you had begun to describe your flight from Paris. Continue.'

As we know better than Livarot what happened, we will substitute our story for his : it may lose thereby in vividness, but will gain in length, since it will include what had occurred in the Louvre. Towards the middle of the night, Henri was wakened by an unaccustomed noise;

oaths, blows of halberds, rapid steps resounding in the corridors, and in the midst of all this, these ominous words were heard :—

'What will the King say ?'

The King leaped out of bed, crying, 'Chicot ! Chicot !' The latter, opening one eye, replied, 'You do wrong to waken me, Henri. I was dreaming that you had a son.'

'Listen, don't you hear ? "What will the King say ?"' repeated Henri. 'Help me to dress, Chicot.'

'What a misfortune !' was repeated in the ante-chambers.

'We shall do well to arm ourselves,' said the King.

'We shall do better still to hurry out by the secret door, that we may see and judge the trouble for ourselves.'

Presently, leaving by this secret exit, they found themselves in the corridor leading to the Duc's room. There they saw arms raised to heaven, and heard the most desperate exclamations.

'I guess what it is,' said Chicot; 'your unhappy prisoner has strangled himself. You are a greater politician than I thought, Henri.'

In the Duc's room the window was open, and a crowd of curious people pressed round it to look at the rope ladder fastened to the iron balcony.

'Escaped ! flown !' cried Henri, in resounding tones, which made all the noblemen turn round. 'It is a terrible calamity. I am lost ! Civil war has broken out in my kingdom. Who did this ? who furnished the ladder ? I will have all the town hanged.'

Profound terror seized the bystanders.

'Who is the culprit ?' demanded Henri; 'ten thousand crowns to the one who reveals his name.'

'Who could it be but some Angevin ?' suggested Maugiron.

'You are right. Ah ! the Angevins, they shall pay me for this !'

As if this word had been a spark setting fire to gunpowder, a fierce explosion of cries and threats broke out against the Angevins.

Chicot could not remain dumb in this universal uproar, so drawing his sword he beat the walls, repeating : 'Oh ! the Angevins, *mordieu !* death to the Angevins !' which was heard by the whole town.

Henri, meanwhile, had disappeared. He had thought of his mother, and, slipping away, went to find Catherine,

who having been rather neglected of late, was waiting
a good opportunity of displaying her power. When
Henri entered, she was reclining in an arm-chair, resembling more a wax statue of meditation than a human being
reflecting. At the startling news, the statue seemed to
waken, and shook its head without saying anything.

'So you do not call out, my mother ?' asked Henri.

'Why, my son ?'

'Why ? does this escape of your son not appear to you
criminal, threatening, worthy of the greatest punishment ?'

'My dear son, liberty is well worth a crown, and remember that I myself advised you to flee when you were in
a similar position.'

'I have been insulted, defied.'

'Not at all, a prisoner has escaped; that is all.'

'That is how you take my part ! Evidently with age,
one's feelings become dulled; you do not love me as
formerly.'

'You deceive yourself,' said Catherine, with growing
coolness; 'you are my well beloved son, Henri. But he
you complain of is also my son.'

'Adieu, madame, I see what must be done. Since my
mother has no compassion for me, I will find counsellors
capable of encouraging my resentment, and enlightening
me on this matter.'

'Go, my son,' advised the Florentine quietly, 'and may
God's spirit be with your counsellors, for they will need it
to extricate you from this embarrassing situation.'

'Farewell, madame,' repeated Henri; but near the door
he stopped.

'Farewell, Henri; one word only: beg your counsellors
to reflect well before expressing their opinion, and to reflect
still better before carrying any plans into execution.'

'Yes, for the affair is difficult, is it not, madame ?'

'Grave, very grave,' answered Catherine slowly, raising
eyes and hands to heaven.

'Who spirited him away ? have you any idea, my
mother ? I suspect the Angevins.'

Catherine smiled. 'The Angevins ?' she repeated.

'You do not think so, yet every one else does.'

'Let others hold their opinion; but you, my son,
really !'

'What, madame, what do you mean ? Explain yourself, please; I am listening.'

'It is useless. The old Catherine to give advice worth anything at her age! my son, it is impossible.'

'So be it, refuse your assistance. But in an hour, whether agreeable to your wishes or not, I will have all the Angevins in Paris hanged.'

'Madman, fool, child! Do you imagine such men as Bussy, Antraguet, Livarot, Ribeirac can be hanged, without causing rivers of blood to flow?'

'Never mind, provided they are hanged.'

'But they will not be; the standard of revolt will be raised, their bare swords will be in their hands to defend their lives, and your subjects will rise up, not for you, but against you.'

'Yet the Angevins are the traitors; they deserve punishment, and who but my brother's friends would have helped him?'

'It is not your brother's friends; he has none; it is your enemy. You are well aware that you have only one, as your brother Charles had one, and as I have had only one, the same always.'

'Henri de Navarre, you mean? He is not in Paris!'

'Can you say who is in Paris or who is not? have you eyes and ears? have you people around you who see and hear? No, you are all deaf and blind.'

'Henri de Navarre!' repeated Henri.

'My son, at each disappointment, each misfortune, each catastrophe, the cause of which is hidden in obscurity, do not seek, or hesitate; it is useless. Say "It is Henri de Navarre," and you will be right.'

'Oh! that man! he is the sword which God has suspended above the house of Valois.'

'Shall I countermand my orders about the Angevins?'

'This very instant. Hurry, or you will be too late; go, revoke these orders, or you will be lost,' advised Catherine, seizing her son's arm and pushing him towards the door with incredible strength. Henri rushed out to rally his friends, but found only Chicot sitting on a stone, tracing geographical figures in the sand.

CHAPTER LVII

THE KING SHARES THE OPINION OF THE QUEEN-MOTHER
AND CHICOT

'Ah! wretch,' cried the King, 'this is how you defend your King?'

'I defend him in my own way, which is really a good way. I will prove it.'

'I am eager to learn the proof.'

'It is easy; first of all, we have been very stupid in doing what we have done.'

'Ah!' said Henri, struck by the correlation of these two subtle minds, which had arrived independently at the same conclusion.

'Yes, your friends, in crying through the town "Death to the Angevins!" have started that civil war which MM. de Guise failed to arouse, and which is necessary to them; by now either your friends are all dead or they have chased the Angevins from Paris, which would displease you greatly, but would rejoice M. d'Anjou.'

'Do you suppose things are so advanced as that?'

'If they are not more so.'

'But all this does not explain what you are doing?'

'I am tracing the map of the provinces which your brother will raise against you, and calculating the number of men each can furnish. Look at my map. Here, first, is Anjou, whither your brother has fled; well managed, Anjou can provide ten thousand fighters at least. Take Guyenne, an old seat of revolt, which will be delighted to rise against France; we can count upon it for eight thousand men, well drilled, well proved. Then we have Béarn and Navarre; suppose these to supply sixteen thousand men. Let us sum up: Anjou, ten thousand; Guyenne, eight; Béarn and Navarre, sixteen—total, thirty-four thousand.'

'You imagine that the King of Navarre will ally himself with my brother? You believe he has something to do with his flight?'

'Eh! I heard near the Rue de la Ferronnerie a *ventre-saint-gris*! which seems to me now convincing enough.'

'He was in Paris? what makes you think so?'

'My eyes.'

'You saw Henri of Navarre? You did not tell me that my enemy had come to brave me in my very capital!'

'One is a gentleman or one is not; if one is a gentleman, one is not a spy.'

'So, Anjou and Béarn!—my brother and my cousin!'

'Without counting the three Guises, of course.'

'What! you think they will join forces? But Henri de Navarre is an enemy of the Duc de Guise.'

'That will not prevent them from uniting against you.'

'You are right, Chicot, and my mother is right; we must prevent a scandal, help me to marshal the Swiss.'

'Ah, yes! the Swiss! Quélus has them.'

'My guards.'

'Schomberg took them.'

'The household troops, at least.'

'They went off with Maugiron.'

'Without my orders!'

'When did you begin giving orders? Permit me to remark that you begin rather late to discover that you are only the seventh or eighth King of your kingdom.' Henri bit his lips and stamped his foot. '*Ventre de biche!* here are your men, Henri,' said Chicot, looking into the darkness, and pointing out three or four horsemen hastening up, accompanied by other horsemen and many men on foot.

'Schomberg, here!' cried the King.

'Eh! bless me, it's the King.'

'It is; I was coming after you, but ignorant where to go was compelled to wait here impatiently; what have you done?'

'What have we done?' said a second horseman, approaching.

'Ah! come, Quélus, and do not leave again without my permission.'

'There is no need, since all is over,' remarked a third horseman, Maugiron.

'Then you have killed them?' asked the King.

'We had not that pleasure. The cowards escaped like a flight of pigeons. We could barely fight with one of them.'

'They were on their guard?' asked the King.

'*Parbleu!* I should think so,' cried Chicot, 'you howl

"Death to the Angevins!" you move cannon, ring bells, and expect people to be deafer than you are stupid.'

'At any rate, here is a civil war begun,' muttered the King gloomily. The words made Quélus start.

'The deuce! that is true,' he agreed.

'Ah! you begin to see that; it is lucky! Here are MM. de Schomberg and de Maugiron who do not suspect it.'

'We are reserving ourselves to defend the person and crown of His Majesty,' answered Schomberg.

'But, Monsieur Chicot, you thought like us two hours ago, or at least you cried like us, "Death to the Angevins!"'

'I am a fool, as every one knows; you who are intelligent men——'

'Come, peace, gentlemen; presently we shall have enough warfare.'

'What does your Majesty command?' asked Quélus.

'That you employ the same ardour in calming the people as you have done to rouse them; that you bring to the Louvre the Swiss, the Guards, the household troops, and shut the gates, so that to-morrow the citizens may take what has happened for a silly affray of drunken people.'

The young men retired shamefacedly to convey the King's orders to the officers. Henri returned to his mother, who was actively issuing instructions to her servants.

'Well!' she asked, 'what has happened?'

'It is as you foresaw; they have fled, and the town is in an uproar; but I do not worry, for I have control of it.'

'The provinces make you uneasy.'

'Yes, they are going to revolt.'

'What do you intend doing?'

'I see only one step; to arm my militia, withdraw the army from La Charité, and march on Anjou.'

'All you propose is impossible, my son.'

'Ah! I am badly inspired to-day?'

'No, but you are upset; first recover yourself, and then we can discuss the business.'

'Then, my mother, invent some ideas for me; let us bestir ourselves.'

'I was giving instructions, as you perceive, for the departure of an ambassador.'

'To whom shall we send him?'

'To your brother.'

'To that traitor !   You humiliate me.'

'This is no time to be proud.'

'This ambassador will ask for peace ?'

'If need be, he will purchase it, if only to be able afterwards to hang in all security those who have stirred up
this strife.   Did you not say you wished to hold them in
your power ?'

'I would give four provinces of my kingdom for that;
one for each man.'

'Well, then, who wishes the end wishes the means,'
replied Catherine, in penetrating tones which roused a
feeling of hatred and revenge in Henri's heart.

'I believe you are right; but whom shall we send ?'

'Search among your friends.'

'It is useless; there is not a man to whom I could entrust
such a mission.'

'Entrust it to a woman, then.'

'To a woman !   Would you consent ?'

'My son, I am very old, very tired, death perchance
awaits me on my return, but I can travel quickly enough
to reach Anjou before your brother's friends and your
brother himself have had time to realise their power.'

'Oh ! my good mother !' cried Henri, kissing Catherine's
hands, 'you are ever my support, my benefactress, my
good providence !'

'That is, I am always Queen of France,' said Catherine,
glancing at her son with fully as much pity as tenderness.

CHAPTER LVIII

THE GRATITUDE OF M. DE SAINT-LUC

THE day after M. de Monsoreau had presented such
a pitiful aspect at the Duc's table, he rose early and
descended to the courtyard with the intention of finding
the groom from whom he could learn something of Roland's
habits.   The groom was standing watching his master's
horses enjoy their usual meal.

'Ah ! friend,' Monsoreau began, 'is it the custom of
Monseigneur's horses to return alone to the stable ?'

'No, Monsieur le Comte; why do you ask that ?'

'Because of Roland.'

'Yes, he came alone yesterday; that does not surprise me; he is a very intelligent horse. He is usually ridden by Monseigneur le Duc, an excellent horseman, who is not easily thrown.'

'Roland did not throw me, friend. I attached him to a tree before entering a house, and on my return he had disappeared; I concluded he had been stolen, or that some one passing had brought him back for a joke.'

'He came alone, as the major-domo had the honour to inform you yesterday.'

'Monseigneur often rides this horse, you say?'

'He did almost every day till his equipages arrived.'

'His Highness entered late yesterday?'

'About an hour before you, Monsieur le Comte.'

'What horse had he? was it a bay with four white feet and a star on its forehead.'

'No, monsieur, His Highness rode Isolin here. I do not remember any one with such a horse as you describe.'

'Very good; thank you. Saddle Roland for me.'

When this operation was finished, the groom led Roland to the Comte.

'Listen,' said the latter, 'what are your year's wages?'

'Twenty crowns, monsieur.'

'Would you like to earn ten years' wages at once? Discover who rode a bay horse yesterday, with the four feet white and a star on its forehead.'

'What you ask is very difficult, but I will do my best.'

'Your goodwill pleases me. Here are ten crowns to begin with; inform the Prince that I have gone to inspect the woods, in order to arrange the hunt he commanded.'

The Comte had scarcely finished speaking, when a new-comer arrived.

'Monsieur de Bussy!' cried the Comte.

'Good-morning, Monsieur de Monsoreau; you at Angers; what a wonder!'

'And you, monsieur, who were reported ill!'

'I *am* ill, and my doctor has ordered absolute rest; for a week I have not left the town. You are riding Roland, it appears. I sold him to M. le Duc d'Anjou, who is so satisfied that he rides him nearly every day. You must have great skill in horseflesh to choose him straight away.'

'I do not make his acquaintance to-day; I rode him yesterday.'

'Which makes you wish to ride him again; you spoke of preparing a hunt for us. Where will you rouse the animal ?'

'Towards Méridor.'

'Very good,' said Bussy, paling in spite of himself.

'Will you accompany me ?'

'No, a thousand pardons. I will go to bed; my fever is rising again.'

'There is M. de Bussy up without my permission,' cried a voice from the stable.

'Le Haudouin; I am sure to be scolded. Farewell, Comte,' said Bussy, going away.

'What is wrong ? You are so pale that I believe you are ill,' declared Le Haudouin.

'Do you know he is going to Méridor. What will happen ? after what occurred yesterday, *mon Dieu !*'

'Madame de Monsoreau will deny it.'

'But he saw !'

'She will assert that he had a hallucination.'

'Rémy, I feel this butcher is going to make a tragic scene at Méridor. I should have accompanied him to support Diane.'

'Madame Diane will support herself, I tell you,' said Rémy, carrying Bussy indoors, while M. de Monsoreau left Angers by the same gate as on the previous night. He had left Roland's bridle free, and the animal did not fail to do what was expected of him. Almost immediately he struck off to the left, then to the right, M. de Monsoreau letting him go. Then he followed the little flowery path, next entered the copse, and finally the forest. At the end of forty or fifty minutes, M. de Monsoreau found himself opposite the wall at the same place as before; the spot was solitary and silent, no neighing was heard, no horse appeared. Dismounting and taking Roland's bridle in his hand, M. de Monsoreau began to climb the wall; all was as still inside as outside; only a few deer bounded over the vast expanse. It was useless to waste time spying on people who had no doubt been terrified by his appearance the previous day, and had chosen another meeting-place; so remounting, he walked Roland to the entrance-gate. On passing the drawbridge, he perceived the Baron exercising his dogs. The Baron advanced ceremoniously to meet him. Diane, sitting under a sycamore tree, was reading poetry, while Gertrude

'Saint Luc's sword lodged in his chest.'

embroidered at her side. Rising, Diane bowed gravely to the Comte.

'Madame, I beg you to grant me a moment's interview,' began the First Huntsman.

'Willingly, monsieur.'

'Will you honour us by remaining at the château, Monsieur le Comte ?' asked the Baron.

'Yes, monsieur; till to-morrow, at least.'

The Baron retired to see that his son-in-law's room was got ready. Monsoreau, sitting on Gertrude's chair, stared at Diane in a way to frighten the boldest man.

'Madame,' he asked, 'who was in the park with you yesterday?'

'At what hour, monsieur ?' asked Diane, with a clear glance, and in a voice, from which all emotion had been driven.

'At six o'clock.'

'In what part ?'

'Near the old copse.'

'It must have been one of my friends, and not myself walking there.'

'It was you, madame. Tell me the name of this man who was walking with you.'

'That is impossible, since it was not I who was walking.'

'How can you dare to deny that I saw you. How can you dare to deny it was you, since there is no other woman at Méridor.'

'That is another mistake, monsieur, for Jeanne de Brissac is here.'

'Madame de Saint-Luc ? and M. de Saint-Luc ?'

'Does not leave his wife, as you are aware; their marriage was one of love; it was M. and Madame de Saint-Luc that you saw.'

'It was you ! I recognised you perfectly with an unknown man, but I swear I will trace him yet.'

'When you are in your right mind, I will consent to listen; at present it is better I should retire.'

'No, madame, you will stay,' declared Monsoreau, holding Diane's arm.

'Here are M. and Madame de Saint-Luc, monsieur; I hope you will restrain yourself before them.'

Madame de Saint-Luc bowed low to M. de Monsoreau; Saint-Luc held out his hand cordially. The three exchanged compliments; then Saint-Luc, motioning his

C.J.　　　　　　　　　　　　　　　　　　L

wife to go with the Comte, took Diane's arm, and they proceeded to the house for dinner. Diane, separated from her husband, was placed between Saint-Luc and the Baron. The conversation turned upon general topics, the arrival of the King's brother at Angers, and the stir this would cause in the province. Saint-Luc cajoled the angry husband with charming wit, and Diane thanked her friends with eloquent glances.

'This Saint-Luc is a chatterbox; he is the man to disclose the secret,' said the Comte to himself, and he exerted himself to answer the young man in such a way as to double Diane's joy, and render everything peaceable.

Moreover, Saint-Luc was making signs to Madame de Monsoreau which meant : 'Be assured, I am maturing a plan.'

CHAPTER LIX

SAINT-LUC'S PLAN

THE meal over, Monsoreau took his new friend by the arm and led him outside.

'Do you know, I am very happy to find you here,' he said; 'the solitude of Méridor terrified me.'

'Have you not your wife ? I shall never believe you feared a moment's boredom with such a wife, and in such surroundings.'

'Bah ! I have spent half my life in the woods.'

'The more reason that you should not be bored; the more one sees of these woods, the more one loves them. You are certainly fortunate to have such a beautiful park with its spreading trees.'

'Oh ! I shall not be staying here long; I am not so fond of nature as you. Besides, I distrust this park; I do not consider it safe.'

'Really ! Because of the isolated position, you mean ?'

'No, not exactly; for I presume one may receive company at Méridor.'

'Not a soul since I came.'

'Not any gentleman from the court at Angers ?'

'I haven't see the feather of a single one.'

'Then I am wrong. Tell me, dear monsieur, does Madame de Saint-Luc often walk in the park ?'

'Often; she adores the country. But why do you ask ?'

'For no reason. When she walks do you accompany her ?'

'Always.'

'*Nearly* always ? I ask because I was told a man has been seen prowling in the park.'

'Are you hinting that this man comes to see Madame de Saint-Luc !'

'No, ! I do not think that; I fear it may be Diane !'

'Bah ! I should like that better. Then, you think a man entered the park ?'

'I have seen him.'

'Alone ?'

'With Madame de Monsoreau, last night; to the left here, look,' and Monsoreau, who had directed their steps to the old copse, indicated the place.

'Indeed; this wall is in a bad state; I must inform the Baron.'

'Whom do you suspect of climbing this wall to speak to my wife ?'

Saint-Luc appeared to meditate deeply, while the Comte waited anxiously.

'The deuce !' said Saint-Luc, 'I can think of none but yourself.'

'You are joking, my dear monsieur ?'

'No. I did that sort of thing when I was first married; why should not you ?'

'You do not wish to answer; confess it, dear friend, but fear nothing—I am courageous. Come, help me, I hope to get good service from you. Take the matter seriously, for it is important.'

'How does this man come, do you know ?'

'He comes secretly, *parbleu !*'

'Often ?'

'I should think so; his feet are imprinted in the soft stone of the wall; have you never noticed what I have just told you ?'

'Oh ! I suspected it a little, but did not worry, for I thought it was you.'

'But I say it is not.'

'I believe you, dear monsieur ! Then it is some one else.'

The First Huntsman glanced almost threateningly at Saint-Luc, who displayed a most imperturbable calm.

'I have still another idea; suppose it were the Duc d'Anjou.'

'I thought of that, but I have inquired, and it could not be he.'

'Eh! the Duc is very cunning.'

'Yes, but it is not he.'

'I have a further idea. If it was neither you nor the Duc, doubtless it was myself.'

'You to enter the park from the outside, when you can enter from within? You to flee at my appearance? You were doing wrong, therefore?'

'I do not know.'

'You are laughing at me!' cried the Comte, paling, 'and have kept up the farce for a quarter of an hour.'

'You are wrong, monsieur; it is twenty minutes,' said Saint-Luc, drawing out his watch and glancing fixedly at Monsoreau.

'I see now. You are conspiring with the coward, the traitor whom I would willingly have killed yesterday.'

'*Parbleu!* he is my friend.'

'Then, if that is the case, I will kill you instead.'

'Bah! in your house! like this, all at once! how badly trained you are, Monsieur de Monsoreau, the company of wild beasts has corrupted your manners!'

The Comte, becoming exasperated, put his hand on his sword.

'Ah! be careful, you are provoking me. I take you to witness that I am perfectly calm.'

'Yes, minion, I provoke you.'

'Kindly pass to the other side of the wall, where we are on neutral ground. I have no desire to kill you on your own land.'

'Very good!' said Monsoreau, hastening to climb over.

'Take care, Comte! There is an unsteady stone there; do not hurt yourself, for I could never be consoled;' and Saint-Luc climbed over in his turn.

Monsieur de Monsoreau waited for Saint-Luc, sword in hand.

'Are you ready?' he asked.

'You have the advantage with your back to the sun; but don't disturb yourself. Do you wish to kill me out-right?'

'Yes, I wish it.'

'Man proposes and God disposes,' said Saint-Luc,

drawing his sword. 'Look at that clump of poppies and dandelions. That is where I intend to lay you.'

Monsoreau thrust with wonderful agility, while Saint-Luc parried with equal skill.

'*Pardieu!* Monsieur de Monsoreau, you handle the sword very well, and any other than Bussy or myself would have been killed by your last stroke. You are perhaps surprised at finding me so good a swordsman; the King, who is very fond of me, gave me lessons, and showed me a thrust which I will presently show you. If it is fatal, you will have the pleasure of knowing that this thrust was taught by the King, which will be flattering to you.'

'You are very witty, monsieur,' said Monsoreau, dealing a direct thrust which should have pierced a wall.

'One does what he can,' replied Saint-Luc, forcing his adversary by a movement to half turn, thus bringing him into the sunlight. 'That is where I wished to see you. I did that well, eh? So I am very contented. You had fifty chances to a hundred of being killed; now you have ninety-nine.'

With an agility and vigour surprising in an effeminate-looking young man, Saint-Luc thrust five times at Monsoreau, who parried, quite stunned by this onset; the sixth thrust consisted of a double feint, a fence and a thrust, of which the sun prevented him from seeing the first half, and at the second Saint-Luc's sword lodged in his chest. Monsoreau stood for an instant; then his strength failed, his hands opened, his eye clouded over; his knees gave way, and he fell on the poppies, mingling his blood with their purple.

'Ah! you have killed me, monsieur,' he murmured.

'I tried to; but now seeing you there, ready to die, I am sorry for it; you were horribly jealous, true, but you were brave. Have you any last wishes, monsieur? I will see they are carried out.'

Monsoreau made no reply. He had turned his face downwards, and was writhing and struggling.

'Poor wretch! Oh! friendship, you are an exacting goddess.'

Monsoreau, opening heavy eyes, endeavoured to raise his head, but fell back, groaning dismally.

'He is dead; think no more about him! It is easy to talk. I have killed a man, that's what it amounts to. It

cannot be said I have wasted my time in the country,'
muttered Saint-Luc, and, crossing the wall, he betook
himself to the château. The first person he met was Diane,
chatting to her friend.

'Excuse me, dear lady,' said he, 'but I must really say
a word or two to Madame de Saint-Luc.'

'As you please, my dear guest; I will go to the library;
you will come when you have finished,' added Diane to
Jeanne.

'What is wrong ? you look gloomy, dear husband,'
asked Jeanne.

'An accident has happened.'

'To you ?'

'Not exactly, but to the person I was walking with.'

'To Monsieur de Monsoreau ? What has happened to
him ?'

'I believe he is dead.'

'Dead ! he was here a short time ago. Saint-Luc, you
are concealing something from me.'

'Absolutely nothing, I swear; not even the spot where
he died, down there, behind the wall, just where our friend
Bussy used to tether his horse.'

'It was you who killed him, Saint-Luc ?'

'The deuce ! who else could it be ? there were only
two of us; I return living to tell you he is dead; it is not
difficult to tell which killed the other.'

'Unhappy man !'

'He provoked and insulted me; he drew his sword.'

'It is fearful, terrible ! that poor man ! But you
cannot stay here !'

'That is what I decided, and for that reason hastened
to you, that you might make preparations to leave.'

'He did not wound you ?'

'That question comes rather late, but reconciles me to
you; no, I am quite unharmed.'

'Then we can start ?'

'As quickly as possible; the accident may be discovered
any moment.'

'Now I consider, Madame de Monsoreau is a widow.
Whilst I inform her, saddle the horses yourself. But
where are we going ?'

'To Paris. The King will have forgotten everything;
besides, if there is fighting, my place is beside him.'

'Very good, we start for Paris.'

'Yes, only I should like pen and ink to write to Bussy. I cannot leave Anjou like this, without giving the reason.'

Saint-Luc, with trembling hand, hastily wrote the following :—

'DEAR FRIEND,—'You will learn by report the accident which has happened to M. de Monsoreau; we had a little discussion beside the old coppice upon the causes and effects of the breaking down of walls, and the inconvenience of horses which travel without guidance. In the heat of the discussion, M. de Monsoreau fell on a clump of poppies and dandelions, and so unluckily that he killed himself outright.

'Your friend for life,

'SAINT-LUC.'

'PS.—As that may at first appear a little improbable, I will add that, at the time of the accident, we both had swords in our hands. I leave immediately for Paris to pay court to the King, Anjou not appearing safe after what has occurred.'

Ten minutes later, one of the Baron's servants hurried with this letter to Angers, while M. and Madame de Saint-Luc set out by a side-gate, leaving Diane weeping, and, above all, very embarrassed at having to relate to the Baron the sad story. She had glanced away when Saint-Luc passed.

'Serve your friends,' said the latter to his wife, 'decidedly every one but myself is ungrateful.'

CHAPTER LX

THE QUEEN-MOTHER'S ENTRY INTO ANGERS

AT the very hour when M. de Monsoreau fell beneath Saint-Luc's sword, a loud fanfare of trumpets resounded at the gates of Angers, which were closed with the utmost care. The guards, raising a standard, replied by like symphonies. It was Catherine de Médicis approaching Angers with an imposing enough retinue. Bussy was immediately informed, and proceeded to tell the Prince, who retired to bed. Catherine leaned from her litter, hoping that the majesty of a royal countenance would effect more than the trumpets. The militia, seeing the Queen, saluted even courteously, but the gates remained shut. Catherine sent a nobleman to the barriers, who was very politely received. When he demanded an entrance for the Queen-Mother, reply was made that Angers could not be opened without some indispensable formalities. The nobleman, exceedingly mortified, returned to his mistress, and Catherine muttered : 'I am waiting.'

Finally Bussy, who had spent nearly half an hour haranguing with the Duc, came to a resolution. Getting his horse saddled and caparisoned, he chose five noblemen most displeasing to the Queen-Mother, and went to meet Her Majesty. Catherine began to feel tired, not with waiting, but meditating revenge upon those who were treating her so discourteously. Bussy appearing at the barrier, looked about vaguely like a night-guard who listens rather than sees.

'Who goes there ?' he cried.

Catherine's attendant glanced at her to discover her wishes.

'It is Madame the Queen-Mother, who comes to visit the good town of Angers.'

'Very good, monsieur; kindly turn to the left and you will see the postern gate, eighty paces away,' replied Bussy, advancing towards the place with his followers. With sword in hand he moved outside the gate and bowed respectfully before Catherine.

'Be welcome to Angers, your Majesty,' he exclaimed.

The Queen, leaving her litter, walked towards the little gate, leaning on an attendant's arm, after saying merely, 'Thank you, Monsieur de Bussy.' The litter was hoisted over the wall, and the Queen got inside to proceed to the palace, Bussy and his friends accompanying it on horseback.

'My son ? I do not see my son ?' observed Catherine suddenly.

'Monseigneur is ill in bed, madame; otherwise your Majesty cannot doubt that he would have hastened to do the honours of *his* town.'

Catherine played the hypocrite sublimely.

'My poor child ill ! Ah ! let us hurry—is he well attended to ?'

'We do our best,' answered Bussy, looking at her in surprise, doubtful whether any maternal feelings existed in this woman.

'Does he know I am here?' resumed Catherine, after an interval spent in studying the noblemen.

'Yes, certainly, madame.'

'He is surely in great pain.'

'Very great. His Highness is subject to sudden attacks.'

They reached the palace; a large crowd ranged themselves at each side of the litter. Bussy ran on ahead, and entered the Duc's room panting.

'Here she is,' said he; 'beware! she is exasperated.'

'Does she complain?'

'No, far worse; she smiles.'

'What do the people say?'

'The people say nothing, but regard her in dumb terror; if they don't know what she is, they guess.'

'We continue the war, then? Are you all here? Why has Monsoreau not returned?'

'I believe he is at Méridor.—Oh! we shall do very well without him.'

'Her Majesty the Queen-Mother!' proclaimed the usher from the doorway.

Immediately Catherine appeared, livid, dressed in black as was her custom. The Duc made a movement to rise, but Catherine threw herself into his arms, kissing him affectionately. She even wept. After finishing her embraces, Catherine sat down at the bedside. Bussy motioned to the bystanders to leave, and waited calmly himself.

'Will you not attend to my poor followers, dear Monsieur de Bussy?' said Catherine suddenly; 'after my son, are you not the master of this establishment? I beg this favour.'

There was no hesitation possible. 'Madame, I am but too pleased to be able to oblige your Majesty.'

'Wait,' he muttered, 'you don't know the doors here as you do the Louvre. I will return,' and he withdrew.

Catherine, mistrusting him, followed him with her glance. Then she set out to discover whether her son was ill, or simply feigning. François, worthy son of such a mother, played his part well. She had wept, so he assumed fever. Catherine believed he was ill; she hoped to have more influence over a mind weakened by bodily suffering.

She overwhelmed the Duc with tenderness, weeping till he asked the reason.

'You ran such a great danger, my child!'

'In escaping from the Louvre?'

'Oh! no, afterwards. Those who helped you in that unfortunate escape were your bitterest enemies.'

('She knows nothing,' thought the Duc, 'but would like to know.')

'The King of Navarre! the eternal scourge of our race—I recognise it well.'

('Ah! she knows,' cried François.)

'Would you believe that he boasts of it and thinks all is won.'

'That is impossible, my mother, because he had no share in my escape. It is two years since I saw the King of Navarre.'

'It is not only of this danger I speak, my son.' Catherine, approaching François, tried to make her voice appear dismayed, as she added, 'The King's wrath! that furious wrath which threatens you.'

'I am safe.'

'Do you think so?' The tapestry shook.

'I am sure of it; and it is so true, that you come to announce it.'

'How is that?' asked Catherine, uneasy at his calmness.

'Because had you been entrusted to carry only threats, you would not have come, and, in such a case, the King would have hesitated to give me such a hostage as your Majesty.'

'A hostage! me!'

'The most saintly and venerable of all,' replied the Duc smiling, and kissing Catherine's hand, not without another triumphant glance toward the door.

Catherine dropped her arms as if crushed; she could not guess that Bussy, by a secret door, surveyed his master, holding him in check by looks which sent him courage at each hesitation.

'My son,' said she, at length, 'they are all words of peace I bring you; you are perfectly right.'

'I listen, my mother, you know with what respect; I believe we are beginning to understand one another.'

Catherine had distinctly the disadvantage in the first part of the interview. Bussy, as we said, in a secret corridor leading into the Duc's alcove, was so placed as to

be visible only to the Prince. The cause he advocated was
war at all costs; he must keep in Anjou, as long as M. de
Monsoreau was there, in order to watch the husband and
visit the wife. This extremely simple reason complicated
in the highest degree the policy of France; great effects
often have small causes. That is why, with many glances,
gestures, terrifying play of eyebrows, Bussy urged his
master to firmness. The Duc, afraid of Bussy, allowed
himself to be influenced, and became furious. Catherine,
defeated on all points, thought of beating an honourable
retreat, when a little event, almost as unexpected as the
obstinacy of M. le Duc, came to her assistance. Suddenly,
in the heat of this conversation, Bussy felt somebody
pull the edge of his cloak. Curious not to miss anything
of the interview, he put out his hand to the place without
turning round; his hand encountered a wrist, then an
arm, a shoulder, finally a man. Turning round he saw
Rémy. Bussy wished to speak, but Rémy, laying a finger
on his lips, gently drew him into the adjoining room.

'What is wrong, Rémy, and why do you disturb me
at such a time ?' asked the Comte impatiently.

'A letter from Méridor.'

'Oh ! from Méridor ! Thanks, my good Rémy ! Where
is this letter ?'

'Ah ! that is why I judged it to be important; the
messenger will give it to you alone.'

'He is right. Is he here ?'

'Yes.'

Rémy, opening a door, signed to a groom to approach,
saying,—

'Here is M. de Bussy,' while Bussy laid a half pistole
in his hand. Bussy turned aside to read and to hide his
emotion; hardly had he finished than the blood rose to
his head and swam in his eyes; from pale he became purple,
and, dazed, fell into a chair near the window. Rémy
signed to the groom to retire; rushing to Bussy, he shook
him by the arm.

'*Mordieu !*' he cried, 'answer me at once, or by Saint-
Esculape, I will bleed you.'

Bussy rose; he was neither red nor dazed now, he was
gloomy, and held out the letter to Rémy, who read it
eagerly.

'It seems to me that this is all very agreeable, and M. de
Saint-Luc is a noble gentleman.'

'Monsoreau dead! I must be dreaming, Rémy. I shall no longer see this spectre, always ready to rise between me and my happiness? But then, Diane cannot remain at Méridor. She must go elsewhere, that she may forget.'

'Paris would be good for that; one forgets fairly well there.'

'You are right; she will live in the little house Rue des Tournelles, and we will spend the ten months of widowhood in obscurity.'

'True, but something is necessary to go to Paris—peace in Anjou.'

'Oh! *mon Dieu!* what time wasted, and wasted in vain.'

'That means you are going to rush to Méridor.'

'Not I but you; go to the old copse where she may be expecting me, or if not, go to the château; tell her I am half mad;' and Bussy, pressing the young man's hand, returned to his place in the corridor. Catherine, in his absence, endeavoured to regain lost ground.

'My son, it seemed to me that a mother could not fail to come to an agreement with her child when she wishes.'

'Madame, you mean when they wish,' retorted the Duc.

'But I wish it! do you hear, François? I wish it.' The tones of Catherine's voice contrasted with the words which were imperative, whilst the voice was almost suppliant.

'Yes, I wish it and all sacrifices will be easy to attain that end. Tell me, what do you require? Speak! command!' she resumed.

'Oh! my mother!' said François, almost overcome at such a complete victory.

'Listen, my son; you do not seek to drown a kingdom in blood, do you? it is not possible. You are neither a bad Frenchman nor a bad brother.'

'My brother insulted me, and I owe him nothing, either as a King or as a brother.'

'But myself, François! you have never had a complaint against me?'

'Yes, for you have abandoned me!' said the Duc, thinking Bussy was still listening.

'You wish my death? So be it, I will die, as a mother must who sees her children slaughtering one another.'

'Oh! don't say that, madame; you break my heart!' cried François.

Catherine burst into tears. The Duc, taking her hands, tried to console her, while he glanced uneasily towards the alcove.

'But what do you want ?' asked she; 'at least state your terms, that we may know where we stand.'

'What do you wish, yourself ?'

'I wish you to return to Paris, to your brother, who holds out his arms to you.'

'*Mordieu!* madame, I understand; it is the Bastille drawbridge which extends its arms.'

'No, return; and on my honour, on my mother's love, you will be received by the King as though you were the King and he the Duc d'Anjou. Accept, my son; do you wish a retinue—guards ? you shall have a captain, if necessary, and he shall be M. de Bussy.'

The Duc, shaken by this last offer, which he thought Bussy would appreciate, looked once more at the alcove, dreading to meet a flashing eye, and white teeth showing angrily in the shadow. But, to his surprise, he saw Bussy, smiling, joyful, and applauding by numerous signs. 'What does that mean ?' he asked himself; did Bussy only wish to become captain of my guards ?

'Then, I should accept ?' he added aloud.

'Yes! yes! yes!' said Bussy, with hands, shoulders, and head.

'I must therefore leave Anjou to return to Paris ?'

'Yes! yes!' continued Bussy, in a fury of approbation.

'Well ? what do you reply?' asked Catherine anxiously.

'I will reflect,' said the Duc, 'and to-morrow——'

'He surrenders. Then, I have won the battle.'

'Indeed, Bussy is perhaps right,' said the Duc to himself.
The two separated after embracing one another.

CHAPTER LXI

CONCERNS M. DE MONSOREAU

A FAITHFUL friend is a good thing, the more so that it is rare. Rémy confessed this to himself while galloping over the fields on one of the best horses of the Prince's stables.

'I am very fond of M. de Bussy, and on his side M. de

Bussy likes me very much,' Le Haudouin soliloquised; 'that is why I am so happy to-day; I have the happiness of two people. Now, what compliments shall I pay to Madame Diane ? if she is ceremonious and gloomy, mute reverences with a hand on my heart; if she smiles, I will execute a polonaise. Ah ! I am approaching.'

The horse, after turning to the left, then to the right, and traversing the copse, had entered the wooded part leading to the wall. Suddenly it stopped with dilating nostrils and fixed eye; Rémy dug the spurs into it, but Mithridate did not move. Rémy looked at the ground in astonishment, seeking the obstacle which stopped his horse; but all he saw was a great pool of blood gradually sinking into the earth.

'Hallo ! is it here M. de Saint-Luc wounded M. de Monsoreau ?' he exclaimed. Then, ten paces away he noticed two stiff legs and a body seemingly stiffer. The body was propped against the wall.

'Here lies Nimrod. If the widow leaves him thus, exposed to the crows and vultures, it is a good sign for us, and the funeral oration will be composed of pirouettes and polonaises.'

Dismounting, Rémy advanced towards the body.

'It is queer ! here he is quite dead, and yet the blood is over yonder. Ah ! here's a trace; that good Saint-Luc must have propped him up here. Yes, that's it, dead, with eyes open and no expression—stark dead.'

Suddenly Rémy drew back, gaping; the eyes had closed, and a more livid pallor spread over the face.

'If he shut his eyes, he cannot be dead,' thought Rémy, slipping to the foot of the tree opposite the corpse.

'I have read that after death certain actions take place, indicating that mortification has set in. Yes, not only have the eyes closed for ever, but the pallor has increased; there is a means of ascertaining whether he is dead or not—that is to drive my sword into his breast; if he does not move, he is really dead.'

Rémy, preparing to try this charitable test, grasped his sword, when Monsoreau's eyes suddenly opened. Rémy drew up as though moved by a spring, and a cold sweat broke out on his brow. The dead man's eyes remained wide open.

'He is not dead; but, if I kill him, he will be,' murmured

Rémy, looking at Monsoreau, whose startled eyes seemed to be reading his intentions.

'Fie! what a horrible thought. God knows, if he stood there brandishing his rapier, I would kill him with the greatest pleasure; but as he is now, without strength and three parts dead, it would be more than a crime, it would be an infamous deed.'

'Help! I am dying,' murmured Monsoreau.

'*Mordieu!* it's a critical situation. I am a doctor, and so obliged to succour my fellow-creature. Let me forget that I am Le Haudouin, the friend of M. de Bussy, and do my duty.'

'Help! fetch me a priest, a doctor,' repeated the wounded man.

'The doctor is here at hand, and may do instead of the priest.'

'Le Haudouin?' cried M. de Monsoreau, 'by what chance are you here?' True to his character, he was suspicious, even in his great agony.

'I met M. de Saint-Luc a league away, and he said, "Run, Rémy, into the wood, to the old copse; you will find a dead man." I came, and saw you.'

'And now, tell me, am I mortally wounded?'

'The deuce, you ask too much; however, I will find out,' said Rémy, carefully removing Monsoreau's cloak, doublet, and shirt. The sword had penetrated between the sixth and seventh rib.

'Do you suffer much?' he asked.

'Not in my breast, but my back, beneath the shoulder.'

'The sword will have encountered a bone,' said Rémy, looking at the place; 'no, I was wrong; the steel has gone right through. What a pretty thrust, Comte; there is pleasure in nursing those whom M. de Saint-Luc wounds; you are pierced through and through, my dear sir.'

Monsoreau fainted, but Rémy took no notice of his weakness.

'Ah! that's it; syncope, pulse feeble; extremities cold; absence of any sound of breathing. Madame Diane's widowhood can only be a matter of time.'

Just then, a faint reddish foam appeared on the wounded man's lips. Rémy, quickly producing a case of instruments and a lancet, bound up his arm.

'We will see if the blood flows; Madame Diane is perhaps not a widow. But if it does not—ah! it flows.'

The blood gushed out from the vein; the wounded man opened his eyes.

'Ah! I thought it was all over,' he stammered.

'Not yet, my dear monsieur; it is even possible——'

'That I may recover?'

'Yes; but first let us close the wound. Do not move; nature is caring for you within as I do without. She is a great surgeon.'

'At first I spat up quantities of blood!'

'Now the hæmorrhage is stopped already. Good! that's going on all right. My dear Monsieur de Monsoreau, I am afraid I have the good fortune to cure you.'

'You think I will recover?'

'Alas!' and Rémy, having stopped the bleeding, rose.

'You are deserting me?'

'You speak too much, dear monsieur. I go to the château for help. Which is the nearest house?'

'The Château de Méridor.'

'And the way to it?' asked Rémy, feigning complete ignorance.

'Cross the wall and you are in the park, or follow the wall till you reach the gate.'

'Good; I fly,' and Rémy galloped off. In five minutes he arrived to find the inhabitants hurrying about like ants disturbed in their home, searching all over without finding where their master's body lay. We must consider that Saint-Luc, to gain time, had given wrong directions. Rémy, falling like a meteor in their midst, dragged them after him. He was so eager in his instructions that Madame de Monsoreau could not help looking at him in surprise. A secret thought came into her mind, and in a moment sullied her soul's angelic purity.

'I thought he was the friend of M. de Bussy?' she murmured, as Rémy retired with everything necessary for bandaging.

CHAPTER LXII

THE DUC D'ANJOU GOES TO MÉRIDOR

As soon as the interview with his mother was finished, the
Duc d'Anjou hurried to Bussy to investigate his extraordinary change of front. Bussy, in his room, was reading
Saint-Luc's letter for the fifth time, while Catherine made
preparations to leave the next day, or in two days at
latest.

'Your Highness condescends to visit me?' said Bussy,
with a charming smile.

'Yes, and I come to demand an explanation. You
order me to be armed from head to foot against my
mother's suggestions, and to withstand the shock bravely;
I do so, and, at the height of the struggle, you say, "Take
off your cuirass, monseigneur."'

'I gave you these instructions, monseigneur, because
I did not know why Madame Catherine had come. But
now that I see she comes to advance your glory and
fortune——'

'My glory and fortune; how do you see that?'

'What does your Highness wish—to triumph over your
enemies? For I do not think you meditated becoming
King of France, as some asserted. Some will advise you
to do this, monseigneur, but they are your bitterest
enemies; moreover, examine yourself; have you a hundred
thousand men, ten million pounds, alliances abroad? In
short, do you wish to go against your lord?'

'He did not scruple to go against me.'

'If you take that footing, you are right; have yourself
crowned, and take the title of King of France; I ask
nothing better than to see you rise, since I will rise with
you.'

'You are discussing a question which I have never
asked any one to settle,' said the Duc sharply.

'Then, all is said, monseigneur, and we are agreed on
the chief point; have a company of guards and five
hundred thousand pounds given you. Before peace is
signed, ask for a subsidy at Anjou to wage war; once you
have it, keep it. Appoint Bussy captain, Antraguet

and Livarot lieutenants; Ribeirac ensign. Then you will see if people, even the King, will not salute you as they pass.'

'I believe you are right, Bussy; I will consider it; but what were you reading so attentively when I came in?'

'A letter which interests you still more than me; I should have shown it to you at once.'

'It has great news?'

'Yes, and sad even; M. de Monsoreau is dead.'

'Excuse me!' said the Duc, with such marked surprise that Bussy thought he distinguished extravagant joy in it.

'Dead, monseigneur. Are we not all mortal?'

'Yes; but one does not die all at once like that.'

'That depends. If one kills you.'

'He has been killed?'

'By Saint-Luc. Here is a note from Saint-Luc announcing it, and as I was as incredulous as you, monseigneur, I have sent my surgeon, Rémy, to make sure, and give my sympathy to the old Baron.'

'Dead! Monsoreau dead! dead all by himself!'

'He is not dead by his own hand, since Saint-Luc killed him. Did you give some one else orders to kill him?'

'Faith, no, and you?'

'Oh! I am not a great enough prince to have this work done by others, and I am obliged to do it myself.'

'Ah! Monsoreau,' said the Prince, with his horrible smile.

'Hallo! monseigneur! one would say you bore him a grudge.'

'No, it is you who bear the grudge.'

'It is natural I should. Did he not make me submit to a horrible humiliation on the part of your Highness.'

'Come, have the horses saddled, Bussy, to go to Méridor on a visit of condolence; besides, this visit should have been paid long ago.'

'Faith,' soliloquised Bussy, 'since Monsoreau is dead, and I have no fear of his selling his wife to the Duc, it matters little if I see her again. Let us use the opportunity.

A quarter of an hour later, the Prince, Bussy, and ten noblemen were proceeding to Méridor. At sight of the cavalcade, the porter came to ask the visitors' names.

'The Duc d'Anjou!' cried the Prince. At once a fanfare

was sounded, which summoned the servants to the draw-bridge. Soon there was hurried commotion in the apartments and corridors; the turret windows opened, the old Baron appeared with the keys of his castle.

'It is incredible how little Monsoreau is regretted; all these people appear as usual. There is the fair Diane, do you see, Bussy?' said the Duc, as a woman appeared on the steps.

'Certainly I see, monseigneur; but I do not see Rémy,' he added. Diane indeed was emerging from the house, but immediately behind her came a litter on which Monsoreau, with eye blazing with fever or jealousy, was carried more like an Indian sultan on his palanquin than a dead man on his bier!

'Long live Monseigneur le Duc d'Anjou!' he cried, raising his hand in air.

'Softly! You will break that coagulum,' said a voice behind him. It was Rémy, faithful to his rôle of doctor. Surprises do not last long at court—on faces at least; the Duc changed his stupefaction into a smile.

'My dear Comte! what a happy surprise! Do you believe it, we were told that you were dead?' he exclaimed.

'God be praised! not only am I not dead, but I will recover, I hope, to serve you with more ardour than ever,' said the wounded man.

Bussy felt a cold sweat break out on his temple as he looked at Diane. To see this treasure, twice lost to him, standing so near her possessor made him feel ill.

'And Monsieur de Bussy, receive my thanks, for I owe my life to you—indirectly, it's true, but my gratitude is not less on that account, for here is my saviour,' said Monsoreau, showing Rémy, who, raising his arms despairingly in air, would have liked to sink into the earth. In spite of the gestures made to him to keep quiet, Monsoreau related the skill and attention Le Haudouin had bestowed upon him. The Duc frowned; Bussy looked at Rémy with a terrifying expression, while the poor young man replied by a gesture, implying 'Alas! it is not my fault.'

'Besides,' resumed the Comte, 'I heard that Rémy found you one day dying as he found me; it is a bond between us. Count on my friendship, Monsieur de Bussy: when Monsoreau loves he does it well; it is true that when he hates, he also does it heartily.'

Bussy noticed that the flashing eyes of the Comte rested on the Duc in pronouncing these words. The latter, seeing nothing, dismounted, and gave Diane his hand. 'Fair Diane, kindly do the honours of this dwelling to us. As to you, Monsoreau, rest; rest befits the wounded.'

'Monseigneur, it shall not be said that you came to my house and another did the honours; my servants will carry me wherever you go,' said the Comte.

The Duc seemed to divine his real thoughts, for he released Diane's hand. 'Approach her,' whispered Rémy to Bussy. The latter did so, and Monsoreau smiled on them; Bussy took Diane's hand, and Monsoreau smiled more. 'This is indeed a change, Monsieur le Comte,' said Diane softly. 'Alas! would that it were greater,' replied Bussy.

CHAPTER LXIII

DIANE'S STRATEGY

Bussy did not leave Diane; Monsoreau's gracious smile gave him a freedom which he took care to use.

'Madame, I am indeed the most wretched of men,' said he, 'on the news of your husband's death, I advised the Prince to return to Paris and make peace with his mother; he agreed, and now you remain in Anjou.'

'Oh! Louis, can you say we are unhappy? So many days of happiness, of ineffable joy, do you forget them?'

'I forget nothing, madame; rather I remember too well, and that is why, in losing this happiness, I complain. Do you understand what I will suffer, if I must return to Paris, a hundred leagues from you?'

'You will go to Paris, Louis, and I also,' said Diane, after a moment's silence.

'You will leave M. de Monsoreau?'

'I would leave him, but he would not leave me; no, believe me, it is better he should come with us.'

Diane, leaving Bussy, approached the Prince, who was answering Monsoreau ill-humouredly enough. At sight of Diane the Comte's brow cleared, but this calm did not last long. Diane approached the Duc. 'Monseigneur,' said she, smiling graciously. 'I believe your Highness is fond of flowers. Come, I will show your Highness the finest flowers in all Anjou.'

'Where are you taking Monseigneur ?' asked Monsoreau uneasily.

'Into the conservatory, monsieur.'

'Ah! carry me into the conservatory.'

'Do not let M. de Monsoreau suspect that you are leaving Anjou, and I undertake the rest,' whispered Diane to Bussy.

Bussy approached the Prince. 'Monseigneur, no indiscretion; do not let Monsoreau know that we are preparing to make peace. He might warn the Queen-Mother of our intentions, and she might not be so disposed to deal generously with us.'

'You are right; you distrust him, then ? I, also; I think he feigned the dead man purposely.'

'No, faith; he was honestly wounded, and that imbecile Rémy thought for a moment that he was dead.'

They arrived at the conservatory, Diane smiling to the Duc more charmingly than ever. The Prince entered, then Diane, but when Monsoreau wished to follow, it was found impossible; the door was long and high, but not wider than a large box, and the litter was six feet wide. Monsoreau groaned; Diane paid no attention to the despairing gestures of her husband.

'Monseigneur! do not enter that conservatory, there are deadly exhalations, strange flowers shedding poisonous perfumes,' cried Monsoreau; but Francois was not listening. Bussy encouraged Monsoreau to be patient in suffering, but the inevitable happened; he fainted. Rémy ordered the wounded man to be taken to his room, while Bussy announced the news to Diane. The latter left the Duc at once and proceeded to the château.

'Have we succeeded ?' asked Bussy.

'I think so; in any case, see Gertrude before leaving.'

The Comte soon opened his eyes, and, seeing Diane at his bedside,—

'Ah! it is you, madame;' he said; 'I am happy to see you that I may inform you that we leave to-night for Paris.'

'Do you mean this, monsieur ?' asked Diane calmly; 'and your wound ?'

'No wound impedes me. I would rather die than suffer, and we start to-night, should I die on the way.'

'As you please, monsieur; but may I know the cause of this sudden resolve ?'

'I will tell you madame, when you have no flowers to show the Prince, or when I have had doors made wide enough for my litter to enter everywhere.'

Meanwhile the Duc d'Anjou prepared to leave Méridor. He expressed the greatest gratitude to the Baron for the welcome he had given him, and mounted his horse. Just then Gertrude approached and informed the Duc that her mistress was prevented from presenting her homage; to Bussy she said that Diane was leaving that night. They set out; the Duc, ignorant of the First Huntsman's resolution, meditated all the way upon the danger of obeying too easily his mother's requests. Bussy had foreseen this, and was prepared for this desire to remain.

'Bussy,' said the Duc, 'I have considered, and it is not right that I should immediately comply with my mother's wishes.'

'You are right; she thinks herself a shrewd enough politician already.'

'Whilst, in demanding a week, or delaying for a week, in giving some fêtes to which we will invite the nobility, we will show her how strong we are.'

'Powerfully reasoned, monseigneur; exact new concessions, but see that your affairs do not suffer by this delay. The King, not knowing your intentions, may become exasperated.'

'You are right, I should send somebody to my brother to announce my return; that gives me the necessary time. But then, nobody would undertake this mission. Do you know of any one?'

'Yes, I know one.'

'Who?'

'Myself, monseigneur. I like difficult negotiations.'

'Bussy, if you do this, count upon my eternal gratitude.'

Bussy smiled, knowing the extent of this gratitude. The Duc noticed that he hesitated.

'And I will give you ten thousand crowns for your journey,' he added.

'Be more generous. Some things cannot be paid for.'

'So you start?'

'Yes, to-night if you wish it, monseigneur. It is agreed, then. You may live happily here, and secure some fine abbey for me from the Queen-Mother. Then, farewell, monseigneur.'

'Farewell, Bussy! do not forget one thing : take leave of my mother.'

'I will have that honour.'

Bussy, more joyful than a schoolboy out at play, visited Catherine, and prepared to leave as soon as the signal came from Méridor. This was delayed till the next day; Monsoreau, weakened by emotion, had judged a night's rest necessary. Towards seven o'clock, the groom who had brought Saint-Luc's letter came to announce that the Comte, despite the Baron's tears and Rémy's opposition, had left in a litter, escorted by Diane, Rémy, and Gertrude on horseback. Bussy, leaping on his horse, saddled the night before, took the same route.

CHAPTER LXIV

SAINT-LUC RETURNS TO COURT

SINCE Catherine's departure the King, whatever may have been his confidence in his ambassador, thought only of arming himself against his brother's attempts; he knew all that a claimant to the throne could do, a new-comer against a legitimate possessor, that is against a man bored and warned. He amused himself by drawing up lists in which those who were not eager to take their King's part were inscribed in alphabetical order. At S and L the King inscribed every day the name of M. de Saint-Luc. His rage against his former favourite was fed by the remarks and perfidious insinuations of the courtiers; indeed, might not Saint-Luc, fleeing to Méridor, be regarded as the quartermaster of Duc d'Anjou, gone to prepare his way. In the midst of all this emotion, Chicot encouraged the favourites to have their rapiers ready to slash the enemies of His Most Christian Majesty. While apparently acting an insignificant part, Chicot was playing a very serious one; he was gradually gathering together an army for his master's service. Suddenly one day, as the King supped with the Queen, whose society he cultivated more assiduously at each political crisis, Chicot entered with arms thrust out and legs stretched like a Jack-in-the-box.

'Ouf!' said he, 'M. de Saint-Luc.'

'In Paris—in the Louvre ?'

'Yes.'

The King rose from the table, flushed and trembling. It would have been difficult to say what feelings moved him. The Queen wished to rise to leave the room free for her husband.

'No, remain, madame. I will go to my study,' said Henri, rushing from the room, followed by Chicot.

'What is he here for, the traitor ?' asked Henri.

'Who knows ?' replied Chicot.

'He comes, I am sure, as a deputy from the States of Anjou. He comes as an ambassador from my brother, for that is how rebellions are managed; they are troubled and muddy waters in which the revolters fish for benefices. This one has scented the rebellion, and has procured a safe conduct by means of it to come and insult me.'

'Who knows ?'

'It may be that he comes to beg for his property, of which I keep the revenues; it is rather an abuse, perhaps, as he committed no definite crime ?'

'Who knows ?' continued Chicot.

'Ah ! you are like my popinjay—always repeating the same thing; you exasperate me with your eternal ''Who knows ?'' '

'What do you want me to reply ? Do you take me for an Ancient Fate or for Jupiter or Apollo ? You exasperate me with your stupid conjectures !'

'Chicot, my friend, you are rude to me when I am suffering.'

'Do not suffer, *mordieu* !'

Henri, lost in conjectures, descended to find Saint-Luc surrounded by many of the household, with Crillon at their head, his eyes flashing, his moustache bristling like a dog preparing for a combat. Saint-Luc stood in their midst, untroubled; he had brought his wife with him, and she was sitting on a footstool. Saint-Luc, his cloak draped proudly around him, waited in an attitude which seemed rather to call forth provocation than to fear it. Henri entered, agitated, wholly absorbed in his excitement; Chicot followed, calm and dignified as the King of France should have been, and studied Saint-Luc's demeanour, which was what Henri should have done.

'Ah ! monsieur, you here ?' cried the King.

'Yes, your Majesty,' answered Saint-Luc simply and modestly, bowing reverently before him.

'Truly, your presence in the Louvre surprises me strangely.'

A dead silence fell between the King and his favourite at this rude attack; Saint-Luc broke it first.

'Your Majesty, I am only surprised at one thing,— that is, that your Majesty, under the circumstances, was not expecting me,' said he. 'Your Majesty is in danger : great, real, serious danger, in which the King has need of the help of all devoted to him, from the greatest to the smallest; I come to lay at my King's feet the offer of my humble services.'

'Ah! do you see, my son, I was right to say "Who knows?"' said Chicot.

Henri did not reply at first; he looked at the by-standers, who seemed to be moved and offended; but Henri soon distinguished in their glances that jealousy which is found in most hearts. He concluded from that that Saint-Luc had done something of which most of them were incapable, that is something good. Yet he did not wish to give in all at once.

'Monsieur, you have only done your duty, for your services are due to us,' said he.

'The services of all the King's subjects are due to the King, I know; but, nowadays, many people forget to pay their debts. I come, your Majesty, to pay mine, happy that I am still counted among the debtors of your Majesty,' answered Saint-Luc.

'So you return without other motives, with any mission to fulfil or safe conduct ?'

'Your Majesty,' said Saint-Luc, knowing by the King's tones that his reproach and anger had vanished, 'I return purely and simply for that reason. Your Majesty may throw me into the Bastille or have me shot; but I will have done my duty. Your Majesty, Anjou is aroused, Lorraine is about to revolt, La Guyenne is rising, M. le Duc d'Anjou is stirring up the West and the South of France.'

'He is well aided, I think ?'

'Your Majesty, neither advice nor representations stop the Duc; and M. de Bussy, firm as he is, cannot reassure your brother about the terror with which your Majesty has inspired him.'

'Ah! he trembles, the rebel.'

'A clever fellow,' said Chicot, stroking his chin; then

elbowing the King, he added, 'Stand aside, Henri, till I shake hands with M. de Saint-Luc.'

This movement decided the King. Walking slowly towards his old friend, he laid his hands on his shoulders, saying : 'Be welcome, Saint-Luc.'

'Your Majesty, I have found my beloved master!' said Saint-Luc, kissing the King's hand.

'Yes, but I do not find you the same; you are so thin that I should not have recognised you.'

At these words a feminine voice was heard saying,—

'Your Majesty, it grieves me to displease your Majesty.'

Though the voice was sweet and respectful, Henri started.

'Madame de Saint-Luc! True; I had forgotten.'

Jeanne fell at his knees.

'Rise up, madame; I like all who bear the name of Saint-Luc,' said the King. Jeanne, seizing his hand, kissed it, but the King hastily withdrew it.

'Go, and win over the King; you are pretty enough for that,' said Chicot to the young woman.

Henri, turning away from Jeanne, drew Saint-Luc into his apartments. Jeanne was uncertain what to do.

'Madame, a good wife should never leave her husband— especially when her husband is in danger,' said Chicot, pushing her after the King and Saint-Luc.

CHAPTER LXV

THE JOURNEY TO PARIS

THERE is one character, there are even two characters, in this story about whose actions our readers have a right to inquire. The first is a huge monk with big hands and broad shoulders, whose neck daily grows shorter; the second a very large ass—the one dwells in a cell in the convent of Saint-Geneviève, the other in the stable of the same convent. The first answers to the name of Gorenflot, the second should answer to that of Panurge. Both are enjoying the happiest fate of which an ass and a monk have ever dreamed. The abbey kitchen is constantly busy preparing food; the choicest wines of Burgundy flow into the biggest glasses.

Yet, sometimes, in the midst of all this splendour, a cloud passes over Gorenflot's brow, the poultry of Le Mans tempts him in vain, the wine is untouched; Gorenflot is sad, and no longer hungry; he dreams. The monks withdraw out of respect; the Prior alone waits till Brother Gorenflot gives some sign of life, raises his head and gazes with dazed eyes.

'What were you doing, noble brother?' asks the Prior.

'I was composing a sermon, father.'

'Like that one you so bravely delivered on the night of the Holy League?'

'Yes, like it. What a pity I did not write that one!'

'A man like you has no need to write. He opens his mouth, and the word of God flows from his lips.'

Indeed, from time to time, Gorenflot, understanding the exigencies of the situation, meditates a sermon.

'You are working too hard, dear brother; it is making you sad,' says the Abbot sometimes.

'Who knows,' answers Gorenflot.

'Perhaps our meals are somewhat coarse; would you like the cook changed? Or, perhaps you have the desire to travel again, for you caress your dear Panurge?'

'Oh!' answers Gorenflot, sighing.

'Alas!' says a young brother timidly, 'I believe you are right, worthy Prior, and that his life in the convent tires the reverend father.'

So, seeing his sadness increasing daily, the Prior says one morning, 'Dear brother, one should not struggle against one's vocation, yours is to fight for Religion; go, then, accomplish the mission with which the Lord has entrusted you; only take care of your precious life, and return for the Fête-Dieu.'

'But, give me some money that I may influence by my alms.'

The Prior fetched a bag of money, which he held out to Gorenflot; the latter plunged his big hand into it, and transferred a sum to his own pocket. Gorenflot was helped on to Panurge, and left the convent towards seven o'clock; on the same day Saint-Luc arrived from Méridor. After traversing Rue Saint-Etienne, Panurge suddenly started: a strong hand had been placed on his croup.

'Who goes there?' asked Gorenflot, terrified.

'A friend,' answered a voice.

'What do you wish?'

'Could you tell me the way to the Corne d'Abondance ?'

'*Morbleu !* it is Monsieur Chicot himself.'

'Exactly; I went to the convent for you, and then followed you for a time, as I was afraid to speak; but now we are alone, I have come; *ventre de biche !* I find you thinner.'

'And you, I find you fatter, Monsieur Chicot; but what have you there ? You seem loaded.'

'It is a piece of venison which I stole from His Majesty.'

'And under the other arm?'

'A flagon of Cyprus wine, sent by a king to my sovereign; it is my favourite wine. What about yourself, brother monk ?'

'Oh !' cried Gorenflot, rocking on Panurge, 'oh ! oh !' In his joy the monk raised his arms and sang in a voice which made all the windows shake. It was the first time he had sung for nearly a month.

Leaving the two friends to enter the Corne d'Abondance, where Chicot never took the monk without intentions whose gravity the latter did not suspect, we will return to M. de Monsoreau and Bussy. Not only is it easy for a well-mounted horseman to overtake foot passengers, but he also runs the risk of passing them. This is what happened to Bussy. As it was very hot at midday, M. de Monsoreau gave orders to stop in a little wood by the wayside; meanwhile Bussy passed. He had obtained satisfactory information at the village of Durtal, and convinced that Diane was in front he was standing in his stirrups at the top of each hill, to distinguish the little company. But suddenly all information failed him; nobody he met had seen any one, and at La Fleche, he was certain of being in front and not behind. Putting up at the worst inn in the place, he stationed himself at the window, hiding behind the curtain. This inn was opposite the best hotel of the town, where he had no doubt Monsoreau would stop. Towards four o'clock a courier arrived at the hotel, and in half an hour the company followed. Bussy waited till nine o'clock; the courier came out, and five minutes later eight men approached the hotel, four of them entering.

'Oh ! will they travel by night ? That would be a splendid idea for M. de Monsoreau.'

Everything supported this probability; it was a beautiful, starry night, with a soft breeze blowing. The litter came out, then Diane, Rémy, and Gertrude on horseback.

Diane looked keenly around; but the Comte called her, and she was obliged to return to the litter. The four relay men, lighting torches, walked at each side of the road. Bussy, saddling his horse, started in pursuit; there was no mistaking the route this time, for the torches lit it up clearly. Monsoreau never let Diane away for an instant; he spoke to her, or rather scolded her, the visit to the conservatory having occasioned much bitter questioning. Rémy and Gertrude sulked at one another, or rather Rémy was dreaming, while Gertrude sulked at him. The cause of this attitude was easily explained : Rémy saw no more necessity for being in love with Gertrude, since Diane was in love with Bussy. The procession was advancing thus when Bussy, to warn Rémy of his presence, blew on a silver whistle, with which he usually summoned his servants. Rémy, recognising it, made an affirmative sign to Diane, who had started and looked at him. 'It is he,' said he, in low tones, approaching her.

'Who is it, and who speaks to you, madame ?' asked Monsoreau.

'To me; nobody, monsieur.'

'Yes, a shadow passed near me, and I heard a voice.'

'It is M. Rémy's voice; are you jealous of him, too ?'

'No; but I like to hear people speaking out loud.'

'There are some things which cannot be said before Monsieur le Comte,' interrupted Gertrude; 'for two reasons : first, because the things might not interest monsieur at all; second, that they might interest him too much.'

'What was Rémy saying to you, madame ?'

'I was saying that if you exerted yourself thus, you will die before going a third of the way.'

Monsoreau's face became as pale as a corpse. Diane was silent.

'He is waiting for you behind; slacken your pace and he will overtake you,' said Rémy. Monsoreau, hearing a murmur, glanced round at Diane.

'Another movement like that, and I won't answer for the hæmorrhage,' said Rémy.

Diane, taking courage, waited, while Rémy, dismounting, approached the litter. In five seconds Bussy was near Diane. Without speaking, they embraced tenderly.

'You see, I have followed you,' said Bussy at length.

'Oh! how happy my days and my nights will be if I know you are thus near me!'

'But, he will see us during the day.'

'No, you will follow at a distance,,and I alone will see you. At the corner of the roads, the plume of your hat, the embroidery of your cloak, your waving handkerchief, all will speak to me in your name. And when we travel by night, as we will do often, for Rémy has said that the night air is good for the Comte's wound, I will loiter behind from time to time to press you in my arms, to tell you, with a hand-clasp, all I have been thinking about you.'

The horses were close together, the two lovers, embracing, had forgotten the world, when suddenly a voice made them start—Diane in fear, Bussy in anger.

'Madame Diane, where are you? Answer,' cried this voice.

'Oh! it is he! I have forgotten. I was dreaming! Sweet dream and horrible awaking!' murmured Diane.

'Listen, Diane; let us flee. Who can prevent us? Look around you; before us is space, happiness, freedom! One word and we start! One word and you are lost to him for ever and belong to me.'

'And my father?'

'When the Baron knows that I love you?'

'Oh! a father? what are you saying?'

This recalled Bussy to himself.

'Nothing by violence, dear Diane; command and I shall obey.'

'Listen, our destiny is there; let us be stronger than it, fear nothing, and you will see if I know how to love.'

'Comtesse! answer, or I jump out of this infernal litter, though I should kill myself,' cried the voice.

Diane rushed forward to find the Comte almost in a swoon.

'Ah! where were you?' he asked.

'Where do you think, monsieur, if not behind you?'

'Keep alongside, madame; do not leave me.'

They reached the halting-place; Monsoreau, after resting for some hours, set forth again. From time to time the scene we have just related kept occurring. Rémy kept saying: 'Let him die of rage, the doctor's honour will be maintained.'

But Monsoreau, instead of dying, arrived in Paris in ten days' time, visibly better. Rémy was certainly skilful, more skilful than he could have wished. During the journey, Diane had succeeded in destroying Bussy's great pride, and had persuaded him to visit Monsoreau, to profit by the friendship professed by the latter. The excuse for the visit was quite simple—the health of the Comte. Rémy nursed the husband and delivered love letters to the wife. 'Esculapius and Mercury,' said he, 'I double my rôles.'

CHAPTER LXVI

THE DUC D'ANJOU'S AMBASSADOR ARRIVES AT PARIS

As neither Catherine nor the Duc d'Anjou appeared at the Louvre, the news of a dissension between the brothers daily assumed more importance. The King, receiving no news from his mother, instead of concluding, 'No news, good news!' said, 'No news, bad news!' And the minions added, 'François, wrongly advised, will have detained your mother.' Indeed, the whole policy of this strange reign and the three preceding ones was summed up in these words, 'François, wrongly advised.' Nobody could say to a king, 'Your brother, having bad blood in his veins, seeks, as is the custom in your family, to have you dethroned or poisoned; he wishes to do to you what you did to your elder brother, what your mother has instructed you all to do to one another,' so the favourites said to Henri III., 'Your Majesty, your brother is wrongly advised,' and, as one person alone could be advising François, the storm burst forth against Bussy. Suddenly word came that Monseigneur le Duc d'Anjou was sending an ambassador. The King became pale with rage, the favourites livid, and many oaths were registered—to scoff at, deride, and imprison this ambassador if an old man; to cleave asunder this ambassador if young, and cut him in pieces, which would be sent throughout France as specimens of the kingly wrath. The King, seeing Chicot reflect, remembered that he had on one occasion shared the Queen-Mother's opinion, which turned out to be the true one. Therefore he understood Chicot to stand for wisdom, and questioned him.

'Your Majesty,' replied the latter, 'either the Duc

d'Anjou sends you an ambassador, or he does not; if he does, it is because he believes himself able to do so; if he believes himself able, then he feels he is strong; if he feels strong, we must treat him with caution; let us receive the ambassador, expressing our great pleasure at seeing him; but if he is not sending you an ambassador, why let all your friends bellow in this way? It sickens me, Henri, to see them, like small boys, playing at ghosts and trying to frighten people by whooping. If the Duc sends nobody, they will imagine they are the cause, and will think themselves important personages.'

'Then, what do you advise me to do?'

'I advise you to wait. If an ambassador arrives, receive him graciously; if nobody comes, do what you like; but, at least, do not be hard upon your brother, who must not be sacrificed to your friends. He is a rogue, I know, but he is a Valois; kill him, if that suits you, but don't deprive him of dignity; he takes care to do that himself.'

'That is true, Chicot.'

'Still another lesson you owe me; fortunately we have stopped counting; now let me sleep; a week ago I was obliged to make a monk intoxicated, and when I undertake these performances, I suffer for a week from the effects.'

'A monk! Is it that monk of Sainte-Geneviève, of whom you have already spoken?'

'Exactly. You promised him an abbey. It is the least you could do after what he did for you.'

'Is he still devoted to me?'

'He adores you. By the way, my son, the Fête-Dieu will be in three weeks. I hope you are preparing some fine procession for us?'

'As His Most Christian Majesty, it is my duty to show my people an example of piety.'

'And you will stop as usual in the four great convents of Paris? The abbey of Saint-Geneviève is one, I think?'

'No doubt; it is the second I intend visiting. But why do you ask?'

'For nothing. I am inquisitive. Now I know what I wanted to know. Good-night, Henri.'

Chicot was preparing to slumber, when a loud noise was heard in the Louvre. The Captain of the Guards entered, looking scared.

'Your Majesty, the envoy of M. le Duc d'Anjou has arrived,' said he.

'With a retinue ?' asked the King.

'No, quite alone.'

'Then he must be specially well received, Henri, for he is brave.'

'Come,' said the King, trying to appear calm, though looking pale, 'let us assemble the court in the Great Hall, and I will attire myself in black; one must be dressed in lugubrious fashion when one has the misfortune to deal with a brother through an ambassador !'

The throne of Henri III. was erected in the Great Hall, and a noisy crowd seethed around it. The King took his seat, sad and gloomy looking. All eyes were turned towards the gallery by which the Captain of the Guards was to introduce the ambassador.

'Your Majesty, do you know the name of this ambassador ?' said Quélus, leaning forward.

'No; what does it matter to me ?'

'Your Majesty, it is M. de Bussy; is it not a triple insult ?'

'I do not see wherein the insult consists,' said Henri, striving to preserve his coolness.

'Perhaps your Majesty does not see it, but we all do,' said Schomberg. Henri made no answer; he felt the rage and hate fermenting around him, and congratulated himself in having raised two such ramparts between himself and his enemies. Allowing his favourites to excite themselves, Henri smiled, and gave the order, 'Let him enter.'

A dead silence fell, and then a step resounded in the gallery and Bussy entered, his head high, and carrying his hat in his hand. Advancing straight to Henri, and bowing low, he waited proudly to be questioned.

'Monsieur de Bussy ! I thought you were buried in Anjou.'

'Your Majesty, I was there; but, as you see, I have left it.'

'What brings you to our capital ?'

'The desire to present my humblest respects to your Majesty.'

'And—nothing more ?'

'I will add, your Majesty, the command I received from His Highness Monseigneur le Duc d'Anjou, to join his respects to mine. He told me that, being on the point of returning with the Queen-Mother, he wished your

Majesty to know of the return of one of your most faithful subjects.'

The King, suffocated with surprise, could not continue his questioning. Chicot, profiting by this interruption, turned to the ambassador.

'That is all you have to say to me, Monsieur de Bussy?' resumed the King.

'Yes, your Majesty; if there is any other important news, Monseigneur le Duc d'Anjou will have the honour to announce it himself.'

'Very good,' said the King, descending in silence from his throne. The audience was over; the groups dispersed. Bussy noticed that he was surrounded by the four favourites, while the King conversed in low tones with his Chancellor. Feigning to see nothing, Bussy talked to Chicot till the King called the latter away. Then Bussy assumed a gracious air. Seeing Quélus approach, he said to him,—

'Good-morning, Monsieur de Quelus, may I ask how you are?'

'Not very well, monsieur; there is something troubling me.'

'Excuse me, monsieur,' said Maugiron, thrusting Schomberg aside, 'it is not *something* but *somebody* that M. de Quélus meant.'

'Ah! Monsieur de Schomberg, I did not recognise you.'

'Perhaps I have still some blue on my face?'

'Not at all, you are very pale; are you ill, monsieur?'

'Monsieur, it is with anger I am pale.'

'Really! then you are annoyed by somebody, like M. de Quélus?'

'Yes, monsieur.'

'It is the same with me,' said Maugiron.

'Indeed, gentlemen, the more I look, the more your troubled countenances strike me.'

'You forget me, monsieur,' said d'Épernon, proudly placing himself in front of Bussy.

It was a curious sight to see Bussy's smile and easy bearing before these four furious men, whose intentions were easy to see. To feign not to see them was possible only to Bussy.

'Make an end of this!' burst forth Quélus, stamping his foot.

'Monsieur, do you notice that there is an echo here? Nothing sends back sounds like marble walls, and voices are doubly sonorous under roofs of stucco,' said Bussy, raising his eyes to the ceiling.

Maugiron approached Bussy to whisper in his ear, but the latter stopped him.

'No confidences here, I beg, monsieur; you know how jealous His Majesty is.'

Maigiron withdrew furious. Schomberg took his place, and began in weighty tones: 'I am a German, very heavy and dense, but very frank; I speak loud that my listeners may hear, but when my words are not heard because my listener is dead or will not hear, then I——'

'You?' said Bussy, gazing at the young man with a tiger's glare which seemed to shoot fire, 'you——?'

Schomberg stopped. Bussy, shrugging his shoulders, turned his back on him. D'Épernon launched forth.

'Do you see how provincial M. de Bussy has become, gentlemen; he has no riband on his sword : he has black boots and a gray felt hat,' said he.

'That is just what I was remarking to myself, my dear Monsieur d'Épernon. Seeing you so well apparelled, I asked myself to what a state a few days' absence could reduce a man; here am I, Louis de Bussy, Seigneur de Clermont, forced to take a petty Gascon noble as a model. But let me pass, pray; you are so near that you trod on my foot, and M. de Quélus, too.'

Bussy, passing between Quélus and d'Épernon, held out his hand to Saint-Luc, who had just entered. Saint-Luc found this hand damp with perspiration, and, under-standing that something extraordinary was happening, drew Bussy out of the hall. Just then the King approached the favourites, while Chicot whispered in his ear.

'Well! what was M. de Bussy saying?'

'Faith, nothing good, your Majesty; he is no longer a Parisian,' said Quélus.

'What is he, then?'

'He is a countryman. He draws back.'

'Oh! what does that mean?'

'It means that I will have a dog trained to bite him—and yet, who knows whether he will feel it through his boots.'

'I have a quintain at home which I will call Bussy,' added Schomberg.

'I will go farther,' said d'Épernon; 'to-day I trod on his foot, to-morrow I will box his ears.'

'What! gentlemen,' said Henri, feigning rage, 'you have dared to ill-use in my palace one of my brother's followers?'

'Alas, yes! and though we treated him very badly, I assure you he said nothing,' said Maugiron, feigning humility.

The King looked smilingly at Chicot.

'Gentlemen, I leave you; I go to dine with the Queen,' said he, retiring by the principal door, while the company bowed respectfully. M. de Saint-Luc entered at that moment, and stopped the minions, as they were leaving.

'Excuse me, Monsieur de Quélus,' said he, 'do you still stay in the Rue Saint-Honoré?'

'Yes, dear friend; why?'

'I have a word to say to you. And you, Monsieur de Schomberg, may I inquire your address?'

'I stay in Rue Béthisy,' said Schomberg, in surprise.

'D'Épernon, I know yours. And you, Maugiron?'

'My home is in the neighbourhood of the Louvre.'

'I will begin with you, if you permit; no, rather with you, Quélus.'

'I think I understand. You come on behalf of M. de Bussy?'

'I do not say on whose behalf I come. I wish to speak to you all.'

'Well! if you do not wish to speak to us in the Louvre, you can come home with one of us. We can all hear what you have to say to each of us.'

'Perfectly.'

'Let us go to Schomberg's rooms, then, in Rue Béthisy, two steps away.'

'Very good; show us the way, Monsieur de Schomberg.'

The five noblemen left the Louvre, arm-in-arm; behind them walked two lackeys fully armed. Arrived at the Rue Béthisy, Schomberg had the drawing-room prepared while Saint-Luc waited in the ante-room.

CHAPTER LXVII

M. DE SAINT-LUC DELIVERS BUSSY'S MESSAGE

LEAVING Saint-Luc in Schomberg's ante-room, let us see what conversation he had had with Bussy. Once out of the Audience Hall, Saint-Luc looked anxiously at Bussy, and asked him,—

'Are you going to turn ill, my friend ? You are so pale that one would imagine you are about to faint.'

'No, but I am choking with rage.'

'Goodness, are you heeding what these rogues said ?'

'The deuce, you are going to see if I heed it.'

'Come, come, Bussy, be calm.'

'You are a nice person to talk of calmness; if they had said to you the half of what they said to me there would have been bloodshed already.'

'What do you want ?'

'You have already given me a terrible proof of your friendship, Saint-Luc.'

'Ah ! dear friend, please don't mention that affair; the stroke was a fine one, and succeeded admirably, but I take no credit for it; the King taught me it when I was his prisoner here. Let us leave Monsoreau to speak of Diane. Was she just a little bit glad, poor thing ? Does she forgive me ? When will the wedding be ?'

'Dear friend, wait till Monsoreau is dead; poppies are not such dangerous plants as you think, and he did not die with falling upon them; on the contrary, he is alive, and more furious than ever.'

'He lives ?'

'Alas ! yes.'

'And what fool of a doctor nursed him ?'

'My own, dear friend.'

'I am overcome. But I am disgraced now, for I have announced his death to every one; he will find his heirs in mourning. But I won't contradict the news; I will wound him four times instead of once at the next meeting, if need be.'

'I appeal to you now, Saint-Luc, to calm yourself; indeed, Monsoreau does me more service than you imagine; he suspects the Duc of having despatched you against him; it is of the Duc he is jealous, while I am an angel, a treasured friend, his dear Bussy. It is quite natural, seeing that silly Rémy restored him; in short, thinking he owes me his life, he has entrusted his wife to my care. You see, then, that this is no time to speak against M. de Monsoreau. You have done me a half service, Saint-Luc; pay me what you still owe in some other way. You are on very good terms with Messieurs the minions ?'

'Faith, we are like cats and dogs basking in the sun together; as long as the rays warm us all, we say nothing; but should one usurp the light and heat of another, then I no longer answer for anything; claws and teeth would come into play.'

'Well ! friend, let us assume that the heat has been intercepted; show me your fine white teeth, stretch out your formidable claws, and open warfare.'

'I do not understand.'

'You will go, if you please, and accost M. de Quélus. You begin to understand, don't you ?'

'Yes.'

'Good ! You will ask him which day suits him to cut my throat, or to have his cut by me. On your way to M. de Quélus, you will oblige me by calling on M. de Schomberg, to whom you will make the same request.'

'Ah ! M. de Schomberg, too ! The deuce ! how you manage matters, Bussy. I will carry out your instructions.'

'Then, dear Saint-Luc, since I find you so complaisant, you will call on M. de Maugiron at the Louvre, and make him join the others, won't you ?'

'Oh ! three; what are you thinking of, Bussy ? At least, that is all ?'

'No; afterwards you will visit M. d'Épernon; I don't attach much importance to him, but he will make up the number.'

'Four !' said Saint-Luc, dropping his arms in amazement.

'That is so, dear friend, four; needless to say, I will not impress upon a man of your tact, courage, and courtesy the necessity for dealing with these gentlemen in the most refined and polite fashion, for I know you to excel in these matters. I trust to you to do this—as a gallant gentleman.'

'You will be satisfied, dear friend. Now for the conditions.'

'I make none; I will accept theirs.'

'And weapons?'

'I will accept their choice of weapons, day, place, and hour; do this quickly, dear friend. I will walk in the Louvre garden, where you can rejoin me when your task is accomplished.'

Let us now return to Saint-Luc, waiting in the anteroom of Schomberg's house, till the four favourites, who expected his visit, had stationed themselves at the four corners of the large drawing-room. When this was done, the folding doors were thrown open, and an usher announced 'M. d'Épinay de Saint-Luc.' Schomberg, in his quality of host, rose to meet his guest, who, instead of bowing, replaced his hat on his head, thus revealing the nature of his visit. Schomberg, bowing, turned to Quélus.

'I have the honour to present to you Monsieur Jacques de Lévis, Comte de Quélus,' said he. Saint-Luc bowed low. This ceremony was gone through with Maugiron and d'Épernon; then Schomberg introduced himself, and the four friends sat down, while Saint-Luc remained standing.

'Monsieur le Comte,' he said to Quélus, 'you have insulted M. le Comte Louis de Clermont d'Amboise, Seigneur de Bussy, who, presenting his very humble compliments, summons you to single combat, at such time as will suit you, that you may fight with whatever weapons you choose, until death ensues. Do you accept?'

'Of course,' answered Quélus calmly; 'M. le Comte de Bussy honours me exceedingly.'

'The day?'

'I have no preference; only I should like to-morrow rather than the day after; or the latter rather than the following days.'

'The hour?'

'Morning.'

'Your weapons?'

'The rapier and the dagger, if M. de Bussy is suited with these.'

'All you decide in this respect will be regarded as law for M. de Bussy.'

Then Saint-Luc addressed Maugiron, who replied in like terms; afterwards the other two were questioned.

'But there is one thing we forget,' said Schomberg,

who, being host, was asked last; 'it is that should we all choose the same day and hour, for chance produces strange happenings, M. de Bussy might find himself in some difficulty.'

Saint-Luc bowed, smiling most graciously.

'Of course, M. de Bussy would be in some embarrassment, as any gentleman would in the presence of four such gallants; but he says that the situation would not be novel, since the same thing occurred at the Tournelles, near the Bastille.'

'And he would fight all four?' asked d'Épernon.

'All four,' answered Saint-Luc.

'Separately?' asked Schomberg.

'Separately or together; the challenge may be taken up individually or collectively.'

'That is very noble on M. de Bussy's part,' said Quélus, red with rage, 'but, insignificant as we are, we can each play our part separately; we will accept the Comte's proposal, to fight in turn, or, what would be still better, as we do not intend to assassinate a gallant man, let chance decide which of us will meet M. de Bussy.'

'But the other three?' asked d'Épernon sharply.

'M. de Bussy has certainly too many friends and we too many enemies to allow the other three to remain with arms folded; do you approve of my idea?' added Quélus, turning to his companions.

'Yes,' they replied with one accord.

'I would be particularly pleased if M. de Bussy invited M. de Livarot to this fête,' said Schomberg.

'If I dared express an opinion, I should like M. de Balzac d'Entragues to be of the party.'

'And the affair would be complete if M. de Ribeirac cared to accompany his friends.'

'Gentlemen, I will transmit your requests to M. le Comte de Bussy, and I think I can promise you beforehand that he will be too courteous not to comply with them. There only remains for me, gentlemen, to thank you very sincerely on behalf of M. le Comte,' said Saint-Luc, again bowing. The four young men, returning his bow, conducted Saint-Luc to the withdrawing-room door.

CHAPTER LXVIII

SAINT-LUC GIVES SOME LESSONS TO BUSSY

SAINT-LUC returned, very proud at having executed his commission so well. Bussy, who was waiting, thanked him, but Saint-Luc noticed that he appeared disconsolate.

'Have I arranged matters badly? You seem quite upset,' he said.

'Faith, dear friend, I regret that instead of agreeing to a date, you did not say "Immediately." '

'Patience, the Angevins are not here yet. Give them time to arrive. Where is the necessity to have a litter prepared so quickly for dead and dying men ?'

'Because I wish to die as soon as possible. I shall kill four of them, I feel sure, and receive a thrust which will quieten me for ever.'

'Gloomy thoughts these for Bussy !'

'I wish *you* were in my shoes. A husband, supposed to be dead, who returns to life; a wife who cannot quit the bedside of this supposed dying man; never to smile, never to speak to one another, touch one another's hand. *Mordieu !* I should like to slash somebody.'

Saint-Luc replied to this outbreak by a burst of laughter, which startled a whole flock of sparrows.

'Ah ! there's an innocent fellow for you !' he cried. 'To say that women love this Bussy—a schoolboy ! You are losing your wits, dear friend : there is no more fortunate lover than you on earth.'

'Very good; just prove that to me, you, a married man !'

'Nothing is simpler; you are M. de Monsoreau's friend ? Well ! be his friend. But is he really your friend ?'

'He says so.'

'He is not, since he makes you unhappy; then you can either treat him with indifference, or as an enemy, by taking his wife from him, and killing him if he resents it.'

'The fact is, I detest him. Do you believe he is not fond of me ?'

'Try him. Take away his wife and you will see.'

'Is that the logic of Father Triquet, the Jesuit ?'

'No, it's my own. It convinces you ?'

'No, I prefer to be a man of honour.'

'And leave Madame de Monsoreau to cure her husband ? For, if you are killed, it is certain she will cling to the only man remaining. But, besides, here is Madame de Saint-Luc, who is a wise counsellor. Listen to her, for she talks most sensibly.'

Jeanne approached, radiant with happiness and brimful of mischief. Bussy bowed to her; she gave him her hand.

'How is the love affair ?' she asked.

'It is dying,' answered Bussy.

'It has received a wound and has fainted; I wager you will revive it, Jeanne,' said Saint-Luc.

'If I am shown where the wound is.'

'I will show you; M. de Bussy does not like smiling at the Comte de Monsoreau, and he has decided to withdraw.'

'And to leave Diane to him ? Poor Diane ! Decidedly all men are ungrateful.'

'I ungrateful ! because I will not lower my love by submitting to the low practice of hypocrisy ?'

'Ah ! monsieur, that is but a sorry pretext. If you were really in love, you would fear only to be no longer loved. Confess that you no longer love Diane; it would be worthier of a gallant man.'

Bussy paled at the mere idea of it.

'You dare not tell her. I will tell her.'

'Madame ! madame !'

'He is still reflecting ! he does not fall on his knees to confess his fault !'

'You are right, I am only a man, an imperfect creature, and inferior to the commonest woman.'

'It is very lucky that you are convinced of it.'

'What do you advise me to do ?'

'To go straightway to visit——'

'M. de Monsoreau ?'

'Who says so ?—Diane.'

'But they are always together, it seems to me.

'When you went to see Madame de Barbezieux so often, she had that great monkey near her, who bit you, had she not ?'

Bussy began to laugh; Saint-Luc imitated him, and Jeanne followed suit; the hilarity attracted to the windows all the courtiers who were strolling in the galleries.

'Madame,' said Bussy, 'I am going to call on M. de Monsoreau. Farewell,' and they separated. Bussy found

the Comte in bed; he exclaimed joyfully on seeing him.
Rémy had told him that the wound would be healed in
three weeks. Diane laid a finger on her lips; it was her
greeting. The Comte had to be informed of the Duc
d'Anjou's commission, the visit to the court, the King's
uneasiness, the cold looks of the minions. Monsoreau,
quite thoughtful at this news, begging Bussy to lean
forward, whispered in his ear, 'There are still some plans
projected ?'

'I believe so.'

'Believe me, do not compromise yourself for this
wretched man; I know him; he is false; he does not
hesitate at treachery.'

'I am aware of it,' said Bussy, with a smile which
recalled to the Comte the circumstance in which Bussy
had suffered from this treachery.

'You are my friend, and I wish to put you on your
guard. And more, whenever you find yourself in a
difficult position, seek my advice.'

'Monsieur ! you must sleep after the dressing,' interposed Rémy.

'Yes, dear doctor. My friend, take a turn with Madame
de Monsoreau. I believe the garden is lovely this year.'

'At your service,' answered Bussy.

CHAPTER LXIX

M. DE MONSOREAU'S PRECAUTION

BOTH Saint-Luc and Jeanne were right, and by the end of
the week Bussy, perceiving this, rendered them full justice.
Diane, being simple and natural, yielded to the two
instincts which the misanthrope Figaro asserts to be
innate in the human species, to love and to deceive.
To love Bussy comprised her logic; to belong to him alone
summed up her morality. M. de Monsoreau was improving
daily; he had escaped fever, thanks to the applications of
cold water, a new remedy discovered by chance by
Ambroise Paré, when suddenly he experienced a great
shock; he learned that M. le Duc d'Anjou had just arrived
in Paris with the Queen-Mother and his Angevins. The
day after his arrival, the Prince came to the Rue des

Petits-Pères, under pretext of inquiring after the Comte's
health. M. de Monsoreau received the Prince, who was
charming to him and also to his wife. Immediately the
Prince had departed, M. de Monsoreau summoned Bussy;
he had a satisfied air, and Diane guessed from his smile
that he was meditating some cunning stroke.

Let us now, however, return to the Duc's arrival in
the Louvre. As might be supposed, it was not allowed to
pass unnoticed. This is what the observers saw : much
haughtiness on the King's part; considerable coolness on
that of the Queen-Mother; a humble insolence on the part
of M. le Duc d'Anjou, which seemed to say, 'Why do you
recall me if you can do nothing better than make grimaces?
The reception was brightened up by the fiery, flashing
glances of MM. de Livarot, de Ribeirac, and d'Entragues,
who, advised by Bussy, made it clear to their future
adversaries that no obstacle to the encounter would be
raised by them.

Two days later the Duc d'Anjou visited the wounded
man a second time. The latter, informed of the details
of the interview with the King, was particularly pleasant
to the Duc, endeavouring to inflame his anger against his
brother. When the Duc departed, the Comte made a tour
round his room, leaning on his wife's arm, after which he
sat down, looking even more satisfied than the first time.
The same night Bussy was informed by Diane that M. de
Monsoreau was certainly meditating some project. A
moment later, Monsoreau and Bussy were alone.

'When I remember that this smiling Prince is my
deadly enemy, and that he induced M. de Saint-Luc to
assassinate me,' began Monsoreau.

'Assassinate ! be careful, Monsieur de Comte; Saint-
Luc is a true gentleman, and you confess you provoked
him, drawing sword first, and your wound was received in
the fight.'

'Granted, but nevertheless he obeyed the Duc's
orders.'

'I know the Duc and Saint-Luc; I may say the latter
is entirely on the King's side, and not on the Prince's. Had
you been wounded by Antraguet, Livarot, or Ribeirac—
but Saint-Luc——'

'You are not acquainted with the history of France as
I am, my dear monsieur,' said Monsoreau, tenacious of his
opinion, preparing to descend to the garden.

'That will do,' said he, ascending again, 'to-night we will remove.'

'Why ?' asked Rémy, 'have you not fresh air here, or is there not sufficient amusement ?'

'On the contrary, there is too much; M. d'Anjou tires me with his visits; I have given orders to prepare my little house at the Tournelles. Only four people at the outside can be received there. It is a fortress, and from the window one can see visitors three hundred paces off, so that one can avoid them if one wishes, especially when one is in good health.'

Rémy, who was reflecting, was the first to speak.

'You cannot do this,' said he; 'the First Huntsman of France must hold receptions and maintain a staff of servants. He may lodge his dogs in a palace, but it is impossible for him to live in a dog-kennel. Then, it is not your remaining here which troubles me, but madame's. Let madame remove.'

'Be separated from her !' cried Monsoreau, gazing at Diane with more anger than love.

'Then resign your office of First Huntsman; it would be wise; for, really, either you will discharge the duties or not; if you do not, the King will be displeased; if you do——'

'I will do what is necessary; but I will not leave the Comtesse,' declared Monsoreau, with clenched teeth.

The Comte was finishing this statement, when a noise of horses and voices was heard in the courtyard. Monsoreau shuddered.

'The Duc again !' he murmured.

Thanks to his privileges as Prince, the Duc entered without being announced. Monsoreau was on the lookout; the first glance of François had been for Diane; he brought her a rare present of a charming dagger, with carved gold handle in form of a flagon; on the blade was engraved a hunting scene.

'To you, who are a hunter, the blade,' said he to Monsoreau; 'for the Comtesse, the handle; Bussy, you are an intimate friend of the Comte's nowadays ?'

'Monseigneur, you forget that your Highness commanded me this morning to inquire for M. de Monsoreau. I obeyed, as usual.'

'That is true,' said the Duc, sitting near Diane, and conversing in low tones.

'Comte, it is very hot in this invalid chamber. The Comtesse is gasping for air, so I will offer her my arm to walk in the garden,' said he presently.

The husband and the lover exchanged an angry look.

'Give me your arm,' said Monsoreau to Bussy, and he followed his wife downstairs.

'Ah !' said the Duc, 'it seems you are quite well ?'

'Yes, monseigneur, I hope soon to be able to accompany madame wherever she goes.'

'Comte,' said he to Bussy, 'if you vere very obliging, you would escort madame to my little Hôtel de la Bastille; I should like her to be there, truly. Having snatched her from this vulture's claws at Méridor, I will not allow him to devour her in Paris.'

'No, monsieur,' said Rémy to his master, 'you cannot accept, because you belong to M. d'Anjou, who will never forgive your helping the Comte to play such a trick on him.'

'What does it matter to me !' the rash young man was about to exclaim, when a glance from Rémy showed him that he must keep quiet.

'Rémy is right,' said Monsoreau, reflecting; 'I cannot exact this service from you; I will conduct her myself, for to-morrow or the following day I shall be able to inhabit this house.'

'Folly ! you will lose your office,' Bussy urged !

'Possibly, but I shall keep my wife.'

That very night the Comte accompanied his wife to the little house, Rémy aiding him in the installation. As he was a devoted man, and understood that Bussy would require his services, Rémy made fresh overtures to Gertrude, who after her first outburst of anger forgave him. Diane occupied her old bedroom, with the white and gold damask bed. A corridor separated this room from the Comte's. Bussy tore his hair, while Saint-Luc asserted that rope-ladders, having been brought to perfection, could replace staircases splendidly. Monsoreau, rubbing his hands, smiled as he thought of the Duc's vexation.

CHAPTER LXX

A VISIT TO THE MAISON DES TOURNELLES

In some men intense excitement fills the place of real passion, as hunger gives to the wolf and the hyena a semblance of courage. Under the influence of such a feeling, M. d'Anjou, whose vexation at not seeing Diane at Méridor cannot be expressed, returned to Paris; he was almost in love with this woman, precisely because she was being taken from him. As a result of this, his hatred for Monsoreau, which had been born the day he learned of the Comte's treachery, had become a sort of wild fury, all the more dangerous because, having tested the Comte's energetic character, he wished to be in a position to strike without giving any hold to his adversary. Moreover, he had not renounced his political hopes, but had rather taken a deeper idea of his own importance, and had renewed in Paris his dark and secret machinations. The moment was propitious; numerous conspirators, reassured by the sort of triumph which the King's weakness and Catherine's astuteness had afforded the Angevins, had rallied round the Duc, mingling his cause with that of the Guises, who remained prudently in the background.

The Duc displayed no more frankness towards Bussy, but, instead, a friendly hypocrisy. Vaguely disturbed at having seen the young man in Monsoreau's house, he grudged him the latter's confidence; he was terrified to see the joy which brightened Diane's face, since it must have been occasioned by happiness. The happiness of others appeared to the Duc like a hostile challenge. One day, after sleeping badly, he ordered his carriage to go to call upon Monsoreau; the latter had left for the house in the Tournelles. The Prince, smiling at this turn of affairs, inquired, as a matter of form, where the house was situated, and, turning to Bussy, 'Since it is at the Tournelles, let us go there,' said he. The Prince was well acquainted with the house: Bussy knew it just as thoroughly. The Prince entered the apartments, Bussy remaining on the stair. As a result, the Prince saw only

Monsoreau reclining on a couch, while Bussy was received
in Diane's arms.

'Monseigneur!' said Monsoreau, livid and trembling
with annoyance, 'Monseigneur in my humble dwelling!
truly this is too much honour for such an insignificant
person as myself.'

'Wherever a suffering friend is, there I go to inquire
after him,' said the Prince, feigning not to notice the
irony.

'Indeed, your Highness used the word friend, I believe.'

'I did, dear Comte; how are you?'

'Much better, monseigneur; in a week I will be perfectly well.'

'Was it your doctor who prescribed the air of the
Bastille?'

'Yes, monseigneur.'

'Were you not comfortable in the Rue des Petits-
Pères?'

'No, monseigneur, I received too much company,
which caused too much noise.'

'You know, Comte,' said the Duc, after a silence,
'your office of First Huntsman is much sought after?'

'Bah! under what pretext?'

'Many assert that you are dead.'

'Oh, monseigneur, inform them I am not dead.'

'I make no answer at all; you bury yourself, therefore
you are dead.'

'Well, monseigneur, I will lose my appointment; there
are other things I value above it; I am constituted that
way.'

'In that case, you would not care though the King
knew this.'

'Who will tell him?'

'The deuce! if he questions me, I must perforce repeat
our conversation.'

'Faith, monseigneur, if one repeated to the King all
that is being said in Paris, his two ears would not suffice
to hear.'

'What is being said in Paris, monsieur?' asked the
Prince, turning sharply to the Comte, who, seeing that
the conversation had taken too serious a turn for a con-
valescent without full liberty of action, repressing his
rage, replied in indifferent tones,—

'What do I know, poor paralytic? events happen

without my noticing them. If the King is annoyed with me for performing my duties so badly, he is wrong. Without doubt, my accident was partly his fault.'

'Explain yourself.'

'The deuce! M. de Saint-Luc, who wounded me, is one of the King's best friends. The King showed him that secret thrust which caused my overthrow, and it would not be surprising if the King had set him on my track.'

'You are right, but, after all, the King is the King.'

'Until he ceases to reign.'

The Duc started.

'By the way, is Madame de Monsoreau living here?' he asked.

'Monseigneur, she is ill at present, otherwise she would have come to present her homage to you.'

'I hope the illness will be short, my dear Comte. You have such a skilful doctor.'

'The fact is, that dear Rémy nursed me splendidly.'

'But that is Bussy's doctor you are naming!'

'The Comte, indeed, lent me his services, monseigneur.'

'Are you very intimate with Bussy?'

'He is my best, I should even say, my only friend,' answered Monsoreau dryly.

'Farewell, Comte,' said the Prince, lifting the *portière*.

At the same moment he imagined he saw the edge of a robe disappear into the adjoining room, and Bussy suddenly appeared at his post in the middle of the corridor. Suspicion increased in the Duc's mind. Bussy descended to give orders for the departure, perhaps, too, to conceal his agitation from the Prince. During the journey the Duc and Bussy did not exchange a word. When the Duc was left alone, Aurilly slipped mysteriously into his room.

'Well! I am beaten by the husband,' said the Duc.

'Perhaps also by the lover; listen, monseigneur, I hope you will pardon me, since it was for your Highness's sake. I watched in a shed in the courtyard after you ascended. I saw a woman's robe, I saw this woman bend forward, I saw two arms clasped round her neck, and heard very distinctly the sound of a long, tender kiss.'

'But who was the man? Did you recognise him?'

'I cannot recognise arms; gloves have no countenance, monseigneur.'

'But one can recognise gloves.'

'Indeed, it seemed to me that these were M. de Bussy's gloves.'

'Buckskin gloves, embroidered in gold, were they?' cried the Duc, from whose eyes a veil seemed to have fallen.

'Yes, exactly.'

'Ah! Bussy; yes, it is Bussy! blind that I was or rather, no, I was not blind; only I could not credit such audacity.'

'Be careful, your Highness is speaking very loudly.'

'Bussy!' repeated the Duc, recalling a thousand circumstances which had passed unnoticed, but which now assumed gigantic proportions in his mind.

'Still, monseigneur, one must not be sure on such slight evidence; might there not be a man concealed in Madame de Monsoreau's room?'

'Yes, doubtless; but Bussy, being in the corridor, would have seen him; and then the gloves, the gloves.'

'That is true; then, besides the sound of the kiss, I heard three words: "Till to-morrow night"!'

'Oh, good gracious!'

'So that, if we recommence that exercise we practised formerly, we can make sure.'

'Aurilly, to-morrow night we will begin again.' The Duc, smiling with an infernal joy, dismissed Aurilly to meditate at ease.

CHAPTER LXXI

THE WATCHERS

AURILLY and the Duc decided upon their action, and the Duc kept Bussy beside him during the day, so as to let none of his actions escape him. Bussy desired nothing better than to pay court to the Prince during the day, for in this way his evenings were left free. At ten o'clock, wrapping himself in a cloak and carrying his ladder under his arm, he proceeded toward the Bastille. The Duc, ignorant of the fact that Bussy possessed a ladder in his ante-room, and thinking he would return to his hotel for a horse and attendant, lost ten minutes in preparation. During that time, Bussy had gone three-quarters of the distance; he had met nobody, and, approaching the house, perceived a light through the panes. It was the signal agreed upon between him and Diane. He threw his ladder to the balcony; it was provided with six hooks, and was continually becoming entangled in something. At the sound Diane, extinguishing the lamp, opened the window to fasten the ladder, and then signed to Bussy to mount; Bussy scaled the rungs in five seconds. The moment was well chosen, for, just as he ascended, M. de Monsoreau, after listening for more than ten minutes at his wife's door, descended the staircase, leaning on a valet's arm.

Monsoreau, arriving at the street, saw nothing.

'Were you wrongly informed ?' he asked his servant.

'No, monseigneur. I have just left the Hôtel d'Anjou, and the head groom assured me that monseigneur had ordered two horses for to-night.

'Perhaps it would have been better to remain in Diane's room. But they may have signals for correspondence, and she will have warned him of my presence. Better watch outside, as we agreed. Take me to that hiding-place, where one can see everything.'

'Come, monseigneur,' said the valet. Monsoreau advanced, half clinging to the wall, until they reached a huge heap of stones, serving as a fortification for the children of the district in their mock fights. In the midst of this heap the valet had contrived a sort of sentry-box capable of holding two people. Monsoreau crouched upon a cloak laid on these stones, the valet placed himself at his feet. Beside them was set a musket, fully loaded. The Comte's eyes, glowing like those of a wolf hidden near a sheep-fold, turned from Diane's room to the depths of the faubourgs and the adjoining streets, for wishing to surprise, he feared to be surprised. He had been in ambush ten minutes when two horses appeared at the opening of Rue Saint-Antoine. Without speaking, the servant pointed in their direction. The two riders dismounted at the corner of the Hôtel des Tournelles, attaching their horses to iron rings.

'Monseigneur,' said Aurilly, 'I believe we come too late; he will have gone directly from your hotel, and, having ten minutes' start, he has entered.'

'So be it, but we will see him come out.'

'Would it be too presumptuous to ask how you intend to catch him, monseigneur ?'

'Nothing is simpler. One of us—you, for instance, can knock at the door under pretext of asking for M. de Monsoreau. All lovers are afraid of noise. When you enter, he will leave by the window, and I, remaining outside, will see him.

'Do you hear what they say?' asked Monsoreau.

'No, monseigneur; but if they continue to talk, we cannot fail to hear them, since the voices come toward us.'

'Monseigneur,' said Aurilly, 'here is a heap of stones which seems expressly made to conceal your Highness.'

'Yes, but wait; perhaps we may see through the curtains.'

Indeed, Diane lit the lamp, or carried it closer, since a faint light shone from inside the room. The Duc and Aurilly kept turning and returning for more than ten minutes, seeking a point from which they could see inside. Meanwhile Monsoreau boiled with impatience, as he fingered the musket.

'Oh! shall I endure this? shall I suffer this insult? No, my patience is at an end. *Mordieu!* to think that I cannot sleep, keep awake, or even suffer in peace because a shameful fancy has arisen in the sluggish brain of this wretched Prince! No, I am not an obsequious valet, I am Comte de Monsoreau, and should he come here, upon my honour, I will blow his brains out.'

Precisely at this moment the Prince, finding it impossible to peer through the obstacles, had returned to his project of hiding amongst the stones while Aurilly was preparing to knock at the door, when suddenly the latter laid his hand on the Duc's arm.

'Come, monseigneur, come; don't you see something shining to the left?' he asked.

'Indeed, I see something like a spark in the middle of these stones.'

'It is the match of a musket or an arquebuse, monseigneur.'

'Ah! who the deuce can be in hiding there?'

'Some friend or servant of Bussy's. Let us go away, and return from another direction. The servant will raise the alarm, and we shall see Bussy descend by the window.'

The two crossed the street to the spot where their horses were fastened.

'They are gone,' said the valet.

'Yes. Did you recognise them?'

'It seemed to me that it was the Prince and Aurilly.'

'Exactly. But presently I shall make sure. Come!'

Meanwhile the Duc and Aurilly passed into Rue Sainte-Catherine, intending to skirt the gardens and return by the Boulevard de la Bastille. Monsoreau, entering the house, ordered his litter. What the Duc had foreseen happened. At the noise made by Monsoreau, Bussy, taking alarm, was obliged to flee like Romeo. As he set foot on the ground, the Duc and Aurilly turned the corner of the Bastille, in time to see a shadow suspended beneath Diane's window, between heaven and earth, but this shadow immediately disappeared into Rue Saint-Paul. Monsoreau, having sent for two servants, who stayed in Rue des Tournelles, set out in his litter, and soon reached the Hôtel d'Anjou, arriving on the threshold just as the Duc handed his boots to a valet. Another valet announced the First Huntsman.

'Monsieur de Monsoreau!' cried the Prince, his uneasiness betraying itself in his pallor and the emotion of his voice.

'Yes, monseigneur, myself,' said the Comte, making such violent efforts to control himself that, his legs giving way under him, he was compelled to sink into a chair.

'But you will kill yourself, dear friend; you are so pale that you seem on the point of fainting.'

'Oh, no, monseigneur. I have some very important matters to treat of with your Highness. Perhaps I may faint afterwards; it is possible.'

'Speak, my dear Comte.'

'Not before your servants, I presume?'

The Duc dismissed them all, even Aurilly, so the two were left alone.

'Your Highness has just entered? It is very rash of your Highness to walk in the streets at night.'

'Who informed you that I was in the streets?'

'The deuce! The dust that covers your clothes.'

'Monsieur de Monsoreau, have you another office besides that of First Huntsman?'

'The office of spy? Yes, monseigneur.'

'What makes you assume this office, monsieur?'

'The desire to know what is happening.'

'Tell me what you have to say to me.'

'I came for that purpose.'

'You will permit me to sit ?'

'No irony, monseigneur, towards a faithful, humble friend like myself who comes at this hour and in this state to render you a service. If I am sitting, monseigneur, it is because I cannot remain standing. I come to your Highness on the part of a powerful prince, Monseigneur le Duc de Guise.'

'Ah ! approach, and speak low.'

CHAPTER LXXII

HOW THE DUC D'ANJOU FIRST SIGNED AND THEN SPOKE

FOR an instant there was silence between the Duc d'Anjou and Monsoreau, which was broken by the former.

'Well ! Monsieur le Comte, what have you to tell me on the part of MM. de Guise ?'

'Many things, monseigneur.'

'They have written to you ?'

'No, they have come to Paris, monseigneur ?'

'Why have they come ?'

'To keep an appointment which you made with them. The same day your Highness was arrested, a letter came from MM. de Guise, to which your Highness sent a verbal answer by me to be in Paris from the 31st May to the 2nd June. This is now the 31st; if you have forgotten MM. de Guise, they have not forgotten you, monseigneur.'

François paled. So many events had happened since that day that he had forgotten this appointment, important as it was.

'That is true; but the relations which then existed between MM. de Guise and myself exist no longer.'

'If that is so, monseigneur, you would do well to inform them of it, as I believe they judge things differently. They continue to count themselves your allies. When you reached Anjou, was I not commissioned to inform you that you could always count on them as they could count on you, and that the day you marched on Paris, they would also march from their side ?'

'True again; but I have not marched on Paris. I am here as my brother's ally.'

'Monseigneur will permit me to observe that he is more than the ally of the Guises. He is their accomplice.'

The Duc bit his lips.

'You say they instructed you to announce their arrival. Did they not communicate the motives for their return?'

'They communicated everything, monseigneur—motives and plans.'

'So they have plans. What are they?'

'The same as ever.'

'And the object of these plans is——?'

'To make you King of France, monseigneur.'

'But is the moment propitious?'

'Your wisdom will decide that. These are the facts, patent, indisputable. The King's nomination as Head of the League was merely a farce, quickly appreciated and rightly judged. Now the reaction has begun, and the whole State rises against the tyranny of the King and his minions. Sermons are appeals to arms; the churches, buildings where people, instead of praying to God, curse the King. The army thrills with impatience, the citizens unite, our emissaries report the names of fresh adherents to the League; in short, the reign of Valois nears its end. In such a state of matters, MM. de Guise require to choose a competent candidate for the throne, and on you this choice has fallen. Now, do you renounce your former aim?'

The Duc made no answer.

'Well! what does monseigneur think?'

'My brother has no children, his health is poor, and after him, the throne reverts to me. Why should I compromise my name, my dignity, my affections by connecting myself with this project? Why, in short, run risks to grasp what will come to me without any?'

'That is where your Highness makes a mistake: your brother's throne will revert to you only if you seize it. MM. de Guise cannot be kings themselves, but they will permit only a king of their making to reign; they had hoped your Highness would be this king; in the event of your Highness refusing, I warn you, they will seek another.'

'Who will dare to sit on Charlemagne's throne?'

'A Bourbon in place of a Valois, that is all; a son of Saint-Louis for a son of Saint-Luc.'

'The King of Navarre?'

'Why not ? he is young and brave.'

'He is a Huguenot.'

'He! Was he not converted at the Saint-Bartholomew ?'

'Yes, but he abjured again.'

'Eh! monseigneur, what he did for his life, he will do for the throne.'

'Do they imagine I will yield my rights without defending them ? I will fight them desperately. I will set myself at the head of the League.'

'They are the soul of it.'   .

'I will unite with my brother.'

'He will be dead.'

'I will call the kings of Europe to my aid.'

'The kings of Europe will willingly engage in war against kings, but they will consider twice before fighting against a people.'

'How a people ?'

'Doubtless, MM. de Guise are determined to do everything, even to form a republic.'

'But my party will not permit France to be turned into a republic.'

'Your party ? Monseigneur, you have been so disinterested, so magnanimous, that your party is composed now of M. de Bussy and myself.'

'My hands are tied, then !'

'That is, monseigneur, you can do nothing without MM. de Guise, but everything with them. Say one word and you are King.'

François rose, very disturbed, and walked about the room; then he stopped in front of Monsoreau.

'Speak, faithful servant, I listen,' said he.

'Well, monseigneur, here is the plot briefly. In a week it is the Fête-Dieu, when the King intends to have a great procession to the principal convents of Paris. He will be unguarded, or at least his guards will remain at the door. He will stop, kneel, and repeat five "Paters" and five "Aves" before each altar. He will visit the Abbey Sainte-Geneviève among others, where an accident opposite the convent will have caused a drain to fall in, so that the altar, instead of being in the porch, will be placed in the very courtyard. The King having entered with four or five people, the doors will be shut. Then, your Highness can understand that the monks who will do the honours of the abl ey to His Majesty, are those who were present at your Highness's coronation.'

'They will dare to lay their hands on the Lord's Anointed ?'

'Oh ! to give him the tonsure; that is all. Have you never heard of a Brother of Sainte-Geneviève, a holy man, who delivers discourses whilst he performs miracles ?'

'Brother Gorenflot ?'

'The same. The King will be taken to his cell; once there the Brother undertakes to make him sign his abdication, and afterwards Madame de Montpensier enters with the scissors. They are already bought, of massive gold, and beautifully chased. You understand the rest. It is announced that the King, feeling a holy repentance for his sins, has expressed the desire not to leave the convent; if some doubt that this calling is a true one, M. le Duc de Guise commands the army, M. le Cardinal the Church, M. de Mayenne the burghers; with those three powers, the people can be forced to believe anything.'

'I shall be accused of violence.'

'You are not supposed to be there.'

'I shall be regarded as a usurper.'

'Monseigneur forgets the abdication.'

'The King will refuse.'

'It appears that Brother Gorenflot is extremely strong.'

'Are they not afraid that I shall denounce the plot?'

'No, monseigneur, since there is another not less vigorous against you, should you betray them.'

'Then, Comte, I yield; what must I do ?'

'Approve.'

'Well ! I approve.'

'It is not sufficient to approve in words, but in writing.'

'They wish to have my name as a safeguard ? I refuse. I shall have chosen my own danger, at least.'

'Take care, monseigneur, not to choose wrongly. In refusing to sign, you kill yourself; the conspirators must succeed at any cost.'

The Duc fell into a state of indecision, easy to understand. 'I will sign to-morrow.'

'No; if you sign, it must be immediately,' declared Monsoreau, drawing a paper from his pocket. It was a full and complete adherence to the project with which we are acquainted. The Duc read it through, paling as he did so; when he finished, his legs failed him, and he sat down at the table.

'I must sign then ?' asked François, pressing his hand to his brow, for his brain was dizzy.

'If you wish; nobody is forcing you.'

'Yes, I am being forced, since you threaten me with assassination.'

'I do not threaten you, monseigneur; I warn you, which is very different.'

As though by a great effort the Duc, taking the pen from the Comte's hands, signed, Monsoreau following the writing, his eyes glowing with hatred and hope. When the Duc had finished, he seized the paper, and, folding it, placed it between his shirt and his waistcoat, buttoning his doublet over it. The Duc watched him in astonishment, understanding nothing of the expression of fierce joy which passed over his companion's pale face.

'And now, monseigneur, be cautious; do not walk with Aurilly at night in the streets, as you have been doing.'

'What does this mean ?'

'It means that to-night, monseigneur, you have been pursuing a woman whom her husband adores, and of whom he is jealous to the point of killing whomsoever approaches her without permission.'

'Do you happen to be speaking of yourself and your wife ?'

'Yes, monseigneur; since you have guessed so correctly, I shall not attempt to deny it. I have wedded Diane de Méridor, who is mine, and no one shall have her in my lifetime, not even a prince. And see here, monseigneur, in order that you may be thoroughly convinced, I swear by my name on this dagger,' added Monsoreau, laying the blade almost on the Prince's chest.

'Monsieur, you threaten me,' exclaimed François, drawing back, pale with rage.

'Not at all, my Prince; as before, I warn you that no one shall make love to my wife.'

'And I, consummate fool, answer that you are too late with your warning, for somebody has made love to her already.'

Monsoreau clutched his hair with both hands, uttering a terrible cry.

'It is not you, monseigneur ?' he stammered.

'You are mad, Comte,' observed François, stepping back again.

'No, I am perfectly sound in mind and speak reason. You have just told me that some one possesses my wife; name the person to prove it.'

'Who was watching with a musket to-night, twenty paces from your house ?'

'Myself.'

'Well, Comte, during that time a man was with your wife.'

'You saw him enter ?'

'I saw him leave.'

'By the door ?'

'By the window.'

'You recognised this man ?'

'Yes.'

'Name him, name him, monseigneur.'

The Duc passed his hand over his brow and half smiled.

'Monsieur le Comte, on my honour as a Prince, before God, I will tell you in less than a week who this man is. Return in a week; that is all I have to say.'

'That is better. In a week I shall be quite strong, and he who wishes to avenge himself needs all his strength,' answered Monsoreau, leaving with a gesture of farewell which might easily have been taken as a threat.

CHAPTER LXXIII

A STROLL TO THE TOURNELLES

THE noblemen of Anjou had now returned to Paris, though we cannot say they did so with confidence. They knew the King, his brother, and his mother too well to hope that the trouble would end in a general family embrace. Remembering the pursuit of the King's friends, they hardly prepared themselves for a triumphal entry, and returning cautiously, they slipped into the town, armed to the teeth, ready to fire at the slightest suspicious gesture, drawing swords fifty times before reaching the Hôtel d'Anjou, where the Duc received them kindly.

'My friends,' he began, 'people are contemplating killing you, it appears; such receptions are in fashion at present, be very careful.'

'Certainly, monseigneur,' answered Antraguet; 'but

would it not be correct to offer His Majesty our humble respects ? If we hide ourselves, it will do no honour to Anjou. What do you think ?'

'You are right; go, and if you care, I will accompany you.'

The three young men exchanged a questioning glance. At that moment Bussy, entering the room, embraced his friends.

'Eh ! you are very late !' exclaimed he, 'but what's this I hear ? His Highness proposes to go to the Louvre to be killed like Cæsar in the Senate-house. Consider that each one of the King's minions would willingly carry off a piece of monseigneur under his cloak. Let us go to the Louvre, whilst monseigneur knocks off poppy heads in the garden.'

François affected to laugh joyfully, and at heart he was happy at not having any more difficult tasks to perform. The Angevins dressed in gorgeous style, being young lords who gladly spent the revenue of their fathers' estates on silk, velvet, and lace. As Henri III. was unwilling to receive these gentlemen, they waited vainly in the gallery. MM. de Quélus, de Maugiron, de Schomberg, and d'Épernon announced this news, bowing politely and expressing deepest regret.

'Ah !' remarked Antraguet, for Bussy kept himself in the background, 'it is sad news, but, told by you, it loses much of its unpleasantness.'

'Gentlemen, you are the soul of grace and courtesy. Would you be willing to change this reception which has fallen through into a walk ?'

'Oh ! we were going to ask that,' interposed Antraguet quickly.

'Where can we go ?' asked Quélus reflectively.

'I know a charming spot beside the Bastille,' observed Schomberg.

'Gentlemen, proceed and we will follow,' said Ribeirac.

The four friends left the Louvre, followed by the four Angevins, and proceeded toward the old enclosure of the Tournelles, then called the Marché-aux-Chevaux, a flat piece of ground, planted with some scraggy trees. On the way, the eight noblemen, taking arms, conversed laughingly, to the unbounded astonishment of the burghers who met them. When they arrived, Quélus spoke first.

'See what a splendid piece of ground it is,' said he;

'look how deserted, and what a good footing one can get.'

'Faith, yes,' answered Antraguet.

'Well!' continued Quélus, 'we thought you might be so kind as to come some day to be a second, a third, and a fourth to M. de Bussy, your friend, who has done us the honour of calling us out, all four.'

'He said nothing of it!' cried Antraguet.

'Oh! M. de Bussy knows what he is about. Do you accept, gentlemen of Anjou?'

'Most certainly; we rejoice in the honour.'

'Good. Then, will you choose your opponents?' asked Schomberg, rubbing his hands.

'I like that method very well, and then——' began Ribeirac.

'Not at all,' interrupted Bussy, 'that is not fair. We all think alike, therefore we are inspired by God. Let us leave to God the task of pairing us off. Let us draw lots as the Horatii did.'

'Yes, let us imitate them,' Quélus agreed.

'One moment. Before beginning, let us consider the rules of the fight.'

'They are simple; we will fight till death ensues, as M. de Saint-Luc said,' answered Schomberg.

'Doubtless; but what weapons shall we use?'

'The sword and the dirk; we are all expert with these,' suggested Bussy.

'On foot?' asked Quélus.

'Yes. One has no freedom of action with a horse.'

'Which day?'

'As soon as possible.'

'No,' said d'Épernon, 'I have a thousand matters to attend to—a will to make; I prefer to wait. Three or four days will suit us.'

'Then, let us draw lots,' Bussy suggested.

'Wait a moment,' said Antraguet, 'here is what I propose. Let us allot the ground as impartial people. The names will emerge two by two at random; let us cut out four divisions for each of the four pairs. I propose for number one, the long square between two lime trees; it is a good position.'

'But the sun?'

'All the worse for the second of the pair; he will face the east.'

'No, gentlemen, that would be unfair,' said Bussy, 'let us kill one another, but do not let us assassinate. We will describe a semi-circle, and stand so placed that the sun will strike on our side face.'

The position was accepted, the names drawn. Schomberg came first, Ribeirac second, thus forming the first pair. Quélus and Antraguet were the second, Livarot and Maugiron the third. At the name of Quélus, Bussy, who expected to have him as antagonist, knit his brow. D'Épernon, finding himself paired with Bussy, paled, and tugged his moustache to bring back some colour to his cheeks.

'Well, gentlemen, from now to the day of the meeting, we are friends. Will you accept an invitation to dinner at my house?' asked Bussy.

All signified their acceptance, and proceeded to Bussy's hotel, where a sumptuous repast kept them together in the highest spirits until the morning.

CHAPTER LXXIV

CHICOT FALLS ASLEEP

ALL these arrangements of the Angevins had been noticed, first by the King, then by Chicot. Henri, in the Louvre, waited impatiently till his friends should return from their walk. Chicot, having followed at a distance, being convinced of the intentions of Bussy and Quélus, had turned back towards Monsoreau's dwelling. Though the First Huntsman was decidedly cunning, he could not hope to cheat the Gascon, and Chicot being the bearer of numerous sympathetic messages from the King, how could he receive him otherwise than well? Monsoreau was in bed; the last evening's visit had exhausted him, and Rémy watched with anxiety for the first symptoms of the fever which threatened to seize him anew. Nevertheless Monsoreau was able to carry on a conversation, dissembling his hatred for the Duc d'Anjou cleverly enough to have deceived any other than Chicot. But, the more discreet he became, the more Chicot divined his real thoughts. The jester wished to ascertain whether the Comte's fever was but a piece of acting similar to Nicolas David's; but Rémy never deceived, and Chicot quickly concluded, 'This one is really ill, and can undertake nothing. There remains M. de Bussy; let us discover of what he is capable.'

Proceeding to the Hôtel de Bussy, he found it all blazing with light, and giving forth odours of cooking which would have elicited joyful exclamations from Gorenflot.

'Is M. de Bussy being married ?' Chicot asked a lackey.

'No, monsieur, M. de Bussy, becoming reconciled to some gentlemen of the court, celebrates the event by a feast, and a splendid one, too.'

Chicot returned to the Louvre, where Henri was walking up and down, fuming and impatient. At sight of Chicot he exclaimed loudly,—

'Oh! dear friend, have you learned what has become of them ?'

'Of your minions ? They should be very low down at this moment.'

'They are killed !' cried Henri, drawing himself up with anger in his eyes; 'they are dead!'

'I am afraid so.'

'You know it, and you laugh, pagan!'

'Don't be impulsive, my son; dead, yes, but dead drunk.'

'You are still joking. Seriously, now, are you aware that they went out with these Angevins ?'

'Perfectly.'

'What happened, then ?'

'What I told you : they are dead drunk, or very nearly. Bussy is making them drunk; he is a dangerous man.'

'Chicot, for mercy's sake!'

'Yes, Bussy is entertaining your friends to dinner; do you consider that all right ?'

'Bussy entertaining them! Oh! impossible; they are sworn enemies.'

'Precisely; were they friends, they would have no need to get drunk together. Listen, can you walk well ? Will you go as far as the river ?'

'I would go to the end of the earth to witness such a spectacle.'

'Well! simply go to Bussy's house, and you will perceive this extraordinary thing.'

'Will you accompany me ?'

'No, thanks, I have just come from there. Go you, my son.'

The King glanced at him angrily.

'You are very kind to trouble about these people. They laugh, feast, and oppose your government. Take the matter philosophically; let us laugh, have something nice and hot served up, and go to bed after supper.'

The King could not help smiling.

'You may flatter yourself on being wise; there have been in France bold kings, great kings, lazy kings; I am sure you will be called Henri the Patient. Ah! it is such a fine virtue—when one possesses no others.'

'Betrayed! those fellows have not even the manners of gentlemen.'

'Ah! you are uneasy about your friends; you lament them as if they were dead, and when you are told they are not, you become more uneasy. You are always whining, Henri,' cried Chicot, pushing the King into the room where supper was served.

'I should like to be able to count on my friends.'

'Oh! count on me; I am here, only feed me,' answered Chicot, holding out his plate.

Henri and his only friend went early to bed. The following day, MM. de Quélus, de Schomberg, de Maugiron, and d'Épernon were announced at the King's levée. Chicot was still sleeping; the King, leaping out of bed, exclaimed, 'Begone!' The amazed usher explained to the young men that the King dismissed them.

'But, your Majesty, we wished to tell you——' stuttered Quélus.

'That you are no longer drunk?'

Chicot opened one eye.

'Excuse me, your Majesty is making a mistake——'

'I have not been drinking Anjou wine, however.'

'Ah! very good! I understand,' observed Quélus, smiling; 'if your Majesty is alone with us, we will explain.'

'I hate drunkards and traitors.'

'Gentlemen, His Majesty has slept badly. A few words will put him in better mood,' Quélus declared.

This impertinent excuse impressed Henri, who argued that those bold enough to say such things could not have done anything dishonourable.

'Speak, but be brief,' he commanded.

'It is possible, but difficult, your Majesty.'

At a sign the usher withdrew; Chicot, opening his other eye, observed, 'Do not mind me, I sleep like a top,' and shutting both his eyes, he began snoring loudly.

'Monsoreau laid the blade almost on
the Prince's chest.'

CHAPTER LXXV

CHICOT WAKES UP

WHEN they concluded that Chicot was sleeping soundly, they paid no more attention to him. Moreover, he was usually considered as a piece of furniture belonging to the King's bedroom.

'Your Majesty knows only the half of the matter, and I venture to say the less interesting half,' Quélus began. 'Most assuredly we have been dining with M. de Bussy, and I must say we have dined very well. During the repast, and especially before it, we engaged in some most serious and interesting talks concerning your Majesty's interests.'

'The introduction is very long; it is a bad sign,' Henri remarked.

'*Ventre de biche!* what a chatterer that Valois is,' cried Chicot.

'Oh! Master Gascon, if you are not sleeping, retire,' commanded Henri loftily.

'If I am not sleeping, it is because you prevent me; your tongue is going like a rattle.'

Quélus, seeing that serious conversation could not be carried on where every one seemed to be frivolous, shrugging his shoulders, rose with annoyance.

'Your Majesty, grave matters are in question,' said d'Épernon, 'if the lives of eight brave gentlemen seems to your Majesty worth troubling about.'

'What does this mean?'

'It means that I am waiting till the King chooses to listen,' said Quelus.

'I am listening, my son.'

'I was saying, then, your Majesty, that we had spoken seriously, and here is the result of our conversation. Royalty is threatened, weakened. It resembles those strange gods which fell into old age without the power of dying, becoming more and more decrepit, until the noble devotion of some votary was the means of rejuvenating them. Then, by the transfusion of young blood, they began to live anew, strong and powerful. Your

C.J.   N

Majesty, royalty, like those gods, can only live by sacrifices.'

'He speaks wisely,' said Chicot; 'Quélus, my son, go and preach in the streets of Paris, and I wager that you will extinguish even that great orator Gorenflot.'

Henri made no reply; a great change was taking place in his mind; at first he had addressed haughty glances to the minions, but gradually a sense of the truth was borne in on him, causing him to become reflective, gloomy, and uneasy.

'Continue, you know that I am listening, Quélus,' said he.

'Your Majesty, you are a very powerful King, but you have no horizon in front of you; the nobility have erected barriers beyond which you can see nothing, unless it be the barriers which the people raise. Tell me, your Majesty, what is done in warfare when one battalion is placed thirty paces from another battalion ? Cowards, looking behind them and seeing empty space, flee; brave men, with heads down, charge forward.'

'So be it; forward !' cried the King; 'am I not the first gentleman of my kingdom ? Who has led finer battalions than I did in my youth ? Forward, then, gentlemen, and I will march first in the *mêlée*.'

'Yes, forward ! your Majesty,' cried the young men, electrified by this warlike demonstration.

'Peace, you others; permit my orator to continue,' exclaimed Chicot, sitting up.

'Yes, I will continue to tell His Majesty that the time has come for a sacrifice such as I mentioned. Against all these ramparts which close round your Majesty, four men are to march, sure of meeting with your encourage-ment. These gentlemen and I devote ourselves to your safety, against your enemies.'

'The mere rivalry of young people,' exclaimed Henri.

'That is an expression of vulgar prejudice under which your Majesty hides his great tenderness for us; but we recognise it. Speak as a king, your Majesty, not as a burgher of the Rue Saint-Denis. It is no rivalry of man to man which makes us draw swords; it is the quarrel of France against Anjou, the quarrel of the people's right against Divine Right; we present ourselves as champions of royalty in the struggle against champions of the League, and we have come to say : ''Bless us, and smile on those who go forth to die for you, our Liege Lord." Your blessing will perhaps help them to conquer, your smile will help them to die.'

Henri, overcome, opening his arms to Quélus and the others, gathered them to his heart; it was an interesting scene, where manly courage was allied to emotions of deep tenderness, which devotion seemed to sanctify.

'Ah! what a noble ambition, and how proud I am of being your friend to-day. Yet I will not accept a sacrifice, the result of which, should you fail, would hand me over to my enemies. To wage war with Anjou, France is sufficient, believe me. I know my brother, the Guises, and the League; often have I tamed horses more fiery and more intractable.'

'But, your Majesty, soldiers do not reason thus,' cried Maugiron.

'Excuse me, Maugiron, a soldier can act blindly, but a captain considers.'

'Consider, therefore, your Majesty, and let us act, as we are only soldiers; moreover, I do not know what bad luck is, for I am always lucky,' said Schomberg.

'Your Majesty, when are we to cross swords with MM. de Bussy, de Livarot, d'Entragues and de Ribeirac?' asked Quélus.

'Never, I forbid you absolutely; never, do you hear?'

'Pray excuse us, your Majesty; the spot was chosen yesterday, the words are spoken and cannot be recalled.'

'Excuse me, monsieur, the King recalls statements by saying, "I wish, or I do not wish"; for the King is all powerful. Tell these gentlemen that I threaten you with my wrath if you meet, and, that you have no doubt yourselves, I swear to exile you if——'

'Stop, your Majesty, for, if you can release us from our oaths, only God can release you from yours. Therefore, do not swear, for should we incur your wrath for such a reason, and be punished by exile, we will gladly go, because, being no longer in your Majesty's dominions, we can keep our word and meet our opponents.'

'If these gentlemen approach you within range of an arquebuse, I shall have them thrown into the Bastille.'

'Your Majesty, the day that happens, we shall go, barefoot and with a rope round our necks, to Maître Laurent Testu, to be imprisoned with these gentlemen.'

'I will have their heads cut off, *mordieu!* I am the King.'

'If such a thing happen to our enemies, your Majesty, we would cut our throats at the foot of their scaffold.'

'There is fine nobility for you. If God does not bless a cause defended by such people!' Henri exclaimed, after a long silence.

'Do not blaspheme!' said Chicot solemnly, rising from the bed. 'Yes, they are noble hearts. Do what they wish. Fix a day for these young people: it is your business.'

'Your Majesty, we beg you,' cried the four noblemen, bending down.

'Very well! so be it. Indeed, God is just; he owes us the victory, but let us prepare for it in Christian fashion. We will engage in devotion; let us fast together and sanctify on the Fête-Dieu; then the following day——'

'Thanks, your Majesty—that is in a week,' cried the young men, kissing the King's hands; after embracing them, Henri, bursting into tears, returned to his oratory.

'Our challenge is written out; only the day and the hour have to be added. Write, Maugiron, the day after the Fête Dieu!' said Quélus.

'There it is; who will bear this letter?'

'I will, if you please,' said Chicot, 'only I wish to give you advice; His Majesty spoke of fastings and scourgings; that's very well after a victory, but before fighting I prefer to try the efficacy of good food, wine, and an eight hours' sleep.'

'Bravo! Chicot!'

'Farewell, my lions, I go to the Hôtel de Bussy,' answered Chicot; then returning, he added: 'By the way, don't leave the King on the Fête Dieu; stay in the Louvre like a group of Paladins. That is agreed, eh? then I execute your commission,' and with the letter in his hand, Chicot disappeared.

CHAPTER LXXVI

LA FÊTE-DIEU

DURING the eight days, events developed as a tempest brews in the sky on calm, heavy summer days. Monsoreau, up again after two days of fever, watched for his rival, but, discovering nobody, he remained more than ever convinced of the Duc d'Anjou's hypocrisy and evil intentions with regard to Diane. Bussy did not discontinue his visits, only, warned by Rémy, he stopped coming at night by the window. Chicot divided his time between two occupations: one half he devoted to his beloved master, Henri de Valois, leaving him as little as possible, watching over him as a mother over her child; the second half was devoted to visiting his dear friend Gorenflot, whom he had with difficulty induced to return to his convent, himself accompanying him, and receiving a most charming welcome from the Abbot Joseph Foulon. At this first visit, the King's piety was much discussed, the Prior appearing inexpressibly grateful to His Majesty for the honour he did him in visiting the abbey. This honour was even greater than was at first expected; Henri, at the Abbot's request, had agreed to spend a day and a night in retirement in the convent. Chicot confirmed the Abbot in this expectation, and was invited to return, since it was known that he enjoyed the King's confidence.

Chicot, returning, was shut up for hours in the monk's cell, presumably sharing his studies. Two nights before the Fête-Dieu, he even spent the whole night in the convent, and the next day report ran that Gorenflot had persuaded Chicot to turn monk. The King spent his time giving fencing-lessons to his friends, especially training d'Épernon, to whom fate had assigned such a formidable antagonist. Any one walking in the town at certain hours might have encountered near Sainte-Geneviève the strange monks we have already mentioned, resembling foxes rather than priests; to complete this picture, we may add that the Hôtel de Guise had become a most mysterious, noisy den, that conferences were held there every night after the blinds had been carefully drawn, these meetings being preceded by dinners to which men only were invited, but at which Madame de Montpensier presided. Thus matters stood when the morning of the great religious fête approached. The weather was splendid, and the flowers strewing the streets exhaled their sweet perfumes.

That morning Chicot wakened Henri early, before any one had entered the royal chamber.

'Ah! my poor Chicot, a plague on you! You rouse me from the sweetest dream I have ever had,' cried Henri.

'What were you dreaming of, my son?'

'That Quélus had wounded Antraguet, and was swimming in his blood. But this is the day. Let us pray to the Lord that my dream comes true. Call, Chicot, for my haircloth and my rod.'

'Patience! it is scarcely eight o'clock, so there is abundant time to flog yourself before the evening. Let us chat in the first place. How do you propose dividing the day, my son?'

'Into three parts. First, mass at Saint-Germain-l'Auxerrois; on returning to the Louvre, a repast will be served. Then, a procession of penitents through the streets, stopping at the principal convents, beginning with the Jacobins, finishing with Sainte-Geneviève, where I have promised the Prior to remain till to-morrow in the cell of a saintly monk, who will spend the night praying for the success of our arms.'

'I am acquainted with this saint.'

'All the better; you will accompany me, Chicot; we will pray together.'

'Yes, be reassured.'

'Then, dress and come.'

'Wait, I have still some details to ask. What is your court to do?'

'It follows me.'

'Your brother?'

'He accompanies me.'

'Your bodyguard?'

'The French guards are to wait with Crillon in the Louvre; the Swiss at the abbey door.'

'Very good! I have my information.'

'Then I can ring!'

'Do so; but, Henri, have you nothing else to tell me?

Is it quite arranged that you go to Sainte-Geneviève and that you spend the night there ?'

'I have promised.'

'Well, my son, I will admit this : this ceremony does not suit me, and after dinner will confide to you another plan I have thought of.'

'I agree.'

'Whether you agree or not, it would be the same thing.'

At this moment the ushers, opening the door, admitted those in charge of the King's toilet, and when it was partly finished His Highness Monseigneur le Duc d'Anjou was announced. Henri, turning toward him, smiled graciously. The Duc was accompanied by M. de Monsoreau, d'Épernon, and Aurilly, the last two remaining in the background. At sight of the Comte, pale and more terrible looking than ever, Henri could not restrain a movement of surprise, which was noticed by the Duc as well as by the Comte.

'Your Majesty, M. de Monsoreau comes to do homage to your Majesty,' the Duc announced.

'I thank you, monsieur; I am all the more touched by your visit because you have been wounded, I believe.'

'Yes, your Majesty.'

'At the hunt ?'

'At the hunt, your Majesty.'

'You are better now ?'

'I am perfectly restored to health.'

'Your Majesty, when our devotions are paid, would you care for M. le Comte de Monsoreau to prepare a hunt for us in Compiègne ?' asked the Duc.

'But to-morrow, don't you know——' began Henri, then paused.

'I know nothing, and should your Majesty wish to inform me——'

'I meant to say that, spending the night in prayer at the Abbey of Sainte-Geneviève, I might not be ready to-morrow; but let Monsieur le Comte go all the same; if not to-morrow, the hunt can take place the following day.'

At this moment, Schomberg and Quélus, entering, were received with open arms.

'Still another day,' said Quélus.

'But only one day, luckily,' Schomberg replied.

Meanwhile Monsoreau was saying to the Duc : 'You are banishing me, it appears, monseigneur.'

'Is it not the duty of a First Huntsman to prepare the King's hunting parties ?'

'I understand, and see what it means. To-night the eight days your Highness asked for end, and rather than keep the promise, your Highness despatches me to Compiègne. But, let your Highness take care; from now till evening I can, with one word——'

François grasped the Comte's wrist.

'Be quiet,' said he, 'I am keeping the promise.'

'Explain yourself.'

'Your departure for the hunt will be known by all, since the orders are official. But you will not leave; you will hide near your house; and your unknown visitor, thinking you gone, will come. The rest is your concern, for I did not bind myself to anything else. You have my word.'

'I have something better, your signature.'

'Eh ! yes, I know that,' answered the Duc, leaving Monsoreau to approach his brother. Aurilly touched d'Épernon's arm.

'It is settled. M. de Bussy will not fight to-morrow,' said he.

'What will prevent him ?'

'No matter ! provided he does not fight.'

'If that happens, my dear sorcerer, you shall have a thousand crowns.'

'Gentlemen, we will go to Saint-Germain-l'Auxerrois,' announced Henri, when his toilet was complete.

'And thence to the Abbey of Sainte-Geneviève ?' asked the Duc.

'Certainly.'

'Count upon it,' repeated Chicot, buckling his sword-belt, as Henri passed into the gallery, where all his court awaited him.

CHAPTER LXXVII

EXPLAINS THE PRECEDING CHAPTER

THE preceding evening, when all had been arranged between the Guises and the Angevins, M. de Monsoreau, returning home, found Bussy there. Thinking the brave gentleman, for whom he still felt great friendship, might compromise himself next day if he were not warned, he drew him aside.

'My dear Comte, will you permit me to give you some advice?' he said.

'Do, I beg you.'

'In your place, I should be absent from Paris to-morrow. All I can hint is that your absence will, in all probability, save you considerable embarrassment.'

'Embarrassment! what kind?' asked Bussy, looking keenly at the Comte.

'Are you ignorant of what is happening to-morrow?'

'Completely.'

'M. d'Anjou has confided nothing to you?'

'Nothing. M. d'Anjou tells me only what he can proclaim aloud, and, I will add, only what he can tell everybody.'

'Well, I who am not the Duc d'Anjou, but who love my friends for themselves, warn you that grave events are preparing for to-morrow, and the Anjou and Guise factions are meditating a deed which may possibly result in the King's downfall.'

'Comte,' answered Bussy, 'I am the Duc's; that is, my life and my sword are his. The King, against whom I have done no evil, bears me ill-will, never missing an opportunity of hurting me by word or deed. And to-morrow—I tell you this only, do you understand? I am risking my life to humiliate Henri de Valois in the person of his favourites.'

'So you are determined to suffer all the consequences of your devotion to the Duc? You know what that will entail, perhaps?'

'I know where I intend to stop; I will never lift my hand against the Lord's Anointed; I will let others act, and will follow M. le Duc to defend him if he be in danger.'

M. de Monsoreau laid his hand on Bussy's shoulder.

'Dear Comte,' said he, 'the Duc is cowardly, treacherous, capable of sacrificing his most faithful servant, his most devoted friend, for an emotion of jealousy or fear; abandon him and spend the day at Vincennes—go where you please, but do not go to the Fête-Dieu procession.'

'But why do you follow the Duc d'Anjou?'

'Because for matters concerning my honour, I still have need of him.'

'That is like me; I will follow the Duc also because of what concerns my honour.'

The Comte clasped Bussy's hand, and the two parted. We have already told what took place next morning at the King's levée. Monsoreau, on returning home, announced his departure for Compiègne, giving orders that all preparations should be made. Diane received the news joyfully. She knew from her husband of the prospective duel between Bussy and d'Épernon, but the latter had no remarkable reputation for skill and bravery, so she thought of the fight with feelings of pride mingled with fear. Bussy, accompanying the Prince to the Louvre, waited in the gallery for him. At the sight of Bussy, so frank, loyal, and devoted, the Prince felt some remorse, but two things combated these kindlier promptings—the strong sway Bussy had exercised over him, as any powerful nature does over a weak one, and which inspired him with the fear that, standing so near his throne, Bussy was the real king; again, there was Bussy's love for Madame de Monsoreau, a love awakening agonies of jealousy in the Prince's heart. Yet, as he had said to himself, 'Either Bussy will accompany me, and help my cause to triumph, and in that case it matters little what Monsoreau may say and do; or Bussy will abandon me, and then, owing him nothing, I will abandon him.' As a result of this reflection, the Prince kept his eyes fixed on Bussy. He saw the young man enter the church, calm and smiling, and kneel behind d'Épernon. When the mass had continued for some time, Rémy, entering, knelt near his master, and, after speaking in low tones, handed him a note. The Prince felt a thrill pass through him; the note was addressed in a fine, charming hand.

'It is from her, announcing that her husband leaves Paris,' the Duc concluded.

Bussy, hiding the note, opened and read it, then, kissing

it, he placed it next his heart. The Duc looked round him; had Monsoreau been there, the Duc would not have had patience to wait until evening before denouncing Bussy. After mass, the company returned to the Louvre, where a meal was served in the gallery. Bussy approached the Duc.

'Excuse me, monseigneur,' said he, 'I should like to say a few words to your Highness.'

'Could you not say them during the procession ? We will walk together.'

'Monseigneur will excuse me, but I approached him precisely to ask his permission not to accompany him.'

'How is that ?' asked the Duc, unable to hide the change in his tones.

'Monseigneur, to-morrow is a great day, since it settles the quarrel between Anjou and France; I should therefore like to spend the day in retirement in my little house at Vincennes.'

'But, still, should I have need of my friends during the day ?'

'As monseigneur could only need them to draw swords against the King, I crave leave to stay away, even more strongly; I am pledged to fight M. d'Épernon.'

'So you abandon your lord and master, Bussy.'

'Monseigneur, the man who is risking his life in a desperate and deadly encounter, as ours will be, I swear, has only one Master, and to Him I will pay my devotions.'

'Knowing that for me it is a question of the throne, you leave me ?'

'Monseigneur, I have worked hard on your behalf, and will do my best to-morrow; do not ask more than my life.'

'Good; you are free; go, Monsieur de Bussy.'

Bussy, without troubling about this sudden coolness, bowed and left the Louvre. The Duc summoned Aurilly.

'He has condemned himself,' said he.

'He is not accompanying you ?'

'No.'

'He goes to the meeting-place named in the letter ?'

'Yes.'

'Has M. de Monsoreau been informed ?'

'Of the meeting-place, yes; not yet of the man he will find there.'

'So you are resolved to sacrifice the Comte ?'

'I am resolved to avenge myself. Now I fear only one

thing—that Monsoreau trusts to his strength and skill, and that Bussy may escape.'

'Let monseigneur be reassured. If he escapes from one Monsoreau, he will not escape another.'

'Who is this other ?'

'M. d'Épernon.'

'D'Épernon, who is to fight with him to-morrow? Tell me about that.'

Aurilly had just begun the narrative, when the Duc was summoned by the King. 'Tell me during the procession,' said the Duc, following the usher. Let us now inform our readers what had passed between d'Épernon and the lute player. The former had arrived at daybreak at the Hôtel d'Anjou, asking to speak to Aurilly, with whom he had been long acquainted. Aurilly had taught him the lute, so that a firm friendship united the two musicians. Moreover, M. d'Épernon, a wily Gascon, practised the art of insinuation, which consists in reaching the master's secrets through the servants, consequently few of the Duc's secrets were unknown to him. In this visit he wished to talk to Aurilly of his duel with Bussy, which disturbed him greatly. The salient point in d'Épernon's character had never been bravery; now it was necessary to be more than brave, even rash, to face a duel with Bussy calmly : to confront him meant to confront certain death. At the first word spoken by d'Épernon on this subject, Aurilly pitied his pupil sincerely, and told him that for a week M. de Bussy had been practising two hours each day with a clarion player in the Guards, a sort of artist in sword thrusts, a wanderer and philosopher, who had borrowed from the Italians their prudent play, from the Spaniards their subtle feints, from the Germans their steadiness of wrist and logical parries, from the wild Poles their sudden turns and confusing gyrations. D'Épernon listened to this long enumeration.

'Ah ! but I am dead,' said he, half laughing, half paling. 'It is absurd to meet a man who is certain to kill me.'

'You should have thought of this before.'

'The deuce, I will withdraw. I am not a Gascon for nothing. But, *mordieu !* yes, this is logical—wait— M. de Bussy is sure to kill me ?'

'I do not doubt it for a moment.'

'Then it is no longer a duel, it is an assassination; and, if so, deuce take me——'

'Well ?'

'It is permissible to avert an assassination by—a murder.'

'Doubtless.'

'What hinders me from killing him first, since he intends to kill me.'

'Oh ! *mon Dieu !* nothing at all, and I even thought of it.'

'Only, instead of killing him cruelly with my own hands, I who detest blood, will leave it to others.'

'That is, you will pay men to kill him ?'

'Faith, yes ! as M. de Guise and M. de Mayenne did for Saint-Mégrin.'

'That will cost a great deal.'

'I will expend three thousand crowns on it.'

'That sum, when it is made known who the victim is, will scarcely engage six men.'

'Is that not enough ?'

'Six men ! M. de Bussy will kill four before he receives a scratch. Do you remember that affray in the Rue Saint-Antoine, when he wounded Schomberg in the thigh, you in the arm, and nearly beat Quélus to death ?'

'I will lay out six thousand crowns, if need be. If I do the thing, I wish it so well done that he cannot escape.'

'If your men fail, they will denounce you.'

'The King is on my side.'

'That is always something, but the King cannot keep you from being killed by M. de Bussy.'

'That is perfectly correct,' said d'Épernon, reflecting.

'I could tell you of a means, but perhaps you would object to make common cause ?'

'I should object to nothing which would increase my chances of getting rid of this mad dog.'

'Well, a certain enemy of your enemy is jealous. So that even at this moment, he is laying a snare for him.'

'And afterwards ?'

'But he lacks money; with the six thousand crowns he could manage your business along with his own. You are not anxious that the credit of the affair comes to you ?'

'*Mon Dieu*, no ! I only ask to remain in obscurity.'

'Send your men to the place without disclosing yourself, and he will make use of them.'

'Still, even if my men do not know me, I must know this man.'

'I will show him to you this evening in the Louvre.'

'He is a nobleman ?'

'Yes.'

'Aurilly, before the meeting terminates, the six thousand crowns will be at your disposition.'

'Then it is settled ?'

'Irrevocably.'

We saw in the preceding chapter how Aurilly said to d'Épernon : 'Be reassured, M. de Bussy will not fight with you to-morrow !'

CHAPTER LXXVIII

THE PROCESSION

As soon as the repast was over the King, retiring with Chicot to clothe himself as a penitent, emerged a moment later with bare feet, a cord round his waist, and hood pulled down over his brow. Meanwhile the courtiers had made a similar toilet. Crowds had gathered on the route leading to the four stopping-places—the Abbeys of the Jacobins, Carmes, Capucins, and Génovéfains. The clergy of Saint-Germain-l'Auxerrois headed the procession; the Archbishop of Paris bore the Holy Sacrament; between the clergy and the Archbishop walked boys shaking censers and girls scattering rose petals. Then came the King barefooted, followed by his four friends, also barefooted and wearing robes. The Duc d'Anjou in ordinary dress, with his suite, succeeded; the burghers and the common people brought up the rear.

It was after one o'clock when the procession left the Louvre, and nearly six o'clock when the doorway of the old Abbey of Sainte-Geneviève was reached, where the Prior and monks waited to receive His Majesty. During the journey, the Duc d'Anjou, becoming weary, had asked the King's permission to return to his hotel. His noblemen accompanied him, in order to show that they followed the Duc, not the King. The King, insisting that Quélus,

Maugiron, Schomberg, and d'Épernon needed rest, in
view of the combat, dismissed them at the Abbey door.
The Archbishop and other officiating clergy, who were
overcome with fatigue, were also dismissed, and the King,
turning to Joseph Foulon, observed : 'Here I am, father,
like the sinner I am, I come to seek repose in your
solitudes.' The Prior bowed, and the King, addressing
those who had followed him, added, 'I thank you, gentlemen; go in peace.' Each bowed respectfully, and the
royal penitent, beating his breast, ascended the Abbey
steps. The doors were immediately shut behind him.

'We will first conduct your Majesty to the crypt, which
we have adorned to the best of our ability in honour of the
King of heaven and earth.' The King, bowing to
express his consent, followed the Prior.

As soon as he had passed beneath the gloomy archway,
twenty hoods were thrown back from the faces of the two
rows of monks, and in the semi-darkness eyes were seen
shining with joy and with the pride of triumph. Certainly,
these were not the faces of lazy monks; the heavy
moustaches and swarthy complexions denoted strength
and activity. Many of the faces were scarred, and,
beside the proudest of all, the one with the most celebrated
scar, appeared the triumphant visage of a woman, who
waved a pair of gold scissors, exclaiming, 'Ah ! brothers,
at last we hold the Valois.'

'Faith, sister, I am of your opinion,' answered Le
Balafré.

'Not yet,' murmured the Cardinal; 'shall we have
sufficient citizen troops to restrain Crillon and his guards ?'

'We have what is better than citizen troops, and,
believe me, not a single shot will be fired,' replied the
Duc de Mayenne.

'How is that ? I should have liked some noise,' said
the Duchesse de Montpensier.'

'Well, sister, I regret to say, you will be deprived of it.
When the King is arrested, he will cry out, but none will
answer. We shall then compel him to sign an abdication,
by persuasion or violence, without our appearing. The
news will spread through the city, disposing in our favour
the citizens and soldiers.'

'It is a good plan, and cannot fail now,' observed the
Duchesse.

'It is a little brutal,' said the Cardinal de Guise.

'The King will refuse to sign the abdication; he is brave, and will rather die,' added Le Balafré.

'Then let him die!'

'No, not so!' exclaimed the Duc de Guise decidedly; 'I do not object to succeeding a prince who abdicates and is despised; but I should not care to replace a man who has been assassinated, and, therefore, will be pitied. Besides, you are forgetting, in your plans, the Duc d'Anjou, who will claim the throne, should the King be killed.'

'Let him claim it, *mordieu!* our brother the Cardinal has anticipated that; M. le Duc d'Anjou will be included in his brother's abdication. Having coquetted with the Huguenots, he is unworthy to reign. Then, another clause in favour of our house follows the forfeiture of rights : this clause will make you Lieutenant of the kingdom, and there is but a step between that post and royalty itself.'

'Yes, yes, I have foreseen all that; but it may be the French Guards will force the Abbey to be convinced that the abdication is genuine and voluntary. Crillon cannot appreciate a joke, and would be the man to say : 'Your Majesty, 'tis true that your life may be in danger; but, before all, let us save your honour.'

'That concerns the general, who has taken precautions. We have here eighty noblemen to withstand a siege, and arms have been distributed to a hundred monks. We could hold out for a month against an army.'

'And what is the Duc d'Anjou doing ?'

'As ever, he has become irresolute at the hour of danger. He has gone, with Bussy and Monsoreau, to his house, where he is doubtless waiting for news of us.'

'Eh, *mon Dieu!* He should be here, and not at home.'

'I believe you are wrong, brother; the people and the nobles would have guessed at a conspiracy against the family, from this meeting of the two brothers; and we must, above all things, avoid acting as usurpers. We inherit, that is all. Leaving the Duc d'Anjou free, the Queen-Mother independent, we shall be blessed by all, and nobody will have a word to speak against us. If not, we shall have to reckon with Bussy and a hundred others.'

'Bah! Bussy fights the King's friends to-morrow.'

'He will kill them; what a fine affair, and then he will belong to us. I will make him general of an army in Italy, where war will assuredly break out. He is a man I esteem greatly, the Seigneur de Bussy.'

'Who is with the King ?' asked the Duc de Guise.

'The Prior and Brother Gorenflot, I believe.'

'Is he in the cell ?' asked the Duchesse, eager to give the King the tonsure, that third crown which she had for long promised him.

'Oh, no; first, he will see the great altar in the crypt and adore the holy relics.'

'And afterwards ?'

'Afterwards, the Prior will address some weighty remarks to him upon the vanity of this world's goods; then the Brother Gorenflot, he who delivered that splendid discourse on the evening of the League, will endeavour to obtain from conviction what we hesitate at dragging from his weakness.'

'Bah ! Henri is superstitious and enfeebled; he will yield to the fear of hell,' Mayenne remarked.

'I am less convinced than you,' said the Duc, 'but our ships are burned, and there is no retreating. Now, after the Prior's attempt, after Gorenflot's speech, if both fail, we will try the last method—intimidation.'

'Then I shall have my Valois,' cried the Duchesse.

Just at that moment a bell resounded through the vaults, already darkening by the first shades of evening.

'The King descends to the crypt; let us call our friends, Mayenne, and become monks again,' advised the Duc de Guise. Immediately the hoods covered the bold brows, keen eyes, and eloquent scars; then thirty or forty monks, led by the three brothers, proceeded toward the opening of the crypt.

CHAPTER LXXIX

CHICOT THE FIRST

THE King was plunged in meditation, which augured an easy success for the plans devised by MM. de Guise. Visiting the crypt with all the community, he kissed the shrine, finishing all the ceremonies by beating his breast, and mumbling the most lugubrious psalms. The Prior began his exhortations, and the King listened with every sign of fervent contrition. Then, at a gesture from the

Duc de Guise, Joseph Foulon, bowing before Henri said,—

'Your Majesty, would you be pleased now to come and deposit your earthly crown at the feet of the Eternal Master?'

'Let us go,' answered the King simply.

Immediately the whole community, ranging up before him, proceeded toward the cells, the principal corridor of which could be seen on the left. On the threshold of the cell stood Gorenflot, his face lit up, his eye shining like a carbuncle.

'Here?' asked the King.

'Even here,' replied the big monk.

The King might well hesitate, for at the end of this corridor was a door, or rather a mysterious looking grating, opening on a steep decline veiled in thick darkness. Henri entered the cell. 'Leave us,' ordered Gorenflot, with a majestic air. Immediately the door was shut; the company retired. The King sat down on a stool in the depths of the cell, clasping his knees with his hands.

'Ah! there you are Hérodès, Pagan, Nabuchodonosor,' began Gorenflot, placing his thick hands on his hips.

'Is it to me you address yourself, brother?' asked the King, in apparent surprise.

'Yes; to whom else? Can one use an abusive term which does not fit you?'

'Brother!' murmured the King.

'Bah! you have no brother here. For quite a long time I have been preparing a discourse. You shall have it. I divide it into three heads, as is the custom of all good preachers. First, you are a tyrant; second, you are a satyr; third and last, you are dethroned—there's my text.'

'Dethroned, brother!'

'Neither more nor less. It is not the same here as in Poland, and you will not escape——'

'An ambush!'

'Oh! Valois, learn that a king is only a man, when he is even that.'

'Violence, brother.'

'*Pardieu*, do you think we imprisoned you to treat you gently? Come, are you ready, Valois?'

'To do what?'

'To deposit your crown; I have been instructed to invite you to do this; I invite you.'

'But you are committing a deadly sin.'

'Oh! I have the right of absolution, and absolve myself beforehand; come, renounce the throne of France, Brother Valois.'

'I would rather die.'

'You shall die, then. Here's the Prior returning—make a resolve.'

'I have my Guards, my friends; I will defend myself.'

'That is possible, but you will be killed first.'

'Leave me a moment for reflection.'

'Not an instant, not a second.'

'Your zeal transports you, brother,' said the Prior, with a sign to the King which implied, 'Your Majesty, your request is granted,' and he shut the door again.

Henri fell into a deep reverie.

'I will accept the sacrifice,' he declared presently.

Ten minutes had passed while Henri reflected; somebody knocked against the door.

'It is done, he accepts,' said Gorenflot. The King heard a murmur of joy and surprise in the corridor.

'Read him the act,' commanded a voice which caused the King to start. A roll of parchment was handed by a monk to Gorenflot, who painfully read it to the King; the latter, in great sorrow, hiding his face with his hands.

'And if I refuse to sign?' he asked, shedding tears.

'You will be doubly lost,' retorted the Duc de Guise, his voice stifled by his hood. 'Consider yourself dead to the world, and do not force your subjects to shed the blood of one who was their King.'

'They shall not force me.'

'I had anticipated this; go, brother,' turning to Mayenne, 'have every one armed, and let them be prepared.'

'Prepared for what?' asked the King, in gloomy tones.

'For everything,' answered Joseph Foulon. The King's despair redoubled.

'*Corbleu!* I hated you, Valois; but now I despise you. Come, sign; or you shall perish by my hand.'

Suddenly a dull noise resounded outside the convent. 'Silence!' cried the Duc de Guise. Soon the sound of blows, struck at regular intervals on the Abbey door, was heard. Mayenne rushed up as fast as his stoutness would permit

'My brothers, a troop of armed men stands before the portal,' he announced.

'They come to seek him,' suggested the Duchesse.

'All the more reason that he should sign quickly.'

'Sign! Valois, sign!' cried Gorenflot, in terrible tones, seizing the King's wrist and offering him a pen. The noise outside redoubled.

'A fresh troop!' announced a monk; 'it is surrounding the parvis.'

The King dipped his pen in ink.

'The Swiss!' cried Foulon; 'they have invaded the cemetery on the right; the whole Abbey will be invested shortly.'

'Well! we will defend ourselves,' answered Mayenne emphatically; 'with a hostage such as we possess, a place is never surrendered at discretion.'

'He has signed!' shouted Gorenflot, seizing the paper from Henri, who, overcome, buried his head in his hood.

'Then we are King. Carry off this precious paper,' exclaimed the Cardinal to the Duc.

The King absently overturned the lamp, but the Duc de Guise already held the parchment.

'What is to be done?' asked a monk, whose robe concealed the form of a gentleman fully dressed and armed. 'Crillon has arrived with his Guards, and is threatening to break down the doors. Listen!'

'In the King's name!' cried the powerful voice of Crillon.

'Good! there is no longer a King,' answered Gorenflot through a window.

'Burst open the door, Monsieur Crillon,' said a voice which caused all the real or false monks to start violently. This voice belonged to a man who had advanced to the Abbey steps.

'It is done, your Majesty,' was the answer, as Crillon struck the door a vigorous blow with his axe which made the walls tremble.

'What is wanted?' asked the Prior, appearing trembling at the window.

'Ah! it is you, Messire Foulon,' said the same calm, haughty voice. 'Give me back my jester, who has been spending a night in one of your cells. I need Chicot; I am dull in the Louvre.'

'I am amusing myself splendidly here, my son,'

answered Chicot, coming forth from his hood, and dis-
persing the crowd of monks. At that moment the Duc de
Guise, producing a lamp, read at the foot of the act the
signature which had been obtained with such difficulty :—

'CHICOT THE FIRST.'

'Chicot the First,' he cried; 'a thousand damnations !'
'We are lost; let us flee,' urged the Cardinal.
'Bah !' said Chicot, striking the nearly fainting Gorenflot
with the cord of his robe.

CHAPTER LXXX

PRINCIPAL AND INTEREST

As the conspirators recognised the King, their stupefaction was changed into terror. The abdication, signed
'Chicot the First,' transformed this terror into rage.
Chicot, throwing back his robe and crossing his arms,
smilingly sustained the first shock of the attack. It was
a terrible moment, for the infuriated nobles rushed on the
Gascon, determined to be avenged for the cruel mystifica-
tion of which they were the victims. But this unarmed
man, with a mocking expression which seemed to defy
the strongest attack, stopped them even more effectually
than the remonstrances of the Cardinal, who argued that
Chicot's death would be terribly avenged by the King.
So the daggers and rapiers were lowered before Chicot,
who continued to laugh jestingly.

Meanwhile the King's threats and Crillon's blows
became more pressing; it was clear the door could not
long resist such an onslaught. The Duc de Guise issued
orders to retreat, which made Chicot smile, since, during
his nights of retirement with Gorenflot, he had examined
the underground passage, and had pointed out the exit
to the King, who had placed Tocquenot, the lieutenant
of the Swiss Guards, at it. The Leaguers were about to
cast themselves into the wolf's jaw. The Cardinal retired
first, then the Duc, finally Mayenne, all accompanied by
noblemen. Ten minutes passed, while Chicot listened
attentively, expecting to hear the Leaguers returning,
but the sounds died away. Suddenly an idea occurred to
the Gascon ! Had the Leaguers, perceiving that the exit

was guarded, discovered another door ? Chicot prepared
to rush from the cell, when, suddenly, the door was
blocked by a shapeless mass, which spread itself at his
feet, tearing out handfuls of its hair.

'Ah ! wretch that I am. Oh ! good Seigneur Chicot,
pardon me !' cried the monk; 'pardon your unworthy
friend who repents at your knees.'

'How is it you did not flee with the others, you rogue ?'

'Because I could not pass where they have passed;
because the Lord, in His wrath, has afflicted me with
corpulency. Ah ! why am I not thin like you, Monsieur
Chicot ?'

'The others have gone somewhere—the others flee,
then ?'

'*Pardieu !* what would you have them do ? wait for
a robe ?'

'Silence ! answer me, how are the others escaping ?'

'By the air-hole leading into the cemetery vault.'

'Is that what you call the underground passage ?
answer quickly.'

'No, dear Monsieur Chicot. The door of the under
ground passage was guarded outside. The great Cardinal
Guise, about to open it, heard a Swiss saying, "I am
thirsty." '

'I understand that; so the fugitives have taken another
road ?'

'Yes, they escape by the cemetery vault.'

'Where does it lead ?'

'On one side into the crypt, on the other under the
Porte Saint-Jacques.'

'You lie; had they escaped by the vault leading to the
crypt, I should have seen them repassing.'

'Precisely; thinking they had no time for this detour,
they have passed by the air-hole leading into the garden,
and I, being too fat, could not get through, though I made
frantic efforts.'

'Then he who is even fatter than you will not have
passed ? Rise up, priestling, and lead me to the air-hole.
Walk in front.'

Gorenflot began to trot as quickly as he could, from
time to time raising his arms in the air, while Chicot
dealt him blows with his cord. Both crossed the corridor,
descending into the garden. Gorenflot reached a clump
of trees from which groans seemed to issue.

'There, there,' said he, falling breathless on the grass. Chicot, advancing a few steps, saw something moving on the ground; beside this object lay a sword and a robe. Evidently the individual so unfortunately caught had divested himself of everything that served as an obstacle, and was making vain attempts to disappear entirely.

'*Mordieu! ventrebleu! sangdieu!*' the fugitive was crying with stifled voice, 'I would rather fight a way through the whole guard. Do not pull so strong, friends, I shall slip through quite gently; I feel myself advancing, though not fast. I was not nicknamed Hercules for nothing; I will raise this stone,' and he made such a violent effort the stone really shook. Chicot made a noise with his feet as if running up very quickly.

'They are coming,' cried several voices underground.

'Ah! it is you, wretched monk,' cried Chicot, as if arriving breathless.

'Say nothing, monseigneur. He takes you for Gorenflot.'

'Ah! so it's you, heavy mass, ah! there!' exclaimed Chicot, striking at the monk with the cord, and using all his force. Mayenne uttered stifled groans, while he redoubled his efforts to raise the stone.

'Ah, conspirator! ah, unworthy monk! this is for drunkenness, this for laziness, this for anger, this for luxury, this for gluttony. I regret that there are only seven deadly sins; take that for the vices you have!'

'Mercy! dear Monsieur Chicot,' murmured Gorenflot, imagining he felt all the blows which fell on Mayenne. Chicot, becoming intoxicated with his revenge, increased the strokes.

'Ah! why does it not please God to substitute for your vulgar body the powerful shoulder blades of the Duc de Mayenne to whom I owe a shower of blows, of which the interest has accumulated for seven years!'

Gorenflot fell down, sighing.

'Chicot!' shrieked the Duc.

'Yes, Chicot, that weak arm, who should have the hundred arms of Briareus for this occasion,' answered Chicot, raining blows with such fury that his victim, summoning all his strength, raised the stone and fell, with torn and bleeding back and sides, into his friends' arms. Chicot's last blow struck the air. Turning, he saw that the real Gorenflot had swooned, if not with pain, at least with fright.

CHAPTER LXXXI

WHAT WAS HAPPENING IN THE BASTILLE QUARTER

It was eleven o'clock at night; the Duc d'Anjou waited in his house in the Rue Saint-Jacques till a messenger should announce the news of his brother the King's abdication. Suddenly, hearing a horse pawing the ground in the courtyard, he ran to the balcony, thinking it might be the messenger. The horse, however, was being held by a groom for its master, Bussy, who came from the inner apartments where, as Captain of the Guards, he had been giving the countersign for the night, before setting out to keep his appointment. At sight of this handsome, brave young man, the Duc felt remorseful for an instant; but, as Bussy approached, the Duc read in his face so much joy, hope, and happiness that all his jealousy returned. Unconscious that the Duc watched his expression, Bussy, throwing on his cloak, mounted and set out noisily under the echoing archway. For a moment the Duc thought of sending after him, for he concluded that Bussy would stop at his hotel before proceeding to the Bastille; but, as he thought of the young man laughing with Diane over his own despised love, and so putting him on a level with the flouted husband, his worse instincts prevailed. Had Bussy appeared sad and gloomy, he might have summoned him back. Arriving at his hotel, Bussy handed his horse to a groom who was listening respectfully to a lecture on veterinary art given by Rémy.

'Ah, it is you, Rémy! not in bed yet?' asked Bussy, recognising the young doctor.

'I shall be in ten minutes, monseigneur. I was returning from your room. Now that I have no patient, the day seems to consist of forty-eight hours.'

'Are you wearied, by chance?'

'I am afraid so!'

'And your love?'

'Ah! I have often explained that I mistrust love, and simply make useful studies of it.'

'Then Gertrude is abandoned?'

'Utterly.'

'And your heart does not speak of her this evening ?
I might have taken you with me.'

'You are going to the Bastille. And Monsoreau ?'

'He is at Compiègne, dear fellow, preparing a hunt for
His Majesty.'

'Are you sure, monseigneur ?'

'The orders were issued to him publicly this morning.'

'Ah !' observed Rémy thoughtfully, then he added,
'So ?'

'So, I have spent the day thanking God for the happiness
He sends me to-night, and I will spend the night in enjoying
this happiness.'

'Good. Jourdain, my sword,' ordered Rémy.

'So you have changed your mind ?'

'Yes, I will come to the house with you for two reasons.
First, lest you have any unlucky meetings in the street.
I know you are utterly fearless, and that Doctor Rémy
is but a poor companion; still, two men are less easily
attacked than one. The second reason is that I have
a number of excellent counsels to give you.'

'Come, my dear Rémy. We will talk of her; next to
the pleasure of seeing the woman one loves, there is none
greater than speaking of her.'

'Here I am at your orders, monseigneur; let us start,'
replied Rémy, taking his rapier from the groom.

Hardly had they set out than the doctor began to quote,
in Latin, some imposing statements, proving that Bussy
was wrong to visit Diane that night, instead of quietly
resting in bed, inasmuch as a man fights badly when he
has slept badly. Bussy smiled; Rémy grew insistent.

'But Rémy, when my arm holds a sword it becomes so
attached to it that the fibres assume the suppleness and
rigour of steel, whilst the steel seems to become warm and
animate like living flesh. From that moment, my sword
is an arm, my arm a sword. Do you understand ? there is
no question of strength or aptness. A blade does not
become tired.'

'No, but it blunts. Ah ! my dear seigneur, to-morrow
the fight must be like that of Hercules against Antæus,
of Theseus against the Minotaur—like Bayard's, something
Homeric, gigantic, impossible; people are to say in future
years, "Bussy's fight," as being *the* fight *par excellence*,
and I do not wish your opponents even to scratch you.'

'Be reassured, my brave Rémy; you will see miracles.

This morning I had a duel with four men who, in eight minutes, did not succeed in touching me once, while I had their doublets in rags. I was as active as a tiger.'

'I do not contradict you; but will you be as supple to-morrow ?'

Here Bussy and his doctor began a dialogue in Latin, frequently interrupted by their bursts of laughter. They arrived in this way at the High Street of Saint-Antoine.

'Adieu; we are there,' observed Bussy.

'Supposing I stay, in order to make sure you return before two o'clock; you need at least five or six hours' sleep before the duel.'

'If I give you my word ?'

'That will suffice. Bussy's word—the deuce, as though I should doubt that.'

'Well, you have it. In two hours, Rémy, I shall be at the hotel.'

'Agreed. Farewell, monseigneur.' The two separated, but Rémy remained. He saw the Comte advance to the house and enter by the door which Gertrude opened to him. Then Rémy resumed his homeward walk; but as he left the Place Beaudoyer, he saw five men wrapped in cloaks and thoroughly armed, approaching, so he hid in the angle of a house. The five stopped, and four took different directions, whilst the fifth remained motionless and thoughtful in his place. The moon, emerging from a cloud, shone on this man's face.

'M. de Saint-Luc !' exclaimed Rémy. Saint-Luc raised his head. 'Remy !' he cried.

'Rémy in person. Is it indiscreet to ask what your lordship does at this hour so far from the Louvre ?'

'Faith, I am studying the look of the town, by the King's orders. He said to me, ''Saint-Luc, stroll about the streets, and should you hear that I have abdicated, boldly contradict the statement.'' '

'Have you heard that mentioned ?'

'Nobody has breathed a word of it. Now, as it is near midnight, all is quiet, and I have met only M. de Monsoreau. I have dismissed my friends, and was about to return when you saw me reflecting.'

'You met M. de Monsoreau ?'

'With a troop of armed men—ten or twelve at least.'

'Impossible. He ought to be at Compiègne.'

'He ought to be, but he is not there.'

'But the King's command ?'

'Bah ! who obeys the King ?'

'You met M. de Monsoreau with ten or a dozen men. Did he recognise you ?'

'I think so !'

'There were only five of you, and he did not attack you ?'

'On the contrary, he avoided me, which astonishes me. In recognising him, I was prepared for a terrible encounter.'

'In what direction was he going ?'

'Towards Rue de la Tixeranderie.'

'Ah ! *mon Dieu !* Monsieur de Saint-Luc, a terrible disaster is going to happen.'

'To whom ?'

'To M. de Bussy !'

'M. de Bussy ! speak, Rémy; I am his friend, you know.'

'M. de Bussy, believing Monsoreau was at Compiègne, thought to profit by his absence.'

'So that he is——'

'With Madame Diane.'

'Ah ! the affair becomes complicated.'

'Yes, he will have had suspicions, or some one has suggested them to him, and, feigning to leave, he has returned unexpectedly.'

'Wait,' said Saint-Luc, considering, 'the Duc d'Anjou has a hand in this.'

'But it was the Duc who instigated M. de Monsoreau's departure !'

'An additional reason. Have you good lungs, my brave Rémy ?'

'*Corbleu !* like the bellows of a forge.'

'In that case, let us run without losing an instant. You know the house ?'

'Yes.'

'Then, go in front.'

'Has he much of a start ?' asked Rémy as he ran.

'Nearly a quarter of an hour,' was Saint-Luc's reply.

'Let us hope we may arrive in time,' said Rémy, drawing his sword to be ready for every emergency.

CHAPTER LXXXII

THE ASSASSINATION

BUSSY had been received without fear by Diane, who felt certain of her husband's absence. Never had the beautiful young woman been so joyful, never had Bussy been so happy. Diane appeared more tender, being filled with fears as she thought of the next day. She wished to tell the young man to-night that his life was her life; to discuss with him the surest means of flight. To conquer was not all; afterwards one had to flee from the King's wrath, for Henri would probably never pardon the defeat or death of his favourites.

'And then, are you not the bravest man in France?' asked Diane, gazing into her lover's face. 'You are already so superior to other men that it would not be generous to wish to increase your glory. Louis, defend your life. I do not say, "Think of death," for it seems to me no man is strong and powerful enough to kill my Louis except by treachery; but think of the wounds which, as you are well aware, can be inflicted.'

'Be sure I will guard my face; I have no wish to be disfigured,' replied Bussy, laughing.

'Oh! take care of yourself altogether. Think of the sorrow you would feel at seeing me bleeding and wounded; I should feel the same sorrow at seeing you wounded. Be prudent, my brave lion, that is all I ask you. Do as that Roman whose story you were reading to me; let your three friends fight, and aid the one who is most pressed; but, should two or three attack you at once, flee, turning like Horace, to kill them from a distance.'

'Yes, dear Diane; besides, I am well seconded, believe me; you do not know my friends, but I do. Antraguet handles the sword as myself; Ribeirac is cool in encounter, and his eyes which gaze on his antagonist, and the arm with which he strikes, seem the only living parts of him; Livarot is agile as a tiger. I really wish the danger were greater, so that I could obtain higher distinction.'

'I believe you, dear friend, and I smile hopefully; but listen to me and promise to obey.'

'I promise, unless you ask me to leave you.'

'Exactly. Now I appeal to your reason. Dear friend, you are tired and need a night's rest; leave me.'

'Oh! already!'

'I will say my prayers, and you will embrace me.'

Kneeling down, Diane prayed with all her heart. She was just finishing, and Bussy was stooping to clasp her in his arms, when suddenly a pane of the window broke into splinters; then the whole window was smashed, and three armed men appeared on the balcony, a fourth, masked and armed with pistol and sword, strode over the balustrade. Bussy stood for a moment motionless, stunned by the fearful cry uttered by Diane, who fell on his neck. The masked man beckoned; his three companions, one of whom had an arquebuse, advanced a step. Bussy, thrusting Diane away with his left hand, drew his sword with the right. Then, falling back, he lowered it slowly, still looking on his adversaries.

'Come, my brave men,' said a sepulchral voice from under the velvet mask, 'he is half dead; fear has killed him.'

'You are wrong, I am never afraid,' retorted Bussy.

'Ah! it is really M. de Bussy; I did not believe it, fool that I was. Really, what a friend, what an excellent friend!'

Bussy was silent, glancing around for what means of defence he could use when the combat began.

'Learning that the First Huntsman was absent, and had left his wife alone, he comes to keep her company,' resumed the voice with a mocking intonation; 'even on the eve of a duel. I repeat it, what a faithful, excellent friend is the Seigneur de Bussy!'

'Ah! it is you, Monsieur de Monsoreau. Throw off your mask. Now, I know with whom I have to do.'

'I will do so,' answered the First Huntsman, casting aside the velvet mask. His face was pale and corpse-like, with the smile of a damned soul. Diane uttered a faint cry.

'There, let us stop, monsieur. I do not like these blustering ways; it was all right for Homer's heroes, demi-gods, to make speeches before fighting. I am only a fearless man; attack me, or let me pass.'

Monsoreau responded by a hoarse laugh, which caused Diane to start, but provoked Bussy's burning anger.

'Let me pass,' he repeated, the blood mounting to his brow.

'Oh, pass! what a curious request, Monsieur de Bussy?'

'Then, let us cross swords and have done with it; I need to return to my house, which is some distance away.'

Meanwhile two more men appeared at the balcony railings, and they crossed the balustrade to their companions.

'Four and two make six; where are the others?' asked Bussy.

'They are waiting at the door,' was the reply.

Diane fell on her knees; Bussy heard her sob in spite of her efforts. He glanced quickly at her, then, looking at the Comte, he said, after a moment's reflection,—

'My dear monsieur, you know that I am a man of honour?'

'Yes, you are an honourable man, as madame is a chaste woman.'

'Good, monsieur,' answered Bussy, bowing slightly; 'that is sharp but deserved, and will be paid for. Only, as I have an engagement to-morrow with four noblemen of your acquaintance, and they have the right of priority over you, I crave to retire to-night, pledging my word to meet you when and where you shall choose.'

Monsoreau shrugged his shoulders.

'Listen, monsieur,' Bussy resumed; 'I swear to God that, after satisfying MM. de Schomberg, d'Épernon, de Quélus, and de Maugiron, I shall be wholly at your service. If they kill me, well! you will receive payment at their hands, that is all; on the contrary, should I find myself in a position to pay you myself——'.

Monsoreau turned to his men.

'Come, my braves.'

'Ah! I was wrong; this is more than a duel, it is an assassination. I see we were mistaken in one another; but, consider, monsieur, the Duc d'Anjou will not like this.'

'It is he who sends me,' replied Monsoreau.

Bussy shuddered; Diane raised her hands to heaven, groaning.

'In that case, I appeal to Bussy alone. Guard yourselves, my braves,' exclaimed Bussy, overturning the praying-desk, drawing forward a table, and throwing a chair above the two so that he had a sort of rampart

erected between himself and his enemies. The movement
was so rapid that the bullet fired from the arquebuse
simply lodged itself in the praying-desk. Bussy meanwhile knocked over a splendid credence-table of the time
of François the First, to add to his fortifications, and Diane,
hidden by this piece of furniture, prayed for his safety.
The hirelings, urged by Monsoreau, moved towards the
wild boar awaiting them with gleaming eyes; one of the
men stretched out his hand to draw him forth, but before
he could touch the desk Bussy's sword had ripped his arm
right to the shoulder. The man dragged himself to the
window with a cry. Hearing rapid steps in the corridor,
Bussy rushed to the door, which opened before he could
reach it. Two men rushed in.

'Ah! dear master,' cried a familiar voice, 'do we come
in time?'

'Rémy!' exclaimed the Comte.

'And I!' called a second voice; 'surely there is murder
going on here.'

'Saint-Luc!' exclaimed Bussy joyfully, recognising
this voice.

'Ah! now, I think, dear Monsieur de Monsoreau, you
would do well to let us pass, for, otherwise, we shall pass
over you.'

'Three men to my assistance!' cried Monsoreau.

Three fresh assailants appeared above the balustrade.

'My God, protect him,' prayed Diane.

'Infamous woman!' cried Monsoreau, advancing to
strike Diane.

Bussy perceived the movement. Agile as a tiger, he
leaped over the barricade, struck Monsoreau's sword,
then aimed at his throat; the distance was too great, and
he merely grazed it. Five or six men rushed at Bussy,
one falling beneath Saint-Luc's sword.

'Forward!' cried Rémy.

'No, rather carry off Diane!' ordered Bussy.

'But you?' asked Rémy, hesitating.

'Carry her off! I entrust her to you.'

'Bussy! help!' cried Diane, no longer able to distinguish
friends from enemies; all that separated her from Bussy
was to her fatal, deadly.

'Go, I will rejoin you,' urged Bussy.

'Yes, you will rejoin her; I hope so,' screamed
Monsoreau.

Bussy saw Le Haudouin totter and fall, dragging Diane with him.

'It is nothing, my master; I received the bullet; she is safe,' said Rémy.   Three men advanced on Bussy, but just as he turned, Saint-Luc passed between him and his foes, felling one of them.   The other two drew back.

'Saint-Luc, by her whom you love, save Diane !' cried Bussy.   Rushing to Diane, Saint-Luc raised her in his arms and disappeared.

'Help ! those on the staircase !' cried Monsoreau, retreating behind his men.

'Ah ! scoundrel, coward !' exclaimed Bussy, splitting one man's temple with a back stroke, and wounding another in the chest.

'That has cleared a space,' said he, returning to his entrenchment.

'Flee ! master, flee !' murmured Rémy.

'I, to flee—before assassins !' retorted Bussy.   Then, bending over Rémy, he added, 'Diane must be saved; but what about yourself ?'

'Take care !' said Rémy.

Four men had entered from the stair.   Bussy was caught between two troops, but had only one idea. 'Diane !' he cried.   Then, without losing a second, he leaped at the four men, two of whom fell, one wounded, the other dead.   As Monsoreau advanced, Bussy retired behind the rampart.

'Draw the bolts, turn the key,' ordered Monsoreau; 'we have him.'

Meanwhile Rémy, with a final effort, had dragged himself in front of Bussy, adding his body to the protecting barrier.   Bussy glanced around.   Seven men lay on the floor, nine stood erect.   On seeing the nine swords flash, on hearing Monsoreau encourage his men, on feeling his feet swimming in blood, this valiant man, who had never known fear, seemed to see the image of death calling him with a gloomy smile.

'Out of nine, I can kill five, but the other four will kill me !   I have strength left for ten minutes' fighting : well ! during these ten minutes, let us do what man never has done or will do,' soliloquised Bussy.

Unfastening his cloak, which he rolled round his left arm, he sprang into the middle of the room, where he thrust into any open space there was; three times he heard the leather of a baldric creak, while a stream of warm blood flowed down on his right hand. Meanwhile he had parried twenty thrusts with his left arm. The cloak was cut in pieces. The assassins, seeing two men fall and a third retreat, changed their tactics; abandoning their swords, some attacked with the butt-end of a musket, others fired with pistols, but he escaped the shot. In this supreme hour he not only saw, heard, acted, but even guessed his enemies' most subtle, secret thoughts; less than a God, being mortal, he was certainly more than a man.

Believing that the death of Monsoreau would end the combat, he searched for him among the assassins. The latter, as calm as Bussy was excited, loaded pistols for his men, or taking them ready charged from their hands fired, keeping himself in the background. It was easy for Bussy to force a way through the hirelings and bring himself face to face with Monsoreau. Just then the latter fired at Bussy; the shot broke his sword-blade six inches above the hilt. Bussy, retreating, picked up the broken blade to fasten it with his handkerchief to his wrist. The battle recommenced, presenting the wondrous spectacle of a man almost unarmed, but almost unwounded, terrifying ten well-armed men from behind a rampart of ten corpses. Bussy was surrounded; the stump of his blade, twisted and blunted, shook in his hand; fatigue began to stiffen his arm; as he glanced round, one of the fallen men rose to his knees, putting a long rapier into his hands. It was Rémy, whose last act was one of devotion.

Uttering a joyful cry, Bussy leaped back to unfasten his handkerchief that he might release the now useless blade. Meanwhile Monsoreau, approaching Rémy, discharged a pistol full at his head; Rémy fell to rise no more, while Bussy uttered an angry roar. Strength had returned with means of defence. Making his sword circle with a hissing sound, he beat down a wrist on the right hand and slashed a cheek on the left, thus leaving a clear space. Lithe and vigorous, he rushed at the door, attempting to burst it open with a blow which shook the wall; but the bolts held firm. Exhausted by the effort, Bussy let his right arm drop, while with the left he tried to draw the bolts behind him, facing his enemies the while. During the interval, he received a pistol-shot in the thigh and two sword-thrusts in his side, but he had drawn the bolts

and turned the key. Howling with rage, he crushed with
a back-stroke the keenest of the bandits, and lunging at
Monsoreau, wounded him in the chest. The First Huntsman shrieked out a curse. 'Ah!' said Bussy, 'I begin
to think I shall escape.'

The four men, throwing down their arms, clung to
Bussy. Unable to finish the struggle by firing, as his
wonderful skill rendered him invulnerable, they attempted
to throttle him. But with blows from the pommel of his
sword, he beat and slashed at them incessantly.
Monsoreau, twice approaching, was twice wounded.
Picking up a carved wooden footstool, Bussy felled two
men, but the stool broke on the shoulders of a third, who
drove his dagger into Bussy's chest. Drawing it out by
the hilt, and turning it against his adversary, Bussy forced
him to stab himself. The man leaped through the window;
Bussy was preparing to follow, when Monsoreau, rising,
slashed at his leg. The young man uttered a cry, and,
picking up the first sword he could see, plunged it so
vigorously into the First Huntsman's chest as to fix him
to the floor. 'Ah!' he cried, 'I may die myself, but at
least I shall have seen you die.' Monsoreau endeavoured
to reply, but just then breathed his last. Bussy dragged
himself towards the corridor; he was losing all his blood
from the two wounds.

Casting a last look at this battlefield, peopled by him
with the slain, he felt a sublime pride, wounded and
dying as he was. As he had said, he had done what none
other could have accomplished. Now he had to flee, to
escape; this was easy, since he retreated before the dead.
But all was not over; arriving on the stair, he perceived
arms shining in the courtyard; a shot sped, burying
itself in his shoulder; the courtyard was guarded. Then
remembering a little window from which Diane had
promised to watch the next day's combat, he dragged
himself in this direction. The window was open; mounting
with difficulty, and climbing the hand-rail, he measured
the iron railing so as to jump clear on the other side.
'I shall never have the strength,' he muttered. He heard
the second troop ascending the stair. Gathering all his
force and aiding himself with one hand and foot, he leaped
forward, but his boot, covered with blood, slipped on the
stonework, so that he fell on the iron points; some of
them penetrated his body, others caught in his clothes,

and he remained suspended. At this moment he thought of the sole friend left to him.

'Saint-Luc!' he cried, 'help! help!'

'Ah! it is you, Monsieur de Bussy,' came a voice from out a clump of trees. Bussy started; this was not Saint-Luc's voice.

'Saint-Luc! help! fear nothing for Diane. I have killed Monsoreau!' continued Bussy, hoping that Saint-Luc, if near, would approach at this news.

'Ah! Monsoreau is killed?' asked another voice; 'good,' and two masked men emerged from the trees.

'Gentlemen, in Heaven's name, help a poor man who may still escape, with your aid!'

'What do you think, monseigneur?' half-whispered one of the strangers.

'Imprudent!' retorted the other.

'Monseigneur!' cried Bussy, who had heard with senses sharpened by the despair of the moment. 'Monseigneur! deliver me, and I will pardon you for having betrayed me.'

'Do you hear?' asked the masked man.

'What are your orders?'

'Well! deliver him.' Then with a laugh, stifled under his mask, he added, 'From his sufferings!'

Bussy turned his head in the direction of this voice which dared to speak jestingly at such a moment.

'Oh! I am lost,' he groaned.

Just then the barrel of an arquebuse was placed on his chest; the shot sped. Bussy's head fell on his shoulder; his hands stiffened.

'Assassin! be accursed!' said he, and expired with Diane's name on his lips. His blood fell from the railing on the person addressed as monseigneur.

'Is he dead?' called several men appearing at the window.

'Yes; but flee; remember that Monseigneur the Duc d'Anjou was the friend and protector of M. de Bussy,' answered Aurilly.

'Now, Aurilly, go upstairs and throw me down Monsoreau's corpse,' ordered the Duc.

Aurilly, recognising the First Huntsman's body amid the incredible number of corpses, placed it on his shoulders and threw it over the window to the Duc, who was bespattered with the blood. François, searching in

the coat pocket, drew out the act of alliance signed by
his royal hand.

'That is what I wanted; we have no more to do here,'
said he.

'And Diane ?'

'Faith, I am no longer in love, and as she did not
recognise us, set her free; Saint-Luc also, and let them go
where they choose.' Aurilly disappeared.

'I shall not be King of France yet,' said the Duc,
tearing the paper into pieces, 'but neither shall I be
beheaded for the crime of high treason.'

CHAPTER LXXXIII

BROTHER GORENFLOT FINDS HIMSELF BETWEEN THE GALLOWS AND AN ABBEY

THE affair of the conspiracy was a comedy to the end.
The Swiss Guards, placed at the mouth of this river of
intrigue, no less than the French Guards, stationed to
catch the important conspirators at the confluence, failed
to seize even the small fry. As every one had disappeared
by the underground passage, no one was seen leaving
the Abbey. As soon as the door was burst open, Crillon
entered Sainte-Geneviève, along with the King, at the
head of thirty men. A silence of death reigned in the
huge, gloomy buildings. Crillon feared some ambush,
but in vain were doors and windows opened and the crypt
searched; all was deserted. The King marched first,
sword in hand, calling, 'Chicot! Chicot!' No one
answered.

'Have they killed him ?' asked the King. '*Mordieu !*
they shall pay for him at a gentleman's price.'

'You are right, your Majesty, for he was a gentleman,
and one of the bravest,' observed Crillon.

Chicot did not answer, because he was deriving such
deep pleasure from his occupation of flogging M. de
Mayenne, that he saw and heard nothing of what was
happening. When the Duc finally disappeared and Gorenflot fainted, Chicot recognised the King's voice calling
him.

'Here, my son, here,' cried he lustily, placing Gorenflot

against a tree. The efforts he spent on this charitable work robbed his voice of some of its power, so that the King imagined he detected something mournful in the tones. This was not the case; Chicot was quite exalted and triumphant, only, observing the monk's pitiable condition, he was debating whether to put an end to the traitor or to treat him with leniency. Gorenflot was gradually recovering consciousness, and in spite of his stupidity was quite clear as to what awaited him; moreover, he resembled slightly these animals, constantly menaced by men, who feel instinctively that they are touched only to be beaten. In this frame of mind he opened his eyes.

'Seigneur Chicot,' he exclaimed.

'Ah! so you are not dead?'

'My good Seigneur Chicot,' continued the monk, trying to clasp his hands in front, 'is it possible that you were delivering me to my persecutors—me, Gorenflot?'

'Scoundrel,' remarked Chicot, in an accent of tenderness badly disguised.

Gorenflot began to howl, wringing his hands.

'Me, Gorenflot, who enjoyed such good dinners in your company, who drank so gracefully, who loved the pullets which you ordered at the Corne d'Abondance so much that he left only the bones!' cried he, choking.

Chicot was now quite resolved to be merciful.

'There they are! I am dead. Oh! good Seigneur Chicot, help me!' cried Gorenflot, endeavouring in vain to rise, but throwing himself face downwards on the ground.

'Get up,' commanded Chicot.

'Will you pardon me?'

'We will see.'

'You have beaten me so soundly that I have been sufficiently punished.'

Chicot burst out laughing. The poor monk's mind was so confused that he imagined he had received the blows given to Mayenne.

'You are laughing; then I shall live?' he asked.

'Perhaps.'

'You would not laugh if your Gorenflot were going to die.'

'That does not depend on me but on the King!' answered Chicot.

At this moment lights shone in the darkness; a number of embroidered cloaks and flashing swords surrounded the two men.

'Chicot! my dear Chicot! how pleased I am to see you again!' cried the King.

'Well! your Majesty, how many have you captured?'

'Not one,' answered Crillon. 'The traitors! they must have found some exit unknown to us.'

'Probably,' remarked Chicot.

'But you saw them?' asked the King.

'Certainly I saw them, from the first to the last.'

'You recognised them, no doubt?'

'No, your Majesty. That is, only one.'

'Which one?'

'M. de Mayenne.'

'M. de Mayenne? He to whom you owed——'

'We are quits, your Majesty.'

'Ah! tell me about it, Chicot!'

'Later, my son; let us think of the present.'

'Ah! you have a prisoner,' observed Crillon suddenly, laying his heavy hand on Gorenflot's shoulder. The monk lost the power of speech. There was a moment's silence, during which he seemed to hear the trumpet of the Last Judgment.

'Your Majesty, look well at this monk,' said Chicot.

One of the bystanders thrust a torch in Gorenflot's face, who closed his eyes.

'The preacher Gorenflot!' cried the King. 'He who——'

'Precisely.'

'Ah! ah!' said the King, with a satisfied air.

Swords were heard clanking; some of the Guards approached menacingly. Gorenflot, hearing them come, uttered a faint cry.

'Wait, the King must know all,' said Chicot. Then, drawing Henri aside, 'My son,' said he, 'thank the Lord for having permitted this holy man to be born some thirty-five years ago; he has saved us all. He revealed the whole plot almost a week ago; so that if your Majesty's enemies find him, he will be a dead man.'

Gorenflot, hearing only these words, 'A dead man,' fell forward on his hands.

'Worthy man,' said the King, glancing kindly at this mass of flesh, 'we will cover you with our protection.'

Gorenflot, catching this glance, remained, like the mask

of the ancient parasite, laughing with one side of his face
and weeping with the other.

'What do you suggest should be done with him ?' asked
the King.

'I think he runs a great risk in remaining in Paris.'

'Supposing I gave him Guards ?'

'No, there is no need; simply permit me to take him
home.'

'Very well, and afterwards return to the Louvre, where
I am going to prepare our friends for to-morrow. Take
good care of him, my friend.'

'Ah ! be reassured, your Majesty.'

'Monsieur Chicot ! where am I to be taken ?' cried
Gorenflot.

'You will know presently. Meanwhile, thank His
Majesty, monster of iniquity.'

'For what ?'

'Thank him, I tell you.'

'Your Majesty,' stammered Gorenflot, 'since your
gracious Majesty——'

'Yes, I know all you have done—in the journey to
Lyons, during the night of the League, and, finally,
to-day. Be sure you shall be rewarded for your merits.'

Gorenflot sighed.

'Where is Panurge ?' demanded Chicot.

'In the stables; poor animal !'

'Go for it, mount, and return here to me.'

'Yes, Monsieur Chicot,' replied the monk, retiring as
fast as he could, and surprised at not being followed by
the Guards.

'Now, my son, keep twenty men as escort, and send ten
with M. de Crillon to the Hôtel de Guise to fetch your
brother,' said Chicot to the King.

'Why?'

'That he may not escape a second time.'

'Does my brother——?'

'Do you regret having followed my advice to-day?'

'No, faith !'

'Then, do as I suggest.'

Henri commanded the Colonel of the French Guards to
bring the Duc d'Anjou to the Louvre. Crillon, who was
not deeply attached to the Prince, left immediately.

'And you ? Will you rejoin me at the Louvre ?' asked
the King.

'In an hour.'

'Then I leave you,' said Henri, retiring.

Chicot, proceeding to the stables, found Gorenflot, mounted on Panurge. The poor rascal had not even thought of escaping the fate which awaited him.

'Come, let us hurry, they are waiting for us,' said Chicot, seizing Panurge.

Gorenflot wept copiously, but offered no resistance. Chicot drew Panurge towards him, shrugging his shoulders.

CHAPTER LXXXIV

HOW D'ÉPERNON RETURNED TO THE LOUVRE

ON returning to the Louvre, the King found his friends sleeping peacefully. Henri advanced softly towards them, followed by Chicot, who, after placing his patient in safety, had rejoined his master. One bed, d'Épernon's, was empty.

'Not in yet, the rash one!' muttered Henri; 'ah! the fool! to fight with Bussy, the bravest man in France, the most dangerous in the whole world, and not to prepare for it! Let him be sought! let him be brought here! Then tell Miron to come to me; I wish him to send that thoughtless scamp to sleep, even against his will. He needs all his strength and suppleness for this combat.'

'Your Majesty, here is M. de Épernon entering,' announced the usher. Hearing of the King's return, and expecting a visit would be made to the sleeping quarters, d'Épernon was going there in the hope of being unnoticed. But his arrival was noted, so, seeing no means of escaping the reprimand, he appeared, all confused, on the threshold.

'Ah! there you are at last; come here, wretch, and see your friends,' cried Henri.

D'Épernon, glancing round the room, indicated that he had actually seen them.

'Look at your friends; they are wise and understand what an important day to-morrow is; you, unhappy being, instead of praying and sleeping like them, go and amuse yourself. *Cordieu!* how pale you are! you will

do well to-morrow if you are exhausted to-night already !'
continued Henri.

D'Épernon was in reality very pale, so pale that the
King's remark caused him to redden.

'Come, go to bed, will you, and sleep. You will sleep ?'

'Soundly, your Majesty.'

'I don't believe it. You are agitated, thinking of to-
morrow. Alas ! you are justified, for to-morrow is now
to-day. Yet, in spite of myself, I cannot help wishing
that the fatal day had not yet arrived.'

'Your Majesty, I will sleep, I promise you, but your
Majesty must allow me to sleep,' said d'Épernon, undres-
sing, and lying down with an air of calm satisfaction, which
seemed to the King and Chicot of good augury.

'He is as brave as a Cæsar,' observed Henri.

'So brave that, on my honour, I don't understand,'
answered Chicot.

'See, he is sleeping already.'

Chicot, doubting this, approached the bed.

'Oh ! oh ! look here,' he exclaimed suddenly, showing
the King d'Épernon's boots.

'Blood !'

'He has walked in blood, my son; what a brave fellow !'

'Hallo ! his doublet too, is stained; whatever has
happened ?'

'Perhaps he has been killing some one for practice.'

'*Mon Dieu !* what is happening around me, and what
does the future hold in store ? Luckily, I shall be reassured
to-morrow, for they will have killed these cursed Angevins.'

'You believe so, Henri ?'

'I am sure of it; they are brave.'

'I never heard that the Angevins were cowardly.'

'Perhaps not; but see how strong my friends are; look
at Schomberg's arm, what a fine muscle.'

'Ah ! but if you saw Antraguet's arms.'

'Look at Quélus's proud lip, Maugiron's brow, haughty
even in sleep. With such a countenance, one must
conquer. Ah ! when these eyes blaze, the enemy is already
half beaten.'

'Beneath as haughty brows as those, eyes I know shoot
as deadly glances as those on which you are relying. Is
that all you have to reassure you ?'

'No, come into my apartment and I will show you
something.'

'And this something gives you confidence of victory?'

'Yes.'

'Come, then.'

'Wait,' said Henri, approaching the young men, 'I do not wish to distress them to-morrow, so I will say farewell at once.'

'Do so, my son,' remarked Chicot, in such gloomy tones that the King felt a shudder pass through him, and a tear came into his eyes.

'Farewell, my friends; farewell my dear friends,' he whispered, as he bent over to kiss the young men.

Chicot was not superstitious; but when he saw Henri touch with his lips the brows of Maugiron, Quélus, and Schomberg, his imagination represented a living person coming to bid farewell to the dead already in their tombs.

Hardly had the King finished when d'Épernon opened his eyes to see whether he had gone. Henri had just left the room, leaning on Chicot's arm. Leaping out of bed, d'Épernon began to efface the stains of blood from his boots and clothes. This occupation led his thoughts towards the scene near the Place de la Bastille.

'I should never have had enough blood for this man, who shed so much to-night, by his own hands,' he muttered, lying down again.

Henri, leading Chicot to his private room, opened a long ebony case, lined with white satin.

'Look here,' said he.

'Swords! I see quite well,' answered Chicot.

'Yes, swords, but blessed by our Holy Father the Pope himself, who granted me this favour. This coffer, as you see it, cost me twenty horses and four men for its journey to Rome and back; but I have the swords.'

'Do they cut well?' asked Chicot.

'Doubtless; but their supreme merit is that they have been blessed.'

'Yes, I am aware of it; still I should be pleased to know that they cut.'

'Pagan!'

'See, my son, let us speak of other matters.'

'Very well; but be quick, I wish to pray.'

'In that case, let us talk of important affairs. Have you sent for M. d'Anjou?'

'Yes; he is waiting below.'

'What do you intend to do with him?'

'I mean to throw him into the Bastille.'

'That is very wise. Only, choose a dungeon, very deep down, very secure; that one, for instance, under the charge of Saint-Pol or Jacques d'Armagnac.'

'Oh! keep your mind easy.'

'I know where they sell beautiful black velvet, my son.'

'Chicot! he is my brother.'

'That's true, and, at court, purple is family mourning. Will you speak to him?'

'Yes, certainly, if only to shatter his hopes, by showing him that his plans are discovered.'

'Hum! in your place, I should suppress the speech and double the punishment.'

'Bring the Duc d'Anjou,' commanded Henri.

A moment later the Duc entered, disarmed, and very pale. Chicot followed, holding his sword.

'Where did you find him?' asked the King, as though the Duc were not there.

'Your Majesty, His Highness was not at home; but a moment after I had taken possession of his dwelling in your Majesty's name, His Highness entered, and we arrested him without any resistance.'

'That was very fortunate,' said the King scornfully.

'Where were you, monsieur?' he continued, turning to the Prince; 'what were you doing while your accomplices were being arrested?'

'My accomplices? Your Majesty has certainly received wrong information with regard to me.'

'Oh! this time, monsieur, you will not escape, and your career of crime is finished. After all, you will not succeed me, my brother.'

'Your Majesty, for mercy's sake, calm yourself; there is certainly some one who rouses you against me.'

'Wretched man! you shall die of starvation in a cell of the Bastille.'

'I await your orders and bless them, your Majesty, though I suffer death through them.'

'Where were you, hypocrite?'

'I was saving your Majesty, and working for the glory and peace of your Majesty's reign.'

'Bah!' remarked Chicot, 'tell us about this, my Prince; it must be curious.'

'Your Majesty, I would relate it, had your Majesty

treated me as a brother; but as I am treated as a culprit, I will wait for events to speak for me,' answered the Duc, bowing again to the King; then, turning to Crillon and the other officers, he added,—

'Which of you, gentlemen, is to lead the First Prince of the blood to the Bastille?'

Chicot, who had been reflecting, had an inspiration.

'Ah! ah! I believe I begin to understand now why M. d'Épernon had blood on his feet and so little on his cheeks,' he muttered.

CHAPTER LXXXV

THE MORNING OF THE COMBAT

THE morning dawned fair over Paris; as we said in the preceding chapter, the King did not sleep at all, but prayed and wept. Towards three o'clock in the morning, he set out with Chicot, to render his friends the sole service in his power, to visit the spot where the encounter was to take place. It was a remarkable spectacle, though one which attracted very little attention. The King, enveloped in a large cloak, his sword by his side, his hair and eyes hidden under his hat, followed Rue Saint-Antoine till within some distance of the Bastille; but, perceiving a great throng of people a little above Rue Saint-Paul, he turned into Rue Sainte-Catherine, so reaching the Tournelles from behind. Chicot, who had been present at the conference a week before, explained to the King the special position allotted to each man, and the terms of the fight. Henri immediately began to measure the ground and to calculate the sun's reflection.

'Quélus will be exposed; he will have the sun on his right, straight in his sole remaining eye,[1] whilst Maugiron is wholly in the shade. That is a bad arrangement, so far. Schomberg, whose legs are weak, has a tree near him in case of need, which reassures me on his behalf; but my poor Quélus!' said Henri, shaking his head sadly.

'Come, don't torment yourself like that,' urged Chicot; 'the deuce! they will only have what they get.'

The King sighed, raising his eyes to heaven.

[1] Quelus had lost an eye in an earlier fight.

'How he blasphemes; but God knows he is a fool,' he murmured. Chicot shrugged his shoulders.

'And d'Épernon,' resumed Henri; 'what a position! Look, my brave Chicot: on the left a barrier; on the right a tree; behind, a ditch; d'Épernon, who will need to give way every minute, for Bussy is a tiger, a lion, a serpent; Bussy is a living sword, bounding, coiling on itself.'

'Bah! I am not anxious about d'Épernon.'

'You are wrong; he will be killed.'

'He! he's not so stupid; he will not fight, *mordieu!*'

'Come, now! did you not hear him a little while ago?'

'Precisely; that is the reason I repeat that he will not fight. I know my Gascon, Henri; but let us return to the Louvre, your Majesty, the great day has arrived.'

'Do you imagine that I shall remain in the Louvre during the fight?'

'*Ventre de biche!* you must remain, for were you seen here, and your friends were the victors, people would accuse you of sorcery, or of bringing bad luck, should they be conquered.'

'What would these rumours matter to me? I shall love them to the end.'

'I compliment you on your affection for your friends, it is a rare enough virtue in princes; but I do not want you to leave M. d'Anjou alone in the Louvre.'

'Crillon is there, is he not?'

'Eh! Crillon is only a buffalo, a rhinoceros, all that is brave and untameable; whilst your brother is a rattle-snake, or any other animal whose power is less in its strength than in its venom.'

'You are right, I should have had him lodged in the Bastille.'

'I warned you against seeing him.'

'I was won over by his assurance, by this service he claims to have rendered me.'

'Another reason that you should mistrust him. Let us return, my son.'

Henri followed Chicot's advice, after one more glance at the field of combat. Everybody was stirring in the Louvre; the young men were being dressed by their valets. Henri entered their room, his calm, almost smiling, countenance displaying none of his emotion.

'Good-morning, gentlemen,' said he; 'I find you in excellent spirits, it seems.'

'Thanks be to God! yes, your Majesty,' replied Quélus.

'You look gloomy, Maugiron.'

'Your Majesty, I am superstitious, and, having had bad dreams, am taking a little wine to fortify myself.'

'My friend, remember that dreams depend upon impressions of the previous day, but have no bearing on events of the following one, except by God's will.'

'So, your Majesty, you see I am disciplined. I, too, had bad dreams last night; yet, in spite of them, my arm is strong and my eye clear,' said d'Épernon.

'My brave friends, you know that your Prince's honour is at stake, since it is his cause you, in some measure, defend; but only the honour, understand; do not trouble about the security of my person. I have established my throne so that, for some time at least, no shock can affect it. Fight, then, for honour's sake.'

'Your Majesty, be reassured; we may perhaps lose our lives, but in any case, honour will be saved,' said Quélus.

'Gentlemen, I love you dearly and respect you. Let me give you some advice; no false bravery; not in dying, but in killing your enemies, you will please me.'

'Oh! I give no quarter,' observed d'Épernon.

'I answer for nothing, but will do what I can,' promised Quélus.

'I pledge His Majesty that I will kill my man even should I die,' was Maugiron's statement.

'You fight with the sword only?'

'The sword and the dirk,' Schomberg answered.

The King laid his hand on his heart. Perhaps this hand and heart betrayed his fears by their trembling and beating; but, outwardly, with dry eyes and haughty lip, he was the King, sending soldiers forth to the fight, not friends to their death. The noblemen were ready; they had only to take leave of their King.

'Do you ride?' asked Henri.

'No, your Majesty, we will walk; it is a healthy exercise and lightens the head, and your Majesty has said a thousand times it is the head rather than the arm which directs the sword,' answered Quélus.

'You are right, my son. Give me your hand.'

Quélus, bowing, kissed the King's hand; the others did

the same. D'Épernon, kneeling down, said, 'Your Majesty, bless my sword.'

'No, d'Épernon; give your sword to my page. I reserve better swords than those for you. Carry these away, Chicot.'

'No, give that commission to the Captain of the Guards, my son; I am only a fool, a Pagan; the blessings of Heaven might be changed into dark sorcery should my friend, the devil, notice what I am carrying.'

'What swords are these, your Majesty?' asked Schomberg, glancing at the case which an officer had brought.

'Swords from Italy, my son, forged at Milan; the guards are good; as you have all delicate hands but Schomberg, you need to be well protected.'

'Thank you, your Majesty,' exclaimed the four young men together.

'Go; it is time,' said the King, overcome by emotion.

'Your Majesty, are we not to have the encouragement of your presence?'

'No, that would not be fitting; give no solemnity to the combat; let it be thought the result of a private quarrel,' answered the King, dismissing them with a majestic gesture. When they had gone, he fell upon an estrade, exclaiming: 'Ah! I die.'

'And *I* want to see this duel; I have an idea, I don't know why, that something strange will happen with regard to d'Épernon.'

'You leave me, Chicot?'

'Yes; should one of them fail in his duty, I should be there to replace him and uphold the honour of my King.'

'Go, then.'

Returning to his own rooms, the King had the shutters closed, and forbidding any one to utter a sound in the Louvre, he issued orders to Crillon, who alone knew what was about to happen.

'If we are the victors, Crillon, you will report to me,' said he; 'if, on the contrary, we are defeated, you will knock three times on my door.'

'Yes, your Majesty,' replied Crillon, shaking his head.

CHAPTER LXXXVI

BUSSY'S FRIENDS

IF the King's friends had spent the night sleeping peacefully, those of the Duc d'Anjou had taken the same precaution; after a good supper they had retired to rest in Antraguet's dwelling, which was nearest the field of battle. A groom who was a keen hunter and skilled armourer, had spent the whole day cleaning and sharpening their weapons; he was also commissioned to waken the young men at daybreak. At three o'clock the latter were already up, fresh, active, and well equipped for the duel. Before leaving the house, they had sent to the Duc d'Anjou for news of Bussy; the messenger reported that he had gone out, accompanied by Rémy, and armed, at ten o'clock the night before, but had not returned. However, they were not at all uneasy in the Comte's household, as he often absented himself in this way; besides, he was so strong, brave, and clever that even his prolonged absences caused little anxiety. The three friends had all these particulars repeated to them.

'Have you not heard, gentlemen, that the King had given orders for a stag-hunt in the forest of Compiègne, and that M. de Monsoreau left yesterday to make preparations?' said Antraguet.

'Yes,' answered the others.

'Then, be assured, gentlemen, he is nearer the place of combat than ourselves, and will be there before us.'

'Yes, but probably not in good trim for fighting,' retorted Livarot.

'Bussy is always fit,' said Antraguet, shrugging his shoulders. 'Come! let us start, we shall meet him on the way.'

All the streets were deserted, save for sleepy peasants coming from Montreuil, Vincennes, or Saint-Maur-les-Tossés with milk and vegetables. On reaching Rue Sainte-Catherine, all three glanced with a smile at Monsoreau's little dwelling.

'One can see well from there; I am sure poor Diane will often come to her window,' remarked Antraguet.

'Hallo!' cried Ribeirac, 'she is there already, for it is open.'

'It is true. But why is that ladder placed before the window, when the building has doors?'

The three drew near, feeling they were about to witness some horrible sight. They arrived under the balcony, where a gardener seemed to be examining the ground.

'Eh! clown, what are you doing there? Did you place that ladder?' called Livarot to this countryman.

'God forbid, gentlemen! Look up there,' was the answer. They raised their heads.

'Blood!' cried Ribeirac.

'The door has been forced,' cried Antraguet's page. Antraguet, seizing the ladder, was on the balcony in a second. Gazing into the room, he uttered a cry of horror. Livarot mounted behind him.

'Corpses! death, death everywhere!' he exclaimed, and both entered the room. Ribeirac remained below, while the countryman, by his remarks, attracted all the passers-by. The room bore the traces of the awful struggle. A river of blood deluged the floor; the hangings were riddled by sword-cuts and pistol-shots; the furniture lay, broken and stained, in the debris of human flesh and clothing.

'Oh! Rémy, poor Rémy!' cried Antraguet suddenly.

'Is he dead?' asked Livarot.

'Cold already.'

'But surely a regiment of German soldiers has been here.'

Seeing the corridor door open, Livarot followed the blood-stains right to the staircase. The courtyard was empty and deserted. Meanwhile Antraguet passed into the adjoining room; there was blood everywhere, leading to the window. Leaning over the window he gazed wildly into the little garden; the iron railing still supported the livid, stiff corpse of the unfortunate Bussy. At this sight, a roar escaped from Antraguet which caused Livarot to run up.

'Look, Bussy dead!' shouted Antraguet.

'Bussy murdered and thrown out of window. Ribeirac, enter,' cried Livarot, rushing into the courtyard. Meeting Livarot at the foot of the stair, he dragged him into the garden.

'It is really he,' cried Livarot.

'His hand is cut to pieces.'

'He has two bullets in his chest.'

'He is riddled with dirk-cuts.'

'Ah! poor Bussy, vengeance!' roared Antraguet. Livarot, turning round, knocked against a second corpse.

'Monsoreau!' he cried. 'Ah! surely all our friends have been murdered last night!'

'And his wife, Diane, Madame Diane!' called Antraguet, but nobody answered. The people were now swarming round the house. It was just then that the King and Chicot turned aside to avoid the crowd.

'It is infamous! cowardly!' cried the young men.

'Let us go up and complain to the Duc,' suggested one of them.

'No, let us give nobody the trouble of avenging us; we should be badly avenged in that case; friends, wait for me,' said Antraguet, descending to rejoin Livarot and Ribeirac.

'Friends,' said he, 'look at the noble countenance of this bravest of men; see the drops, still red, of his blood; he gives us an example; he would entrust no one with the duty of avenging him. . . . Bussy! Bussy! we will act like you, and, be sure, we will be avenged.'

As he spoke, Antraguet laid his lips on Bussy's, and, drawing his sword, laid it in his blood, saying,—

'Bussy, I swear on your corpse that this blood shall be washed in the blood of your enemies!'

'Bussy, we swear to kill or die!' vowed the others.

'Gentlemen, no mercy, and no quarter,' exclaimed Antraguet, replacing his sword in its sheath.

'No mercy, no quarter,' repeated the two, stretching their hands over the corpse.

'But, we shall be three against four,' observed Livarot.

'Yes, but we have not murdered any one, and God will strengthen the innocent. Farewell, Bussy!' said Antraguet.

'Farewell, Bussy!' cried the others, leaving the house, with terror in their soul and pallor on their brow. Arriving at the place of combat, they found their opponents waiting.

'Gentlemen, we have had the honour of waiting for you,' observed Quélus, rising and bowing haughtily.

'Excuse us, gentlemen; we should have arrived before you, but for the lateness of one of our companions,' replied Antraguet.

'M. de Bussy ? indeed, I do not see him. It seems he is very reluctant this morning,' remarked d'Épernon.

'M. de Bussy will not come,' answered Antraguet.

A profound astonishment was depicted on all the faces, d'Épernon's alone expressing another emotion.

'He will not come ? ah! the bravest of the brave is therefore afraid ?' said he.

'That cannot be the reason,' declared Quélus.

'Why will he not come ?' asked Maugiron.

'Because he is dead,' was Antraguet's reply.

'Dead!' exclaimed the minions. D'Épernon, paling slightly, said nothing.

'Dead, assassinated! Are you not aware of it, gentlemen ?'

'No, why should we be ?'

'Besides, is it certain ?' asked d'Épernon.

'So sure that this is his blood on my sword,' said Antraguet, drawing his rapier.

'This blood cries for vengeance; do you not hear it, gentlemen ?' asked Ribeirac.

'Seek whom the crime benefits,' muttered Livarot.

'Ah! gentlemen, will you make your meaning clear ?' cried Maugiron, in a voice of thunder.

'We have come for that purpose precisely,' retorted Ribeirac.

'Then, swords in hand quickly and let us get to work,' exclaimed d'Épernon, drawing his weapon from its sheath.

'Oh! you are very hurried, Monsieur le Gascon; you were not so eager when we were four against four,' said Livarot.

'Is it our fault there are but three of you ?' asked d'Épernon.

'Yes, it is your fault,' cried Antraguet; 'he is dead, because he is less dangerous lying in the grave than standing on the ground; he is dead, and his hand cut off that it may not longer hold a sword; he is dead because it was necessary to blind, at all costs, these eyes whose glance would have dazzled you, all four. Do you understand ? Am I clear ?'

Schomberg, Maugiron, and d'Épernon howled with rage.

'That will do, gentlemen,' ordered Quélus. 'Withdraw, Monsieur d'Épernon; we will fight three against three. Come, gentlemen, and seeing us fight under the open sky and beneath God's eye, you will be able to judge whether we are murderers. Space! space!'

'Ah! I hated you before; now I loathe you,' exclaimed Schomberg.

'On guard, gentlemen,' cried Antraguet.

'Hallo! I have lost my dirk,' said Quélus, taking off his doublet. 'It was loose in the scabbard, and must have fallen out.'

'Perhaps you left it in M. de Monsoreau's dwelling, in a scabbard from which you did not dare withdraw it,' suggested Antraguet.

Growling with rage, Quélus fell on guard.

'But he has no dirk, Monsieur Antraguet,' cried Chicot, who had just arrived.

'All the worse for him; it is not my fault,' replied Antraguet, taking up his position.

CHAPTER LXXXVII

THE COMBAT

THE piece of ground where this terrible encounter was to take place was shaded with trees. It was usually frequented in the day-time by children, who came to play, and at night by drunken men and thieves, who came to sleep. Chicot, with a beating heart, sat in front of the lackeys and pages on a wooden balustrade. He had no affection for the Angevins, he detested the minions; but all were brave young people, and in their veins flowed generous blood, which was soon to gush forth. D'Épernon wished to show some bravado again.

'What? so you are afraid of me?' he cried.

'Be quiet, chatterer,' answered Antraguet.

'I am in my rights; the meeting was arranged for eight.'

'Come, keep off!' cried Ribeirac impatiently.

D'Épernon returned with haughty bearing, and put up his sword.

'Come, flower of bravery, or you will lose a pair of shoes, as you did yesterday,' said Chicot.

'What says this master fool?'

'I say there will be blood on the ground presently, and you will tread in it as you did last night'

D'Épernon became pale. All his bragging vanished at this terrible reproach. Sitting down near Chicot, he glanced at him in terror. Ribeirac and Schomberg, after the customary salute, approached one another. Quélus and Antraguet were already crossing swords. Maugiron and Livarot, each leaning on a barrier, were making feints so as to place their swords in their favourite guard. The fight began as five o'clock was ringing from Saint-Paul. For a few minutes a clashing of swords was heard, but not an effectual blow was struck. Presently Schomberg, stepping rapidly forward, dealt Ribeirac a blow, which was as the first lightning flash from the cloud. Ribeirac's face became livid, the blood gushed from his shoulder; Schomberg tried another thrust, but Ribeirac, parrying skilfully, dealt him a blow in the side. Each had received his wound.

'Now, let us rest for a few seconds,' said Ribeirac.

Meanwhile Quélus and Antraguet were becoming excited. The former, having no dirk, was at a disadvantage; he was compelled to parry with his bare left arm, so that each time he received a wound. In a few minutes his hand was completely covered with blood. Antraguet, grasping his advantage, and being not less skilful than his opponent, parried with the utmost care. Three times the blood flowed from Quélus's chest, but at each thrust, he repeated, 'It is nothing.' Livarot and Maugiron were still using caution. Ribeirac, furious with pain, feeling he was losing his strength, rushed upon Schomberg, who did not retreat a step. Both thrust successfully : Ribeirac had his chest run through and Schomberg was wounded in the neck. The former, mortally wounded, placed his left hand on the gash, while Schomberg dealt him a second blow. But Ribeirac, with his right hand seized his enemy's hand, and with his left drove his dirk into his chest. The blade pierced the heart. Schomberg, uttering a hoarse cry, fell on his back, dragging with him Ribeirac, still transfixed by the sword. Livarot, seeing his friend fall, ran rapidly to him, followed by Maugiron. Winning in the race, Livarot dragged the sword from Ribeirac's chest.

Then, rejoined by Maugiron, he was forced to defend himself, with the disadvantages of slippery ground, a bad guard, and the sun in his eyes. In a minute Livarot fell on his knees, letting his sword fall, his head cut open by a rapier thrust. Quélus was closely pressed by Antraguet; Maugiron hastened to run Livarot through, and the latter fell prostrate. D'Épernon uttered a loud cry. Quélus and Maugiron remained against the sole Angevin. Quélus was bleeding all over, but from slight wounds, whilst Maugiron was almost unharmed.

Antraguet understood his danger; he had not received the least scratch, but he began to feel fatigued; yet this was no moment for demanding a truce. Violently thrusting the sword of Quélus aside, he leaped lightly over a barrier. Quélus replied with a cut, which fell on the wood. At this moment Maugiron attacked Antraguet from the side. The latter turned round, and Quélus, profiting by the movement, passed under the barrier.

'He is lost,' said Chicot.

'Long live the King!' cried d'Épernon; 'be bold, my lions.'

'Monsieur, silence, if you please,' said Antraguet; 'do not insult a man who will fight to his last breath.'

'And who is not yet dead,' cried Livarot, rising, covered with blood, and plunging his dirk into Maugiron's shoulder. The latter fell in a heap, muttering: 'My God! I am killed.' Livarot fell back in a swoon, the movement and his rage had exhausted his remaining strength.

'Monsieur de Quélus, you are a brave man; surrender; I offer you your life,' said Antraguet, lowering his sword.

'Why should I surrender? Am I defeated?'

'No; but you are covered with wounds, and I am uninjured.'

'Long live the King!' cried Quélus, 'I have still my sword, monsieur,' and he lunged at Antraguet, who parried the thrust, rapid as it was.

'No, monsieur, you have not it any longer,' answered Antraguet, seizing the blade near the guard and twisting Quélus's arm so that he loosened the sword.

'Oh! a sword! a sword!' yelled Quélus, rushing at Antraguet, and enveloping him with his arms. The latter, with sword in one hand and dagger in the other, struck incessantly at his enemy, who, refusing to relax his hold, cried out at each fresh wound inflicted: 'Long live the King!' He even succeeded in catching the hand which struck him, and in pinioning his enemy with his arms and legs. Antraguet felt his breath stopping; tottering, he fell, but in falling, stifled the unhappy Quélus.

'Long live the King!' muttered the latter, in his death-agony.

Antraguet, freeing himself from the embrace, rose on one arm, and ran Quélus through the chest.

'There, are you satisfied?' he asked.

'Long live the K——' articulated Quélus, his eyes half closed. That was all; the silence and terror of death reigned on the field. Antraguet rose, covered with his enemies' blood; he had but a scratch in the hand. D'Épernon, terrified, crossed himself, and fled as though pursued by a spectre. Antraguet cast on his companions and opponents, dead and dying, the same glance with which Horace must have viewed the battle-field that decided Rome's destiny. Chicot, coming forward, raised Quélus, bleeding from nineteen wounds. The movement revived him, and he opened his eyes.

'Antraguet, on my honour, I am innocent of Bussy's death,' said he.

'I believe you, monsieur, I believe you.'

'Flee; the King will not pardon you.'

'Monsieur, I will not leave you thus, though the scaffold should await me.'

'Save yourself, young man, and do not tempt God; you have escaped by a miracle; do not ask for two on the same day,' advised Chicot.

Antraguet approached Ribeirac, who still breathed.

'Well?' asked the latter.

'We are conquerors,' answered Antraguet in low tones.

'Thanks. Go,' said Ribeirac, falling back in a swoon.

Antraguet picked up his own sword, then those of Quélus, Schomberg, and Maugiron.

'Finish me, monsieur, or give me my sword,' said Quélus.

'Here it is, Monsieur le Comte,' replied Antraguet, offering it with a respectful bow.

A tear shone in the eyes of the wounded man.

'We might have been friends,' he murmured.

Antraguet held out his hand to him.

'Good! that is quite knightly,' observed Chicot; 'but flee, Antraguet, you are worthy of life.'

'And my companions?'

'I will take care of them, equally with the King's friends.'

Antraguet, throwing on his cloak to cover the blood stains, disappeared by the Porte Saint-Antoine.

CHAPTER LXXXVIII

CONCLUSION

PALE with anxiety, shuddering at the least sound, the King paced up and down his fencing-room, calculating the time his friends should have taken to meet and to fight their adversaries, also the good or ill luck which their nature, strength, and skill gave each of them.

'If only Quélus remembers the parry and thrust I showed him, parrying with the sword and striking with the dirk!' said he. 'As for Schomberg, that self-possessed man, he should kill Ribeirac. Maugiron, unless extremely unfortunate, should soon get rid of Livarot. But d'Épernon! oh! he is dead. Fortunately he is the one of the four I like least. His loss will not be overwhelming; but Bussy, after killing him may attack the others. Ah! my poor Quélus! my poor Schomberg! my poor Maugiron!'

'Your Majesty!' said Crillon's voice at the door.

'What! already!' cried the King.

'No, your Majesty, I bring no news, except that the Duc d'Anjou desires to speak to your Majesty. He says the time has come to reveal the service he rendered your Majesty, and what he has to say will calm some of the fears which are agitating the King at present.'

'Go, then,' answered the King. Just as Crillon turned away, a rapid step was heard and a voice exclaimed, 'I wish to speak to the King this very instant.' The King, recognising the voice, opened the door.

'Come, Saint-Luc; who else is there? But what is the matter with you? what has happened? are they dead?' cried he.

Saint-Luc, pale, bareheaded, without a sword, all bespattered with blood, rushed into the room.

'Your Majesty! vengeance! I come to demand vengeance!' he cried.

'My poor Saint-Luc, whatever is wrong? speak; what causes you such despair?'

'Your Majesty, the noblest of your subjects, the bravest of your soldiers was murdered last night—treacherously murdered.'

'Butchered, murdered, last night; of whom are you speaking, Saint-Luc ?'

'Your Majesty, you dislike him I know, but he was faithful, and, if the occasion had arisen, would have given his life for your Majesty; but for that, he had not been my friend.'

'Ah !' said the King, who began to understand. A flash of hope, if not of joy, illuminated his face.

'Vengeance, your Majesty, for M. de Bussy, vengeance !'

'For M. de Bussy ?' repeated the King, dwelling on each word.

'Yes, for M. de Bussy, whom twenty assassins stabbed last night. Just as well there were twenty, for he killed fourteen of them.'

'M. de Bussy dead ! Then he is not fighting this morning,' cried the King impulsively. Saint-Luc darted a glance at the King, which the latter could not bear; turning aside, he beckoned to Crillon to bring the Duc d'Anjou.

'No, your Majesty,' added Saint-Luc, in severe tones; 'M. de Bussy did not fight, and that is why I come to ask, not for vengeance, as I wrongly said, but justice; for I reckon my King's honour above all things, and consider that, in stabbing M. de Bussy, a deplorable service has been rendered your Majesty.'

The Duc d'Anjou arrived at the door and stood, motionless as a statue. The words of Saint-Luc had enlightened the King; they recalled the service which his brother claimed to have rendered.

'Do you know what people will say now ?' cried Saint-Luc. 'They will say, should your friends be victorious, that it is only because you had Bussy murdered.'

'Who says that, monsieur ?'

'Pardieu !' everybody,' said Crillon, joining in the conversation.

'No, monsieur, they will not say that, for you will expose the murderer for me.'

Saint-Luc saw a shadow fall across the floor; it was the Duc d'Anjou, advancing a few steps into the apartment.

'Yes, your Majesty, I will name him, for I wish, at all costs, to vindicate your Majesty from such an abominable crime,' cried Saint-Luc, recognising the Duc. The latter stopping, waited calmly.

'Your Majesty, last night, Bussy was led into a trap.

Whilst he was visiting a woman who loved him, the husband, warned by a traitor, returned to his house with assassins; they were everywhere : in the street, in the courtyard, and even in the garden.'

The Duc, in spite of his self-control, paled at the last words.

'Bussy defended himself like a lion, your Majesty, but numbers overwhelmed him, and——'

'He died, and justly, for I certainly will not avenge an adulterer,' interrupted the King.

'Your Majesty, I have not finished the story. The unfortunate man, after defending himself in the room for nearly half an hour, after triumphing over his enemies, escaped, wounded and bleeding, but alive. It only needed to stretch forth a helping hand to him, and this I would have done, had I not been captured by his murderers, along with the woman he had entrusted to me ; had I not been pinioned and gagged. They had not, however, deprived me of sight as well as speech, and, your Majesty, I saw two men approach the wretched Bussy, hanging on the spikes of an iron railing; I heard the wounded man ask for help, for in these two men he had a right to recognise friends. Well ! one of them—your Majesty, it is horrible to relate ! but, it was still more horrible to witness and to hear—one gave orders to fire, and the other obeyed.'

Crillon clenched his fists and knit his brows.

'And you know the murderer ?' asked the King, moved in spite of himself.

'Yes,' answered Saint-Luc, and, turning to the Prince, he cried with all his pent-up hatred in his voice and gesture, it is monseigneur; the murderer is the Prince ! the murderer is the friend !'

The King was expecting this declaration; the Duc heard it calmly.

'Yes,' said he, 'Monsieur de Saint-Luc saw and heard aright; I caused M. de Bussy to be killed, and your Majesty will appreciate the action. M. de Bussy was my servant, it is true, but this morning, in spite of my efforts, he was to bear arms against your Majesty.'

'You lie ! murderer ! you lie !' cried Saint-Luc; 'Bussy, pierced with cuts, his hand hacked, his shoulder shattered by a bullet; Bussy, hanging downwards from the railing, could only have inspired his bitterest enemies with pity, and his bitterest enemies would have helped him. But you, the murderer of La Mole and Coconnas, you killed Bussy, as you have killed all your friends; you killed Bussy, not because he was the enemy of your brother, but because he was the confidant of your secrets. Ah! Monsoreau knew well, why you committed this crime?'

'*Cordieu!* why am I not the King?' muttered Crillon.

'I am insulted in your presence, my brother,' murmured the Duc, livid with terror.

'Crillon, retire,' commanded the King.

'Your Majesty, punish me for having saved your friends this morning, and for having confirmed the justice of your cause, which is mine.'

'And *I* tell you that the cause you speak of is an accursed one, and that, wherever you go, the wrath of God ought to fall upon you! Your Majesty, your brother has protected our friends, woe to them!' cried Saint-Luc, losing his self-control.

The King felt a thrill of terror pass through him; at this very moment a vague noise was heard outside, followed by hurried steps, then eager questionings. Finally came profound silence, in the midst of which, as though a voice from heaven were justifying Saint-Luc, three knocks, from the powerful hand of Crillon, shook the door. Henri's face quivered with emotion.

'Defeated! my poor friends defeated!' cried he. The Duc clasped his hands in terror. The King covered his face with his hands.

'Oh! my poor friends, they are defeated, wounded?' he moaned. 'Oh! who will give me news of them?'

'I, your Majesty,' answered Chicot. 'Two are already dead, the third is about to breathe his last.'

'Who is this third who is not yet dead?'

'Quélus, your Majesty.'

'And where is he?'

'In the Hôtel de Boissy, where I had him conveyed.'

Without listening longer, the King rushed from the room, uttering mournful cries. Saint-Luc had taken Diane to her friend, Jeanne de Brissac; hence the delay in presenting himself at the Louvre. Jeanne watched for three days and three nights beside the unhappy woman, who was in wild delirium. The fourth day Jeanne, overcome with fatigue, sought some rest; on returning, two hours later, to her friend's room, she missed her.

Quélus, the sole survivor of the three defenders of the
King's cause, died at the Hôtel de Boissy, in the King's
arms, after enduring thirty days of agony. Henri was
inconsolable. He had magnificent tombs built for his
three friends, with life-size marble statues upon them.
For nearly three months Crillon kept close guard over the
Duc d'Anjou, whom the King, in his profound hatred,
never pardoned. The month of September arrived, when
Chicot, who had never left his master, and could have
consoled Henri, had such a thing been possible, received
the following letter, addressed from the Priory of Baume, in
a clerkly handwriting :—

'DEAR SEIGNEUR CHICOT,—
    'The air is balmy in our district, and the vintage
promises to be a good one in Burgundy this year. I am
told that our Liege Lord, the King, whose life I saved,
is still very sad; bring him to the Priory, dear Monsieur
Chicot, he shall drink a wine of 1550, which I have discovered in my cellar, capable of making one forget the
greatest sorrow; that will gladden him, I have no doubt,
for I have found this admirable sentence in Holy Writ :
"Good wine rejoices the heart of man !" It is very fine
in Latin; I will make you read it. Come, then, dear
Monsieur Chicot, come with the King, come with d'Épernon, with M. de Saint-Luc; you will see that we will all
grow fat.
        'THE REVEREND PRIOR DOM GORENFLOT
    (who inscribes himself your humble servant and friend).
    'Postscript.—Tell the King I have had no time to pray
for the souls of his friends, as he instructed me, on account
of the trouble of my installation; but, as soon as the
vintage is past, I will certainly do so.'
    'Amen,' observed Chicot,' the poor wretches are well
recommended to God !'

LONDON AND GLASGOW: COLLINS' CLEAR-TYPE PRESS.

Illustrated Pocket Classics

Cloth, 1/- net.   Leather, gilt edges, 2/- net
(In Great Britain only)

THIN PAPER EDITIONS AT POPULAR PRICES
Over 2000 New Illustrations

LIST OF TITLES

LONDON AND GLASGOW

COLLINS' CLEAR-TYPE PRESS